# The Girls of Jerusalem
# and Other Stories

# THE GIRLS OF JERUSALEM

# AND OTHER STORIES

*Marsha Lee Berkman*

These stories appeared previously in the following publications:
"Deeds of Love and Mercy" (as "Deeds of Love and Rage" and "Acts of Mercy")
in *Sonora Review, Lilith, Writing Our Way Home, Shaking Eve's Tree,
Mothers, The Shocken Book of Contemporary Jewish Fiction,
Feldspar Prize Stories 2*, and *Chicago Quarterly Review*;
"Kreuzlingen," "Grisha," and "How I Found My Life"
in *Jewish Women's Literary Annual*;
*Kreuzlingen: The Secret Life of Freud's Anna O.* as a Kindle eBook;
"Ghosts" in *Cottonwood*; "In The Time of Dreams" in *The Long Story*;
"My Grandmother's Eyes" in *The New Laurel Review*;
"Sudargas" in *Riversedge*; "Vilna" and "Passion" in
*History, Memory and Belles Lettres as a Response to the Jewish Past*.

Yehuda Halevi's poem adapted from *Jewish Portraits* by Lady Katie Magnus.
Published by David Nutt in *The Strand*, 1897. Courtesy of Project Gutenberg.

Cover: *Hosannah!*, 1863–81. Dalziel Brothers, engravers, after Simeon Solomon.

Text design by Julie Fry
Typeset in Galliard and Interstate



Printed in the United States of America.

ISBN 979-8-9893417-0-2 (hardcover)
ISBN 979-8-9893417-1-9 (paperback)
ISBN 979-8-9893417-2-6 (e-book)

O city of the world most chastely fair

In the far west, behold I sigh for thee

Oh! had I eagle's wings, I'd fly to thee

And with my falling tears make moist thine earth.

I long for thee.

—YEHUDA HALEVI (1075–1141)


One doesn't go to Jerusalem, one returns to it.

—ELIE WIESEL (1928–2016)

# CONTENTS

# In Sudargas

ENTER THE PHOTOGRAPH and you are there. A village—no, not even a village, a hamlet, perhaps—between Vilna, that great city, the Jerusalem of Lithuania to the east, and the treacherous Baltic Sea to the west.

The train comes even here, or at least somewhat nearby: then you have to take a wagon and a driver for the rest, or walk the twenty kilometers to Sudargas, where there is a street of the Jews and a wooden synagogue with a balcony for the women, a dance hall for weddings, a study house where the old men and beggars gather and children learn their *aleph-bet*, a *mikvah*, ritual bath for purification, a marketplace, and outside the town a cemetery where lovers seek their beloved and tryst among the silent, sunken stones whose occupants will not tell tales.

A small town, in other words, but almost every town has a photographer now, and if not, an itinerant one will pass through from time to time, traveling from village to village, carrying a large black box with a bellows resembling an accordion, which is placed on a three-legged stand. A drape of black fabric to keep out the light. A makeshift studio with a large painted backdrop for the family who wait silently for their picture, boots firmly resting on a wooden floor.

Morning or afternoon? Winter or summer? Enclosed in this room, we'll never know—but let it be late spring then, a morning when the air is fresh and fragrant, the scent of honeysuckle carried in the breeze, and in the rustling leaves of the newly fringed trees the sound of birdsong; in the evening the nightingales have returned and ice has melted in the river where pagan gods still dwell. Even the ground is warming. Bushes grow full with tender flowers that will ripen into berries, and blossoms and mushrooms flourish in the woods and propagate beneath the fir trees.

The cold winter is over: the heavy outer clothes discarded at last. The sky is soft, a pale blue. The sun plays tag with the clouds and finally wins, growing bolder, and shines brazenly for a short time before the gloomy skies return. The snow has taken flight, pulling back, and all that remains of the long, bitter nights and frigid days are the muddy streets pocked by horses and carriages.

## THE PHOTOGRAPH

Stand behind the photographer before he releases the shutter. Look into the family's eyes, and you will know everything about them. Mongolian eyes from somewhere north of the Steppe, faces that carry within them a glint of the *galut*—exile. You will never see them except here; in this photograph they are still alive. Hear the beating of their hearts. The passions that are hidden beneath their stiff, drab clothes.

The older children have left for America or for other lands. Most of these in the photo will leave too, over that sea where gales of wind toss ships about like toys. Three sons remain: Reuven, a young man now, who will follow his brothers and sister in a few days, eager to leave this place, and the younger ones, Eleazar and Shlomo-Aaron, dressed in their best suits. And two daughters: the little one, Sarah, and her older sister, Rachel Rivka, who stands apart, wearing her beauty lightly, like a treasured shawl tossed carelessly over her shoulders. Only their slender, virginal arms and hands are visible.

The tsar rules even here. Pogroms erupt without warning. In Kishinev not long ago, bodies such as theirs were had for the taking: raped, murdered, mutilated.

### GITTA-LEAH

At the center, the mother. She has brought nine children into the world. She knows it's a blessing from above that these have lived. She is at the center of their universe. Yet one by one they have set off on that faraway sea, and these younger ones will leave too.

Her strong hips held these children in her womb, felt their soft limbs descend into the light; her large breasts, spilling over with drops of milk, nourished them. There is one thing that she knows in her heart: She will never see them again. A letter or two may arrive by mail, which a son will read to her, or a learned man in the village — perhaps one letter a year at most, and later, nothing. They have begun their own families now — she hears news of the birth of grandchildren, far-off infants she will never see or hold, whose lives in that strange country she cannot even imagine. Their names are strange on her lips; their faces in photographs unfamiliar, as hers must be to them. Even the language they speak, she cannot understand.

Still, though she will never know it, in those strange countries she can never see in her mind's eye, they will remember their mother, pausing in the completion of some task to see her face. And at once she is there with them — her touch, her admonitions, even her rare tenderness. They remember her moving about from early morning, even before the first cracks of light came through the windows, to darkness falling: stoking the fire, washing clothes, preparing meals, tending to them.

In the photograph, her lips curve slightly downward — pride at what she has accomplished, weighted by weariness from the never-ending toil. Her dark hair parts in the middle (or perhaps it is a *sheitel*, a wig, covering her own hair lest it distract men from prayer) and is drawn back in a bun.

Hands that are never idle are idle now, free of their burdens, unencumbered objects that rest in her lap, captured forever by this man with his strange black box, visible reminders of her life long after she is gone. This morning she awoke again while darkness still stretched across the sky to finish ironing the girls' dresses and pressing the boys' suits and ties and shirts. She got the little ones up, bathed them, and fixed their hair. There was the breakfast to be made ready and the house to clean. And then, at last, she laced boots over tiny feet as she rushed them along.

"Hurry or we'll be late!"


## NAHUM MOTEL

He works as one of the drivers who deliver freight or passengers between towns. A wagon for hire, a horse, a place to rest tired feet until they arrive at the next village. A story, a quip is always on his lips, a bit of levity to lighten a heavy load, an apt saying, sometimes a drop of liquor too.

Younger than his wife, Nahum sits beside her, but he is alone with thoughts that amuse him and he tries to suppress a smile. His lips begin to part, but he closes them again, determined to stay still, a jaunty cap perched atop his head and a book in his hands that belies his workman's clothes. A simple man who likes a smoke now and then. Driving from town to town, listening to the clop of the horse's hooves, feeling the rough swaying of the wagon as he travels on his way, he thinks of treats to bring home for the children, of a time when he likes to tease his daughters gently and enjoy a quiet moment with his sons.

His family has lived in this village for generations. He knows the earth beneath his feet better than he knows the lines of his own palm, as well as he knows his own wife, Gitta-Leah—the touch of her hands, the shape of her body as much a part of him as his own since they were children. Their youth has slipped away, but the sons and daughters they have brought into the world remain. It was he who drove the older ones in his wagon to begin their journey by train, and from there a boat, pressing into their departing hands a few coins to see them through the voyage, and then the long ride returning home alone with a heavy heart.

One son has followed the pioneers to Palestine; another has become a freethinker in Berlin, a supporter of those who have turned their backs on God. A third has gone to Vilna and become one of the pious who wears a black hat; his eldest daughter traveled to meet her husband in another land, big with child. And now Reuven. Splendid in his new suit, a pleasant, angular face

with a straight nose and earnest eyes that reveal how impatient
he is to be free. And so they have come for this final memento. A
family photograph so that he can remember them.

### REUVEN

Years later he will still feel their breath next to his own and recall
the pain of knowing he was leaving them behind. He will never
come back. He will never see any of them again unless they, too,
cross that sea to where his new life waits.

Reuven has memorized this village where he was born,
knows in his heart the wooden houses, crooked paths, and
winding streets, the churches and synagogues, the *cheder*, where
he learned to read the ancient script, the smell of the stables and
the blacksmith's shop, and the way the trees glisten wetly in the
fall rain before the snow begins.

Here are the faces of his parents and brothers, of his sister
Rachel, her full lips and raven hair and pale skin. He will remember her beauty long after he has left. In the spring he used to
gather bouquets of wildflowers to bring to her, and she would
take a glass and fill it with their fragrance, and laughing, bury
her face in them.

He'll remember the aroma of his father's pipe and the scent
of his mother bending down to kiss him goodnight. And then
the night noises while the others slept, when he dreamed of a
world beyond the sea, beyond this house and this place, where
*Jew* was not a dirty word.

### RACHEL RIVKA

She is Nahum's favorite. Standing behind him, she touches her
father's shoulder lightly. She is the daughter of a poor man, but

her eyes, nose, full lips, are arranged to form a comely countenance that shines with incandescent grace.

Everyone else will go, even the little ones, but she will stay. She has not been farther than the next town, but she has heard of Vilna where her brother lives, with its many synagogues and cobbled streets and fine houses and women with elegant clothes. But her world is here. Why would she leave? Sun, moon, sky, water. The fields and rivers, where great bonfires are lit on holidays and goblins dwell.

She has not gone to school like the boys, but she can make out letters and words. She sews and embroiders and made the pretty lace collar that brightens her dress. She plucks feathers and stuffs the pillows and winter comforters. Every night, she heats water in a samovar and brings her father a glass of tea that he drinks with a cube of sugar, and relieves his swollen feet of their muddy boots. She feeds the hens and gathers the eggs, bakes the bread, draws water from the well.

She has helped to bring up the younger children, attended her mother at their births, placing amulets and red string on the bedposts to keep the she-demon, Lilith, from harming them. She cleans the house and goes to market, hurrying past the coarse, drunken men who call after her.

"Look at the pretty Jewgirl!"

But she is more than this. Inside her is a soul. She feels every rustle of the fresh spring breeze as she rushes through the streets on her way to the center of town, her steps hastening past the church where passersby cross themselves. She has felt the first stirrings of desire, can already see the children she will have one day.

The seasons pass, as this one will too. The holy days appear one by one, each succeeding the other. This pleasant morning will finally turn into the trembling of the Days of Awe, when lives hang in the balance, and then to the short dark nights of the winter solstice when thin, slender candles that remember a long-ago victory provide the only light. Then comes again the airing of beds at the turn of spring, the house to be made ready for the journey into freedom, not a piece of leaven left in the cupboards.

And yet they are still in exile.

Yes, she will remain while the others go, close to her mother and father. There are times when she has visions of what is ahead, can feel it just beyond her, feel the quickness of being alive and then the fear that their lives will end. When they have all left, even the little ones, she will be known as the one who remained. Secrets press against her as her life stretches through the days.

Beyond this room, beyond this moment, she senses the earth shuddering. The future comes closer and closer: years pass, and she is no longer young. She hears in a time that is still to come the firing of distant guns, the trucks with their soldiers and killing machines that will roll across this soil where she has lived. She does not understand the men's words, but she understands the firm resolve of their faces.

The soldiers will take away their lives—Rachel Rivka's, Nahum Motel's, Gitta-Leah's—and everything else on the Jewish street, until nothing is left but this photograph, this moment in eternity where they rest without moving now, alive forever.

# Vilna

Joseph finished the doll three days before the Germans came in 1941. It was a June day, just after the first day of summer, and his daughter Batya's seventh birthday. The day was warm, the sky was clear, cloudless and blue. Not even a bird stirred in the courtyard.

On days like this when he was a child, he and his younger brother Jacob would have skipped school and gone to the Vilnia River to bathe or to the forests beyond the town to play between the somber shadows. Now he remembered it as one remembers photos stippled with the gauzy film of the past. Oh, the strength of their young bodies burnished with sunlight! The sinewy cords of firm flesh! The radiance of their youthful faces! And years later, the small town where he and Miriam had stayed, wedding-tinsled, their hot breath and passionate hearts unknowingly making fodder for the onslaught of the cold Nazi machines and their masters.

Run! Flee! Joseph had told Jacob before they came, and

miraculously his brother was able to climb out of the net that was enveloping them just in time. The Communists escaped first, followed by armed Lithuanians who slaughtered helpless Jews who tried to reach the Russian border. Only a few made it. On the 24th of June German forces entered Vilna. Within days synagogues were burned and Torah scrolls desecrated. The enemy went from house to house searching for Jews.

Joseph had urged Jacob to flee, even though he didn't think he would ever see his brother again. The oldest, Joseph stayed behind to take care of his parents. Now, they too were dead but he was still here. Sitting at his bench fashioning a new pair of pants, his breath sucked in, he thought of Jacob in America. Now it was too late, too late to join him.

"And what will you do?" Jacob had asked when they parted. His eyes were the same washed lapis as Joseph's, bleached stones that burned like ice. People thought they were twins. Jacob's hair flamed coppery red around his face, like ribbons of fire against his skin — fair and milky white.

"I'll think of something," Joseph answered. "Meanwhile go, and don't worry. We'll get along somehow. After all, I still know how to make a fine suit of clothes!"

Sitting at his bench working, he often thought of his brother. Whole sentences composed themselves in his mind. Letters he never wrote. He closed his eyes and tried to picture Jacob in America. Even when he said the *Shema*, it was Jacob's pale mirror image of himself that rose before him. At that very moment, he thought, perhaps Jacob was thinking of him, too.

When they were young tailors together, working next to each other every day, the same thought had often come to each of them at exactly the same time, and when they began to speak they were astonished to find that the same words came out of their mouths.

Now Joseph tried to imagine the streets where Jacob walked, the people he talked to, the foods he ate, the height of the buildings. Was it possible that the same sun shone over both of them, the same moon lit their paths at night? In America, Jacob wrote, there were so many lights that night was like day. Only fools still believed that the streets were paved with gold, but riches could be acquired. Here in Vilna, despite the trees, vernal and lush, tessellated with light and dark against the outlying hills, the serpentine blue of the water that had levitated his childish body in its palm, there was only poverty, dust, and fear.

In America, Jacob was no longer a poor tailor but a man who sold clothes made by machines to elegant stores that in turn sold them to wealthy men. Jacob sent pictures, and Joseph stared at them for hours. His brother was clean-shaven, and his unruly hair was covered with a dapper-looking hat instead of a skullcap. He wore a suit with a vest that even in a photograph, Joseph could see, was made of fine, expensive cloth. But for years they had sat side by side in this small room, first with their father and then just the two of them, the smell of tailor's dust and musty bolts of fabric penetrating their nostrils. Every day they listened to the identical hum of their machines turning out pants and shirts and jackets until Joseph's wife, Miriam, brought down a lunch of rolls and cheese or they went upstairs for their meal.

Jacob wrote that in America he feasted on tomatoes, pineapple, grapefruit, and oranges, even in winter. Pineapple, grapefruit, oranges! Their names slipped over Joseph's tongue. Jacob shopped in stores where there were aisles of food, choosing whatever struck his fancy. In restaurants, food appeared automatically behind closed doors that revolved, ready to be devoured, and clothes that would have taken Joseph several lifetimes to make were lined up on racks and sold without even a fitting. Houses were heated from pipes instead of brick stoves between the walls that might catch fire, and people bathed every day. It was a wonder their skin didn't fall off!

Now another man, Feitel, worked alongside him. He had weak eyes, framed by spectacles, a long face and nose, a high forehead and sparse hair that grew in grassy tufts on his chin and out of his ears. Joseph had taught him how to take a measure, that the right arm was often longer than the left, and one shoulder higher than the other.

"Batya will be pleased," Feitel said, as he eyed the doll and nodded appreciatively, his lips rising over ragged, yellow teeth.

Joseph looked into a doll's face that was as sweet and sad as his daughter's. Like a golem, an inanimate being, who had suddenly come to life, the doll appeared to wink one glassy eye, as though to exclaim, Ah, fool, so you think I am not alive!

For a dress he had found some scraps of flowered material, and over that stitched a white pinafore with a narrow border of lace. He finished the final touches as the heat rose and a shallow shaft of sun crept down the walls of the narrow cobbled street outside.

And beyond the street: Soldiers. Stink of vodka! Peal of church bells! The clamor of an ever-flowing throng of people carrying their few possessions on their backs, German boots marching just behind them. They were scurrying like animals, fleeing from towns he had never heard of, knocking on his door and begging for food and money. At once he had seen that they were Jews. *Yidn*. Oh, shameful, shameful! Stars of yellow and white, a haunting specter of all shapes and sizes, dazzled his eyes, a squeezing hum that tore at his heart.

"Nu, where are you from?" Joseph always asked. But when they answered he shook his head. Could there be so many towns on this earth and people to inhabit them? Even the children begged. Occasionally Joseph put a *grosz* into their outstretched hands, or a piece of hard candy, and in their frightened eyes meeting his, whole conversations passed between them:

*Yes, I know you are only a child, but still you are a Jew, despised and scorned by the world. A Jew chased by hooligans and peasants who do the Germans' dirty work, chased and hunted like dogs before the wild wolves that roam the forests beyond the river.*

And what was a Jew? Simply a human being, no more, no less, who hungered and thirsted, who needed a place to lay down his head. They slept in thick glades of trees, hidden under bridges and archways, in doorways, feeding whole families from scraps, their bodies and feet swaddled in rags. Is it any wonder that the stench of death followed them wherever they went?

The stories they told were enough to turn a young man gray. Had the whole world gone mad? From people passing through he had heard unspeakable things: children lying dead in the street, or dying of hunger. In the winter, hundreds had frozen to death. In the cities people committed suicide by jumping from windows. In one town after another, Jews had been rounded up and killed like cattle before the slaughterer. Beards were pulled off along with pieces of flesh, women and girls defiled and shamed; the precious Torahs piled with excrement and spat upon, *hillul hashem*, the desecration of the Name, fires made from the sacred parchment, letters ascending back to God whence they came;

religious Jews forced to eat pork, or harnessed to wagons and *droshkies* and made to pull back-breaking loads.

Had yet another Haman come to terrorize peaceful people who wanted nothing more than to enjoy their simple lives? If such a thing happened to him, what would he do? He posed questions and tried to answer them, torturing himself without mercy. Whom would he save if his parents were still alive: those who had given him life, or those to whom he had given it? If he were threatened with death or eating ritually forbidden food, would he eat the food and live, or die a martyr to *kiddush hashem*, the sanctification of the Name.

At night he lay awake tossing and turning, plotting escapes, remembering the places where he'd hidden as a child. Yet no matter how desperately he tried to conjure up such terrible things he could not—just as on this summer day he could not remember the bitter winds and freezing cold of winter. The day still blossomed serene and beautiful, and the delicate fragrance of summer flowers drifted in the air. No matter what happened, the sun still shone, inviting promise.

Shavuot, the Feast of Weeks, had come and gone, including the reading of the Ten Commandments. *I am the Lord your God who brought you out of the land of Egypt.*

Joseph didn't consider himself a religious man, but still he prayed. Yet what could God do if men were intent on committing evil? Must the whole world be destroyed before the Messiah showed his face? Even Jews lied, cheated, blackmailed, and murdered to save their own skin, sold their brothers, especially now, for a mess of pottage. Though the earth endured, men appeared and disappeared like flowers that vanished with the first frost, while others miraculously pushed their sleepy heads above the earth with the first tidings of spring.

A line from the Talmud, like a lost melody, played its way through his thoughts:

*Life is a passing shadow. Is it the shadow of a tower or a tree? A shadow that prevails for a while? No, it is the shadow of a bird in his flight—away flies the bird and there is neither bird nor shadow.*

Feitel, who jumped at every noise like a schoolboy, turned expectantly toward the door at that very moment and wrung his hands nervously.

"So?" Joseph said, dismissing the danger, "I still have work to do and I will finish it, God willing."

At Joseph's words his assistant peered into the empty courtyard, shrugged his shoulders and went back to work.

"Let them come," Joseph muttered through half-closed teeth. It seemed that he worked more slowly than ever, that time itself had slowed down or nearly come to a stop. He was determined not to rush, to savor the juice that still flowed in his veins, to fill his lungs with air that was not yet rent with the stench of murderers. In the summer light, shining with gold like a painting he had once seen, everything glowed and grew soft and balmy. In the corners of the room spiders spun intricate webs, and motes of dust, miniature worlds, danced through the air.

Everything reminded him of the past, as though it had already disappeared into the shadows and taken him with it. The streets of his boyhood! Scents of his youth! The sweet spice of Sabbath! He clung stubbornly to life, pulled into a nether world where neither space nor time existed.

"No," he said aloud, and again, "No."

At the corner of his eye he saw Feitel raise one quizzical eyebrow.

"No," Joseph said once more to himself, quietly.

As long as he drew breath he would not give in. He returned to work, stilling the chatter of his thoughts, until the sun threw its light over the far corners of the room. He stopped his foot on the treadle and set his work aside, listening with one ear to Batya's footsteps upstairs, still light and free, tripping over the floor as a bird flies through the air. He arose from his bench, closed the shutters, nodded to Feitel and went up, the doll behind his back. Batya greeted him at the door. He bent down to kiss her, taking in the clean sweet smell of her hair and skin like food and drink.

Batya! His beloved! A round face like a full moon, resonant with light. The tender nape of her neck, the smooth delicate curve of her legs and arms, the sweet berry stain of her mouth over neat chips of even teeth, shining as pale and luminous as precious pearls, set his heart astir.

"What did you bring me, Papa?"

"What makes you think I brought you anything?" Joseph answered solemnly.

"Then what are you hiding?"

"Why should I hide anything?"

Her eyes grew mournful, reminding him of bruised fruit.

"Why tease the child?" Miriam said, irritation creeping into her voice.

"Ah, since you insist," Joseph said, and instructed Batya to hold out her arms and close her eyes. He took the doll from behind his back and laid it in the cradle that she had formed to receive his gift, watching her eyes leap with excitement when she opened them.

"Did you really make her for my birthday, Papa?" Batya stood on the tips of her toes and kissed him, then gazed at the same face that Joseph had created out of discarded cloth, glass buttons for eyes and red thread turned into lips.

"I think that she looks exactly like me," she said.

"But you are far prettier and livelier, and I would rather have you," Joseph answered.

He sat down at the table and ate herring, rolls, a slice of cheese. The baby, Lubba, cried, seeking Miriam's breast. They seldom spoke except for desultory comments about the weather. Now whole sentences were contained in a gesture or an expression. Once they had laughed, held hands, felt the heady taste of life stretching unbroken and untainted ahead of them.

The heat affronted him, dense and heavy, obliterating what little sweetness was left. At night they slept fitfully or not at all, eyes nearly open, dreaming or not dreaming, waiting and watching like beasts, barely daring to move, hoping to escape like turtles into their shells until all this was over. Joseph imagined that in each house people slept the same way, their hearts as dark as the sky that covered them.

In the middle of the night, he often awoke and walked from room to room. The baby whimpered, the doll's eye enfolded in Batya's arms winked, caught in a mocking ray of light. He lay down again and waited for sleep to overtake him, swimming within Miriam's embrace, caught in his own terror, feeling in the dark for her breasts, still heavy with milk. They clung to each other, touching limbs and flesh with desperate abandon, his arms clasping her so tightly that she cried out.

In the morning, Miriam stood at the window, drawing back the curtain.

"What are you looking at?" he asked, his body still longing for sleep.

"What should I be looking at?" she said, adding bitterly, "We should have fled instead of staying here like hares before the hunter."

Her words were like stones weighing him down. Where could they flee now with a baby, a child? They would die on the roads or in the forests, like others before them. Or else fall prey to animals or peasants, human savages, who would eventually catch them and turn them in for a few *zlotys*.

And still they waited, moving about completing tasks, like ordinary people. The cooking had to be done, the wash hung out, the children fed and put to bed, clothes to be mended or made. At dusk he left for the tailor's synagogue while Miriam raged, hurling after him before he shut the door, "Fool! The world crumbles and you pray!"

Perhaps she was right. He listened as the pious rebelled at their fate and watched the righteous beat their chests as on the Day of Atonement. Others prophesied and saw God's design even in this.

On Sunday at noon as church bells pealed and people strolled in the streets, the enemy turned the peaceful summer day into a vision of hell.

The Germans had routed the Russian troops in hours, moving eastward in a few days: Bialystock, Polotsk, Pskov. Confusion reigned. Men and women swarmed out into the countryside, bewildered as they carried bundles, babies, a lifetime of possessions winnowed to what they could hold in their arms, fleeing from the plague of German planes that swooped overhead like locusts, scattering them with fire until they dropped to the ground, discarded rags.

Later came the tanks, with their black swastikas, the devils on motorcycles and truckloads of soldiers with shiny gray helmets barking commands in a language that was at once familiar and strange.

Joseph and his family hid in the cellar the first day and night. The air was damp and cold in spite of the heat. They made a barricade of bricks and had to relieve themselves in front of each other. The baby screamed and grew red in the face until Miriam put a cloth in her mouth dampened with wine and she finally dozed off to sleep. Their bellies grew ravenous. At night they crawled out briefly for air. The sky was aflame with bursts of red light and the sound of artillery echoed in their ears. By the next day it was over. They climbed out like sewer rats, covered with soot and cobwebs, opened the door, and heard the sound of German voices.

"Look," Joseph said. He stood at the window, a ghost who watched behind closed curtains as the conquerers took over the city, fanning out until they had covered every street, every alleyway, every courtyard. In the next few days Joseph looked for a sign that they were human and found none. He had never seen an enemy like this before. Such clever wily ways! Such practiced deceit! An enemy that wanted to kill no one but Jews. Exaggerated politeness that confused and tricked them, alternating with bestial brutality. They learned quickly that Jewish brains were helpless against Nazi cunning.

The pronouncements were fast and fierce. When they grew accustomed to one order, it was changed and something else was substituted. The chaos unsettled them. Jews had to be registered. Jews had to wear a white armband of ten centimeters with a yellow circle and the letter "*J*" in the center. As soon as this was carried out, another demand was sent in its place: Jews had to wear two badges, one on the chest, one on the back with a yellow Star of David. Jews were not allowed to walk on pavements nor to use public transportation. Jews were forbidden to be in the center of the city. Jews were not to swim in public beaches, to enter public parks, playgrounds, coffee houses or restaurants, theaters, cinemas, libraries, museums, or hospitals, and were forbidden to own cars or radio sets. Jews who refused to work on the Sabbath were to be shot, as were Jews who did not follow orders. All able-bodied Jews were subject to forced labor. Jews were vermin, lice, beneath human contempt.

Jews were counted, numbered, their names written down. Jews were dragged from their homes and never seen again; others were spared; but no one knew their fate until it was too late. Men were shot in the streets, including Joseph's apprentice Feitel, who was killed in front of his own children only because he was wearing glasses, but not before the glasses were torn from his face and crushed on the ground. His oldest son brought Joseph the news.

Ten men, including the ritual slaughterer, were killed in the slaughterhouse and hung from meat hooks. On the street of Ulica Niemiecka a child of five impeded the passage of a German staff car. The officer whose car it was, in a fit of rage, grabbed the child up by his legs and dashed him against a brick wall. The car then resumed its progress through the narrow streets without looking back, oblivious to his mother's screams. The blood took three days to dry. The enemy went from house to house searching for Jews. Jews were decapitated, thrown into the river, Jewish homes set on fire.

Nonetheless, in every courtyard children impersonated Nazis and their victims. The children who took the part of the Nazis strutted, cracked imaginary whips, buried corpses, miming men who showed no mercy. Joseph forbade Batya to play with them, but as the days grew hotter and hotter and she grew steadily more sorrowful, watching at the window, he at last gave in.

"Very well," Joseph said, when Miriam insisted the child had to get outside, "Even victims can learn to become persecutors."

The heat gave way to dark, incessant rain, interrupted by violent bursts of thunder and lightning that mirrored the blackness of his heart. Joseph sat in his shop next to the empty bench that Feitel had occupied, his absence a black pit that screamed, *murderers!* every time he looked at it.

Feitel's table was just the way he had left it, his work folded to one side as though he would at any moment walk in the door and pick it up again—one pant leg sewn, the other still to be done. Eventually, Joseph finished it, still feeling the touch of Feitel's hand upon the material, imagining as the treadle rocked dully the puzzled expression that must have been on his helper's face as he met death.

How is this happening to me, of all people, a quiet tailor who has been no further than Kovno, a poor man who only wanted to earn his daily wage and enjoy the fruits of his labors?

Joseph's heart hardened, like Pharaoh's. The days grew hot as fire again, suffocating him, a punishment. Sweat gathered on his forehead and chin and ran down his chest, collecting in large pools beneath his arms. Hunger and heat made them all weak. At night they lay naked on their beds, the windows open as far as they would go, trying to find a breath of air. He had never felt such hate. Hate that consumed him.

As in Pharaoh's time, pestilence reigned and the water grew red with the blood of the murderers. Events moved swiftly. Thugs and criminals, collaborators with the enemy, roamed the streets with iron bars, looking for Jews. The synagogues were turned into public latrines, or else stables for the enemy's horses. Men met secretly, pulling the curtains closed and bolting the doors, praying in the darkness, their hearts rising in agitation, speaking in whispers to rail against the Creator or plead for mercy.

The Germans took hostages and demanded money as the price of their release. Every day men, women, and children were gathered in the center of town and marched beyond the city limits to the forests. The pleasant pine forests of Ponary where they spent their summer holidays became forests of death. No one ever returned. The net narrowed, sweeping over those who were still left, each certain that an exception would be made in his case, each man secretly hoping that it would be someone else who would be taken and that his family would be spared.

People fought for work passes. First white, then yellow and blue, and last pink, to confuse the mind, to snare even the quick-witted. Those without a pass were snatched from the street. A nod to the right meant life; a quick toss of the head to the left meant death. On such impetuous decisions whole families were wiped out. Staying alive meant constant vigilance and a refusal to give in to despair. The enemy replaced reason with whim; intelligence with lawless disorder. Resistance that flamed with a manifesto declared by the great poet Abba Kovner was punished by death, rose again and was crushed, then burned with Kovner's Avengers, who fled to the forests. Rebellion and subservience met the same reward. Yet somehow life continued. Theater performances were held, classes and readings organized, children studied in temporary schools, and hope, against all odds, glimmered with belief in the future.

In the midst of this a young couple was married. The groom broke the traditional glass under foot; the bride wore a white dress that belonged to her mother and encircled the groom seven times. But there were no wedding jesters, no band, no dances, no toasts to a long and happy life.

When the Germans came he was ready for them. Three of them burst into his shop early one morning demanding to see his papers, muttering *verfluchte Juden*, accursed Jews. He stood up as soon as they entered, bowed slightly, uttered the few words of German he knew, *guten morgen*, and concealed his ritual fringes. Two of them tore the place apart while the third nodded him up the stairs. A rifle butt opened the door. Miriam screamed. Batya stared straight ahead with frightened astonishment, saying nothing and clutching her doll; the baby smiled and cooed.

The German took his rifle and prodded her in the stomach until a chubby fist reached out to grab it. He laughed, a heinous laugh, Joseph thought, a laugh like something he might hear at the gates of Gehenna. Then just as suddenly he lowered it, flipped through Joseph's papers, and with an exaggerated motion, herded him back down the steps.

He was given work to do: sewing uniforms for the German army. It meant life prolonged a little longer, a little longer to stay alive. By that afternoon black-booted soldiers, immaculately dressed, delivered the fabric. He admired the way they looked, even as he knew that he would kill them, given the chance.

He worked day and night meeting quotas. The faster he sewed, the more material they brought. At once he felt like a novice. He pricked his fingers, blood veined through the whites of his eyes, and a black spot appeared, always floating, just beyond him. He sewed furiously, ticking off the minutes, as though each minute that he endured had turned into gold.

After the children were asleep, Miriam came to help. One night he awoke before the first light and found they had fallen asleep over their work. Miriam's head lay on the garment that she had just finished, her arms flung outward, like a rag doll someone had discarded.

He sewed and plotted ways to resist. Every time the enemy came to collect his goods he gauged his chances to divert and overcome them. But then he asked himself, To what purpose? To die a little sooner and leave his family to fend for themselves? He devised terrible deaths and imagined carrying them out—an eye for an eye. No, worse, for they deserved worse. No human being lived who could imagine fit punishment for the crimes that were carried out with a shrug of the shoulders, an eye to expedient detail, a meticulous recording of every evil act.

The population dwindled. Hunger overcame the young and the weak. Despair carried off others. The Germans dispensed with the rest. Orphans roamed the streets, no older than Batya, begging piteously for food. He felt himself turning into a madman in the disguise of a tailor that he wore like a clown's costume. A clown who wept. He sought revenge, but he thought that even revenge would not be sweet enough. In the end he did nothing.

Miriam's eyes grew deeper in their sockets. Batya's, too, were sunken. Lubba, the baby, turned as yellow as a pinch of saffron. In the courtyard where they lived, there were nine deaths in three months, two of them suicides, three from hunger, one a poisoning, and a mother who went berserk and murdered her own children so they would not have to suffer.

At the end of summer, when the nights were beginning to grow chilly, a wooden wall was built in the old quarter, a wall surrounded with barbed wire. Rumors spread that the Jews were to be resettled there. But for what reason, and how, when there were already people living there?

The rumors were not idle gossip. To remove the Jews who lived there the enemy used eager townsmen to stage a provocation: shooting at German soldiers from one of the houses, then blaming it on the residents of the ghetto. Forewarned, Christians painted crosses on their doors to distinguish them from their neighbors. Within a day, the Jewish occupants were removed, obliged to remit the keys to their apartments, and taken away.

The screams of the dispossessed tore through the night. Dragged forcibly from their flats, mothers were separated from children, husbands from wives, infants disposed of with one blow to the skull to save time, old people abandoned. No one ever saw them again. They left rooms pulsating with lives: half-eaten meals, furniture, possessions, photographs, clothes and personal necessities, hairbrushes and lipsticks, provisions and memories. The rooms were soon occupied by other Jews who had been given a night's warning to move. As in as all previous actions everything was accelerated, everything accomplished to shouts.

*Schnell! Schnell!* Hurry! Hurry! *Alle Juden raus!*

Joseph and his family walked out of their lives like people walking into a dream, wondering how such things could happen. Everything was chaos, everything turned upside down, displaced, nothing where it should have been. They stumbled around like those searching for what they had lost by staring into mirrors.

They were allowed to take only what they could carry. They took their clothing on their backs, as much food as they could, pillows and blankets, some household items.

Miriam dressed in layers, wrapped in sweaters and a heavy coat against the coming of winter; Batya would not part with her doll. The baby grasped a rattle. Joseph slipped spools of thread, needles, and bobbins into his pocket. He walked out of the house where he had been born, looked back once, and thought that like Lot's wife he would be turned into a pillar of salt.

In that moment, a ghostly image of Jacob appeared. Then he blinked, hurried down the steps. It was gone.

He was no longer Joseph, but simply a Jew, one of thousands as far as the eye could see, like ants beneath a blazing September sun, marching without stopping, without a drop of water. When Batya's legs could no longer carry her, he lifted her on his shoulders, feeling the throb of her frail limbs, his flesh and blood, his beloved.

Those who fainted were killed; those who wept because

they were frightened and in despair were beaten. And still they walked. Through the narrow, winding streets to a second ghetto that loomed ahead of them: a prison of death.

He became as before, Joseph, a tailor, but this time in a German factory. Every day he passed through the ghetto gate and went to work. Hundreds of needles tapped in unison for the enemy. He sat quietly at his place, his fingers growing numb and stiff in the advancing cold.

At night he searched for firewood, stealing what he could, along with food: potatoes, flour, onions, groats, and butter, from which Miriam could make soup — or milk for his children, whose bellies were bloated with hunger. At the gate a woman was killed for just such a crime. He watched her blood freeze into scarlet ice. The cold became bitter and unforgiving, sweeping through the unheated rooms. He longed again for the punishing heat of summer, but it seemed as remote as his own life.

At night they huddled together, their own flesh no longer enough to keep them warm. Miriam's bones felt like broken twigs. Her fingers and toes seemed to Joseph the color of turnips. Batya's eyes grew fearful. Her thin arms clasped the doll.

"Cold!" cried the baby. "Cold! Cold!"

At last he tore apart the walls, stripped down every door, and burned the furniture for fuel. Yet, like their famished stomachs, which were never full, they were never warm. When the light was gone, they suffered in darkness. Drains clogged and became polluted. The cesspools overflowed. Children, left on their own, turned into delinquents and roamed the streets, destroying or stealing whatever they could lay their hands on.

And still the enemy swooped down like hunters, encircling them, cats catching frightened mice.

The boots of the storm troopers thundered over the buildings, and like bewildered animals, sensing the end, people looked for a place to hide, constructing openings behind stoves that led to other rooms, so small only a child could crawl through. Apartment doors were camouflaged to look like solid walls. Stairs were taken down and the shafts closed up with boards to seal off second stories. Cupboards and cabinet doors led to secret places. Crowded together, barely able to breathe, they listened for the thud on the stairway, the pounding against the door, the screams of those who had been discovered and routed, and trembled as the enemy persevered in its purpose, taking them singly or in groups, relentlessly sniffing out hidden places, hunters surrounding the hunted.

Snow came first in soft flurries, making soft hills out of the ruins and abandoned buildings. Then as blizzards covered the ground and the tops of trees, they could glimpse occasionally a world beyond the ghetto walls. Children slid down icy slopes, determined, even here, to enjoy themselves.

On that morning the sky was cloudless and clear, a frozen blue, and Joseph's skin tingled with the knowledge that he was still alive, though he knew how temporary that was. He knew that death would come, if not now, then eventually when he was no longer of use to the enemy. In his fury he wanted to confront them, but with what? He had no weapons, no strength left. Rubbing his hands to kindle warmth, he almost envied those who could no longer feel.

He passed over familiar streets as though he strode through

another world, one strange and unknown, with another life lurking beneath it. He saw his mother's face tucking his childish body into bed, his years at *cheder*, boyhood friends and outings, family gatherings, girls he had known and admired, and some that he had courted. The night he met Miriam and the first time he had taken her in a wooded vale one summer evening...the birth of his children. For a few moments he felt himself buoyed into the man he had been; then in the wink of an eye that other self was gone again.

"Yes, gone," he said aloud, although he still could not believe it. He thought it strange that these events were telescoped now, as if they had occurred in a day instead of a lifetime and an impostor existence had taken over his real life. In the distance a flock of birds flew overhead, squawking and calling to each other, and then another formation joined them and disappeared. His footprints were covered in the falling snow as rapidly as he walked.

Batya and Miriam followed behind with Lubba, through a path of brilliant white, past shapeless forms and figures disguised by snow.

Suddenly Batya cried, "Papa, my doll!"

Joseph turned and saw it trampled on the ground, one arm gone and the right eye broken.

"I will fix it good as new," he said, picking it up, and with this comfort he knew to be a lie, he gave it back to her. She held the doll to her breast as Joseph shut his eyes for a moment and the past receded.

When it happened, it was almost exactly as he had prophesied. Summoned with the others who had served their purpose, Joseph, the tailor, son of Amram, of the tribe of Levi, was led to the synagogue with his family, the doors locked, and the holy scrolls kindled with fire. Hope and desire, flesh and bone were turned into ashes. Only the solitary eye of a child's doll was found among the smoldering ruins.

An ocean away, Jacob suddenly grew still, thinking of his brother, although that life seemed so far away now that it might as well have been a dream. He felt his face become drenched with perspiration as if a great heat had coursed through him, even though it was the dead of winter. The taste of bitterness rose in his throat.

Jacob had heard the rumors and now he felt in his heart that the moment had come. Joseph was dead, and he wept.

# Passion

CONVERSOS

BENTO. This is what he is called, the diminutive of Baruch, blessed. Later he will be known as Benedictus, the Latin form of his name. But now he is still a child, the son of Portuguese Jews, traders, whose family fled from the Inquisition, first Spain, then Portugal, arriving here in 1616, escaping from a golden age that is no more and was never really the refuge that it seemed to be. The poet asked, *How can we sing of Zion in a strange land?* And so they have fled, taking their dreams of a better life with them. Their ancestors endured exile and persecutions. They themselves have been hunted from place to place, slaughtered, flayed, burned alive, and yet they still want to be Jews, instead of *conversos*, forced ones, or *meshummadim*, converted ones, or worse yet, *marranos*, swine. There remains in their hearts and minds the longing for Jerusalem, the City of David, for a home where they are not despised, for the land where they once had their own kings and sat under their own fig trees and were not afraid. Of that place, which they can only imagine now, a place where they tilled the soil and brought their offerings to the great Temple on festivals and holidays, memories have been passed down from father to son. They yearn to return to the faith and the life that lingers in these tales, but they cannot.

They have come to these low-lying lands to be Jews again instead of New Christians, to a city on the Amstel River that is called Amsterdam, where, except on Sunday, the Christian Lord's Sabbath, the loading and unloading of cargo takes place: spices from the Indonesian islands of Maluku and sugar from Brazil, in a maze of canals with its foul stench.

And yet life is not unpleasant. They don't have to dwell in a ghetto, though many of their neighbors are Jews too, here in the Vlooienburg quarter, a square island of recently drained land surrounded by canals and the river, accessible by four bridges. They have good homes on the Breestraat, two synagogues, Beth Jacob, House of Jacob, and Neve Shalom, Dwelling of Peace, and eventually will build another, Beth Israel, House of Israel. They have amicable relationships with their neighbors, and freedom, as well as peace and security. They are finally free from prying eyes and the suspicions of the Inquisition. In 1568 the Dutch had revolted against Philip II, who tried to crush the growing Protestantism of the Netherlands, and won their freedom from the iron hand of Spain.

Yet cut off from the rest of the Jewish world for so long, the Sephardic Jews are different from Jews who had lived in other lands. They have forgotten many of their religious laws and customs, but no matter how pleasant their lives, they are not deceived by the cordiality around them. They are still Jews, after all, the eternal outsiders. Even here, although they can worship, there are limitations. Jews are not allowed to engage in most of the trades that are regulated by guilds. Mixed marriages are forbidden. Jews cannot have Christian servants. Their children are not permitted to attend the city's schools, lest they mingle with the fair-haired children from respectable families. Finally, they have had to promise that they will keep order within their own community, which has made their leaders unyielding in regard to observance, determined not to arouse the attention of the citizens who have allowed them to settle here.

## BENTO

This child Bento, who was born sixteen years after the Jews came to Amsterdam, is dark, with olive skin that contains an unusual paleness, and long, black hair that falls around his pensive face. His raven eyes are slightly hooded and sad, reflective, studious, with shadows that shift according to the light, and seem, in their opaque pupils, to hold secret worlds.

Still, he is not averse to being with others. In his free time he likes to draw, sketching the crowded scene from the windows of his house, the throngs of people on the cobblestone paths and bridges that span the canals, the shops, the fine-looking women. On his way to synagogue with his father, walking along the tree-lined streets in the cold, so sharp it stings his face, he quietly observes the passing scene. Once inside, he watches silently as his father draws a great shawl around his shoulders and over his head, a voluminous black-and-white striped tent bordered by fringes signifying the commandments, which turns him into a stranger. Now he seems to resemble a melancholy creature that might have come from another world, or perhaps an enormous bird, immersed in a prayer book written in that ancient script.

At home, his father speaks of deeds instead of salvation, goodness that will bring the Messiah and allow Jews to enter that other world that lies like a vision beyond them, a world that is truer and holier than the one in which they live now.

As young as he is, Bento doesn't believe in that world. Thinking of his mother, he remembered how still she was at the end, her skin, once the color of his own, had turned ashen. Even her lips were pale and parched. She coughed incessantly and her breathing was shallow and labored. Since she had been ill, her nose appeared longer, drooping sadly at the tip.

He had been brought in to see her. Where before she had always been moving—her quick steps heard throughout the house as she cooked, saw to domestic tasks, or directed the servants, and even when she sat quietly in the evenings her fingers kept busy with her needlework—she lay on her bed, too weak to move. Her hand, which tried to reach for his, barely moved from where it rested limply by her side. He stared at her as though she was a stranger: a small, pitiful form in a large, high bed, with red velvet curtains that enclosed her in another sphere entirely, her face grown so thin and angular that he had to keep telling himself this was indeed his mother.

And then the long trip by barge to the cemetery, before the sun came up, her diminished form resting in a simple coffin made in those same wood factories that surrounded them. He peered down into the water, filled with refuse, on that sad, gloomy voyage to the Jewish cemetery at Ouderkerk, a small farming village south of the city, past sown fields, orchards, and houses, where she would await the resurrection of the dead. Famous Jews had been buried here, as well as ordinary citizens. Scholars' graves dotted the grounds, their tattered volumes of books accompanying them between the stones, as though they might still ponder the words that lay within, which had set their minds on fire during their lifetimes.

"This is the last time you will see your mother," his father said somberly.

The lid of the coffin was lifted momentarily so that he could say goodbye, and, looking into her face, stripped of all expression and emotion, he knew with a certainty that never left him that there *was* no other world. There was no afterlife. There was only death, terrible and unfathomable to him as a child. It seemed even more so when he was grown. He would never love anyone the way he had loved her. Passion could only hurt and lead one astray. It was a thought that would come to him again and again throughout his life.

### A FAMOUS ARTIST

A famous painter lived nearby. Bento was used to seeing him in the street around the synagogue, sketching the Jews of Amsterdam, or on the banks of the Amstel with his easel and paints on balmy summer days.

His father, seeking to have a likeness painted of his mother from a drawing that was all that remained of her, took him to the artist's studio. The house smelled of the pungent vapors of varnish, and the floor was filled with portraits of familiar people. Many of them Bento knew or had seen, and although the painter was not a Jew, he seemed to capture the sweet melancholy of these faces that bore the pain of centuries of exile.

Now the artist looked at the boy with a nod of recognition and asked his father if he could paint a likeness of the child, too.

"Can you sit still until I tell you to move?" the artist asked sternly after his father gave his consent.

"Yes," he said without hesitation. He could feel the older man's approval.

"Very well, we will begin tomorrow."

Even though his limbs ached, he kept his word, while the artist drew sketch after sketch, stopping only occasionally to show him the fine-lined drawings. It was a shock to see himself, not only his face with its solemn expression but also his body. Although he was still young, he was well-formed, but he had his mother's fragile lungs, like his older brother Isaac who would die when he was only nineteen. At night especially, Bento's lungs often felt constricted, as though he could not breathe. He'd occasionally seek relief by sitting up or taking medicinal drops concocted from herbs to ease the congestion.

Yet his brain was strong, clear-thinking, lucid. He looked around and decided he liked being here in the artist's studio. It was different from other places he knew. Here, there was the palpable excitement of creation as he watched the paintings come to life.

Every day that summer he walked to the fine wooden house with its steep roof and sat dully on a stool while the artist made rapid strokes on the paper. Now and then the master would look up and regard him. Winter or summer he wore a head covering, most often a beret. His face was ordinary looking, with its fleshy nose, but his eyes, dark and penetrating, appeared to see everything.

When the portrait was done, he allowed Bento to take a

final look at it, and the child was startled to realize that this stranger had caught something of his hidden thoughts, which were exposed now for the world to see. He wanted to find out how the artist had done this, but he could only nod his head when asked if he liked it and wonder what being had given this man such power that he could see into other people's hearts.

## MENASSEH BEN ISRAEL

Bento's teacher, Menasseh ben Israel, had himself been painted by this man, the renowned artist Rembrandt van Rijn. Menasseh was not averse to paintings or drawings, which were not the forbidden graven images or idols of God. In fact, he is a friend of Rembrandt's, and the artist will illustrate one of his books, the *Piedra Gloriosa* (The Glorious Stone), which explains the dream of Nebuchadnezzar prophesying the coming of the Messiah.

Menasseh was consumed with the coming of the Messiah, believing that it would ease the suffering of his people and end their exile. His whole passion in life consisted of preparing the world for that time, which will only occur, as promised in the Kabbalah, the teachings of the mystics, when the Jews were dispersed to the four corners of the earth. He was heartened to learn that the Native Americans in the New World were believed to be the Lost Tribes of Israel, and now turned his attention to arranging for Jews to be admitted to England for the first time since they were expelled more than three hundred years before. He was eager to hasten the age that would end all pain, a time that he believes will come soon, in his own lifetime, when he himself would lead those tribes of Israel back to Jerusalem.

For Christians that time is important, too. The Second Coming of Christ will only occur after the Tribes of Israel are reunited and restored to their kingdom. Menasseh was a rabbi, an esteemed orator, fluent in many languages, owner of the first Hebrew press in Amsterdam, and one of the most famous scholars in Holland, a man more appreciated in the wider community of non-Jews, who refer to him as "a swelling river of eloquence," than in his own congregation, where he teaches students who often exasperate him.

"Donkeys!" he often exclaimed as he regarded them. He could only think that many would never learn anything without prodding, and even then, when he pushed them laboriously uphill, they lacked the understanding to probe the depths of the text and could only parrot what they heard. He himself, quick of mind, had little patience with those who were not able to keep up with him. Still, in the dark of night, he often awakened and wondered who he was. He has lived many lives. Was he still in his heart the Portuguese *converso*, Manoel Dias Soeiro, or was he truly the Amsterdam Jew, Menasseh ben Israel, whose name had been changed so that he could rejoin his people? His family escaped the Inquisition, like most of the others who have come here, and he often remembered his old life that had fallen away, his father, who bore the wounds of that terrible time and became a broken man before Menasseh was born.

In this child, Bento, he saw himself at the same age. What mysterious thoughts are swirling around in that head? he wanted to ask, seeing the child's serious face as he listened.

Like the other students, the boy studied from early morning until the midday meal, when he went home, a short walk over the canal, and then came back to school until it was dark. In winter the canals were often frozen solid, and he was able to skate over their surface as the bitter cold nearly took his breath away. He had heard his elders speak of the unusually cold winters oppressing them. Food was scarce, and in many other lands there was famine. The cold had caused havoc in these lands, not only famine, but also diseases that killed thousands, causing political upheaval as the peasants starved. Many people thought that it was a punishment sent by God.

Yet the Netherlands was spared from famine and life in Amsterdam did not change. Bento's daily routine was the same except on the Sabbath. He liked to go to school—learning excited him. Before he fell asleep, he traced the stars in their orbits and the precision of their journeys through the heavens. The moon, too, appeared to be bathed in a frosty aura, and as he rose in the dark of early morning and watched the rays of first light overtaking the blackness and a new day unfolding, that too struck him as nothing less than a miracle.

On the Sabbath the whole family rested. To amuse himself Bento placed two spiders in a jar, closed the lid, and watched them fight to the death, an act that he didn't think of as cruel. He simply had a passionate curiosity to see what would happen. When the long day was almost over and he could resume his activities, he was sent outside to watch for the three stars appearing in a sky dotted with flurries of brilliant lights that signaled the end of Sabbath observance.

The world itself seemed luminous to him, guided by a mysterious force that filled him with awe. He looked for answers to the eternal questions in his studies as he examined the portion of the Torah to be read in the synagogue that week, read the prophets who had spoken to God, and contemplated Rashi, the gentle Jewish scholar who lived through the terror of the First Crusade in 1096, when thousands of Jews were martyred.

When Bento was no longer a child, he would immerse himself in the sea of the Talmud, the Oral Law, classical texts, and Hebrew grammar, but nothing would satisfy his inquisitive mind. In the evenings, as in the mornings, he attended services with his father. On the *Yamim Nora'im*, the Days of Awe, the synagogue was full, and the swaying bodies pleaded for mercy from a deity who rewarded or punished them, passing in front of Him to be judged, a capricious God who decided each man's fate.

## A RABBI

As he grew older, Bento had another teacher, an Ashkenazi Jew from Venice who was also a great scholar, a man devoted to his pupils, as different from Rabbi Menasseh ben Israel as the moon is from the sun. He was learned in the Talmud, a rationalist who taught that the key to studying the Law is reason, the kind of reason characterized by the work of the great philosopher Maimonides.

If the prophets came to life, Bento thought, they would look like Rabbi Mortera, with his stern, uncompromising face and strict adherence to Jewish Law, unlike Menasseh ben Israel, known to be lax in his observance at times. Still, he was not unkind. He had made it his life's work to teach these Jews the Law, which they had forgotten in the gardens of Spain, when they'd lapsed into Catholicism, confusing that religion with their own, and had stopped observing the rituals prescribed by the ancient rabbis.

Rabbi Mortera was diligent in this—some believed, perhaps too oppressive. Mortera and Menasseh ben Israel did not agree, and in their sermons they attacked each other. They were so different in their outlook: one a mystic, following the hidden life that connected him to God; the other determined to live a rational life, believing that God could only be apprehended through the intellect. From each of them, Bento learned what it is to struggle with faith and to wrestle with one's own convictions. Yet Mortera was often intractable, unwilling to listen to other opinions.

Perhaps, Bento thought, there would still be another path to knowing God. In the world around him, in the faces of people he loved, even in those he knew only slightly, he saw a divinity, the workings of a mind that moved the tides and the sky, the intricate processes of the body, the seasons that pass each year according to a hidden plan.

Standing in the dim interior of the synagogue as the light of early fall retreated and grew dark and the months and then the years passed, the questions continued to plague him: Who has written Scripture, if not man? Did this God really listen to men's prayers, a separate being who ruled the universe? Or was He, instead, simply part of the processes of nature itself?

As the cold and pestilence persevered elsewhere, fear rose up and entered the hearts of men. People turned against their neighbors and strangers were viewed with suspicion.

"It is a punishment for our sins," they said, certain now that it was an ominous warning from the hand of God that predicted disaster.

Bento would never believe that. God did not parcel out rewards or punishments any more than God rewarded good men and punished evil ones. How could that be—when all around him he could see that this is not always the truth?

Now, as he watched his father immersed in his prayers, he wanted to ask him if he truly believed. Or was it all, instead, merely an outward pretense of piousness to satisfy the demands of others?

There had always been only one answer to his questions: Do not forget Uriel da Costa.

Uriel, formerly known as Gabriel, had been born in Portugal. His family, relatives to Bento's mother, were *conversos* who continued to follow the laws of the Torah, even after they were forced to convert to Catholicism. But eventually Uriel had gone his own way, rejecting the teaching of the rabbis and even the truth of Scripture. Before coming to Amsterdam, he had gone to Hamburg, a place of unbelievers and new ideas, where he had completely lost his faith.

Given the chance to recant his heretical ideas, he refused.

## THE HERETIC

Bento began to wonder what he would have done himself in that moment of no return. Although Uriel had died many years before, when Bento closed his eyes he could still see Uriel's veiled head, his hands tied around a pillar, and imagine the whip of the lashes and the pain that scourged his flesh, while a psalm was sung, as though God had actually demanded this vengeance. Then, the heretic lay at the entrance of the synagogue, and the congregation, one by one, stepped on his inert body as they left, though some said that this could never have happened.

That was the story that had come down to Bento, but the

truth is that shunned by the community and humiliated, Uriel da Costa went home and shot himself. He was to remain a cautionary tale of what could happen if one strayed.

All in all, thirty-nine people from the synagogue had been excommunicated. Even Menasseh ben Israel himself had been put under the *cherem*, censure for heresy, if only for a day, because of a disagreement with the community.

What did Uriel deny? He yearned, it was said afterward, for a pure devotion to the Law of Moses, instead of to the rabbis, who had taken it upon themselves to offer commentary and interpret that Law. Questioning the validity of the Oral Law at the same time, he attacked the doctrine of the immortality of the soul and the resurrection of the dead.

Recalling this distant relative, Bento realized that ordinary life, a life that consisted of only acquiring material possessions—the life of a Jewish merchant of Amsterdam—seemed futile, filled with vain illusions, fine clothes, more food than one needed, and a pomposity of power and riches. Such a merchant lived according to the edicts that had already been declared and followed to avoid the wrath of these other Jews, who were no more tolerant than those they had fled.

It was the life that his father and brother lived. Of all his relatives, only Uriel da Costa had been different.

## A CONFLICT

"What is it that you want?" his father asked, warning him to be careful.

The answer to this question preoccupied and bewildered him for some time. Most of all, he desired to seek the truth that lay beneath appearances, the truth of his own mind, wherever that might take him, resisting the restrictions that had limited him. He began to write down his thoughts in a diary.

"The highest activity a human being can attain is learning in order to understand, because to understand is to be free," he wrote. "Wealth and possessions mean nothing. Rather it is finding true meaning, pursuing a life that is worth living, and dying for what matters." If it came to making a choice, he would not compromise.

"The basis of wisdom," he continued, "is not in the reflection on death, but in the reflection on life." He paused and thought of his mother again. Was she asleep, dreaming? Or was she, instead, alive in that other world that the rabbis were so certain exists? Did her body still lie beneath the ground at Ouderkerk, or was she floating in the celestial bodies above them?

This was a question he would never pose to Mortera. The rabbi was a man who purported to believe in reason, but only when it was consistent with his own beliefs, opposing those who did not follow the rabbinic dogmas. Bento began to disagree with him, quietly at first, then more vigorously. He could see in the old man's face that he was not pleased at this turn his best pupil had taken.

"There are clearly contradictions in Scripture," Bento told him. "It has become clear to me that the Bible is the work of men instead of God."

Mortera flew into a rage. He was not used to being contradicted. "You must never utter such blasphemy in my presence again. I am warning you. These ideas are forbidden. *I* forbid them. Merely to give life and breath to them is heresy. Your father is a good man. I do not want to see him defamed."

In the past he had greeted Bento warmly. Now he either avoids him or gives him a cursory nod.

## REASON

Along with the cold, the plague reasserted itself in the summer of 1654 after a twenty-year absence. Many people died, and it was said that thousands more would surely perish, at least as many as last time, when 17,000 citizens succumbed. Perhaps it has been spread by an epidemic on the ships that dock from faraway lands. Suddenly, poor, sick Jews began arriving from those distant places, some on those same ships, but more on land, carrying their few tattered possessions in wagons and on foot, fleeing pogroms in German towns and Poland, with stories that defy this civilized age.

Yet, despite this violence, the world was changing.

"Reason will prevail," Bento notes in his diary, "I am almost certain of this."

In fact, he knows it, even though in the world of the synagogue everything appeared to stay the same. Yet tensions flared as the *ma'amad* strictly enforced the rules of the congregation. The purchase of kosher meat and the observance of the Sabbath and the holidays were points of contention and non-observers were punished. In the universe outside the walls of the synagogue, however, in the year 1654 there were new currents, new concepts. Bento has already begun to learn about them, secretly at first, at the home of a man who studied for the priesthood in the school of the Jesuits. In those pleasant rooms, he was captivated by the conversation and easy companionship.

He was no less enthralled with the man's daughter—not because of her face, which was ordinary enough, nor for her body, which was even more unremarkable—but for the brilliance of her mind. She was able to teach him Latin, as ably as her father, and spoke of those who have cultivated original ideas as well as any man.

### CLARA MARIA

Her name, Clara Maria, reflected an unfamiliar world. Perhaps, Bento thought, he would marry her at some future time. When he suspected that the way of women was upon her, her pallor alarmed him, but her blue eyes, which changed from one shade to another according to her mood, seemed to him full of understanding and intelligence as they looked shamelessly into his own.

"I have never met a woman like you," he blurted out awkwardly, thinking at the same time that she did not blush at the compliment the way most women would.

"And how should I be?" she answered, turning from the book in which she was engaged.

He had no answer for this.

"My mind is like yours," she continued with quiet forcefulness. "I want to know what people are thinking, what they are feeling and writing. This book I am reading is by a man named René Descartes. He was a great thinker, but his ideas are just becoming known. The world is changing right beneath us."

"And what does he say?" Bento asked with interest.

"He writes of constructing a system of knowledge, discarding perception as unreliable. He says it right here, 'The senses deceive from time to time, and it is prudent never to trust wholly those who have deceived us even once.' You must read him yourself. He is a fine mathematician as well."

He followed Clara's suggestion, and found Descartes to be one of the most important influences on his work. He continued studying Latin to be able to read the significant thinkers of the day, seeking the rewards of knowledge and understanding. At the same time, he stopped attending synagogue and came less and less frequently to Mortera's study group, the Crown of the Torah.

## FRIENDS

Bento became friends with a physician, a much older man named Juan de Prado, also a *converso*, who was born in Andalusia and received his degree in medicine from the University of Toledo. De Prado considered himself a Deist, a critic of revealed religion.

Originally he had practiced Judaism secretly. He even wrote a poem praising another Jew for defying the Inquisition and for helping other friends who were caught in the net of that terrible scourge; ultimately the man had been burnt at the stake in Cordoba in 1655. But after he spent some time in Hamburg where he was influenced by Juan Pinero, another physician, Prado's views had changed. God is not the author of Scripture, he told Bento, nor is there immortality of the soul. The Law is false. There is no reason to give more credit to the Law of Moses than to any other religion. There is no Divine Providence, and therefore no reward and punishment. One by one, Prado demolished the arguments upon which their faith rested, while Bento listened to him.

Prado's views gradually influenced his own, arousing suspicion in the Jewish community. Two young men were sent to ascertain these views, pretending to be friends, and when they pressed him, he revealed his true convictions, believing them to be as earnestly in search of the truth as he is.

"The same thing can at one time be good, bad, and indifferent," he told them. For example, music is good to the melancholy, bad to those who mourn, and neither good nor bad to the deaf."

"Do you not believe, then, in God's absolute laws in the Torah?"

"I believe," Bento said, leaning closer to them, "in the power of man to make laws that are right for him."

"But God has given us commandments that keep us from giving into our desires," one of them protested.

"Desire is the very essence of man," he countered. "If men were born free, they would form no conception of good or evil. I call him free who is led solely by reason and is not constrained by the rigid boundaries of religion."

They continued to listen as he cast doubt on Divine Revelation and instead spoke of the intellectual love of God, the highest blessedness to which humans can aspire, wherein man's mind passes to the highest state of perfection, knowledge of God.

They were silent after he spoke so openly, and in that silence he realized that it had been a mistake. He had been circumspect while his father was alive, lest his beliefs wound a sick, old man. Now, however, he spoke more forcefully, an act that he will regret after they hastily reported his words to the synagogue elders.

"The world would be happier if men had the same capacity to be silent that they have to speak," he wrote of his own failure to be more careful of what he told others.

Many other changes have taken place. His older brother and

his sister, Miriam, have also died, along with his stepmother, providing an opportunity for his half sister, Rebekah, to try to steal his inheritance. He sued her and won, then gave it back to her, asking only for the best bed, the one in which his mother died. He remembers resting his head against her soft breasts in that bed as a young child, feeling the caress of her lips on his forehead, the touch of her hands.

Reflecting on his sister's greed, he was reminded of those spiders in the jar that battled it out until one was triumphant. That kind of desire shocked him. Why did men want to hurt others when their common destiny was to lie with the worms at Ouderkerk?

"The ordinary objects of man's desire, wealth and power," he recorded in his journal, "do not afford permanent satisfaction. Only truth increases power and the accompanying joy, which can be described as happiness or salvation. It is only because of confused knowledge that men desire perishable objects."

## THE INTELLECTUAL LOVE OF GOD

For some time, Bento had been conversant with the medieval Jewish philosophers, especially Maimonides, studying his efforts to reconcile his faith with logic, the logic of Aristotle. Bento's teacher Menasseh had written the *Conciliador* for similar reasons, attempting to explain the apparent contradictions in Scripture.

He himself rejected these efforts as unwise, along with the divine origin of Torah, the omniscience of the Creator, and the life that was supposed to take place in the world to come. Instead, he was interested only in Maimonides' belief that the intellectual knowledge of God led to the highest level of union with the divine to which man could aspire, the love of God. Bento read the ancient Roman writers, including Cicero and Seneca, and studied the work of sixteenth-century and contemporary scholars (Galileo, Machiavelli, Hobbes, Grotius, Calvin, and Thomas More), captivated, most of all, like Clara, by the work of Descartes, who had settled in Amsterdam a few years before Bento was born to find a quiet place to do his work. Descartes was not only a brilliant mathematician, as Clara Maria had told him, but also a philosopher. Descartes' writings began to guide him. He felt amazement and wonder at the mathematical splendor of the universe. Late at night, by the light of a candle, far into the black silence around him, he concentrated on the sentences that seemed to rise from the page with a life of their own and set him afire with excitement.

"I entirely abandoned the study of letters," Descartes observed, "resolving to seek no knowledge other than that which could be found in myself or else in the great book of the world, I spent the rest of my youth traveling, visiting courts and armies, mixing with people of diverse temperaments and ranks, gathering various experiences."

Bento was especially fond of *The Passions of the Soul.* It was the first time he had encountered a mind like his own. For Descartes, as for himself, God was the supreme rationalist, who had created an orderly universe that could be known by following the clear and distinct ideas of reason. Despite that, he began to differ from Descartes on several essential points. He resolved that henceforth he would follow only his own opinions, though with discretion.

"I must be watchful," he wrote to a friend. "I have not forgotten that Galileo was condemned by the Roman Catholic Church more than thirty years ago, and Descartes himself before his death was under attack at the University of Utrecht and forced to abandon plans to publish one of his works."

Even so, Bento was already considering how he would compose his own beliefs. He decided he would cast them into a Euclidean format of theorem and proof to emphasize the importance of following the dictates of rationality. He was aware that Descartes had constructed a new discipline of geometry and had written a treatise in which he explained all of the phenomena of nature. There were times when he felt that there was more beauty in carefully ordered words than in life, words which could create worlds and bring forth ideas that had the power to change men's minds.

Of course, there was always the interruption of the passions. Clara Maria often entered his thoughts when he was not with her: her glance, her hands and delicate fingers, her intellect, which rivaled his own. His feelings bewildered him.

"I already resolved to seek true happiness and joy," he wrote, "after experience has taught me that all the usual surroundings of social life are vain and futile. Men everywhere seem to esteem riches, fame, and the pleasures of the senses, but their pursuit seems to diminish rather than enhance men's lives."

As for himself, he continued to devour every new idea he came across, consuming the sentences like food and drink, pushing through the nights, following the path that he had set for himself, certain that he was coming closer and closer to the truth and moving past Descartes' dualism to a unifying force in the universe. He forgot about everything else, even though he had taken over his father's business of importing fruits and nuts from the south of Portugal. That role had become increasingly like one of the acting roles he assumed at the behest of his teacher, the Jesuit priest, who used plays to help his pupils understand the Latin works they are studying.

## A RECKONING

"Bento!"

Someone called his name as he left the theater one night, in good spirits after performing in a comedy by Terence.

"Bento!"

The voice was wheedling, sharp and unpleasant. He turned quickly, and the man was upon him, spewing obscenities. In that instant he was aware that it could only be another Jew, someone he didn't know—who, nonetheless, drew a dagger and tried to kill him. He felt the sharp point of a knife blade and blood draining from him at the same time that he realized he could actually die.

It was only later that he found out he'd been attacked for his ideas, a fact that stunned him no less than the assault. Rumors and lies had been spread about him.

"I did not die, after all," he recorded in his journal. As it turned out, he was not even badly hurt, merely a graze. But he was shaken for a long time. Worse, he knew from his understanding of the erratic conduct of men that it would not be the only time someone would try to take his life. Again he thought that passions only lead men astray. The attack had taught him something else, as well: the commitment a man has to protecting his own life is unlike his commitment to anything else. He became aware, once more, as he looked at the heavens, of his own place in the calm structure of the universe, the beauty of the dome of the sky, which impassively observed this event in such stark contrast with the volatile nature of human actions.

It was not long after the attack that he received a letter from Rabbi Mortera summoning him to his office.

The rabbi was sitting in his study, waiting for him, the Five Books of Moses open on the table to the portion of the week. He looked up.

"Come in," he said, and gestured to a chair opposite him.

His face, when Bento arrived, was solemn. They spoke of other matters for a few moments. The rabbi lamented the death of Bento's father, a true leader of the community. The mention of his father's name was deliberate, of course. Mortera was a cunning man. He offered Bento something to drink, but he asked only for a cool vessel of water.

The rabbi took a long time composing his thoughts. After a lapse of some moments, he finally spoke.

"Will you relent then?"

"About what is there to relent?" Bento questioned.

"What?" the older man said, and quickly added, "There are rumors—in fact, they are more than rumors."

"And just what are these 'rumors'?"

"It is rumored that you have denied God Himself, that you have become an atheist. Instead of coming to synagogue, you have been studying with a priest."

"He is no longer a priest."

"Well, then, he is not a Jew."

"That's true. He isn't. But he is one of the most learned men I have ever known. He and his daughter have taught me Latin— and other subjects."

"Latin?"

"I have learned what is going on outside these walls. There is knowledge that will reveal the mysteries of the universe."

"And what good will it do?" Mortera asked sharply. "I have read them too, but it has not changed my views. Our Torah has revealed everything."

"I am finding out where they will lead me," Bento said calmly. "I don't believe that the Torah was revealed. There are inconsistencies that I have mentioned before. I believe that it was written by men over a succession of many years."

"I must warn you—such words are dangerous," the rabbi replied sternly. A vein in his forehead throbbed anxiously. "Is it true, then, that you have denied the immortality of the soul and the resurrection of the dead?"

"The soul is not immortal any more than the body. I believe that the soul of each individual dies with the body."

"Blasphemy! This is not what you were taught. That is not what we believe. When the Messiah comes, all the dead will be resurrected."

"That is an impossibility," Bento added quietly. "Death is the end. Reason tells us that this is so. No one can revert to a previous state, according to the laws of the universe. Nor can the Messiah be a human redeemer. It is faith and reason, as well as man's moral nature, that will result in an age of justice and peace."

"What do you know about reason?" Mortera cried out. "Reason? I am the most reasonable of men, but we do not follow our natures. We follow God's commandments. If you do not deny these positions, I must warn you that there will be a *cherem*. I beg of you, in honor of the memory of your father, do not do this. In fact, I am willing to make a proposition in concession to your youth. If you keep these ideas to yourself and come to the synagogue as usual, we will not proceed. It is not only yourself you are putting in danger. The Christian authorities may bring sanctions against our whole community for your heresy. Come to your senses while you still can. Repent or be punished," he said at last, issuing an ultimatum.

He dangled the bait and waited for Bento to take it. The leaders of the community were willing to offer one thousand guilders for him to appear now and then at the synagogue. So, all along, knowing that Bento would never relent, Mortera was willing to compromise for the sake of appearances to the outside world. *Do what you like*, he was saying, *in private, but let us live with the fiction that you are still one of us.*

"I couldn't do that. It would be the height of hypocrisy," Bento said, and rose from his chair.

Mortera sighed and tried another tactic, this time as though he was a sympathetic uncle speaking to a recalcitrant youth.

"You are young. The young often have unorthodox ideas. They have not lived long enough to know that the well-worn path, the proven course of tradition, is the best one. You cannot imagine what it means to be entirely cut off from everyone and everything you have known. You will be severed from your remaining family. You will be excised from members of the synagogue and your people. Other Jews will spit at you in the street. There is no returning. That means *never*. There is no turning back. For the rest of your life, you will not live as a Jew — or die as a Jew. You will be dead. Do you understand? No Jew can see you, nor you them."

There was a pause before Bento replied.

"I am prepared."

"I am losing patience. You were Rabbi ben Israel's pupil as you were mine, and even though Menasseh and I have had our differences, the fact is, you were one of our best students, our shining star. Now you are telling me that you don't even believe in God."

"You are wrong. I do believe in God. Nothing can be conceived without God."

"Yes?" Mortera leaned forward eagerly. Perhaps there was still a chance to salvage this man and bring him back to the fold.

"Knowledge of God is the mind's greatest good; its greatest virtue is to know God. But not a God defined as a personal God. There is but one force in the universe. God is part of that force. He does not reward or punish us. He is a rational God who can be apprehended in the laws of nature — this is the God I believe in."

"Enough!" Rabbi Mortera shouted, despite the frailty of his age. "I have heard enough! Destroyer!" It flashed through his mind that this man's family name meant "thorn." How like a thorn in his side had Bento become. "Then have you no shame?" he asked, before he added, "I will personally announce the *cherem* against you."

"Very well," Bento said with a sharp anger in his voice that surprised him in its ferocity, "do as you wish. I know the gravity of the threat. And in return for the trouble you have taken to teach me, it appears that I will now teach you how to excommunicate those with whom you do not agree."

Rage and defeat were reflected in the rabbi's countenance. Erect and vital despite his years, he suddenly appeared to grow older, collapsing in his chair like someone who has lost the thread that stitched his life together. And yet the thin, stubborn line of his lips, the tight set of his jaw, plainly said, *You will not get away with this arrogance. I will see to that.* It was an expression that Bento would never forget. It meant, *Think what I think; do as I say!* It was clear his former teacher had become his fiercest enemy.

So, he thought, it was not to be death, after all, but another exile.

On the way out, he paused at the sanctuary. On the *bima* the Torahs were hidden behind satin curtains, but he could still see them in his mind's eye, their embroidered covers, the crowns, and the bells that he had loved as a child when they gave forth a pleasant sound as the Torah scrolls were carried about the room. The Eternal Light above the ark shone with a steady glow that defied the centuries, a testament to this people who would no longer be his own.

He knew at that moment that he would never come here again.

## THE CHEREM

On July 27, 1656, a warm, sensuous, golden day, the trees were full of foliage, and in the fields the crops were ripening. Outside, the sun was shining and the air was gentle. Yet, here inside the Amsterdam synagogue, it was cold and barren.

When the harsh words of the *cherem* were read, Mortera was there, as he had promised, but not Menasseh ben Israel, who was in London trying to arrange for the Jews to be readmitted to England. He would never hear of the excommunication of his best pupil, as he would die on the return voyage, accompanying the body of his son Samuel, who died suddenly while they were still occupied with their mission.

Rabbi Mortera read in an impassioned, trembling voice:

The Lords of the ma'amad, having long known of the evil opinions and acts of Baruch de Spinoza, have endeavored by various means and promises to turn him from his evil ways. But having failed to make him mend his wicked ways, and on the contrary, daily receiving more and more serious information about the abominable heresies which he practiced and taught and about his monstrous deeds...they became convinced of the truth of the matter...they have decided that the said Espinosa should be excommunicated and expelled from the people of Israel...

No one was permitted to communicate with him, orally or in writing, nor accord him any favor, nor stay with him under the same roof, nor come within four cubits in his vicinity, nor to read any treatise composed or written by him.

Unlike other *cherems*, it will never be rescinded. For Bento the past was gone. There was only the present and future, the rest of his life to discover the truth. The hurts, the humiliations, the passions, the power that others wanted to exert over him, had vanished. He was only twenty-three years old, and yet it felt to him that he had lived a very long time. Suddenly, he remembered an axiom of Terence, the Roman slave who became free through the power of his mind: "Nothing human is alien to me."

### BENEDICTUS

Passersby looked up, unaware of the drama that was unfolding, and saw a man walking down the road to Ouderkerk in haste, as though he was fleeing from someone. He was dressed in the manner of a city gentleman. His face was handsome and sensitive, but agitated with exertion. Horses clopped along the dusty path next to barges floating down the river as people gazed curiously at this fine figure they did not know. The sweet scent of summer enveloped him, the buzzing of insects and the song of birds, as on any other summer day. The heat rose thickly from the ground into the muted sounds, and wildflowers clustered brightly in tufts of grass.

Children stopped for a moment at their play; men who were still working looked up and then went about their business. It was the hour when the earth was lit with a coppery glow, and in this low land, the sky was enormous as dusk descended, in that time of sadness between day and night when loneliness and death become manifest in the burnished light of the sky as it reflects the earth, the sun burning brightly and then sinking into the horizon, extinguished. Timidly, at first, one by one, the stars appeared, and then spread across the heavens.

It was at that moment, looking into the spangled abyss above him, the slender figure striding down the road thought of that extraordinary man, his friend Christiaan Huygens, the mathematician and astronomer who had just the year before discovered a new moon orbiting Saturn. He had also examined the planet's rings, but most miraculous of all, Huygens had observed and sketched the Orion Nebula, the nearest star formation to earth, which could be seen faintly with the naked eye.

What might that mathematician have thought, Bento wondered, when he saw the splendor of the nebula?

"It seemed as though the vault of that chamber had turned into a glowing fire with blue-tinted dust, reflecting the light of newborn stars," Bento imagined he might have written. "My whole being expanded. I felt as though I had encountered divinity itself, the source of all life, and my heart beat with the rhythm of the universe that will transcend time long after I am gone."

These thoughts calmed him. Nothing can impede the future. It impinges on the present, always moving forward, and those who try to halt the process are finally crushed and defeated. The quest for knowledge advances to conquer ignorance. He feels his fear and sorrow at what took place that day begin to pass. And by the time he reaches the cottage of his companion, one of the Mennonites, who emphasize individual independence in interpreting the word of God, he feels some measure of peace. He knocks. The door is opened and then quickly closed. Despite the danger, he will find a home here from his enemies, for a time, at least.

He is not a Jew anymore, but neither is he a Christian. The constraints of religion will not be able to hold him. He feels a tremor of exaltation and excitement as they sit down to eat. His friend had prepared a meal, the table laid for a feast, if not a celebration. The men raised their goblets and drank to a new beginning. He will never again be called by his Hebrew name, Baruch.

On occasion, in rare moments, he will be able to look to the end of his life. He will think much and publish little in that lifetime, but after his death, when his views and work are more fully known, men will realize the glory of his mind, which they barely appreciated while he was alive.

The leading figures of his day will come to visit and converse with him. He has already become interested in optic lenses, which he will grind to earn a living (even though he has been warned the small particles of glass could damage his lungs). The work is meditative and allows him time to think and to keep up with the latest advances in mathematics. But he will be bound to no one.

He is no longer confused. He has decided that love can only bring unhappiness. Someone else will marry Clara Maria, that intelligent woman, seduced by the gift of a string of pearls, the wealthy suitor, a friend of his, a fellow student who betrayed him.

"All evils seem to have arisen from the fact that happiness or unhappiness," he wrote, "is made wholly to depend on the quality of the object we love."

It was not the first or the last of betrayals. He will never see his younger brother again, nor his childhood friends, nor anyone who called himself a Jew. But his rewards will be many. He will pursue reason. He will change the way men think and guide them in the power of the mind to overcome all obstacles, freeing them from the limitations that states and religion impose.

But most of all, he will himself be free from the prisons that men build to contain their souls.

# A Love Story

Some people said I was a prodigy, an *ilui*. It's true that we had more than our share of them in our town. My mind was like lightning, with brilliant flashes of illumination. Thoughts pierced my brain like shooting stars vaulting across the immense inky dome of the night sky. My father had only to tell me something and I remembered it.

By the time I was three, I knew my *alef-bet*, the blessing for washing my hands, the praise of the Creator after meals, and the words of the *Shema*. Until that age, my mother and sister took care of me. But then my hair was cut and I was left with only *peyot*, sidelocks, and I began wearing the *tallit katan*, a small cloak with ritual fringes, and a cap to cover my curls. And I had to study with my father every evening instead of falling asleep listening to my mother's lullabies.

I wanted to stay with my mother and clung to her skirts. "You are no longer a child," she told me gently.

Now I had to say my morning prayers while my father recited

blessings as he wrapped the straps of the *tefillin* that bound his heart to the Creator around his left arm seven times, fastened the small leather box that contained scrolls of Torah verses above his forehead, and then finished winding the remaining strap three times around his middle finger, a reminder of the covenant, before extending it across his hand as he formed the letters of one of God's names. He faced in the direction of Jerusalem, the place where he longed to return. I watched him as he prayed, yearning toward that unseen being that governed our lives, and was filled with questions that seemed to have no answers.

When I asked why we had to obey all these rules, my father answered, "God is everywhere."

"Why can't I see him then?"

"He is invisible to our eyes. But he knows every act we commit. You must not only know the Law, but to be a good Jew you must follow it."

The tone of my father's voice was firm. There was a law for everything, getting up and going to sleep, washing my hands, the food I ate. From that time on, I would learn these laws, one by one, until they were part of my life and I obeyed them without thinking.

My father was a vintner, like his fathers before him. Yet years before, most of our community had been massacred by the Crusaders on their way to our Holy Land and the rest, seeking protection among their non-Jewish neighbors, were betrayed and chose to kill themselves and their families rather than fall into the infidels' hands again.

However, gradually life resumed once more, and even flourished after a time—until we were accused of ritual murder.

And then again, when we were banished anew, when we were accused falsely of poisoning the wells during the plague in 1349. Then, once more, in the summer of 1438 we were expelled, our cemetery and synagogue desecrated.

The process repeated itself throughout the years. First we were invited back and then we were banished.

During the war between the Catholics and the Protestants that only ended in 1648 after thirty years, the Jews suffered grievously, but so did the rest of the population. Terrible acts were committed. Innocent people slaughtered as heretics, and other savage deeds committed by mercenary soldiers. The land was devastated, with famine and disease rampant across the countryside.

Still, as the years passed, we came back as we had done in the past. First a few and then more, until more than a hundred families were allowed to settle in the Jews' part of the city. With the war that had ravaged our part of the world over, and the hope of peace in the future, my father was one of those who had returned and received permission to begin planting vertical rows of vines on the terraced hillsides to provide wine for our sacred occasions. He often took me when he went to inspect the vineyard for disease and vermin. A good harvest depended on many things: abundant rain, mild winters, and a discerning eye and a quick hand to catch trouble before it happened.

In winter, dark, low clouds brooded heavily in the sky and the land was cold. But in spring the rain softened the ground, the sky became less angry, and by the Feast of Weeks, the grapes had begun to mature. It was the most beautiful season of all.

After the spring rains, droplets of water clung to the leaves and sparkled in the light like glittering jewels. From my hilly perch, I looked down at the town below, glowing in shades of burnt ocher, and imagined the rooms of my timbered house as though there were no walls or roof. I saw our entire house totally open to earth and heaven—my bed, with its ewer of water next to it so that my hands would be washed immediately upon waking, the room where we dined, a seven-branched Sabbath lamp suspended overhead that illuminated our faces on the day when all the hustle and bustle of the week ceased, the great hearth where my mother and her servant girl prepared the food, even the place where I liked to hide and curl up beneath the staircase.

In the spring, summer, and early fall, from Passover to the Jewish New Year, Father was busy with the hired workers until the harvest, and then the grapes were transformed into casks of wine that would later be shipped on the river to countries where other Jews lived.

Behind and in front of me spread the endless exile of our history, like the river itself. Our town lay on the west bank of the water, where Romans had built a fortress centuries before. As I followed the winding pattern of the river below, I thought that long-dead sailors might still swim in those watery depths beneath it.

The perfumed petals of the almond trees floated gracefully to the ground around me, embracing heaven and earth; evil seemed far away in all that beauty alongside the serpentine swath of water between the staggered hillsides, its sound like the inhalation and exhalation of a giant undulating beast. And within it all were the silent lives of people—being born, growing like the turrets and towers of the cathedral of our town, whose spires rose to the celestial height of the sky, then shrinking away until death claimed them to the earth again, beneath the tombstones.

My father had a printing press, invented in our town centuries before.

"They have cathedrals, but we have the word of God," Father often liked to say. After the harvest, during the brilliant colors of autumn and those dark days of winter when the light from the kindling of the holiday lights pierced the gloom and darkness, he printed his prayer books and Bibles as well as other holy works. Our home was filled with many volumes in the ancient letters of our people and drawers full of Hebrew characters that entertained me on rainy afternoons.

New ideas were springing forth that intrigued me and would one day change our lives, but the books that my father printed were the ones that had been read by our people for generations. I would hear him talking to the other men about this, each voicing his opinion.

"God's word has given us everything we need to know. It has served us well in the past. Why should the future be any different?"

Though my father was a pious man, our lives were not without incidents. Violence occurred, often without warning, inflicted not only by men, but also, some said, committed by demons and spirits who lay in wait for the unwary in the opaque cover of night. They hid in jugs of water or privies, in the very river itself. Who knew why a healthy child suddenly died, or why my sister awoke with knots in her hair even though she had combed it the night before? Or what would cause a woman in childbirth to scream in tongues she had never spoken? Both rationality and superstition made their presence known, and they dwelled uneasily among us, strange bedfellows.

During the pleasant summer days, after his work was done for the evening, when daylight lingered longer, my father would study the *Pirkei Avot*, the Ethics of the Fathers, reading it aloud.

The words fell like gentle drops of wisdom on my ears. I pondered the meaning of these sages who had lived so long ago, trying to imagine their lives and the thoughts that had coursed through their minds. Once they had been as alive as I was now.

"Neither silver, gold, precious stones, nor pearls will accompany a person in death," my father read from the *hachamim*, the wise scholars.

"Where are they now?" I asked.

"They are here in the pages of this book. Though they are dead, their words live on."

Years later I realized that my father was still a young man when he said this. His hair beneath his skullcap was black and thick, his eyes piercing and alert, his face still devoid of wrinkles despite the summer sun and heat. His voice was melodious and strong and clear.

The days of my childhood passed without event, even though my mother's health, never robust, began to wane. She had already lost three children before I was born. In the cemetery on a hilly mound of earth far from town, my sisters' graves lay side by side like triplets, although they had been born at different times. The inscriptions bore witness to their short lives.

I tried to imagine them, their bones as fragile and inert as those of dead birds. Instead of playing with my older sister, or spending their afternoons embroidering, helping to prepare meals, and learning the many domestic tasks that occupied my mother, they rested in the shadowy abyss of the netherworld.

Between the New Year and Yom Kippur, the Ten Days of Awe, when my father told me we must repent and be judged, we would visit their graves in the cemetery where my namesake Rabbi Gershom was buried, while at home a memorial candle burned for each of my sisters until the last ember.

My mother remembered them in turn, beginning with the first, murmuring their names as though they could still hear her. "My babies, my babies," she cried, until my father led her away.

Those three sisters haunted my childhood—their deaths the reason why she was always afraid that something would happen to me. I was not allowed to play with other children lest I become infected with some dreadful disease that would spell my end. Nor was I allowed to go anywhere by myself, although as I grew older, I didn't always follow this rule. When she took a basket of cakes and went out visiting the sick, I would sneak away to the hillsides, or seek out a hiding place where I could be by myself.

It was during these interludes that I believed I remembered the time before I was born—a secret that I kept to myself.

Mother had not been allowed to go out without a companion during her pregnancies, because demons might lie in wait. I could recall her hesitation whenever she left the house, even when someone went with her. My mother was slight, with a thin face full of angles and hollows and deeply set black eyes with violet shadows imprinted like delicate flowers beneath them. Her hair was hidden beneath a *sheitel*, a matron's wig, and covered with a bonnet to shield her from the sun. On the Sabbath she went to worship and led the women in their prayers. She had a pleasant voice and often sang as she went about her household tasks. I like to think that I remembered the sound of her voice from the womb.

The week before a baby is born is considered perilous in our tradition, and great caution was exercised before my birth. The key to the synagogue was put under my mother's pillow, as well as a volume of the Psalms and the Book of Raziel, and words from the Scroll of the Torah. The room itself was festooned with red ribbons for good measure to keep the she-devils away.

My mother lay in bed, her damp hair spread out around her, wearing an article of clothing that belonged to my father to confuse the Angel of Death. A circle was drawn around the four posts of the bed where she was to give birth.

As the time grew closer for me to make my appearance, I struggled with the world I was leaving behind as I made my way from darkness to the light beyond, as though Creation had begun with my birth. In the process I forgot the place I had come from, and all at once it seemed that I had always been here, in the dazzling light of dawn, with the sounds of laughter and weeping, aware suddenly of the cruelty of men and the blight of exile. The euphoric face of the midwife who slapped me on the bottom and cleaned me rose before me. The cord still connected me to my mother, who seemed surprised that after all that pain I had actually arrived.

I bid farewell to the life I had lived before I was born, when I had spun dreams and visions as I swam within the armor of my mother's body. From the moment we were separated, my

Creator had sent the highest of the angels to teach me the spiritual laws of nature and life on earth, and the power of speech and the nature of my soul within the confines of this new physical world, familiar shapes and faces grew more distant, and all at once I realized that I could no longer remember the world I had left behind.

"You have a son," someone said, and my father wept with joy as he cradled me in his arms.

Through the haze of birth my eyes adjusted slowly. The only other child I saw was, I found out later, my sister, who helped to take care of me. Then I suckled at my mother's breast and was laid to sleep in a basket filled with soft blankets, while around me men came to pray, keeping watch, reciting psalms as they had at my birth for protection.

Now was the most dangerous time of all, as I waited until the eighth day, when I would enter the community of Israel. There was always a fear that there would be an avenger, although it was never made clear exactly who it would be. Was it God or Satan who had forced Zipporah to circumcise her husband, Moses? She had taken that act into her own hands and done the deed herself to prevent him from being killed.

But our lives were fractious, too. Who knew what might happen if someone got it into their head to snatch or harm me? It had occurred before. It was believed that Satan feared that the Jews would keep the commandment and therefore be saved from *Gehinnom*, where condemned souls are cleansed of their transgressions. Danger might appear and take us by surprise, whether by human hand or demon. I learned early that there are evil forces in the world, and that no matter how we try to evade them, there are people who seek to harm us even though we wish them no ill will.

I was guarded night and day. For the *Wachnacht*, the night of watching, a table was set the night before. The house needed to be full of light to keep the demons and the enemies of the Jews away. Candles would be lit while I was being initiated, thirteen of them to correspond to the twelve tribes of Israel and the two half tribes, the sons of Joseph, Manasseh and Ephraim, in memory of the persecutions during the time of Hadrian, when such observances were forbidden under pain of death and devious subterfuges were necessary.

I was born with a full head of dark hair that grew into bouncy curls that would be shorn at a ceremony when I turned three. Both my mother and I were guarded until the circumcision took place. Neighbors and friends arrived secretly for the ritual, just as in the time centuries before, when it was prohibited.

My uncle took his place on the chair of Elijah. The *mohel* laid out his tools, and my mother was led away, her face ashen, too fearful to remain. A few drops of wine were pressed to my lips and everything grew indistinct and hazy. A jab of pain caused me to cry. Another drop of wine, and in minutes the deed was done, and there were shouts of joy and jubilation.

"Mazel-tov! ... L'chaim! ... To your health! May the Holy One protect this child," and choruses of "For a happy life!"

My father spoke of Rabbi Gershom, the Light of the Exile, for whom I was named, his face glistening with joy and hope. Like my namesake, known for his commentaries and *takkanot*, rulings, I, too, was a stranger in a strange land. I was passed around on a blanket, and when at last I arrived again at my father's open arms, he looked into my face, and for a moment when I opened my eyes, I knew that he was trying to read the future, the person I was destined to be.

The table was laden with festive cakes and food. Neighbor women brought still more in baskets, and while the adults were drinking and talking loudly I was free to dream about the desires of babies, a warm bed, my mother's breast, the sweet taste of her milk.

In this way I grew until my third birthday, the time of my *upshernish*, when I was formally initiated into the world of learning. My father would read to me as I pondered the meaning of the words he spoke. Had not the Word come from God, who created the world with language?

"Yes, the Creator brought the Creation into being through these letters," my father told me. "Their very shapes are holy. Each letter has a story. The letters together connect to the history of our people, with words that contain a message from the Master of the World."

When I drew the letters, I watched the way their very forms complied: some curve and others are closed; still others spiral to the heavens or open their arms and beckon to me with hidden mysterious messages. At night when I fell asleep, I strung them together into words and the words into sentences that spoke to me of ancient times. In the dark, when the canopy above us is dormant between slumber and being, I caught glimmers of the world I had come from, the learning that I had already mastered. But by morning when the first rays of light opened my lids, and I arose and washed to say my blessings, the knowledge had disappeared again, as though it was a phantom I had only imagined.

Then one day when I was five or six, I awoke and went into my father's library while he tended his vineyard and took down a book by my namesake. Miraculously, in my semiconscious state that the sages say is one-sixtieth of death, I began to read by putting the letters together to form words from the commentaries of Rabbeinu Gershom, who lived in this very place where I had been born, the head of the great yeshiva of Mainz, who continued the tradition of Talmudic learning of the Babylonian sages.

The words of this man I had never known spoke to me from the grave, until he was no longer dead, but possessed my very soul. As I read, I saw a passage that startled me.

A Jewish community must accept with compassion a Jew returning to the faith after forcibly being converted to another religion.

It was only later that I learned it was his own son of whom he spoke, a son who was forcibly converted to Christianity and died before returning to Judaism. At his death, Rabbeinu Gershom sat *shiva* for fourteen days, seven mourning for the physical death, and another seven for the spiritual loss.

Even at my young age, I knew that it was a tragic tale of our lives here and now. The story moved me to tears and at the same time compelled me to continue my studies and to find out everything I could about the people who preceded me, the parents who had given birth to me. Soon my eagerness to learn overcame my obedience to my father, who had forbidden me to enter his library secretly, by myself. A hunger consumed me, and eager for knowledge, I began to study whenever I could, despite his warnings. In this way I memorized half the Torah and began making my way through the Talmud, the Oral Law.

Days and months went by like this, until I grew careless, so engrossed that I left out a volume that I had been studying.

One evening my father called me into his presence and asked me to sit down. His face was grave and troubled; he seemed angry.

"Did you help yourself to the books here?"

I waited a moment before I answered. My face was hot.

"I wanted to read them for myself."

"And did you?"

"Yes, Abba."

"And how did you do that?"

"I learned myself. By studying the letters."

My father looked shocked, but he strove to keep his voice steady.

"And what did you learn?"

"I have read the Torah," I explained. "In fact I have memorized much of it. I have studied the Talmud, and I am also memorizing the Law and its teachings. I have learned about Rabbeinu Gershom's son who was forced to convert to Christianity and died before he could return."

"A great tragedy," my father said. "Is that all, then?"

"No, father."

"Yes?"

"Rabbeinu sat fourteen days of *shiva*. He mourned the expulsion of the Jews of Mainz in 1012, and also his son."

"I am beginning to think that you may be the heir to Rabbeinu Gershom," he said.

I did not answer. The tone of my father's voice frightened me. Then he looked at me with great sadness.

"You are already beyond your years. Yet you may be one of

those who have been designated to continue our tradition of great scholars." He mused half to himself. "I cannot hold you back. The law is that a father must not be envious of his son." He stood up, placed his hands on my shoulders, and looked at me intently, "The time has come for you to study with someone else."

Since I was not yet old enough to go to the yeshiva, a place was found for me with Reb Meier.

I had seen Reb Meier when I accompanied my father to worship. He always sat alone, wrapped in his prayer shawl in such a way as to shield himself from everyone else. His beard was white, but the remaining hair on his head was still a mottled gray. Nestled within pockets of flesh beneath his thick brows, his eyes were mournful watery beads. When he was called to the Torah and ascended the steps to the *bima*, his heavy footsteps shook the floorboards, and his voice as he recited the blessings and read from the scroll was so low and halting as to be barely perceptible.

The first day my mother took me to join other boys who were students at Reb Meier's, I was dressed in my best clothes. I carried with me a lunch of boiled eggs, cakes of fine flour and honey, and morsels of fruit. I knew with each step I took that my hours of gazing at the river from my hidden perch were over, except for a few weeks in summer when I helped my father.

We began our lessons an hour or two before daylight. First we studied for a couple of hours; then we were taken to the adjoining synagogue for morning prayers or had a private service in Reb Meier's home. The furnishings there were as simple and severe as Reb Meier himself. A servant girl was usually cooking and tidying up. Several wooden chairs and a table were visible, as well as a desk and reading chair, a lamp, and a shelf of Reb Meier's books. I saw a volume of commentary by the great scholar Rashi, who had once presided in this very place, a vintner, like my father.

I had learned that Reb Meier's wife and children had been murdered by thugs who broke down the door of their house looking for Jews. Reb Meier must have eaten his solitary meals here, even on Sabbath, moving in the desolate circuit of his thoughts. He had a single Torah held in his own ark, a special cabinet for the holy scroll, behind a blue velvet *parochet*, which he took out once a week to read the weekly *parashah*, teaching us with his Torah pointer that he called a *yad*, in the shape of a hand. His voice, as at worship, was so low and mournful that it was difficult to hear him. He was a gentle, peaceful man, unsuited to teach young boys, and so found it difficult to control his students. Still, he persevered.

But over all our youthful voices, the recitation of the prayers, I felt the disturbing presence of those others who had once lived here, as though they might suddenly come to life and appear, startling us with their presence. It was as if Reb Meier's family still existed on another plane, if only we could find them and set them free. I could feel them hovering about, watching us, pleading to come back and resume their lives, and thought how cruelly they had been taken, with no more thought than it would take to kill a fly on a summer's day.

After morning prayers, we ate a simple breakfast, and then our studies recommenced. In a few hours, we would take our midday meal, and then begin our lessons once more, until past nightfall. When our studies were over, the sky was black and dense and cold. Everything was opaque. I returned home the way I had come, carrying a lantern to make my way. The trees leaned toward me like sentries guarding the path, before the illumination of the lantern broke through the shadows.

I stumbled along through the brambles, reciting the *Shema*, praising the one God, as the prayer tapped its way through my mind, to keep me from harm. The wind swept around my head, playing with my prayer cap. I whirled around.

*Listen!* My brain exclaimed.

The trees whistled my name. I was ready to fight off demons. The tree trunks, an impenetrable fortress like huge human forms, moved toward me in odd shapes and my studies swam relentlessly through my mind. I had already mastered everything Reb Meier had taught me. I hoped that I would be one of those who would enlighten the dark places of the world, driving away superstitions that I myself still half believed. When I at last reached the door of my own house I gave thanks to God, and felt the warmth of the welcoming fire, the aroma of dinner being prepared, the sounds of my family stirring around the hearth.

Word began to spread of my knowledge. I began delivering sermons in the synagogue that became a second home for me.

Standing on the *bima*, boosted by a box so that I could see over the lectern, I thought of the way the Torah scrolls unfurled their ancient letters, inscrutable to all but the initiated. The letters spoke to me of those I had never known, all those hidden lives illuminated through the stories of our people. As young as I was, I could hear the footsteps of history, the people who had shaped them, the men and women who had lived and died by them, the sacred spaces of meaning between that guided us through generations.

In those letters I saw the flames that would return to God and would be reborn. The light cascaded through the windows, illuminating the forms of worshipers dipping and bowing like great fluttering birds trying to soar to freedom, the rapt faces, all of them older than myself, but looking up at me on the *bima*.

What did I speak of? My mind brought forth thoughts I didn't even know I possessed, scraps of fabric magically sewn to form a whole cloth, revealing a pattern that had not been obvious before, braiding words together like the woven twists of bread we ate for Sabbath.

Thus did my earliest years pass, until it was almost time for me to enter a yeshiva, at thirteen years old. By now my sister had grown into a young woman. Beneath the bodice of her dress, she concealed a new maturity. She was betrothed to a man she scarcely knew, and yet she was not unhappy. Her dark hair was lustrous and thick, at least what I could see of it, tied back as it was with a kerchief. Her skin glowed with anticipation of the future.

I had not thought about girls yet. Their bodies seemed mysterious to me, with special powers that allowed them to participate in the act of creation. Once a month my sister's face grew pale with tiny beads of perspiration. I had read the marriage laws; soon I would study them again more carefully, with new understanding. Although I could not imagine a time when I would take a bride, it would surely come soon, and my parents would make arrangements.

I saw the passing years most in their faces. Almost overnight my father's hair appeared to lose its color and his face was drained of energy. My mother became more bent, and her eyes grew so weak that she had to wait for someone to help her thread a needle.

On Friday evenings, when my father reviewed my lessons, he would ask me about the portion I had studied. But sometimes we spoke of other things as well. At times I would question the Law or rail against the persecutions of the exile, or decry the Cossack massacre in Poland in 1648, in which thousands of Jews had been murdered.

My father's responses were cautious. There was a fear in his voice that knowledge would lead me astray, or that I would be so taken with the eloquence of my own mind that I would forget my gifts were part of the divine spark of the Creator.

"We must not judge the ways of God," he said with certainty. "There is a reason for everything."

"Even our sages argued with Him," I responded with new authority. "Didn't Abraham, our Father, plead for mercy and compassion, asking God not to destroy good men? Job, too, questioned the justice of God in which the evil prospered and the good were smitten."

"It is not for us to question," my father said with finality. "Only God has the knowledge that is hidden from us."

My father watched me in wonder and puzzlement as I grew. I had skated far beyond him onto the ice of a perilous future. I saw it plainly on his face. From what world had I sprung? Still, he was my father. I stood in his presence and carried his prayer books to worship. I never usurped the seat that was his alone. He would guide me as best he could. He was a religious man, a man who obeyed the word of God even when he did not understand it. I had been sent to him for a reason. He bent low at the essential prayer as though imploring his Creator to give him strength and guidance. The expression on his face said as much, as did his very posture. He would submit to the will of God, who had brought me into the world for a reason, as He had brought each man, for his brief lifetime, whatever its purpose.

As Noah had become the caretaker of the earth, so would he become the custodian of this son who stood before him uttering words that seemed to come from a mysterious place beyond his own wisdom. Surely this child had been brought into the world for a reason.

My new school was famous for its Talmud studies. Students came from many places just to study here, traveling on foot, existing on meager food, their bodies so emaciated that their ribs showed through their clothes.

I had never met the head of the yeshiva, known to his students as "our teacher, the rabbi," Jacob Mintz of Mainz, called the Rav, a demanding man, impatient with those who did not apply themselves to their studies, dismissing them without even a backward glance.

My parents gave me a new Sabbath coat and shoes, and we said goodbye as though we would never see each other again. Although we would surely visit at the turn of the New Year, I would not be back to live with them. Before long, a wife would be found for me, and I would become a teacher myself. In the space of a few short years, I would grow into a man and could no longer live in my parents' home.

When I reached the home of Jacob Mintz to introduce myself, I rapped on the knocker and a young girl opened the door.

"So you're the new student."

The scent of rose petals washed over her, as though she had bathed in them. Her eyes were bright and alert, with a hint of amusement as though she were mocking me. The slender ringlets that poked out of her bonnet were a reddish-gold, framing skin that was resplendent with light. She eyed me intently, boldly, as if judging my worth, without looking away, like other young women I knew.

From another part of the school I could hear the confusion of voices in singsong argument. The rabbi's daughter opened the door, which led to a large study hall, and let me look in.

"These will be your fellow students," she said, that half-mocking tone once more creeping into her voice.

Young men in black frock coats and white shirts that reminded me of magpies swayed back and forth as they disputed with their partners, prayer caps askew, their faces flushed with conviction and anger to prove a point. I was embarrassed to have them see me with a girl, but they were so engrossed in their studies they barely took notice that I was standing there watching them.

"Tomorrow you will be one of them, too," she observed.

She seemed to take delight in that. Her meaning was clear. I began to feel that my very survival was at stake as she led me to meet her father.

The Rav was sitting at his desk reading. I stood there for a few more minutes until he acknowledged me and gestured to a chair. It seemed an interminable time before he closed his book and studied me as intensely as his daughter had.

"Why are you here?" he asked abruptly.

The question startled me. Of course he knew why I had come.

"I want to study the Oral Law."

"Is that all?"

"I'm here to master the wisdom of our fathers," I replied, but even to my own ears my words sounded smug and pretentious.

"Yes, yes, of course," he said impatiently, "but there must be more than this. Reb Meier has spoken highly of you, but there are many such youths here, one more brilliant than the next. You will not be able to rest on what you have achieved."

His words were sharp and to the point, chastising me. I quickly learned as he began to examine me that the Rav did not suffer fools gladly. He questioned me about the chain of tradition, the different schools of thought—Hillel and Shammai, Akiva and Ishmael, famous tractates and arguments—trying to trick me, like a cat teasing a mouse before he pounced for the kill.

"Perhaps you are an *ilui* as your teacher believes; perhaps not," he said slyly. "That is to be seen. You still have much to learn. You will have to prove your worth. Your life here will not be easy. You will learn what it is to love Torah and to love God, to think of Him day and night, when you are sitting in your house and when you are walking by the way, to love Him more than life itself.

"You will study with a companion. As it is said in *Berakhot*, 'Two scholars sharpen one another.' We learn in pairs. I myself will choose your partner."

The Rav had a stern, unyielding face elongated by coils of white hair around a high forehead, a white beard, and a narrow mouth. It was impossible to tell if he was pleased or not.

"You will analyze the text with your *havruta* and organize your thoughts into logical arguments, explaining your reasoning, but at the same time listening to your partner, questioning and sharpening each other until you achieve new insights into the meaning of the text. This is the way that Jews have studied for centuries. We who have lived on this ancient river have been known for our Talmud study. It has stood by us in good times and bad, it has kept us Jews."

"You will have to make your own way, find your own path," he said, as though echoing my own thoughts.

He stood up to dismiss me. He was not tall, but it felt as though he towered over me, his piercing dark eyes peering into the depths of my soul, as if he knew even better than I knew myself the innermost feelings I hid from others.

I was to learn that the Rav wrote responses to questions about the Law posed by Jews in many countries. He was famous as a Talmudist and for his learning, and like my ancestor, wrote rulings for the entire community. But he was much more than this, I was to find, a man who stood by his word and ruled his school with an iron hand.

It took me a long time to sort out the faces and names, the diverse temperaments of the forty other *bochurim*, students. It's not true that all Jews are alike. Some were tall, others short; some handsome, some ugly, so ugly that their ugliness seemed, indeed, to be a gift from God, as surely as the faces of those who were more pleasingly formed. They were young and old—students who had left wives and children and had already lost the black hairs on their head, from either age or lack of nourishment. A few stumbled along, second-rate students who garbled the text as though their minds were clogged with fog or stuffed with straw. Some spoke only when they had to, as though to save their real conversation for study. Others never stopped talking. A number of the students were pleasant and courteous. A few were arrogant and rude.

And yet we slept together, ate together, and studied in unison. At night I listened to the murmurings and rumblings of their bodies, the thoughts that were moving in and out of their dreams as though we were one person. All of us were seekers after knowledge and in pursuit of the holy word of God, each desiring to claim it for ourselves, as though we alone could unlock the secrets that were concealed from others.

But we ourselves were not holy beings. We were as imperfect as our ancestors. Some of us suffered from jealousy; others were cunning and secretive. Many harbored evil in their hearts, even though it was forbidden. *Envy, malice, anger, greed*—yes, these evil emotions, too, described us.

A number of the students had traveled from school to school to study with famous rabbis, learning from dissimilar points of view, moving on restlessly to attain mastery with yet another scholar whose reputation had spread, ravenously craving knowledge like food and drink. Each tried to carve out his territory and curry favor to win a worthy spot distinct from his fellows, trying to advance his own power. Like the Talmud itself, which is filled with conflicting opinions and seemingly contradictory statements, we reflected the perversity and ambiguity of the human condition, the evil impulse that tries to gain ascendancy over our better selves.

But perhaps most important of all, like Jews throughout the ages, we persevered. In the world outside our doors, time moved on. Jews became better off; some assumed important positions at court or with wealthy landowners, the feudal lords.

Most lived ordinary lives, the lives that people have lived since the beginning of time. Babies were born; elders died—the flux of life, like the river that endured, kept flowing into the future. In time, the past was all but forgotten, except within our walls where the words that were uttered nearly two thousand years ago were studied and the lives of sages long dead came to life, their light shining on us from centuries before, as we attempted to decipher their meanings and unravel their intentions. We marveled at the tenacity with which they attempted to construct a moral universe that would reflect the vision of what was possible for humanity, a dream they had seen in the word of God.

Immersed as we were in this world, the days moved seamlessly into one another. Day followed night, and night, day, separated by a veil. As King Solomon said, "The sun rises and the sun sets."

The moon waxed and waned, but was always in the heavens, now full and luminous, then nearly hidden, but always renewing itself. Months passed this way, and then years. We only rested on the Sabbath, the day when man once again assumes the limitations imposed by his mortality, retreating into his own being and allowing the Creator to reign without him.

During these years, I often saw the Rav's daughter. She frequently opened the door to the study hall to listen to the chorus of voices clamoring to be heard, following the arguments. Perhaps she also studied along with the students.

Her father believed in the education of women, which would enable them to educate their children in the ways of our people. He often spoke of this when he instructed us.

"I have followed in the footsteps of Rashi, who taught his daughters Talmud," he was fond of saying.

The Rav's daughter always carried a prayer book, no matter what her tasks, clasping it to her bosom, stopping to recite a passage or a prayer. She often quoted from the Psalms and knew many by heart. She had lost her mocking tone. Her hair still bore those fiery flames, her face shone, but in a different way than before. Now it was alive with knowledge, the knowledge of Torah.

When I spoke to her, she would mention some point I had made that she found illuminating, or with which she disagreed.

"What was your reasoning to reach that conclusion?" she often asked.

Then she would consider it thoughtfully.

"I'll read the passage again. Perhaps I will understand it in a different way."

Her eyes were quick and lively, and in what she didn't say, in the way her gaze lingered, I knew that she was fond of me. I had begun to feel the same way about her, even though I was betrothed to someone else. In the midst of my studies I would think of her, reflecting on something she had said, or merely the way she turned to me with a half smile, the golden glints in her doeskin eyes as she spoke. The tremor of something I had never experienced before whenever she was near made me uneasy.

She was on the verge of womanhood, ready to assume a position as the wife of a scholar. Her betrothed was someone I disliked, a student who had once been my *havruta*. I found him malicious, using every opportunity to try to manipulate the text to prove his own cleverness, instead of concentrating on the meaning of the words. He had a position in another town and the master's daughter would soon join him. Perhaps in that other world I remembered, we had been *bashert*, intended for each other, a connection that was broken as soon as we descended to earth, where we would find each other again.

I knew that it was a sin to think such thoughts, so I forced myself to put them aside. My evil inclination tried to lead me on, the work of the devil, distracting me from my studies, but not enough to do me harm.

I continued to excel. First, I read a page of the tractate, a portion of the Talmud, using Rashi and his descendants as a guide. The next step was in listening to our teacher as he presented and interpreted the text, adding his own commentary, following a dialogue between the students and the master.

In our study sessions, the Rav began by outlining the problem that needed to be solved, asking questions, adding explanations, refuting others. We were to take one side first, and then another, in order to discern the real intent of what we read. Now and then I glimpsed behind his gruffness an admiration for my explanations, a slight nod, the faint tilt of his head, as he listened intently to what I was saying, elucidating a point here and there, chastising me occasionally that in my search for truth I had failed to see a basic premise of the Talmud: *Both arguments are the living words of God.*

We learned that no one holds the entire truth and no opinion should be discarded. Perhaps in time for future generations it, too, will shine with truth. Thus, we were engaged in the holy task of renewing Creation, separating light and darkness, earth from heaven, good from evil, life from death, falsehood from virtue and honor.

"Truth is not found," the Rav said. "It is revealed. And where is it revealed?"

Our glances met, as if he was speaking only to me, even though the room was filled with students.

"It is revealed," he continued, "in our questions, in the search for answers, not in the answer itself but in moving beyond the text and re-creating the cosmos, like the dawning of the day that begins with the gradual coming of light, as though a curtain is being raised, the splendor of the sky as it appears once more before us, not suddenly, but gradually, until our souls are filled, like a jug with water that we drink to quench our thirst. In this way it is similar to Torah. Truth is found in the breath between the words, in the tension of discovery, in striving to manifest the will of the Holy One with human understanding. It is not the answer that is important, but the question."

My thoughts were as sharp as a lion's teeth. My arguments cut to the core of the dispute. My mind throbbed with clarity. The Rav expressed his approval by giving me responsibilities that he customarily performed himself. I began helping with the new students, guiding them to follow the difficult path ahead of them. Looking into their tender faces, I was startled to find myself staring into my own face at their age. I saw the same hunger for study in their eyes, the consuming passion for knowledge, the eagerness to learn.

Yet even here in this hallowed place dedicated to learning, life intruded. The winter days were dark and cold, and when I awoke to perform my ablutions and recite the blessings, the world appeared bleak and cheerless.

A student was inconsolable after his mother died and spent his nights weeping, keeping me awake. I thought of my own mother. I had not seen her for some time. Her health was poor and she walked with difficulty, her eyesight even dimmer than before. My father had become bent with work, climbing the steep hills to tend his vineyards, and had been forced to hire more young men to help him.

I reminded myself that I must visit them soon. But time went by, days and months, and I had not fulfilled the promise. My sister had married and was again large with child; I was scarcely acquainted with her other children. I thought of my betrothed, whom I barely knew, and asked to put off our wedding until I had completed my studies. A few students left to return to the familiarity of home and never came back. Yet holidays were celebrated: joy rose up out of the gloom during this dark period, when we remembered the cleansing and rededication of the ancient Temple with the soft glow of candles that banished the shadows that had crept into my heart.

And then, in just a few months, the world slowly awoke from its slumbers. The black night of winter receded and the budding of the trees burst forth, filling the earth with hope.

I thought of the words of Isaiah the prophet, *The whole earth is full of His glory.*

The soil blossomed and grew green, the skies appeared brighter, the air balmy and light as we marked the journey to the land that was promised and the giving of the Law.

Our teacher's daughter—dare I say her given name, Esther— prepared for her forthcoming wedding, her face alive with a giddiness that was uncharacteristic of her usual somber demeanor.

She was always in a rush. Dressmakers were summoned and hurried in and out of the house in the midst of our lessons, adding to the noise and confusion. Her cheeks were flushed with excitement and her eyes shone with a new fervor. Even so, she stopped to converse with me as though she wanted to say something that still remained concealed. It was as if unspoken thoughts whirled within us and would persist until we met again in the world after this one.

We stood regarding each other.

"I will soon be leaving," she said.

"Yes," I answered, and waited for her to continue, but she smiled a sad smile and was off, as invisible words danced in the air and disappeared, burdening my heart with their weight.

After all the preparations, the wedding took place in a whirlwind, and in days she was gone.

I remembered her in a glaze of merriment and feasting, wine and festivities. Perhaps I had only imagined that she was the soul who was destined to complete me. Possibly my father was right. There is a reason for everything that happens, although we do not always know it at the time. She belonged to someone else, and our unborn children would wait unbidden to descend into the vault of life.

Was everything ordained in the heavens, then, planned before we are born? Yet our wise sages tell us, *even though everything is foreseen, freedom of choice is given.*

Another year passed, and my responsibilities increased after I achieved ordination. I put off marrying once again, much to the dismay of my parents and my betrothed.

With his last child gone, his wife long dead, the Rav often took to staying late in his study reading, or writing to distant communities, handing down opinions or instituting rulings. Sometimes I found him nodding over his books or simply staring into space, as though he had discovered something that was imperceptible to everyone else. Although he was not yet an old man, he seemed weary, as though he was exhausted with life itself—even though his mind was as alert as before, the depth of his vision as perceptive, his grasp of the material far beyond what even his best students could achieve.

Pupils continued to arrive to study with him. Yet more and more, I took over his many duties and the trips to speak in small hamlets and townships that dotted the surrounding areas.

In early summer, golden wildflowers mantled the meadows and the unfolding petals of pink apple blossoms mingled with the bouquet of almond trees, reminding me of my childhood, when I had hidden within the branches of the trees, surveying the land below me as though I, myself, had brought this splendid kingdom into being.

Yet in spite of the beauty, terrible events had happened in these towns: wars, massacres, savage cruelty. Old men who had been young then stumbled along with stumps for legs. Some bore the scars of swords—an ear cut off or a patch worn over an eye. The stones in the cemetery, like my own city, told the story of heinous wrongs perpetrated on Jews, dead before their time, gravestone eulogies for youth cut down in the prime of their lives, brides and grooms slain at their own weddings.

I grieved for the past, but it could not be undone. It could never be undone. I continued as before to pursue my studies, the knowledge that would lead me to God.

Still, when I spoke to the villagers, I saw in their posture, in their inaccessible expressions, in the way they often turned a deaf ear to me, that they did not want to hear about the search for truth, the endless quarrels and tedious sparring between scholars, the splitting of Talmudic hairs. Their lives were hard, their spirits uneasy. The stench of poverty filled their nostrils. Life for some Jews had changed, but their own lives had stayed the same. They yearned for comfort, for freedom from want, for an end to all of their travails. They prayed in their simple wooden synagogues for the time when all wrongs, all sorrow would be defeated and evil banished.

I couldn't blame them, of course, but I also couldn't imagine my own life without the eloquence of thought. So I continued to teach in these small towns as well as in the cities. In this way my reputation grew, and in a few years I attracted a following and became renown for the precision of my thought and the expansiveness of my mind. Life gradually unfolded, following a path that had been destined from the beginning, before I was born. I was no longer a student but had become my master's study partner, sparring with him, although I always acceded when we were together.

The Rav had grown more and more to resemble the prophets of old, as I imagined them, a figure of stern morality who held man accountable, but who had softened, too, in his declining years, weathered by life, like a stone eroded by shifting tides.

He spoke now of the inner conflicts of his heart, confiding in me that his daughter was barren, unable to have a child, even though she had consulted wonder workers famous for performing miracles.

"She is like Rachel of ancient times," he told me, his words heavy with sorrow.

Occasionally, I saw her. She had shorn her own hair, as was

required of all married women, lest she become attractive to other men. Now she wore a matron's *sheitel* that made her look staid and older. Yet in spite of that, her eyes still held the same spark of intelligence and curiosity. A slight teasing expression returned to the corners of her lips as soon as we encountered each other.

"Gershom," she uttered, as softly as a summer's breeze.

She may have murmured my name, or perhaps I imagined it, although I thought I also heard a tremble in her voice, even though we did not speak. I felt the same tremor of familiarity, the pulse of recognition that I strove to suppress. Our eyes met and responded silently.

My travels now encompassed other lands and faraway places. Between the Feast of Weeks, when the Torah was given in the wilderness, announcing the moment of Revelation, and the awe of Elul when the wail of the shofar was heard, I was seldom home, following the river where my father once set out with his casks of wine.

I left at dawn, when the world was awakening and the mist slowly lifting from the water, and in the beauty of that moment and the vernal shades of green all around me, a mosaic of various hues, it was easy to believe that evil had indeed vanished from the earth. My heart rose at the beauty, and in my happiness, which radiated outward like the whorls of water that grew wider and wider as the boat glided on the surface before me, heaven and earth joined together. Like the psalmist, I felt joy burst forth from my heart at the majesty I beheld.

I became one of the great throng of itinerant rabbis of the day who compassed the earth from one place to another, traveling by boat, on foot, by beast, over water and through forests, meadows, and mountains, bringing the news of the age and the word of God—one of the chains of the living tradition, expounding Scripture, settling disputes, delivering public addresses at places of worship, learning on my way other languages and customs to transmit the sum of my own knowledge, and gaining knowledge in return, enhancing my erudition and imparting it to others, all in the service of helping Jews to study the holy texts.

In those days, I forgot everything else, everyone I had left behind. It was as though a haze had settled over the person I had inhabited.

Yet the life of a scholar is hard. I slept on synagogue benches, ate little and sometimes not at all. Knowledge was my food. Truth was my drink. At night the stars were pinpoints of light spreading across the arch of the sky, guiding me through the woods and away from danger, those who lay in wait, especially for a Jew on the road.

The rustling of the trees called my name and beckoned to me.

"Gershom, Gershom, Gershom," a stranger in a strange land, as though in naming me my parents had already known my fate.

When I came into town on a Sabbath evening, the light of the candles spiraling toward the firmament encouraged me to quicken my steps to seek shelter and the warmth of comrades, the sound of a fellow Jew greeting me with the very words that the angel of God uttered to Hagar, adrift in the wilderness as she escaped the wrath of Sarah: "Where have you come from, and where are you going?"

I barely knew the answer to that question, but I was content, making my way from place to place beneath a speckled sky while all around darkness encroached.

Yet an overwhelming sense of loneliness oppressed me at times. Students and disciples surrounded me, but now and then I longed for home, for the steady companionship of another human being, for everything I had relinquished. But I had no home. In spite of my youthful doubts, I had given up all human comforts to follow my destiny.

My parents had embarked on a journey to that other world, my father first, then my mother. With each death, I stared into the open wound before me that rent the earth at my feet as I shoveled dirt upon their coffins—the final act of kindness that can never be repaid—admonished in those moments to reflect upon the image of myself following them one day.

My sister had taken care of our parents, and her brood that stood somberly in the shadows on the grassy slopes grew larger every year so that now I barely recognized my own family.

Even though I had married, I had left my wife and never returned, releasing her from her vows.

My master, too, no longer walked the earth, his piety in the land of the living assuring him a place in *Olam Ha-Ba*, the World to Come. I thought of Esther, the slightly amused smile that teased her lips, the steady gaze of her eyes that pierced my heart, the beauty of her mind that radiated clarity and reason, as though she had just turned to me.

"What do you want from me now?"

What demon possessed me? Who was I? I often asked. For what purpose had the Creator put me here?

I was reminded of the quarrel between Hillel and Shammai, *Was it better for man to be created than not to be created?* Yet my mind burst with sparks of desire, and each spark spurred me on to continue to learn more, to study more, to enter that rare palace on high when everything would be revealed to me. On the Days of Awe, I prayed fervently before the closing of the gates, hoping to come closer to discovering the secrets that I longed to possess.

Once a year I traveled to the fair in Leipzig, the same journey that I had made long ago with my father. When I was a child he had taken me with him to market his wine. A quilt of colors, the smell of smoke, a chill in the air and the brooding of clouds, a foretaste of the biting cold to come, the quickening of life before the despair of winter, the whirl of dancers and the clarion sound of things to do and see, rogues and con men and tricksters, maidens and hausfraus, peasants and burghers, traders and vendors, the dizzying cacophony of voices and music, merchants and families, priests uttering blessings.

Rabbis called out, "Shalom Aleichem," and then the quick response, "And to you, peace."

A gaggle of rabbis as noisy as a wedge of geese, contentious and argumentative in spite of their greeting, quibbling over rulings and ledgers, money and territory, synagogue seats and Sabbath meals—no different from the yeshiva students I had known, each attempting to draw others to his side, each certain that he, and he alone, had found the way to God.

Many of my followers had come to hear me, traveling great distances. In that great din, they alone were silent, waiting for me to speak. I knew what my students desired. They wanted me to guide them to the truth.

"I am no master. I am a seeker like you," I wanted to tell them. There is no certainty, just as there are no answers. There are only questions. All is conjecture and nothing is known."

I began to speak of the four rabbis who entered the orchard in paradise: Ben Azzai looked at the Divine Presence and died. Ben Zoma gazed, and went mad. Elisha ben Abuya destroyed the shoots, the foundation of faith, and became known as *Acher*, the Other, a heretic. Only Rabbi Akiba, whose good deeds brought him fame near and far, entered in peace and departed in peace.

I had nothing more to give. My body ached with weariness. My mind was a pitcher that could hold no more. Yet I continued speaking, cautioning my followers not to give up the bounty of the world to chase an elusive dream. I saw in their stunned faces disbelief, as if I had betrayed them.

"We will be punished in the afterlife for all of the pleasures of the world that we neglected while we lived," I said, and saw at once that it was the truth I had been searching for these many years. "This is the beginning of the path to wisdom."

Thus, I began to speculate on what I had learned as I remembered King Solomon, our wise king, who despite his learning wrote, *He that increaseth knowledge increaseth sorrow.*

First my followers had been curious; then their faces looked disgruntled. Finally, they mocked me.

"Betrayer," one of them said.

"Apostate!" another shouted.

"Deceiver!"

"Deserter!"

As they drifted away, a path was cleared like the parting of the Red Sea. I had not given them what they wanted, and they had turned on me. I felt the echo of despair reverberating from the depths of my being, but at that very moment when I looked up, I was startled to see Esther standing in front of a grove of trees as though an apparition had come to taunt me.

I recognized her at once, even though her flaming red hair was hidden beneath her kerchief, and her eyes as I approached were no longer filled with mockery or merriment, but were dark with sadness.

We looked at each other silently before we spoke, as if each of us was an impostor that would suddenly disappear. She said nothing at first, at last murmuring my name as she had many times before.

"Gershom," she said, as though my entire existence were contained in those few letters.

"What brings you here?" I asked after a few moments.

"I am a seeker like you."

"It's wisdom I seek now."

"Very well, but you are a seeker nonetheless."

She was as direct as she had always been. Her eyes lifted and grew luminous.

"And your husband?"

"There is no husband. There are no children. He has left me and married someone else."

"What will you do?"

"I travel to fairs. I have a stall in the marketplace. I speak about my father. I make known his teachings. If you are looking for wisdom, you need look no further."

I thought of him now, the great Rav who had taught his daughter as he had taught his sons and students, as he had taught me. My rabbi. My teacher. The dead can live again. They guide us when we have lost our way. The words he spoke that enlightened my mind began to return to me then and to linger as radiantly as they had many years ago.

I regarded Esther. She was not old, even now. It was possible that her body would still be able to create life and continue his light. Perhaps we could have the worldly pleasure of bringing that light to life together. A tiny world of soul and breath could stir inside of her. I thought of the children who were still waiting to be born and had not given up hope. Nor had I.

We stood there a long time. The noise of the fair had grown fainter, as if all of the people around us had been silenced. The day was sinking into the softness of evening, and stillness surrounded us. The trees rustled slightly. A wandering troubadour began a song in the distance.

Despite the evil in the world, I drank in the goodness of that moment.

"Then let us begin," I said. "We will be seekers following the same path."

And in the darkness that enclosed us, we began to walk together.

# In the Time of Dreams

It was not a land of milk and honey—that was clear from the outset—but a country of densely wooded forests, of green firs and birch trees. Softly graded hills above the town overlooked the river, with soil that was good for almost nothing unless you dug deeper for coal, copper, and gold.

The first time Anna saw it, in the middle of April 1932, snow had come down those hills and covered the trees with a sheen that turned luminescent in the dim light.

"Can you beat that?" she said to no one in particular, "snow in April."

The few passengers left on the train remained silent. They had barely spoken, even though they'd been on board almost as many days as she. The train ride was tedious. She had spent several nights sitting up, her head nodding off to one side, trying to stay awake. For what, she wasn't certain. Looking out, all she could see was her own reflection, a face as round as the moon that hung like a stage decoration in the sky, a long, pale nose and forehead and shadowed eyes that stared into the opaque shapes that closed in on her, desolate and unfriendly. She hoped it was not an augur of what was to come.

Anna was wearing a shirtwaist and a long coat that had belonged to one of her older sisters, boots and warm undergarments. But she was still cold as ice when she arrived and the conductor unloaded her suitcase and possessions at the station. Some of her fellow passengers were getting off too — a few men, but no other women except for herself.

Someone was there to meet her. A Miss Judith Becker, who wore thick glasses, and who held out a gloved hand.

"Are you Anna, the new girl?"

"Yes," she said, relieved that they had expected her, after all.

It had been arranged in advance, and she was happy that she had arrived soon after the sun had risen.

"It's not that far," Judith said as they walked through the slushy streets. Then she bent down to take one of the suitcases.

"Here, let me help you," she offered. "I expect you're not used to snow this late in the year. But we often get it just when it seems that winter is finally over." Then she added, "You'll be working in the chicken coops and helping in the kitchen, at least at first. The women and men live separately, dormitory style, but they eat together in the dining room. Most of us are new here. After a few days you'll feel right at home."

They passed small wooden houses made out of logs, and dark forms moving through them like swimmers under water. The town looked naked and forlorn. But it was too late now to back out.

Anna came from Lublin, with its fine buildings and houses and renowned schools, where scholars came from all over to study. Her fare had been paid, and she was promised 600 rubles if she stuck it out. She was not the only new girl, though, she found out soon enough. Others had come, too. It was a country for the young, for those who were strong.

At that time the village was a ramshackle place with muddy streets at the eastern edge of Russia, shoring up the Chinese border. It was a raw land, set aside for the Jews, filled with people seeking a new life, hoping they could leave poverty and oppression behind. Some came by rail as she had; others by ship from other continents; and some with horses and wagons filled with their life possessions tied with rope; a few in dilapidated old cars. The houses themselves appeared to lean together, huddled for warmth and companionship. A small number of people in the village still lived in tents and sod houses underground. During the day the children looked about them like moles that had been left too long in darkness, their mothers also pinched and worn with hardship. They came from almost every country, but the faces looked the same. All Jews.

The tsar had been dead for fifteen years, and now the Revolution was still trying to create a new order. Lenin had given them hope. Stalin was continuing the work, while finding a way to solve the Jewish problem, too. Yes, this barren outpost had been chosen for them. So there were Jewish faces, but if you looked deeply into their eyes, you could see the sadness and despair and disappointment, the toll of endless work and poverty, the heat and rain and mosquitoes and disease, and bitter cold in winter, the effort to plant crops and make sure they grew and thrived.

Not far off, wild animals roamed the country. Somewhere out there was danger. Who knew what was out there?

The morning after Anna arrived, she and Lena, another new girl, paired off and went together to feed the hens and gather fresh eggs. It was safer with a companion, protecting them from both man and beast that might take them by surprise.

"There are no rules here," Judith had told her, "except what is good for the new society that is being born."

Eventually there would be a school, a theater where plays were put on, and a group that had services in someone's house, although religion was not encouraged and few people came. In the beginning, there was the expectation that things would be different: Jews would finally be like other people. It was still an age of possibility and a time for dreams.

Lying awake in her simple bed at night, with other young women on either side of her, Anna would listen to the wind rattling the thin panes of glass, and to the howling of wolves. But then she sank deeper and deeper into sleep, worn out, and roamed back to Lublin in dreams so vivid that she was not sure where she was when she bolted awake in the middle of the night. In her dreams, she walked familiar streets and slept in her girlhood bed with a comforter of goose feathers instead of a hard wooden one with only a cloth blanket to keep her warm.

Anna was almost all alone in the world. Her sisters were married and busy raising their own families, and now her mother was dead. She refused to serve as a footstool for her stepfather—who banged on the table for his dinner—as her mother had done. She was pretty because she was young, but she also knew that she wouldn't be pretty forever. As her mother aged, her face had grown wizened: furrows had planted themselves in her forehead, the color in her hair dulled, and her skin grew yellow.

After Anna's father died, her mother took in wash, carrying bundles through the snow and cold, forever at her washboard and iron. Finally, she had married again, a man who beat her every Saturday night after the Sabbath was over. When her mother's heart gave out at last, Anna planned her escape. She decided to apply to an organization that gave girls like her money to come to this forsaken place.

A land for Jews. She couldn't even imagine it: a place where they would speak Yiddish, their own language, have their own schools, work the soil themselves, and own their own homes. After she had been there for a while, though, and the novelty wore off, she found it was not so different after all. There were good and bad people everywhere, cheats and thieves, those she liked and those she didn't, and others who were lazy and just plain stupid too.

One afternoon when her stepfather was sleeping, she had taken a few coins that he owed her and left his loathsome body in bed snoring. She would have liked to murder him too, but she didn't.

"Which way to Tihonka?" she asked.

"And what takes you there?" the stationmaster responded, as though if he didn't like her answer, he would refuse to sell her a ticket.

"My husband lives there," she said quickly, "He's sending for me."

The man looked at her hard, his eyes narrowing with displeasure.

"A likely story," he said, but took her money nonetheless. "The fact is, you can't go straight there. You have to take the train to Moscow first,"

"Well, then, a ticket to Moscow." When he slipped a ticket beneath the grill, she noticed that his fingers were greasy and soiled.

"You tell him hello for me when you get there," he said.

"I'll do that. You bet I will," she returned sharply, giving him back some of his rudeness. He was mocking her, she knew, because she was poor and she was a Jew.

Every day now she awoke at five and went downstairs to make a fire before she baked the bread. The summer passed quickly, hot and rainy, and suddenly it was only a memory. The days grew shorter as fall approached, dark and colder.

Standing in the kitchen, looking out the window at the vast fields and overcast horizon, she could no longer remember a time she hadn't been here. In the summer, Anna and some of the other girls had picked berries in the woods on their days off until their lips turned bright red, eating and drinking the bread and wine they'd brought, and lying in the thick grass before going down to the river. They took off their shoes and lifted their skirts to wade into the cool water. Once, that first summer, after it had rained for weeks, the river flooded its banks, forcing them to move to higher ground. The land was marshy and the mosquitoes unbearable, but they were young, eager to enjoy themselves even here.

Sometimes men would come, too, on these outings—young, single men who wore white tunics, jodhpurs, and jaunty caps on their heads. It was cool on the hillside, and they picked bouquets of flowers to bring back to the bare rooms of the places where they were staying.

One of the men was Avigdor Gurevich. He was tall and strong and well-built, and next to Anna he seemed like a Jewish giant. He had the largest hands she had ever seen. As if to make up for his size, he was quiet and gentle and serious, with a mustache that she thought would tickle if he ever kissed her. He kept stealing glances at her.

"Anna, Anna," he said, "you're as beautiful as your name."

She blushed. How could she tell him that she was wondering what it would feel like to have those large, comfortable arms around her, to have his body pressing down upon her—but suddenly the men were running down the hill, throwing off their boots to jump in the water. Only Avigdor hung back. "I can't swim," he said, embarrassed. "I never learned."

"Neither can I," Anna admitted.

The confession brought them closer together. Anna looked closely at him now. His eyes were deep brown and kind, and beneath his mustache, his lips curved into a smile.

"I want to give you something," he said, and left her waiting for him to return.

When he came back he was holding tiny white flowers shaped like stars. He pulled her to her feet with his free hand and bent down to kiss her on the lips. It startled her and she drew back. Her head was spinning. She had never been kissed before. Not like that. The hard force of his mouth felt wet against her own, his tongue searching out the hidden spaces of her soul so deeply that she shivered even though it was a hot day.

After that he hung around, surprising her in the kitchen, or as she was coming back from gathering the eggs.

Lena told her, "He's after you, Anna. Can't you see that?"

Finally Avigdor cornered her when she was outside, hanging up the wet sheets to dry.

"I'm tired of meeting you like this," he complained. "I know a place where we can be alone."

"And where is that?"

"An abandoned house. The family left. They woke up one morning and walked out after their baby died, leaving everything behind."

All week she debated whether she should go. But when Saturday evening came she found herself hurrying to the place where he had told her he would be. It was on the outskirts of town, and when she lifted the latch and went inside, she knew how Goldilocks must have felt. Nothing had been touched. The table was spread with a tablecloth, and the cupboard still held dishes and groceries. Even the beds were neatly made up. Anna tried to picture this family. She felt like an intruder. Everything was left, even a jar of tea leaves.

She found Avigdor in the garden gathering tomatoes. When she called to him, he came in carrying an armload of them. "They were ripe on the vine, waiting for someone to pick them."

"All this going to waste. What a pity," Anna said, and thought that she would put up preserves for winter.

"We could live here," Avigdor suggested, "if you marry me."

"But I barely know you."

"What does that matter?"

"Love matters," Anna said thoughtfully, because it had just occurred to her.

"But I love you."

Anna didn't say it back. She was not sure if she loved him or not, but his presence made her feel so light-headed that she had to catch her breath, feeling the quickening of her heart beating faster when he was near.

She boiled water and steeped the tea leaves in a teapot she found in the cupboard. Using another woman's things, she tried to slip into that unknown life and the grief that had consumed her, for she felt sure that there had indeed been terrible grief. The baby's empty high chair stared back at her. They drank their tea and sat and talked.

Avigdor told her that he had grown up in a village not far from Moscow, where he had been taunted by his classmates for being so large, and for being a Jew. Once he had gone to St. Petersburg during the White Nights of the summer solstice with his brother, and they had roamed the streets all night, when the light was almost as bright as during the day, joining in the festivities until it was time to come home.

He was the youngest in his family, and now his parents, who had fought poverty ever since he could remember, were old. He wanted a new life, a different kind of life, and that was why he had come here, to work for something with his own hands. Now he was one of the loggers who went out into the forests to cut down trees and transport them along the river.

They talked until darkness had crept over the house and thrown an icy stillness around them, and when he drew his arms around her and pressed his flesh into hers, she knew that eventually she would give in to him. Not long after, she did just that.

As soon as she took off her clothes, he gathered her in his arms, and she could feel her naked breasts growing aroused against his bare skin, as she inhaled the piney scent of the forest where he spent his days. Through the windows, she glimpsed distant stars and wondered what her place was in such a large world. If she hadn't come here, she never would have met him. How strange that was. How many people there must be in the world. She had come to a small place at the far end of the planet that even God must have forgotten, though they were not supposed to speak of God here.

"Anna," Avigdor said, "I hope you will learn to love me."

She had never slept with a man before, but it felt perfectly natural, and when he entered her, she could feel the beating of his heart enclosed within the armor of his body.

Her dreams were no longer of Lublin, but filled with a life that was here with Avigdor.


At the beginning of winter, when ice floes drifted on a gray, silent, river where, it was said, night demons played, her bleeding stopped, and she knew that she was with child.

Gradually, her body began to change. It grew rounder like her face. A seed of new life had been planted in her, and slowly she felt it taking shape. She imagined the tiny head and eyes, like a sea creature she had seen once in a museum, the bones coming together, growing stronger and larger as it swam effortlessly in that interior vessel that nature had created.

Other things had changed as well during the past year. A library and a schoolhouse had been built, and passing by she would hear the children chanting, "Lenin was our leader. Our teacher, our friend..." In the evenings there were clubs and gatherings: political groups and a reader's circle—even a fledgling theater that put on performances in Yiddish. The streets were paved, and more automobiles had appeared. By May the crops were thriving, and on one of the farms, they kept bees and sold pots of honey.

Anna had seen the beekeeper in town one day. He usually wore a mask to go among the hives, but once, unprotected, he had been surprised and stung by swarms of angry bees. He was rushed to the doctor, who treated him with a salve. This was the same doctor, Grunwald, who would deliver Anna's baby—if she wanted him to—otherwise, one of the midwives would do it.

Within a few months, her movements grew slow and heavy, and she no longer flew down the stairs, eager to begin the day's tasks. Avigdor helped her before he went to work. He got out her rolling pin and baking supplies, asking her, as she prepared the dough, to marry him and give the child a name instead of letting the child remain a *mamzer*, a bastard, who would never be accepted among the people of Israel.

"But you said you didn't believe in that," she argued. You said you had to work for the good of the Revolution." She didn't mention the rumors that were beginning to circulate: that they had been lured here so that they could be eliminated more easily.

"But we are still Jews," he insisted. "Nothing, not even Stalin, will change that." So perhaps, she decided, Avigdor had heard the rumors after all.

In the end she gave in and married him. A group of women got together and made her a dress—white, with a lacy bodice—a soft, flowing drapery that concealed a stomach that was growing larger every day. Her breasts, once small and compact, pressed painfully against the fabric, as though they would burst with milk. She was six months along when they became husband and wife, and she wrote her sisters that she was a married woman now and expecting her first child. Anna sent the letter by post, and it was a long time before she heard from them. It was not likely that she would ever see them again.

Anna didn't want to continue living in a place where a child had died, so Avigdor had promised to build her a house. It was not an easy pregnancy, and she was worried, thinking of that other child. Her ankles grew swollen and her good looks disappeared. Avigdor slept and snored while she lay awake at night. She stayed in bed when she could, thinking about the child who was coming into the world. Everyone who was alive had been born once, she reasoned. Yes, every day people arrived and others left, barely leaving a trace, all forgotten, she thought, after a few decades, even by those who loved them the most.

She remembered the biblical story of the lively Hebrew women who had given birth before the midwives came and saved their sons from being thrown into the river. As her time grew near, she cleaned the house in anticipation, searching the cupboards for dirt and scrubbing the floors on her hands and knees until she was barely able to get up. The pains grew worse, and she decided to walk over to Dr. Grunwald's house and wait for him to see her. The room was filled with people—young and old—those who were sick, and others who looked healthy, stricken with some hidden ailment that she could only guess at.

Dr. Grunwald, a *landsman* from Poland, she discovered, was tall and thin, and slightly stooped as he went from patient to patient. One by one, the people in the chairs disappeared, and others took their places. The contractions were coming closer together now, and when she got up and asked if her time to see the doctor had come, the nurse took one look and told her to come in. Waiting in the doctor's examination room, she liked gazing at the cool precision of the medicines, the drawers labeled with various potions and different size bandages, the clean white floors and walls. She was lying on a narrow table when he entered the room, and for the first time she felt calm. His blond hair was thinning, and his eyes, behind his spectacles, were a pale penetrating blue. The doctor looked at her for a moment, and as he began to probe her stomach, she noticed that his fingers were long and tapered, with smooth palms and none of Avigdor's rough calluses. He looked older than he probably was, in his late thirties. After he was finished, he sat down on a stool opposite her.

"I'm afraid this is going to be a difficult birth, Anna. The baby's turned around. We'll have to do something about that."

He looked at the expression on her face and cautioned her.

"Stay calm and everything will be all right. Someone will contact your husband and let him know where you are."

She wanted to ask if she was going to die. He saw the concern that was written on her face.

"You're going to be all right," he reassured her again. "Years from now you'll look back on this and wonder what all the fuss is about."

"Oh, will I?" she managed to say almost flirtatiously, even with her discomfort, and forced a smile.

"Yes," he said, "you just wait and see."

She laughed despite the mounting pain. And would he be there to remind her he had reassured her, she wanted to ask, but the nurse was already helping her up and to the car that would take her to the hospital. Everything settled into a hazy blur. At the hospital, someone guided her to a bed that resembled a crib. The sides came up, and there was no way to get out. When she looked around she saw other women were there too. Some were moaning; others were crying softly. Anna bit her lip until it bled, and bore down with the spasms that rose toward her throat, feeling the baby pressing against her, barely able to catch her breath.

Lena came, hurrying to see her, with a red face and disheveled hair. She had been baking fresh loaves of bread for dinner, but as soon as she heard, she told Anna, she decided to come right over.

"So," she said, "it's finally time, is it?"

Lena had grown stouter in the past year. Her hips spread into a comfortable girth as she sat on the chair. She took out her knitting.

"I'm making something for the baby, but I couldn't decide on the color, so I chose yellow, good for a boy or girl."

She chattered on, but Anna was seeing her whole life fly by. She felt light and airless, and yet melancholy at the same time. Odd scenes from the past rose up and then faded away. She had been given some medicine to soothe her distress, which made her feel as though she was floating, the unpleasant taste of the medicine still lingering in her mouth. She had turned to Lena to say, "Well, we'll soon know whether it's a boy or girl," when Avigdor's face came into view. He towered above her, his large hands resting on the railings.

"Why didn't you tell me it was time?" he said, an edge of anger overtaking his voice.

"I didn't know myself until I got here—that is, to Dr. Grunwald's house."

Looking closely at Avigdor, she thought that he might as well have been a stranger. She tried to close her eyes and sink into the throbbing contractions again. Were the feelings she had for him only a snare that nature had planted to trap young women like herself? All at once she noticed everything that was imperfect about him. The pitted scars from a childhood bout of chicken pox, a nose that was slightly crooked...his large clumsy hands. How could she love such a man? But before she saw anything else, he was being directed to the door and told to come back when the baby arrived.

Suddenly he was gone, and Lena had left, too. Dr. Grunwald came in with an assistant Anna hadn't seen before. One of them gave her a whiff of something powerful. She closed her eyes and waited for it to be over, as she listened to them discussing in subdued voices how best to turn the baby around. They were quiet for what seemed like a very long time, and she was afraid there was something wrong. Had it been minutes or hours before they uttered a word, telling her to push? She kept pushing until a searing pain passed through her body that felt as though it would tear her in two, and at last, Dr. Grunwald spoke.

"You have a son, Anna. Your husband can't deny this one." She would soon find out what he meant.

When she opened her eyes and looked up, the baby was still attached to her. She would never forget that sight as long as she lived—his bloody body, wet and slimy, startled at being thrust into the world, wailing lustily at the insult. It was hard to believe that this giant child had been inside her. She was touched by the well-formed limbs, the mouth, already struggling for survival, that would still find nourishment from her body, his tightly clenched fists. He was perfect—that was all she knew, counting his toes and fingers, marveling at the tiny shell-like spirals of his ears.

"You see, Anna, what did I tell you? It came out right, after all," the doctor said.

She began to cry with relief now that it was over. Dr. Grunwald reached over and touched her hand.

"You can relax now," he said. "All your hard work paid off."

She smiled, tired but contented. The baby—for they had not yet decided on a name—was already nursing. He had Avigdor's dark hair, and the length of his body told her that he would have his height as well. Her husband appeared then and bent down to kiss her.

"So this is our son," he said quietly.

She wished that he hadn't left her so obediently. He should have been there to hold her hand, giving her encouragement until the baby was born.

Now he waited impatiently until his son had finished nursing before he picked him up for the first time and held him in his arms.

"What do you want to name him?" Anna asked as they both looked with astonishment at the new life they had created.

"Iosif," Avigdor replied without hesitation. "We will call him Iosif after our leader."

She went home to the new house that Avigdor had finished building for them. It had two bedrooms and a living room, a tiny corridor of a kitchen, and in the back yard he had planted a fir tree in honor of their firstborn. The fragile limbs spread out against the sky, and she thought of the way the summer birds would come to rest on its boughs, and before long, a dusting of snow would gild its branches.

In the bedroom, her husband had surprised her with a rocking chair. She placed it next to the window facing the front of the house so that she could see people passing by. They settled in, and little Iosif slept in their bedroom in a cradle next to their bed. He was always ravenous, and every few hours Anna had to get up and nurse him until her nipples were raw. Outside, the stars loomed closer than they had in Lublin, and on these nights she would remember her own mother and father, sleeping in their graves.

Time passed oddly, she thought. She could not see it, and yet it passed all the same, leaving its traces on human lives. In the middle of the night, in the midst of this strange land, the wind pressed against the house, threatening to make it disappear in the forceful gusts. It was early fall, but already flurries of snow were piling up at their doorstep.

The months passed uneventfully. All day she looked forward to Avigdor coming home, when they would sit at the wooden table in the kitchen and discuss the day's happenings as they ate their supper. Afterward, he would play with his son, tossing him in the air and then catching him in the nick of time to make him laugh.

First, the baby smiled. Then he was able to sit up in his highchair and eat his first real food, jabbering noisily as he announced his presence. Little chips of white pearl had come through his gums, and Anna spread vodka on them to ease the pain. Then it was summer, and he was nearly a year old, taking his first steps, holding on to the legs of tables and chairs to make his way unsteadily around the house.

The summer rains became heavier; the river grew turbulent for days and at last overflowed. Yet logs still had to be cut and transported. Avigdor left for work early in the morning and came home late. One evening, Anna was preparing dinner when someone knocked on the door. She hurried to answer it, drying her hands on a towel. It was Boris, Avigdor's friend. His face was pale and his voice shook.

"There's been an accident, Anna."

"What do you mean?" she asked, but already she felt herself falling down an endless corridor as he launched into a long story. While transporting logs on the river, Avigdor had lost his balance and was swallowed up before anyone could reach him. She heard the sounds, but not the meaning. Her thoughts spilled out in a torrent of words. How could that be? She was expecting him. Dinner was almost ready, and Iosif would be waiting for his father to come home.

She babbled on until Boris blurted out, "He's dead, Anna. He's dead. They just brought his body here."

"What?" she asked sharply. "Where?"

"To the doctor."

"Then he can't be dead," she said confidently.

Perhaps he was not really dead but needed some food and rest to put him on his feet again. She ran to the bedroom and snatched Iosif, damp and confused, from his nap, tossed a blanket around him, and threw a shawl across her shoulders. Boris led the way to Dr. Grunwald's so rapidly that Anna struggled to keep up, carrying baby Iosif in her arms.

Avigdor was laid out on the same table where she had been stricken with her labor pains.

"There was nothing I could do by the time they brought

him to me," the doctor said wearily. For the first time he looked helpless, a mere mortal and not a god.

That morning Avigdor had been alive. She wanted to shake him and tell him to wake up. Anna tried to picture her husband earlier, eating his breakfast, full of plans, the touch of his lips on her own as he went out the door. His eyes, which had been alive and warm so recently, were now closed. But more than that, his face was blank, as though he was a man who had never lived. His mouth hung slightly open, as if death had completely surprised him. It was not Avigdor's face, but that of an impostor who had come to take his place. His huge hands rested limply by his side, and he looked bloated and blue from the water, his skin bruised by the rocks close to shore. Even so, she was angry that she could no longer reach him. She bent down to kiss him before the doctor pulled a cover over him.

"I'm sorry, Anna."

She was still trying to equate this Avigdor with the man who had held her in his arms the night before. Was it all an illusion, then? Life? The world itself that could disappear in an instant? How fragile we are, Anna thought. She would never believe again in the genuineness of the world around her, or of the people who inhabited it.

"What about your husband's family?" Dr. Grunwald was saying. "How will you inform his parents?"

Avigdor's family? She had never met them and seldom thought about his mother and father. She would have to send a letter right away that she was already composing in her mind.

To Avigdor's Mama and Papa:

I am afraid I have very bad news. I am sorry to tell you that your son, my husband, Avigdor Gurevich, died today in an accidental drowning while transporting logs downstream. I am his wife, Anna, and he has a child now, a boy named Iosif who is a year old. Unless you can arrive within the next few days, we will have to proceed with the burial. He was a good man, a good husband and father, and I will miss him.

She didn't know how to conclude it. *Love* was inappropriate since she had never met them.

When she sat down that night to write those words, her hand trembled. At the bottom she signed it simply, "Your daughter-in-law, Anna Gurevich."

She was certain someone would come and tell her it was a joke. But no one came except Lena, who sat with her until she fell asleep.

At the cemetery she watched in disbelief as the earth opened up, and their friends picked up handfuls of dirt to throw on the coffin after it was lowered into the ground. She felt a swelling of bile creeping into her throat, accompanied by a longing to touch something real to anchor herself to the world she knew. But she was not sure what that would be. The rain had stopped, but the sky was overcast. Around her, fall was already gathering its arsenal in the dark clouds, the chilly breeze that prevailed as soon as the sun went down. The gloom around her crept into her heart and wouldn't go away.

Lena took charge of the food. When they came back from the cemetery there was a spread on the table. She had found the good tablecloth and dishes, both wedding presents, and forced Anna to eat at least a few bites: a hard-boiled egg, a piece of bread with freshly made jam, a concoction of noodles.

Some Party officials stopped by. Were any of them agents of the government she had been hearing about, who were on the lookout for dissenters? But they shook her hand gravely and offered her condolences on the passing of her husband, Comrade Gurevich, who had helped to make possible the construction of new buildings in this utopia, using his strength to build a new country and a new life.

One by one the mourners left, until she was alone again. Dr. Grunwald was the last to leave.

"I wish you well, Anna," he said, and bent down to kiss her on the cheek. "If you need help, come and see me."

She thanked him, and told him the same lie she had told the others: she would be all right. She would never tell them how afraid she was of making her way in the world again, with a child to take care of now too.

The winter set in, and she did not know what she was going to do. Was Avigdor in the World To Come, or was he simply under the ground, as dead as when she had last seen him? She didn't know. Either way, her husband could no longer help her. Avigdor had a small pension, and she would have to live on that for the time being. She was hoping that his family might send something to assist her, but it was months before his brother wrote back.

> Dear Anna,
>
> I regret that it has taken so long to write this letter after Avigdor's death. I am sorry that we were not able to come for his funeral. We all grieved here after we received the terrible news. Poverty is still beating a path to our door. Conditions have been very grave. Since you wrote, my parents have both died, one after the other—a

difficult time. I hope that you and little Iosif are both in good health. Perhaps we will meet some day.

Until then,

Avigdor's older brother, Leib Gurevich

She read the letter over and over. He had not asked her to come and live with his family. Nor did he send her any money to help out, as she was hoping he would.

"So that's that," she said in disgust. She would not write again.

As promised, the desolate skies ushered in a bitter, sullen winter. She stared into the black night and thought of Avigdor buried beneath a blanket of snow, and shivered while the baby slept beside her on the empty side of the bed, sucking his thumb until it was red and swollen.

The constellations were brilliant and cold in the night sky, without comfort or compassion. There was no one to pray to, and God, the God of her childhood, was far away. In her dreams Avigdor was still alive, an invisible presence who talked to her, telling her to take care of their little son without him. What would Avigdor, a man who believed so fervently in the new order, have said about the rumors around town that grew stronger?

"Be careful what you say. There are spies around. They might be your neighbor or friend, or even your own children."

There was no one you could trust. It created suspicion, and beneath the cordial greetings was always a layer of wariness. If that wasn't bad enough, many of the crops failed in the spring, and epidemics were killing the children, who died in their parents' arms.

One night her own child took sick, running a fever, his face flushing crimson as he struggled to breathe. Anna set up a croup tent and woke every few hours to check him. But in the morning his condition had deteriorated. She decided to take him to Dr. Grunwald, bundling the boy up and trudging through the snow.

"Why didn't you have someone come get me?" he scolded as soon as he saw her.

"I didn't want to wait. I couldn't wait. He was too sick."

She threw off her coat and looked at the baby struggling to breathe, reminded of the few minutes after she had given birth to him, when she had glimpsed his whole life unfolding before her.

"He got worse suddenly," Anna explained.

She could hear the baby's breath rattling in his chest and thought that she couldn't bear it if he died too. There was no one who could help her now except this man.

His attention turned to the baby. He put his stethoscope to Iosif's heart and lungs and proceeded to examine him. "He needs to stay here or at the hospital," he told Anna when he had finished. There is a cot where you can sleep and take care of him. A mother's care is always better. I will give him medicine to help him through the night."

She stayed awake by Iosif's bedside until she couldn't keep her eyes open. A nurse went back and forth around the clock while the baby slept, fighting for the life his mother had given him.

Deep in the night, his fever spiked. Anna sponged him down and prayed that he be spared, although she was still not sure to whom she was praying while he hovered between life and death. Anna asked Avigdor, who was already in that other world, to intercede.

And perhaps he did. On the third day the child's fever broke, his forehead was cool when she touched her lips to his brow, and he began to get better. When the boy was allowed to go home, Dr. Grunwald came to see him every day. Afterward, he sat down while Anna made tea. Early in the morning she had baked a cake, and now she cut some slices and put them out on a plate while he helped himself.

The doctor had grown a beard the past year and perhaps it was what made him appear older, but he also looked ill himself. His color was poor, and he had inky smudges beneath his eyes Anna hadn't noticed before. At first they spoke in generalities, and then abruptly, Dr. Grunwald asked Anna to call him Mordechai. She had thought of him as Dr. Grunwald for so long that the name stuck on her tongue when she asked him about the rumors still circulating through the town.

"They are more than rumors," he said. "Some people have already been interrogated. Others have disappeared."

"Who?" Anna asked sharply, shocked at this news.

"Anyone who speaks out, anyone even remotely suspected of not being entirely friendly to the government. There are camps—and worse, executions. I've seen with my own eyes what is happening." He drank the rest of his tea before he said, "You should know that I'm under suspicion too. There are informers everywhere." Lines had etched themselves deeply around the pale blue eyes that looked into her own.

"What will you do?" she asked, because she thought that she could fall in love with him.

"I will stay here as long as I can to take care of my patients."

"And what is your crime?"

"I know too much. It's as simple as that. We Jews are merely an inconvenient deviation from the Party line. I have already spoken out about what is happening. One way or another, we are all doomed."

His words frightened her. She had heard that his wife had died and he left everything behind in Poland to forget. He told Anna that at night, after his patients were gone, he wrote into the long, cold evenings. But what did he write? About the corruption among the officials, he said. He sent letters to the local newspapers and even to Moscow, complaining about the conditions here. He did not have enough medicines and equipment. He had almost no one to help him. Every day children were dying of diphtheria and scarlet fever, smallpox and whooping cough.

One night the doctor stayed longer than usual. Anna put the baby to bed and came back to join him. She had served a dinner of borscht and boiled potatoes, with almond biscuits to accompany a glass of tea.

They finished their supper and Dr. Grunwald sat back to enjoy his pipe. He was silent, thinking, while Anna tidied up. Then he asked her, "Would you mind if I stayed?"

It took her by surprise. She thought about it. She had not slept with a man since Avigdor's death.

"Perhaps it will offer comfort for both of us," Anna said at last.

They made love in the bed she had shared only with Avigdor, although neither of them mentioned his name. At first it was awkward, but then she warmed to his embraces. She did not want him to leave when he rose to get dressed, refusing to spend the night.

"What if someone needs me?" he asked, although he did not expect her to answer.

"Be careful," Anna cautioned, suddenly afraid for him.

"Yes," he replied, as she fell back to sleep and heard the door close behind him. Her body felt satisfied, the way it had not felt in a long time.

Dr. Grunwald began coming to see her several times a week. She had yet to call him Mordechai, his given name, which brought up memories of the ancient Mordechai, the uncle of Queen Esther in that long-ago Persia, who had saved the Jews from wicked Haman and annihilation. What had been their crime then? Was it possible such accusations could threaten them again? Surely some progress had been made. But Stalin had brought them here and now turned against them.

Why had he come from Poland? Anna wondered. He had come to forget the past, he said, not only his own personal past, but the whole unrelenting specter of hatred that had pursued their people through the centuries. He had come here to help forge a new national identity and to put poverty, ignorance, and hatred behind him, but he had arrived at the conclusion that branches severed from the root die an unnatural death.

He said this sadly, even as he played with Iosif and delighted in the boy. He put him to bed and told him a story, making it up as he went along. Anna found out that he had sons of his own, but he had lost track of them after their mother died.

"How did that happen?" she asked, amazed to hear this. It did not seem possible—one's own flesh and blood.

"How does anything happen?" he answered, as though the question itself was absurd.

He was always busy with his patients, he told her, and hadn't had time for his wife or sons. In fact, the sons blamed him for his wife's death because he had ignored the lump that he felt in her breast, not stopping long enough to take care of her properly.

"They were right, of course," he said. "I have only myself to blame." Anna saw at once that his eyes, a color that reminded her of the river after the rain had washed it, were full.

"Sometimes things happen," Anna offered, "and there's nothing we can really do about it except to go on with our lives."

"Yes?" Grunwald said hopefully, as though he longed to believe her.

"That is what I have done," Anna continued, her voice taking on added conviction, feeling his sudden vulnerability. It was only partially true, of course. Looking at Grunwald, she could still see Avigdor's face in front of her. Snatches of remembered scenes would appear unexpectedly before her eyes, as though her husband were still alive.

Anna made herself useful at the doctor's house. His housekeeper had decided to leave and go back to wherever she had come from, and everything was in disarray. Anna cleaned all the cabinets, routing out dirt from the corners, lined the cupboards, threw out food that had been kept too long, washed the sheets, stuffed pillows for the rooms where patients waited, embroidered towels and polished the tables. When the weather warmed she went out to the fields and hillsides and brought back flowers that she put in glass bottles that had been discarded.

"You have performed miracles here," Grunwald observed as he came out of his office one day and looked around at the changes that were taking place.

She tidied up his papers and books, taking notice of the titles that he was reading. Two Yiddish writers, he said with resignation when he came upon her bent over them, were in prison, arrested by the authorities for counter-revolutionary activities: Moshe Kulbak and Izi Kharik. The great poet Osip Mandelstam had been seized for writing an epigram satirizing Stalin, and then released and exiled to starve in Siberia.

In the evenings Grunwald often liked to put a record on his wind-up Victrola and listen to the polonaises of Chopin, their countryman, composed to console a defeated Poland after it fell into Russian hands; or read from one of the medieval authors who centuries before wrote of the Jews' longing for Zion and its golden city bathed in light, even as they were surrounded by Spain's lush gardens and perfumed flowers.

"Perhaps I will still go to Jerusalem," Grunwald said.

Anna remembered pictures she had seen. A golden city on a high hill. What was it like? Would there be a place for her and Iosif? If Grunwald went, perhaps she would go, too. Fewer and fewer patients were coming. Some days they had none at all, or only a few Koreans, who kept to themselves in other matters, performing the most menial tasks that even the Jews did not want to do.

One by one as conditions deteriorated, the nurses left. Schools and businesses had been closed, teaching Yiddish was suddenly a crime, and hundreds of individuals were arrested, even some of the town officials. Grunwald asked Anna to help him with the patients who still came. There was something companionable about working side by side while he taught her how to diagnose a sore throat, or how to treat an earache or bad cough, or how to sew an almost-severed finger back on with a fine stitch. She found that her hands were skilled and efficient and that she was calm in an emergency. When the hospital also closed, Grunwald had to deliver babies in his office, calling Anna in to comfort a woman in childbirth whose son was born dead, the cord wrapped around his neck.

I could have been that woman, Anna thought, as she looked at a frightened girl of about eighteen, but I was luckier.

Once, when the doctor was out, men with hard eyes and grim faces came from Moscow asking questions, men Anna did not like. She did not like the way they looked, or the way they looked at her. They asked for Dr. Grunwald, and when she told them that he was out seeing patients who were too sick to come to him, they began looking around to see if she was telling the truth, turning over supplies and medicines and going through the papers on his desk.

That night when the doctor returned, he heard a dog whimpering outside the window. When he went out to see what was the matter, he found that it had been poisoned. The animal looked at him as if to ask, What did I do to deserve this?

Grunwald had to put him to sleep. A warning, Anna told him.

"They won't frighten me that easily," he said firmly, determined to continue his work.

Coming to his house one day a few months later, Anna saw at once that something was wrong. The doctor was gone, the furniture broken, and his phonograph records were in pieces on the floor. The books had been torn to bits, and everything was in confusion. In the dispensary, bottles of medicine were shattered and supplies tossed aside. A shiver of fear and foreboding passed through her. She began to clean up, wondering what she should do. Finally, she went to Party headquarters and found out that Grunwald had been arrested and taken away.

She never saw him again.

For a while she stayed on, hoping to hear some news, continuing to take care of the patients who came. She was the last person left who knew how to treat a fracture or frostbite or any of the other ailments of those who came to the doctor's doorstep. Gradually, though, the town became a place where only phantoms dwelled.

"We are all doomed," Grunwald had said, as though he had already known that on a sunny summer's day he would be executed by a firing squad.

Since he would never go to Jerusalem, Anna decided to take Iosif and go in his place. She settled on a collective farm to the north, a place where the oranges grew as large as a man's fist. Then came the war, and her sisters and their children were murdered by killing squads who fanned out across the Polish countryside to exterminate every Jew they could find. When it was over, a different war began, another fight for their lives in Israel, the land she had adopted.

In that fierce battle, Anna took care of wounded men, treating bodies after limbs had been blown off, skulls were crushed, and burns seared off the skin.

It had been years since Avigdor and Grunwald had died, but even long after they were gone, at odd moments that surprised her with their brilliant clarity, she would speak of them as though they were still alive — two good men in that forgotten place they had once hoped would be a haven for their lost souls.

# My Grandmother's Eyes

"YOU HAVE YOUR GRANDMOTHER'S EYES," my father says.

I have his also: brooding, dark, filled with desperate longing. I am my father's child. He was his mother's, the favorite son, the adored eldest. I keep searching for a past denied me, a grandmother I never truly knew. My father pursues a past that he has left behind, or perhaps only temporarily mislaid.

My father confronts death daily. He's never certain when it will come but he's ready. Not that he is ill. No, he is old, it's true, but strong and robust, yet he has begun to count his days.

My father is a dreamer. He dreams about the past. The past is more real to him than the present. He dreams about his mother's house, the house where he grew up. Or he is in the old country at *cheder* learning the *alef-bet*. When he was a child, he meditated on the stars. As the end of Sabbath drew near, he would be sent by his mother to find the first three stars of evening that signaled its end, but often he would be so stricken with that splendor, the sharp-pointed brilliance of the evening, so overtaken in the hushed silence of that starry expanse that he would forget to come in. Someone had to be sent to scold him into returning.

In that lost country where he was born, the frozen beauty of the sky filled him with respectful silence. Hazy bands of powdered snow stretched across the galaxy. On clear, dark nights, a burst of fireworks burned occasionally across the heavens, the slim crescent of moon gradually unfolded its cratered face, and spiral arms of luminous fields stretched overhead, punctuated by the reddish disk of Mars and the swirling opalescent clouds of Jupiter.

Eating oranges on the way to the Golden Land, weak and homesick, his mother's pale face beside him, he remembered those boundless nights of radiant visions. Tired and frightened, fleeing pogroms and persecution, my grandmother is carrying feather beds, candlesticks, a samovar, dishes.

"How did she carry all that across an ocean?" my father asks.

It is all in the boxes for me to see, kept there since my grandmother's death. He gestures uncomfortably. He presses his own past upon me, afraid it will be lost forever. Boxes of photographs. Cartons of dishes. Possessions that are no longer part of a home but merely objects now. All the things my grandmother used, her hands passing over the familiar shapes until she knew them by touch, like the blind.

He lifts out an ancient saucer—chipped at the edges and glued together like the jagged parts of a puzzle. He broke it himself when he was five. Angry or bored, he took a hammer and chopped it into pieces. He laughs suddenly, recalling the childish prank, his mother's horror. And then his voice is serious again, even solemn, full of regrets. He handles the brass samovar, picks up the candlesticks and puts them down, opens the prayer book and closes it.

"This is it," he says. "It's all that's left," and his mouth settles once more into that old man's expression that I barely recognize.

"I never knew her," I tell him.

But what I want to say is, *How do you expect me to care about people I never knew? I could have, you know. I could have at least known her. She was still alive.*

"It's a shame," he adds, as though I have spoken out loud, our thoughts automatically traveling the same path. "We lived too far . . . during the war . . . it was too hard." He gestures blankly around the room, looking for an explanation, reviewing the mistakes of a lifetime, too late to correct now. "They didn't get along," he says at last, meaning his mother and my own. As though that explains everything.

He has spoken the truth—his truth at least. But it's somehow insufficient for either of us. Then, embarrassed, he reaches into his pocket and takes out his mother's brooch, as though it is an afterthought. He has kept it secret, God knows how, from my mother all these years.

"Your grandmother would have wanted you to have it," he says and drops it into my hand. Set in a tarnished silver frame, the cameo is still lovely, an offering of peace where he has placed it. My fingers close around it into a fist.

"Go ahead," he urges, "put it on."

How do I explain that it doesn't mean anything now, that it's too late, that I am a grown woman with three children, and my grandmother has been dead for 30 years. Before long I will be a grandmother myself.

"Father, it is too late," I murmur. "Don't you know that? It is much, much too late."

Three pictures—one that I haven't seen before.

"It was taken just after we arrived from the old country," my father says. It catches me by surprise. It's a family portrait, an image recorded for posterity. My grandfather is the only one who is sitting, as befits his position as head of the household. Yet he looks uncertain, as though he's lost his place in life and doesn't know quite how he will regain it. He wears a starched white collar, a tie, and a suit that is too large for him. The sleeves hang down awkwardly on his arms. His face is stoic and long-suffering.

My father, six years old, stands to the left of his mother, her arm resting lightly on his back, her face tilted toward him. He's dressed in the kind of sailor costume popular around the turn of the century. His brother, four years his junior, who will die before him, is dressed in a similar fashion. But, oh, the marvelous figure of my grandmother. She is wearing a ruffled white blouse, the brooch upon her breast, and a skirt of an indefinable color. When I look closely at her face, there is startled recognition. My eyes. Yes, there are my eyes, I think. I have stolen my grandmother's eyes.

"She's still a girl," I say out loud. "She's only a child herself."

The second photograph is familiar. I've seen it before, but I have never seen it in quite the same way. My father is a young man, but he's not the father that I know. He gazes in wonder toward some vision that I'm incapable of seeing, trusting, but at the same time curious, his eyes fixed in delicious anticipation, the lips parted ever so slightly in that charming sweet and sad half smile that he still wears half a century later. His lithe body, lean with the discipline of athletics, stands tall and straight beside his mother's slender form, which is already stooped with age, his arm protectively around her shoulder as he tries to glimpse the future lying beyond the confines of the picture that holds the two of them forever.

The third, a picture of myself taken when I was six, shows me full of pensive longing, my lips caught in that same wistful smile that I have inherited from my father.

"This is the face of an angel," my father says every time he sees it. "Your grandmother would have adored you. Yes, it's a shame the way things turned out," he says again.

Sometimes I think it is the only thing upon which we agree completely. "You were a princess, you know," he will say other times, looking at me uneasily because through the years he has lost control over what I have become.

What I was: I was a child dispossessed of attachments to people I could have loved. My mother's wounds, real and imagined, my father's silent acquiescence, our frequent moves to places where we knew no one and no one cared to know us, conspired to excise the past and sever connections. Consumed by loss, I hungered for all that was left behind—the knowledge of who I was gleaned from what had come before.

I envied the rainy afternoons of other children: box-filled attics yielding the sweet discovery of prior lives, nooks and crannies hiding antique lace, old dresses still smelling of musk and rose water. But even more than these trifles, I yearned for every-thing those children took for granted—and perhaps despised—noisy holidays filled with feasts, backyard gatherings on summer Sundays, indulgent grandparents bringing gifts.

My relatives were few and far away, and my father's mother—my only living grandparent—was a dim figure whom I barely knew. And yet—or maybe because of that—my fierce longing made her the focus of all of my fantasies and invested her with all that she surely was not. If she was arrogant or stubborn, stingy and possessive, as my mother insisted, I wanted to know none of these things. Instead, I was determined to spin a famil-iar cocoon around her to shield my own loss from strangers, and perhaps more important, from myself as well.

I remember seeing her only a few times. My first memory takes place in a kitchen. I remember little else of the house where my father grew up but the kitchen and the flutter of my grandmother's hands as she prepares the food, turns from the stove to the table. She's telling me to eat something, pushing the bowl closer to the spoon that I eagerly bring to my mouth. But whether the words are Yiddish or English, I don't remember. I cannot even recall the sound of her voice, but I know that she is so old and thin that her bones are nothing more than cobwebs spun together. Her fingers are long and narrow, the skin of her hands so translucent that I imagined I could see down to blood and bones.

I don't remember kissing her, or holding her close. I don't remember that she ever called me by name.

Yet the visit lingered in my mind. I was a lonely child—and frightened, of what I cannot recall. The memory of my grand-mother remained an invisible presence, a secret fortress. When

I was small and full of fears, I wanted her to come and gather me in her arms, to ask, Of what are you afraid, my child?

A mother is busy, but a grandmother understands. I was certain that she would say, You must not be afraid—I am here. And the soothing murmur of her words would silence forever the fearful trembling of my heart.

Driven by desire, I dreamed that I went to stay with her, that she lived nearby instead of thousands of miles away. It's cold, cold enough to snow. My brothers and sisters are peering enviously after me, their noses pressed against the frosty panes of glass. It's windy and bitter, the howling of the trees quickening my steps, so that by the time I arrive my head is pulsing wildly and every shadow waits to pounce upon me.

Yet before I even knock at the door, it swings open and grandmother appears, calling my name so sweetly, so softly that it sounds like a caress, and as I take off my boots, she warms my frozen cheeks with her hands. We sit down in the kitchen to eat, our heads bent over our plates. It is the same kitchen that I remember: the cabinets, the drawers, everything is the same.

We eat in silence, and then, leaning back, my grandmother speaks to me in a low voice of forgotten things. Her words fall like broken shards into timeless fragments. The tales seem like islands jutting forth from the secret fathoms of the past. Isolated by space, by age, by grief, they call, sweeping us both to a place that has neither form nor substance, shape nor name.

She becomes a young girl, her skin pulled smooth, a babushka around her dark curls, her eyes two amber jewels, harboring visions, imagining herself once more in the village of her childhood.

Over and over again, the same scene, the same dream.

My father saw his mother's eyes in mine, and within his own I inhabited an invisible circle, a charmed embrace, a place of sorcery where everything was transformed, a special realm where only the two of us were allowed to dwell.

I knew instinctively that this excluded my mother. She understood neither of us. Not our dreaminess, which she called "having our heads in the clouds," or our trips to the library where we devoured stacks of books, or the nights we stood outside meditating on the stars, overcome with their beauty and majesty. Summer evenings, we climbed to the top of a nearby hill, or simply stood behind the darkened profile of the house and gazed at the dust of stars flecking the sky as my father asked the eternal questions—how and when and why all this had come into being—meditating on the marvel that we, two finite dots among all these riches, could even be here to contemplate it.

These visits were somehow stealthy, something we didn't talk about. Our communion with those glittering jewels and winged horses, mighty lions and shining goddesses through which we considered the nature of things, might be misunderstood—or at best construed as merely frivolous.

At my grandmother's house my mother paced the floor, or, if it was warm enough, waited outside on the porch, smoking a cigarette. She didn't like to go there, and after a while, she simply refused.

Inside, I prowled its dark, gloomy interior, so full of unfamiliar objects and pictures of people I didn't know. I tried to imagine my father's lighter childhood body moving through the density of the rooms, my grandmother's younger form, her eyes still bright and full of light.

Perhaps I understood why my mother didn't want to go: My father was different there. He had another family, one that was separate from us. He fit into those rooms as though he had never left. Watching him one day, his head tilted attentively toward his mother, speaking the strong, gutteral sounds and cadences of a strange language, I saw him altered into someone else.

I try to remember my grandmother's eyes that day and cannot. But I remember the touch of her bony hands on my shoulders, her skin next to mine, as dry and withered as parchment. I remember that I longed to go there again, but the next time I saw her, I was older and we weren't at the house where my father had grown up but in a strange hotel in a city I had never seen.

Why must I see my grandmother in a hotel?

It never occurred to me to ask.


The stories that I heard mingle with these memories: Her father was a tailor. She was the oldest of his eight children and worked at his side, bent over his machine all day and half the night until her wedding day. Then the hard work changed, but continued. She was strong, rising at dawn to begin a day's work before my father awoke on dark, cold mornings.

When she was a girl, she had been the best dancer in her village. At sixteen, in a sepia portrait washed with ocher and bronze, she faces the future with determination. But in the hotel room where we meet, she clutches an old-fashioned purse, and her face, creased with age, is filled with doubts and questions. When she takes off her hat, adorned with red carnations,

I see that she is nearly bald. Wisps of white strands are all that is left of her luxuriant hair.

And again, I remember those eyes, sparks of saffron-colored light in which, strangely distorted, I see my own bewildered face. Two generations away, they look at me sadly, as though mutely acknowledging my own melancholy thoughts.

I'm still not too big to climb on her lap, but we are both shy and say nothing. I make a great pretense of playing some game on the rug, and now and then our gazes meet.

Now, I wonder, What did she think of me? Did she speak? But again, I cannot remember the sound of her voice. Did she say something that lingers there beneath the layers of memory? But no, there is nothing.

I never saw her after that, and there is no more to tell except that I feel a longing for her, and a regret that she was withheld from me. Just that, and nothing more.

She never came to visit. We never went there again. When my father saw her, he saw her alone and never spoke about it. Once I came upon him writing a letter in that language I didn't understand, and knew it was to her, a shadowy figure, a mysterious presence.

When she died, there was only a white memorial candle flickering forlornly on my father's dresser.

Gradually the memory of my grandmother receded, her face blurred. Yet when I looked in the mirror, I saw her reflection. I imagined that my bones were her bones; my skin, her skin; my eyes, her eyes. Sometimes I would think that we were linked inseparably together, and I couldn't escape her even if I wanted to. But finally that thought, too, retreated into the past. My face became my own, and I forgot about her. Or thought that I had.

Now my father has brought it all back, and I begin once more to build her out of these scraps and fragments, which will have to substitute for flesh and bones, knowledge and familiarity.

I have become as obsessed as he is to make some sense out of it, to recover with these slender threads some semblance of what has been lost, the sweet, mysterious connection we have to the dead.

# Deeds of Love and Mercy

WE ARE A TROUBLED FAMILY. Ephraim left three months ago, and Cecilia and I have had to confront each other like enemies who suddenly find themselves at the same party. Yesterday we quarreled, and today, dressed in a pair of faded blue denim shorts and a yellow T-shirt that says *Foxy* in flowery, iridescent letters, she moves through the house sulking. She is the only thing in motion on this hot sultry day.

My only child . . . Her dark, uncombed hair straggles around a thin face, and sad thirteen-year-old eyes are swollen from lack of sleep. Last night through the flimsy walls of our apartment, I heard her weeping, and this morning her whole face slumps in sorrow and rage.

It's all my fault.

I can see it in the frown that bridges her forehead. If only I would make concessions and try harder, she thinks, her father would come back.

And so we're doomed to this summer that stretches endlessly before us, a time that hardly seems real at all but just a series of minutes, hours, days to get through and endure together. Ephraim and I have agreed to reach a decision about our marriage for the sake of the child by the end of summer, but now we are still wavering back and forth.

Yes, I can tell from the way her black eyes glow with a fierce fury. She's as tired of me as I am of her. How Cecilia and I have begun to dislike each other.

Ephraim packed up his bags and took an apartment and a job on the other side of the city at the beginning of June.

"I don't have enough space," he said.

How foreign that word sounds on his tongue. We had begun to chip each other into little bits and pieces. Ephraim will not admit it, but sometimes I think it was the strain of the child.

As a baby she was perpetually restless and moody. She came into the world too soon, bounding feet first from the womb. I had nothing prepared. No, not even her name. I had to snatch that also without thought. She cried day and night, refusing to be soothed, and Ephraim and I would take turns rising from our sleep, moaning with fatigue, too tired to comfort each other since this strange being had taken over our lives.

Thirteen years later and she still remains a puzzle to me, her moods flashing back and forth, a new one for every moment of the day. A look, a remark, or some dark demon within can change her in an instant. I was too old to have her. Yes, I am certain it must be that. But Ephraim is a religious man. He used to say that suffering cleanses the soul, that burdens are to be borne.

"It's a sign," he said then, clasping his heavy hands together, closing and unfolding them nervously.

To Ephraim there is a purpose in the world that escapes me. There are things that we're not supposed to understand. He prefers the difficult to the simple, certain that God is testing him. He was not an easy man to live with.

This morning when Cecilia asked if her father would be coming before sundown for the Sabbath, I told her that it was hopeless.

"Your father is impossible," I blurt out in a weak moment, saying it passionately, throwing up my hands in a gesture of despair.

I can hear my voice rising unpleasantly, and I'm sorry as soon as the words are out of my mouth. But it's already too late.

"Bitch," she says without a sound, mouthing the letters with her lips.

At first, I ignored her. It was too hot to respond, to become embroiled in another one of these arguments. Anyhow, what would be the use? Let her vent her wrath on me. Let her get it out of her system and think that her father's absence is all my fault. What harm can it do? But then she says it again.

"Bitch."

This time she whispers it, but loudly enough for the ugly sound to reverberate in the room.

"Bitch," she says a third time, growing bolder. The word explodes from her mouth, chilling me to the bone, although the sun is seeping resolutely through the drapes and the room is sweltering with the heat.

"Bitch," she said again and again, unable to stop, her face contorted with rage. I felt my heart beating faster within the cage of my body, fluttering against the armor of my bones, and rising, I slapped her face, so hard that it stung my hand and left an ugly red mark on her skin.

She ran to her room and slammed the door shut. I could hear the click of her lock snapping closed, then loud sobs as she gasped for breath. I imagined her flung sideways across her bed, her hair falling wildly over the edge, beating the pillow with her tightly closed fists, and suddenly I was filled with pity for her and shame for myself.

Through the long hours of the morning she remained in retreat. I pounded on the door and ordered her to open it, but the only sound was the steady whirring of a fan. Finally, frightened that she had done something rash, racked with guilt that I had lost control, I took a wire hanger and, bending it, worked diligently at the keyhole until at last the door swung open.

Cecilia had stopped crying but her face was splotched with red and there was still an angry imprint where my hand hit her cheek. Her eyes were puffy, her lower lip thrust forward. She was pouting on the bed, and wouldn't look at me. The curtains were drawn against the heat, and in the dim light of the room I could see that she had strewn candy wrappers over the floor. An empty Coke bottle sprawled on its side against the dresser. A lonely sock protruded from beneath the bed. A trail of dirty clothes traced a path through the room and ended in a corner next to a stack of *True Confession* magazines littering the rug.

"Come out," I said, as calmly as I was able, swallowing hard for what we've done to each other, what we continue to do. "We'll make up. Everything will be all right." I tried to appear more confident than I really was. "You're only hurting yourself, you know." The words sounded as hollow and meaningless as when my own mother uttered them, and I knew that this sort of logic would never reach her.

"Look," I said, trying to keep my voice steady. "It has nothing to do with you. It's between your father and me."

At last she lifted heavy lids to look up defiantly. A difficult age, I thought to myself, and she is more difficult than most. Beneath that yellow T-shirt with the ludicrous letters, her breasts were beginning to rise as supple as ripe fruit. Under her arms I saw black prickly hair sprouting like desert scrub. She won't let me see her naked anymore. Once I came into the room, catching her by surprise, and saw with a shock that triangle of womanly hair on her body.

Now we stared at each other without speaking. Suddenly overcome with remorse, I longed to tell her that I was sorry but the moment passed and I said nothing. I retreated and she rose slowly to take a shower.

When I heard the water running full force, I decided to call Ephraim. He's an engineer, capable of correcting the errors of vast machinery. Perhaps it was still possible for him to correct the errors of our lives.

I dialed his number at work and he answered the phone himself, startling me, as though he had been standing there all along, arms crossed over his chest in a familiar posture, waiting for me to call.

"Ephraim," I began, without bothering to ask how he was, "come home tonight. We're eating each other alive."

"Not until Sunday," he said.

We'd been through this before. Ephraim refused to come on Friday for the Sabbath.

"It's too far," he said. He's afraid that something will happen before he gets here and he'll have to travel after sundown, when it is forbidden. A thousand and one disasters passed through his mind. The car could stall and leave him stranded. A train could have an accident, God forbid. A bus could be hijacked on the highway (he's read of this happening), he'll be caught as night falls and the Sabbath descends without a prayer to protect him.

"Too late," I said. "By Sunday we'll both be dead."

"Don't worry," he answered solemnly as though he hadn't even heard me. "I will pray for us."

Suddenly, I can see him standing in the fading light, his prayer shawl draped over his shoulders, a skullcap on his balding dome—at dawn, at dusk, in heat or cold, swaying and rocking on the balls of his feet, summoning the God of Israel, communing with his Maker.

He was in the wrong century, I think, the wrong life. He should have been Abraham journeying beneath a starry sky, Moses adrift in the wilderness, Jeremiah making his lonely vigil through the desolate city of Jerusalem.

"Ephraim, Ephraim," I plead, desperation overtaking my voice. "Live a little! Take a chance. What harm can it do?"

But he was older, more set in his ways. I could hear him sighing and struggling with himself.

"Yes, I'll pray," he repeated again, but he sounded exhausted, as though what was happening to us was all too much for him.

"What good will your prayers do? What good is your God?" I cry, aware that I am beginning to descend over the edge.

Then I decide on another tactic and this time my voice is softer, cajoling.

"Come home, Ephraim," I said, "I need you, I want you."

I could almost hear the catch in his voice, the hesitation as he thought it through.

"For the child, Ephraim . . ."

"It's too difficult."

"Ah, Ephraim," I said, "*life* is difficult."

But he has made up his mind. He refuses to commit himself.

"For shame," I cried, and slammed down the phone.


Tonight, tomorrow he won't answer the phone. Once I let the phone ring a hundred times just to test him, knowing that he was there, swaying silently in the dark.

Cecilia has called him late at night when she thought I was asleep. I could hear her whispering about me, telling him how hard it is for us to get along, how she wishes he would come back.

Now, suddenly, I wondered if *she* had been standing there listening as I spoke to her father just now. I turned on the tap and quickly splashed my burning face with cold water as she paused in the doorway behind me. I could feel myself flushing as if she had caught me in a disreputable act. Her eyes were red and rimmed with fatigue, but she had changed her clothes, and clipped her wet hair back from her forehead. Yet the place where I struck her continued to stain her cheek, forming a barrier between us.

She said nothing, her face an impassive mask. Perhaps she hadn't overheard anything after all and it was only my imagination that tortured me.

"Come," I said, "It's time to get ready for Shabbes."

Before the sun sets we must clean the house, polish the silver, cook the dinner, and bake the bread.

In these matters Ephraim has trained her well. She obeyed me silently, without a word of complaint. I uncovered the dough that we prepared earlier, and we took out the bread tray and the silver candlesticks that needed polishing. On the shelf next to them a sad solitary imprint marked the spot where Ephraim's wine cup had stood.

She placed a board on the kitchen table and separated a small piece of dough that she burned in an ancient ritual offered to the Kohanim, descendants of Aaron, who consecrated it to God. She closed her eyes, and moving her lips in silent supplication as she has seen me do, her face coloring with the heat, her eyes intent on her task, her fingers moved deftly over the remainder, twisting it into thick braids to slip into the oven.

What did she yearn for behind those sorrowful eyes? What thoughts did she think? For the past year she has suffered with nightmares that wake her up screaming in the middle of the night, as though striving to be released from some dread torment that won't leave her alone. In the morning when I come into her room, I see her sheets twisted into knots, as though demons have tied them during the night.

"A stage," the doctor told us, but I know better.

She's always been this way. Now just more so. Sometimes I think that when I'm old and defenseless, unable to take care of myself, I'll have to live with her and she'll be able to vent her stored-up rage upon my helpless body like that dough beneath her hands.

Yesterday I prepared a picnic supper to take to the park. Other families were there, too, and we spread a blanket on the grass and had cold slices of roast beef and potato salad.

When the ice cream man came around, we bought cherry Popsicles and sat at the edge of the playground to eat them. Children were swinging, and watching them, Cecilia decided to pump her own skinny legs high over the sandboxes, soaring higher and higher until her face was filled with a strange gentle joy.

Afterward, she sat very close to me and laid her head upon my shoulder, her eyes tranquil, her expression subdued. But by evening it was obvious that she was brooding. We quarreled, and later I heard her crying until I finally turned over and fell asleep.

Today, she was still working soundlessly as the heat of our oven built to a peak of intensity, and I paused to step outside onto our small balcony, where we have some hanging plants that are rapidly wilting and two old porch chairs that Ephraim kept meaning to paint. We live on a quiet street at the very end of a cul-de-sac, and an occasional car, coming down here by mistake, would turn around beneath our porch. But now there isn't a sign of life.

Across the street, windows are sleepy eyelids, blinds and drapes closed against the broiling sun. From next door I hear the blast of a TV, then a muffled sound as it was quickly turned down.

I joined Cecilia in the house, and we worked side by side without uttering a word. Beads of perspiration gather on her forehead and above her upper lip, and I wonder again what she is thinking behind those inscrutable eyes.

I opened the oven and took out the bread, setting it on the counter to cool. It was dark brown, the top of the braids blackened slightly at the edges, and she glanced at it approvingly. I seasoned the chicken and put it in the oven to roast.

When I reappeared an hour later, I saw that she had spread a white cloth upon the table and set out the best dishes and silver, placing the candlesticks in the center. Over the mound of fragrant bread was a green and gold embroidered cover she made one summer at camp with the word Sabbath embroidered in Hebrew.

She had changed into a clean white blouse and white shorts, and her hair was tied back with a light blue ribbon. I was wearing a long print skirt and a colorful top I bought one year in Mexico. My hair, which was beginning to thread with gray at the sides, was pinned on top of my head with a large tortoise-shell clip.

I turned off the fan and opened the windows, drawing back the curtains. For the first time in days the heat had begun to break. A cool breeze stirred the air as I lit the candles and stood before them, arms upraised to say the blessing that ushers in the day of rest.

Cecilia took her place next to me, and even though my eyes were closed I could feel her hands circling the air next to mine, drawing the Sabbath closer.

"A good Shabbes," I say, forcing myself to reach out and put my arms around her shoulders.

Her spine stiffened at my touch. Her body remained rigid, and she averted her eyes, her front teeth biting down hard on the middle of her lower lip.

I set the dinner on the table and we both sat down, neither of us acknowledging Ephraim's empty place at the head of the table. I could remember his strong blunt hands above

Cecilia's bowed head, intoning the patriarchal blessing that always brought such a quiet joy to her face.

In his absence I said a prayer of thanksgiving over the bread, breaking it apart with my hands, and then we ate it in thick chunks, greedily, suddenly ravenous.

"It's *good*," I said. "*Very* good."

She blushed with the praise, her tan cheeks turning rosy beneath the surface.

"Do you really think so?" she asked, speaking to me for the first time since morning. "You're not just saying that?"

"No. Really. It's good,"

A slight smile passed over her lips.

"It's a pity your father couldn't be here to taste it."

For the second time that day, I was sorry as soon as the words were out of my mouth. A look of pain crossed her face and her eyes lingered longingly on the candles.

"But he's coming Sunday, isn't he?" she asked.

"Yes... Of course. On Sunday."

As we ate, a strong breeze gathered outside and blew through the room. Lengthening shadows fell over the walls in ghostly shapes. Darkness enfolded us, broken only by the bright headlights flooding the living room when cars came to the dead end of our street.

Cecilia's brow furrowed in concentration above the slender bridge of her nose. We made desultory talk. At last I set out two melons and strawberries that we spooned into the hollowed centers for dessert. We lingered for a while longer, not speaking, and then I cleared the table while she rose to help, thrusting her arms into the soapy dishwater.

She handed me the dishes and I dried them, placing them

one by one on the white counter, the light of the candles finally sputtering out. The smell of burnt wax filled the air. A full moon illuminated Cecilia's slight figure, and I saw that the red mark on her cheek was nearly gone.

When we finished, I hung the towel to dry, and our glances met as she turned to go. How fragile she looked, how young. I yearned to cry out to her as she disappeared into the hushed darkness of the hallway.

I was filled with a rush of love for her. Flesh of my flesh. Bone of my bones. Then, as though she had read my mind, suddenly she returned and standing on her tiptoes, kissed me goodnight.

"I'm sorry, Mother," she said. Then just as quickly she was gone.

On Sunday, Ephraim will come, and perhaps things will work out after all. Who knows?

But for a while at least in the stillness of that moment, there was peace at last. And tomorrow or the next day anything seemed possible, anything at all.

~

More than twenty years have passed and now Cecilia and I are at it again.

She is no longer a child, but I am still her mother. An early annulment, and then she married and divorced, and married once more. Now that marriage, too, is unraveling.

Men are drawn to her like bees to the proverbial pot of honey. Something restless in her soul blazes out of her fiery eyes. Where did it come from? What demons conceived her?

Considering Cecilia, Ephraim was wont to fold his hands in despair.

"We are born to suffer," he would say. And so, after he came back, we kept on, days, months, another year, one after another.

At last, nearly weeping, seeking the peace that eludes him, he tells me what he'd decided.

"I am going to Jerusalem."

"If that's what you want," I answered. "Talk to God, but leave me out of it."

Ephraim is a man searching for his destiny. His namesake was the second son of Joseph, whose mother Asenath was an Egyptian woman given to his father by the Pharaoh. And like his father Joseph, Ephraim was given the greater blessing over his brother—a life that should have been cloaked in moments of grace.

Yet he couldn't rest. At dawn I found him saying his morning prayers, *tefillin* strapped to his arm and above his forehead, communing with his Maker, shutting me out.

Before long, he was gone.

I imagined him praying at the City of David. Pale gold over Jerusalem stone. Yet there was no peace, neither there, nor here. When I closed my eyes I could see Ephraim swaying and rocking back and forth on his heels although I could no longer remember his face or his voice.

I sent him letters that he did not answer.

"Write to me, Ephraim," I begged. "Help me. Tell me what to do. Better yet, come home, I need you," remembering the time before Cecilia, when our love was new.

Once he sent back a scrap of paper: "It is all in God's hands."

"Even God needs help," I replied, but there was no one to hear me.

"He's finding his way," a friend advised. "You must be patient."

I told myself I should have given up long ago, but something compelled me to keep trying. How do you stop love? Or mend sorrow? We are a troubled family still. Like whorls expanding each year on the trunk of a tree, our lives repeat the same patterns.

I was reminded of Koheleth's words, a seal over my heart:

Only that shall happen
Which has happened,
Only that shall occur
Which has occurred
There is nothing new under the sun.


After Ephraim left for Jerusalem, I was alone with Cecilia. Mystery surrounds her. Everything is secret, an enigma. I'm still not sure who she is. Perhaps I have never known. Her dark hair already holds silver threads, like my own at her age, and furrows have worked themselves into her brow.

For a time she was contented. The first flush of motherhood became her. With two young children to steady her, the troubles would be over, I thought, and she'll be all right. But it didn't last.

"I'm unhappy, Mother," she told me.

When I called, she was out. Where did she go? What does she do? Who's with the kids?

"I'm with friends," she says.

Strangers all. People I no longer know.

Her eyes accuse me. The mistakes she makes are all my fault. She tells me I withheld love and so she is forever condemned to seek it elsewhere.

"Why can't you understand?" she cries.

And so we seesaw back and forth. Perhaps it's true that I never loved her enough. Yes, perhaps she is right, after all.

"What do you want?" I ask.

The man she couldn't live without is a son-in-law I would never have selected. They quarrel, make up, and quarrel again. Quarrels that grew angrier and more violent. I slept with my clothes on the bed, waiting for the phone to ring.

One night she called me at 3:00 a.m. Her husband was sobbing when I arrived.

"She has a lover."

Though it's still the middle of the night, the children were still up, listening, their bare feet padding on the floor. I stood at the door, looking around at the chaos and disarray.

"He hit me," Cecilia said.

"Move out," I warned her. "This could be the end. Who knows what could happen?"

She didn't appear to hear me and did nothing. Immobile.

I snatched the children, Reuben and Rachel, one in each arm, and Cecilia came with me, a coat thrown over her nightgown.

We plunged into the darkness, cold air stinging our faces, and like a witch I flew through the night, fog and drizzle settling around us, past the lighted reindeer prancing on the lawns, the inflatable Santa Clauses climbing down chimneys, houses emblazoned with luminous icicles against a black sky.

When we got home, I gave the children warm milk to soothe them and put them to bed.

"Daddy," Reuben said.

"Mama," Rachel cried.

I heated up the coffee and put out stale biscotti.

Cecilia and I sat at the kitchen table. In her face, I saw all the ages she has been, all the Cecilias I have known in the past, just as she must see in me all the mothers she has known. Perhaps she has wandered into the wrong life, the wrong mother. An irrevocable mistake has been made, too late to rectify now.

Should I tell her that all mothers age and turn into children? I won't be her mother forever. All we know disappears. The brain tangles. The air is let out. We become confused. We don't remember that we're mothers. One day she'll try to find me and I won't be here.

I'll be the child and she will be the mother, even more powerless than I feel now.

We locked the door and turned off the lights. We sat in the dark and listened to the pounding of his fists on the door until it seemed that at any moment it would shatter it into a thousand pieces.

"Didn't you know what he was like?" I cried. "When will you learn?"

"No," she said, burying her head in her hands. "How could I have known?" as though the question itself was absurd.

Always the same question, the same answer.

A litany of men. Men I never would have let into my life. Men who are fragmented and lost, who crash cars, cry out for their own mothers in their sleep. Men who hurt, and are hurt, men with circumcised pricks and uncircumcised ones, men who father children and men who don't, men who love and those who can never love, men who don't know the meaning of love and will never learn.

In the morning, I took the children to the park. It's the same park where I took Cecilia and yet it is not the same. The old swings and jungle gyms are gone, replaced by shiny new equipment. Even the children are the same and yet different. The same mothers fussing over toddlers. The same toddlers crying for mothers, yet different. The mothers themselves toddlers who have grown into mothers.

The sun comes out from behind the clouds, and sheds a warm spotlight over the grass. The children clamber up and down ladders, swing from bars, run across the lawn squealing, crying, "Mommy...Daddy...*home.*"

When I returned, I found a scribbled note.

"I've gone back...Cecilia."

She was nonchalant when I called.

"Are you crazy? Have you lost your mind?"

"Everything is all right. You must believe me."

I delivered the children. And there he was, smiling this time.

"Hey, don't sweat it, everything's going to be okay."

"He's turned over a new leaf," Cecilia explained.

"You'll be sorry," I told her. "Stop while you're still ahead. Stop while you're still alive."

She turned on me then, a teenager in a woman's body, all her rage focused in my direction, love turned inside out.

"You just don't want me to be happy," she said and slammed the door.

I can't endure the cold. The furnace goes out. The toilet clogs up. The rain and storms keep on. The gutters and streets are flooded. I wander in and out of my dreams. A whisper of a remembered prayer tugs at my soul: *Spread over us your shelter of peace.* I wake breathlessly, afraid she is dead. I don't know if it's day or night. In Jerusalem, Ephraim floats above the city as in a painting by Chagall.

I refused to call. Instead, I drove past her house, the headlights turned off. There was frost on the roofs. The reindeer and Santa Clauses were gone, but real deer's ears quivered at the sound of my car, a doe followed by a fawn, leaping across the street.

I pulled my car beneath the trees and waited until the moon hid behind a cloud, then walked the rest of the way to her house and stood, watching the phantom forms moving from window to window. Shadows against the staircase. Familiar shapes. I went around to the back, put my ear against the window and listened. I listened to what is beneath the world, as well as what is above. I listened to the world turning over. I listened to generations coming and going. I listened to babies entering the planet. I listened to people saying goodbye, never to appear again.

Days go by, weeks without a word.

Then she was rapping frantically at the door, the children in tow.

"I made a mistake," she said. "He hasn't changed. He can never change."

There was a swollen lump above her eye, like a piece of dough.

"When will you learn?"

"He promised."

"And you believed him?"

I stood guard, watching, waiting, ready to murder him if need be. Cecilia wouldn't press charges, afraid of pushing him over the edge.

"The children," she said.

"Yes, the children. For the children's sake you must."

But she won't. She cannot.

We changed the locks and combinations. We checked the power and telephone lines coming in and going out. We bought batteries for the flashlights. We pulled down the shades and closed the drapes. We warned the neighbors. We covered the TV and sat in the dark.

"We're playing a game of hide-and-seek. Daddy musn't find us."

The children loved this game.

"Daddy won't find us!" they shriek.

We let the phone ring and ring and the children laughed, "Don't talk to Daddy!"

I thought about Ephraim and myself a long time ago. I thought back to the beginning, before Cecilia, before anything, when our love was still strong. If Ephraim and I had not met? What then?

"Does her life hang by this slender thread?" Ephraim would ask. "There is a reason she was born. There is a reason for everything."

I thought of the melody that floats beneath the sea, the humming beneath our lives, the thing we don't see or hear until we're dead.

Time reverses, spiraling backwards. I swim through chambers that close, one by one, as I advance, trying to reach Ephraim, but he is always in the distance, just beyond me. I swim farther and farther until my lungs ache and my limbs feel limp, but each time, as soon as I grow closer and my hand extends to clasp his, he slips beyond my reach. I call to him. He responds, but I cannot make out what he is saying, and at last I stop, turn around, and find my way back through the maze. When I wake in the morning, something has broken, like a fever. I've made it through another night. Then I hear him. The familiar sound of his voice explodes in the room. The sun has already risen, and it's the hour for saying the morning prayers.

My heart lifts. I pull on my robe and ascend to meet him.

From the darkened hallway I glimpse Ephraim swaying and rocking on the balls of his feet, a prayer shawl draped over his head. A miracle. An act of mercy that he has come.

I breathe a sigh of relief and hearing me, he turns and nods. Then I see with a shock that it isn't Ephraim.

It's Cecilia. My daughter. My child.

It is she who has brought me this unexpected moment of grace.

# The Girls of Jerusalem

THE MAN SHE HAD LOVED WAS DEAD. His obituary was there in the newspaper, for everyone to read.

Yes, now he was dead, but even though Sora read the words over and over again, trying to take them in, he was still alive in her mind. She hadn't seen him in years, but now it all came back to her—the force of her fierce passion and the sound of his voice, strong and wide like the country he had come from, a place in the Midwest where drifts of snow covered the fences and even the doors of the houses.

He had been her rabbi. She remembered how young they'd been, although he was much older than she was, almost 32, his hair already drawing back from his forehead, and he had a limp, from what she didn't then know, maybe polio or a childhood accident. Sora was barely 20, with two children already, mere babes who had to be tended day and night. How weary she had been then, even though it was years before her hair had become white, and her lips, Clara Bow lips her mother had called them, turned permanently downward in regret.

She had married their father too young. They'd had to. It was her shame. It was a time when there was still shame, when such things weren't done, or if they were, they had to be covered up.

If you slept with someone and got caught, you had to pay the price.

First you play—then you pay.

She had heard that the whole time she was growing up. She remembered what her mother said: "Don't let that happen to you."

But it had, and when Sora became pregnant the first time they made love, it was already too late, and there was nothing she could do. Leonard, the child's father, was a good man, a decent man, though he was still a boy. He had done the right thing. He had married her, and she was supposed to be grateful for it.

"But I love you," he said. "Surely you must know that."

Yet something else had crept into the way he looked at her, and though he had never brought it up, she knew that he was sorry things had turned out this way. A yearning had been smothered in him—the hope that his life would be different from that of his parents, who had been refugees.

On good days she was grateful, but at other times she bore a thin ribbon of sorrow in her heart because he had not married her because he wanted her but had been forced into it, his dreams of becoming an architect put aside. He was a draftsman instead, a good one. Often she would find him up late, half asleep at his drafting table over those precise drawings that promised order and rationality in the world and belied the fact she had discovered over the years—that there was nothing of the sort, that it was all a sham. This was something she had kept to herself, the way she had kept her love of Rabbi Ben a secret.

Now that secret rose up from the past and threatened to envelop her, to take over her life the way it had done long ago, in that time when she was still not much more than a child herself. He entered her dreams, although she was old now, creating a persistent tug that would not go away. She could think of nothing else through the cold winter except that long-ago time when she had loved him.

Sora and Leonard had come to California on a whim, escaping the East, and its pressures of family, the sameness of the place where they had grown up, crowded with buildings and people and houses that were too close to each other. Like pioneers of an earlier day, they were seeking a new life, putting everything behind them, for they had both come from people who had been obliged to scrape by, immigrants who had suffered during the war. And besides, though they were married now, the scandal of her pregnancy clung to them, a brand like the numbers on their parents' arms.

Here in this strange land, the farthest west they could go, they found what they were looking for fifty miles north of San Francisco, not far from Napa Valley. Redwood forests, green hills, the cleanest air she had ever breathed, the sky as clear and blue as a baby's eyes, fruit for the picking in their own backyard, rows and rows of grapes that would be made into wine, a lushness and a vastness she could not have envisioned before, in this land the Native Americans once called the Valley of the Moon.

They settled on one of those green hills. Sora had only to

step out of her door in the morning to pick lemons and limes for pies, cherries in season, plums and apricots and oranges.

They first arrived after the winter rains had stopped, and from their house on the height of a steep incline, held up by stilts, she could see the expanse of the horizon for miles around.

Their first summer there, on the younger child's first birthday, fires ignited and flames ringed the countryside as far as they could see. The acrid smell of smoke drifted toward them and choked their lungs.

"Look at that," Leonard said, peering through his binoculars, although there was little to see beyond the haze that enfolded them. "A fire like that could eat us up alive."

She shivered and drew closer to him. She was afraid for herself and for her children. She could see their little frame house going up in the flames. How small they were. How fragile. Sora was afraid the fire would devour them. Old-timers told her how fast a fire could spread in those hills when the earth was dry. And so they had slept in shifts, staying up every night until it was over, and they saw the patches of scorched earth that remained.

They were alone, and because they were also lonely now, and because they were Jews, they sought out other Jews. There were some even here. A mixed bag: refugees like the parents they had just left, still rebuilding their lives after the war; socialists who had come west to found a utopian commune and raise poultry to support themselves; Jews whose great-grandparents had come in wagon trains looking for gold; couples like themselves, harboring secrets, coming to the end of the world to escape what they had made of their lives or to bury their failures. In a synagogue built of towering redwood trees they went with hats on their heads or without, wore prayer shawls or disdained them, knew how to *daven*, pray, or could barely read the *aleph-bet*. They had a choir, a women's sisterhood, a men's club, and a full-time rabbi, not just an itinerant one who traveled from place to place.

They went to meet the rabbi. Sora noticed his limp right away as he showed them around. He walked slightly ahead of them, slowly dragging his right leg.

"You won't find many Jews in these parts," he said. "We are a small congregation, but a close one."

While Leonard asked questions, complicated ones, she kept her eyes on the rabbi's face, the blaze of his eyes, the intelligence of his expression, a great nose that curved at the bridge like a shofar. Next to him, her husband seemed pale and inconsequential.

A custodian brought them some Cokes. It was a hot day at the end of summer. Late August heat, an empty day. Sun beat against the dull expanse of the windows. They could barely rouse themselves from their stupor.

"Oh, you'll want the heat back once the rains start," the rabbi joked. Then he said more seriously, "It's time you met some of the congregants. We're gathering before the holidays." He scribbled his address on a wrinkled piece of paper he drew from his pocket. "A family affair. Bring the children, of course." She looked at the large loopy letters he had written and suddenly felt her heart drawing closer to him, as though they were a secret sign he had given her.

"I hope you'll join us," he added. Although he didn't say, we're the only show in town, he could have.

She thought how much she liked him, the whole time he was talking. While he was answering Leonard's questions, he was glancing sidelong at her as if to gauge what she was thinking. She blushed, certain he could see right through her.

He didn't look like a rabbi. He was dressed in washed-out jeans, a white knit sports shirt open at the neck, and tennis shoes, not that clean. He had perhaps tried to grow a beard to look older, more rabbinical. They were still calling him "Rabbi" when they parted, but he put up his hand to stop them.

"Call me Benjamin. Or Ben," he said. "That'll do. We don't stand on ceremony here."

The party was on the following Sunday, and as soon as they arrived, she saw that everyone else had brought something to share. Sora and Leonard had brought only their children, who had fallen asleep in the car, one on each parent's shoulder, their bodies damp with the heat, their little mouths twisted to the side, drooling on Sora and Leonard's good clothes.

The rabbi himself had answered the door.

"Ah, so you've brought us gifts," he said, and ushered them in, introducing them to young couples and old, a blur of people who would have to be sorted out later. A fuss was made about the children, as though Sora and Leonard had indeed arrived with something extraordinary. Which of course they had, she thought.

The rabbi drew his arm around his wife, Hannah, a woman who looked as tired as Sora felt. She already had four children in stepladder fashion, and now as he said their names, impish grins appeared on one face after another. Three boys and then the youngest—a girl, but as rambunctious as her brothers.

"Do you sing?" Hannah asked when their husbands had drifted away. "We have a choir, if you do. We're practicing for the holidays. We're running late, same as last year, but it always comes out right somehow."

The question left her flustered. In fact, she had no voice at all, but didn't want to say this straight out.

"But you mustn't worry about it," Hannah said. "I'm sure we'll find something else for you to do. We all have to pitch in here."

And then she was called away, and Sora was left to wander about for a while on her own, examining the books and Sabbath candlesticks and the twisted candle for the Havdalah ceremony to conclude the Sabbath, and the silver set on a tray, carved with Hebrew letters she couldn't read. She wandered over to the buffet table and stood looking over the arrangements of sweets and salads and mounds of food, admiring the flowered teacups and Danish dining-room set, the kind of furniture that young couples at that time aspired to own.

Hannah went back and forth. Other women consulted with her, put out more food, and took platters away to be refilled. Sora wondered if the rabbi's wife was happy. She wondered that about every woman she met, if their marriages were more or less like her own. She concluded that Hannah was happy because she had no reason not to be. But Sora was beginning to realize that you never really knew how happy people were behind their facade.

Exactly at the moment when she wondered how she would get through this—not only this moment here with all these strangers, but the rest of her life, and especially her marriage, which loomed as treacherous as any mountain to be climbed— Rabbi Ben appeared again.

"Have you had anything to eat?"

She shook her head.

"Well, then, you must. Don't be shy. Dig in, Sora." He speared a small tomato on the pronged end of his fork.

"I hope this isn't too much for you. All these people, a roomful of strangers."

He didn't wait for her to answer.

"I have just the thing for you. The pay's not much, but I think you'll like it. Teaching one of the grades in our school. Best of all, since it's a Sunday, your husband can stay with the children. Unless Hannah's gotten to you about the choir."

"No, I'd be hopeless. I didn't dare."

He looked into her eyes, and she was struck by their beautiful flecks of gold and brown. She had to bite her tongue to keep from telling him out loud. His palm rested intimately on her back, and she didn't want him to take it away. Outside, through the sliding glass door, she saw her husband playing baseball, the children deposited with people she didn't know.

Later that evening, at home, the children in bed, Leonard said, "What did you think?'

"Of what?" she asked, though she knew very well what he meant.

"Of the rabbi—his wife—the people we met."

"I talked to a few of the women. The rabbi's wife asked me to join the choir."

"And what did you say?"

"I didn't have to answer. She took one look at me and knew."

Her husband laughed, not kindly.

"Ha! She doesn't know how lucky she is!"

"Benjamin—the rabbi—asked me to teach on Sunday."

"And will you?"

She had already thought about it. It was because of him—the pressure of his hand on her back, the color of his eyes, the sound of his voice—but she didn't say that, of course.

"Yes," she said. "I think I will. It will be a good way to meet people. It will give me a chance to get out once a week, away from the children."

"And where will they be?"

"Why, with you, of course."

"Oh," he said. "So that's the way it is."

Leonard didn't like her to leave the house. He didn't like her to do anything but take care of him and the children. In his own quiet way he had taken charge of her life. Was that the way all husbands were? Or was it a punishment because she had given in to him and gotten herself in a family way?

She could tell from the tone of his voice, his silence when she told him, that he didn't like the idea of her teaching. He didn't say no, though he must have thought it. It was for the synagogue, after all, for the rabbi. On Sundays he liked to catch up on his drawings or hike over the hills, exploring. He didn't want to be bothered with the children on his day off.

"I'll be paid," she added. "Not much, of course."

She thought that she would use the money to buy something new for herself. She was already thinking about Benjamin, shutting off his wife and children from her mind. If she thought about his wife at all, she imagined that their lives were somehow loftier than hers. Perhaps they read to each other after the children were put to bed or had discussions on more profound topics than Leonard and she did. She had actually tried now and then to make an effort, but at night they were both tired. Besides, her husband didn't see the point of it. At heart he was a simple man.

No, the man she had loved was not dead in her mind. He would never be. She could resurrect him. The tremble of excitement before she heard him speak the first time. The clear resonance of his voice, the sermons he gave that were like a light struck in the wilderness to guide her on her way. In spite of the heat, he would dress in a very rabbinical white robe and hat on the high holidays, the kind of garb the rabbis in her childhood wore, although the most observant had clothed themselves in a *kittel* that would one day resemble their shroud. That was what these holidays were all about, wasn't it? To simulate death, to come as close as you were ever going to come, and then to realize that you were still alive.

But she was too young to understand that. Death didn't seem real then. She couldn't feel it the way her parents had, perpetually weeping over family members who had been lost. It was always somewhere in the distant future, unless something terrible happened, something unthinkable.

She marveled at the gift of Rabbi Benjamin's mind, which was quick and brilliant. The way he could take an idea and turn it around, the way he could weave it with other ideas and make you see the world in a different way. It was how she'd felt when she read a book that touched her, and she thought, Ah, so that's what life is all about. Or heard a truth put into words that she had already suspected deep down. His speech swept her along with the intensity of his passion. He knew how to pause for effect. He used silence and spaces like the north country in which they lived. There, on the *bima*, looking larger than he did when he was standing next to her, he turned into another person entirely, his voice thundering across the room like a father admonishing his children.

"We can be the people we want to be," he began. "That is the message of the *Yamim Nora'im*, the Days of Awe. We can change our lives. The message of this day is *teshuvah*, not only repentance and a return to God, a return to all that is best in us, but renewal, to fully realize our lives, to become fully alive, to negate death. To negate everything that numbs us, everything that deadens us while we are still alive."

He paused, placing his hands on either side of the lectern as if he had to gather strength for the message he wanted to deliver.

"On this day the Torah says, 'God will make atonement for you, to purify you.' In the days of the ancient Temple, two goats were chosen, one to be sacrificed; the other, to be sent into the wilderness and set free after the high priest confessed over it the sins of the children of Israel. The ritual of the scapegoat was intended to carry away our sins, to relieve us of this burden. Of course, in our day we think of that as primitive. We make atonement in other ways. We must personally atone for our sins in our souls and with our very bodies, which are today denied food and drink, the pleasures of the flesh . . ."

It seemed that his words were meant for her alone, that they entered her heart and took root there as though they had found a home where they could grow—she must find her own way and make her own life. It was as though he had seen the longing in her life and knew what she must do to change it. Yes, she was certain that he was speaking directly to her.

"We make *teshuvah* by turning to a new way of life, by

putting behind us all of our mistakes and transgressions and offering repentance to God. But those sins against man can only be forgiven by those whom we have wronged by asking their forgiveness.

"It's death that waits for us," he declared in a voice barely above a whisper. "These Days of Awe come to tell us that the time is short. Each of us makes a journey with our life, a journey across the years and a journey into ourselves."

He told the story of a ship that was driven from its course by a great wind and finally, becalmed, dropped anchor at a pleasant island. Beautiful flowers and fruits grew there and tall trees.

"The ship's passengers divided themselves into five parties. The first party decided not to leave the ship, afraid they might be left behind, thus forgoing the temporary pleasures of the island. The second party went ashore for a short time, enjoyed the perfume of the flowers, tasted the fruits, and returned to the ship happy and refreshed, losing nothing, but cheered by the recreation of their short visit there. The third party also visited the island, but they tarried on the way. Meanwhile a fair wind arose, and they hurried back aboard as the sailors were lifting the anchor. Many had lost their places and were not as comfortable as they had been before. They were wiser though, than the fourth party, which stayed so long on the island and tasted so deeply of its pleasures that they minded neither the wind nor the ship's bell that called them. When the last bell sounded, they lingered still, thinking the captain would not sail without them. So they remained until they saw the ship moving, then in haste they swam after it and scrambled up the sides, and the bruises and injuries they encountered in so doing were not healed during the remainder of the voyage. But the fifth party ate and drank so deeply that they did not even hear the bell, and when the ship started, they were left behind. They became prey for the wild beasts on the island, and they who escaped this evil perished from the poison of surfeit.

"My friends," he concluded, "The ship is our good deeds, the voyage of life. The island symbolizes the pleasures of the world, which the first passengers refused to taste or look upon, but which enjoyed temperately by the second party make our lives pleasant without causing us to neglect our duties. True, we may return as the fourth party did at the eleventh hour and be saved, but with many bruises and injuries that cannot be entirely healed. But we are in danger of becoming like the last party, spending a lifetime in the pursuit of vanity, forgetting the future and perishing from the poison concealed in the fruits that attract us.

"*Teshuvah* does not tell us to negate the pleasures of this world but to be cognizant that our voyage will end one day. We must change our lives now; we must do what we can to cleanse ourselves and to turn in the right direction before it's too late without forgoing the pleasures of this world."

He paused before moving away from the lectern. His prayer shawl fell off one shoulder, and he drew it around him. There was silence before the choir began again. It was so still that it seemed to Sora no one breathed. She knew each person there must have thought the same thing she did: that he was speaking only to him or her. Yet she was certain that the sweep of his eyes, his words were destined for her alone.

She started teaching every Sunday morning, from ten to twelve. The children were so young! Not much older than her own. To each she said a kind word. She brought juice and cookies she had baked herself, read to them, and told them stories about Noah and the animals and Father Abraham, who had glimpsed a new life through the one God. Before she married, she had wanted to become a teacher, and she thought if things went right, in a future that still seemed far away, she might yet be. Often Rabbi Ben would come in to observe, making his way slowly up and down the aisles in his white sneakers—himself again instead of that thundering voice from the pulpit.

Then, as she was leaving one day, he opened the door to his study and invited her in.

"Sora, Sora," he murmured, turning her name over and over on his tongue. "How do you like our school?"

She blushed. Her name had always seemed to her to be just a step away from sorrow, from the terrible fate that had overtaken her parents' mothers and fathers, brothers and sisters, who had perished. Sitting across from him on the other side of the wide expanse of his desk, she drew herself up straighter. Her cheeks burned with pleasure, and her skin felt moist.

He was surrounded by books. One lay open on his desk. She thought of the knowledge that lay behind the golden stars of his irises, which stared intensely into her own, and of the way he leaned toward her.

"And how is your soul, Sora?"

*Her soul.*

"But where is my soul?"

"You don't know?" he asked her.

"I don't think of my soul very much," she said.

He sat back, clasped his hands together.

"Oh, but you must."

Then he told her a story about the different levels of the soul.

"The *nefesh* is the first level," he said. "It nourishes the body and becomes a throne upon which the second level, the spirit, *ruach*, rests. The *ruach* in turn becomes a throne for the *neshama*, breath. The *neshama* is hidden, the most concealed, bringing together all the powers of the soul in single devotion to God. Above that is *chaya*, infinite wisdom, the source of all understanding. But in all of these levels, we are still separate from God. It is only when we erase the ego that we can prepare ourselves for the highest level, the *yechida*, to become at one with the Divine."

She remained silent, mesmerized by the sound of his voice and intensity of his eyes upon her.

"And so it is with us. As the powers of the soul ascend, we are accorded insight into divine wisdom. Your soul is hidden now, Sora. But one day it will shine with perfect light."

"And how will that happen?"

"You'll find a way."

Perhaps he meant love, she thought. Yes, perhaps that was the way her soul would shine with a pure white light.

She thought of him while she served her husband his supper and put the children to sleep in their little beds, and then she looked into the black night and thought of her soul, a flame growing brighter and brighter. Why hadn't she met him before she'd married? Why did everything come too late to do anything about it? This was what she was thinking when her husband took her into his arms. She was thinking of another man, and it pained her that she was being unfaithful to Leonard in her heart. Sometimes she thought he knew. Perhaps he guessed. He questioned her endlessly.

"Where have you been?" he asked. "Who did you see?"

When she went out in the evening to get a breath of fresh air after being with the children all day, he waited impatiently for her to come home. Yes, surely he must have felt it. An absence at the center. An inattention. At times she thought that he was going to shake her, as though she was only their daughter's rag doll.

"Where are you?" he asked once after they made love, so sharply that it frightened her. "Who are you now?"

She was weary, she answered, the children, after all…And so he didn't press her again.

On those Sundays, after she was through teaching, Rabbi Benjamin spoke of the land where he grew up, a more isolated place than this, with bleak, frigid winters and bitter winds blowing in from Canada. The few Jewish families lived miles apart. When there was a *bris* they had to send for a traveling *mohel* to perform the circumcision; for weddings a rabbi had to be hired from some faraway town, for they had no rabbi, no synagogue. On holidays they would gather in one of the homes for services.

"But we had books," he said, his gaze sweeping around the room. "All those years I was growing up, I read. I couldn't get enough of it."

"Yes," she said. "I can see you doing that."

It was true. She could. In a corner of her mind she saw him while the snow piled up outside the windows, the way you see people in a dream, a vague shadowy shape in the dim light of those freezing winters, reading until he fell asleep—a younger version, of course, of the man who sat before her.

"We knew we were Jews. We didn't need anything more. My father had a store in town. When he wasn't busy with customers, he studied, and was the most learned man around. He sent for books from Jerusalem. He tutored the boys for their bar mitzvahs. He counseled other Jews on the Law and wrote rabbis from great distances for answers, like a medieval sage. In the opaque days of winter, when we remembered the rededication of the ancient temple, the candles would glow from our windows, light pulsing through the darkness.

"What kind of life could I have hoped for in that small town where the roads were dirt and people still rode their horses to my father's store? I left. I had to. My father insisted. I went away to the university. I met people like myself, eager to learn. But most of all, I met other Jews. I studied philosophy. I asked questions. For a while I wasn't sure I believed. Where is the proof, after all, for God? It has to be felt.

"And then a friend died, one of those tragic accidents. People said it was God's will. What does that mean? That God wanted a person in the bloom of his youth to die, and not someone else? A boy who had done no harm? Other people said that there must be some hidden sin. It is the same thing they said about the Six Million—even Jews said it."

He made a fist and slammed it on the desk.

"No, I will never believe in a God like that. Gradually, I came to trust in a God who did not punish people. Yet I am still searching, occasionally there are doubts..."

She told him about her parents, Leonard's parents, the families who had been left behind, although she was sick of hearing her parents' stories about the war and the camps. Her father had escaped one of them and lived in the woods, eating whatever he could find in the forests. He met her mother afterward in a displaced persons camp. She suffered with headaches from a blow to her head. The one to her stomach had ruined the life she tried to live after the war.

"She wanted to have many children to make up for all the children who were lost, but it was a miracle that she was even able to have one—me. Her womb had almost closed up. If I had been there...if I had been born sooner...I might have been one of those children who perished. I think about it all the time."

She didn't tell him about her unhappiness.

Not yet.

Fall gradually turned into winter. The rains began. Although the trees kept their leaves, she felt cold all the time. It grew colder still and damp—a dampness that entered her bones. In the Sierras to the northeast the snow fell, and people skied down the mountain slopes. She dreamed that she was entering a new country, one she hadn't known before, a country where she and Rabbi Ben were together.

Sora sat on the other side of his desk, primly, her knees straight while he spoke. He wore a wedding band, a thick one, and when she looked closely, she saw the carved letters there in the ancient language.

He followed her gaze.

"Do you know the holy tongue?"

"No," she answered. "I was never taught."

"But you can learn. It is never too late to learn," he said firmly. "The word for letter in Hebrew means sign, or miracle, a revelation from heaven. Everything that exists came into being through combinations of these letters. Each letter is divinely ordained, each has a unique purpose, just as each person's soul is inviolate. *Your* soul, Sora."

She thought about this while he told her a story about a famous rabbi who had discovered how to combine the letters by which heaven and earth were created.

"Yes," he added, "a world came into being through these sacred sparks."

She thought of each letter becoming a sacred spark, part of the very air she breathed, and one by one she learned them. First the *aleph*, a letter that makes no sound of its own.

"And yet," he said, "it is the foundation upon which the unity of the world rests. *Bet* gives rise to the beginning, *b'reishit*, and *b'rakhah*, blessing; from *gimmel* comes benevolence; *dalet*, the secret doors that we must open."

She was *vav*, standing alone but joined to the world through love.

In the long, dark evenings when she studied, after the children had been put to bed, Leonard spoke to her.

"So that rabbi is teaching you things."

"Yes," she said. "He is teaching me about the soul. He is teaching me the holy letters."

"Are you sure that's all he's teaching you?"

Leonard didn't know what to do with this woman who was his wife. She could see it in his eyes, the way he looked at her now, as though she had already moved far beyond him. She wanted to tell him that the knowledge she had been given was like food and drink, a great gift. It was a gift that belonged only to her. At last she could see a way to become her own person, standing her ground against her husband's demands, for their lives had become a tug of wills.

The letters entered her and she became certain that she was not the same person she had been before. She saw everything in a different light. There were layers and layers, some of them hidden and waiting to be discovered. Benjamin had given her a new name, another soul. *Shulammite.* She felt herself becoming that young woman who sought out what she desired and took it for her own.

Benjamin was reading from the Song of Songs, and in his voice the words took flight, like the lovers, rising up from the past and still embracing. *As a lily among the thorns / Such is my darling among the girls.*

I am black, but also comely,
O girls of Jerusalem,
Like the tents of Kedar,
Like the pavilions of Solomon.

Just as she was leaving he rose from his desk and leaned over to kiss her, like a cool breath of air passing over her.

"Forgive me, Shulammite, I am smitten."

I adjure you, O Girls of Jerusalem,
By the gazelles and by the hinds of the field:
That you neither rouse nor disturb love,
Until it so desires.

Her body stirred at the sound of his voice, and the words of a woman she would never know entered her heart. Was she, then, to be the comely girl of Jerusalem that Benjamin desired?

Gradually, in the weeks that followed, she revealed the unhappiness of her marriage, pouring out her grief to him. He reached out and put his hand over hers. She took it as an omen, and in her heart she began to hope that he would love her too.

On Sunday afternoons she stayed longer and longer, reluctant to leave him. Every week she thought about what would happen if he desired her. At the moment he began to caress her she didn't think about Leonard or the children or even the risk she was taking. She didn't even care after a while that he belonged to someone else. It was only important that he belong to her.

It was not only his touch. It was what he said. And as he entered her, he made love to not only her body, but her mind. His words, his ideas, the sound of his voice ravished her. The world grew larger. Time slowed down. Everything became more intense. She could see to the depths of the earth, below the sea, and beyond the heavens, and yet there was only this, here and now, with him.

Naked, at last she saw the withered flesh of his leg and found out that he had been trampled by a horse when he was a child.

"Crushed," he said. "The whole damn leg. I couldn't walk for a year."

It made her love him even more. She discovered what she had known deep down all along. He was a man filled with passion. Passion for the flesh and passion for God. Afterward, he brought her into the empty sanctuary while he prayed. Perhaps, she thought, this time to cross the abyss that still separated him from his Creator.

Sora saw his wife occasionally. Once, standing in the kitchen setting out the cakes after services, Hannah turned to her.

"I know what you're doing. Don't think I don't."

"It isn't the way you think," Sora said quietly.

"Oh, I know all about it," Hannah replied. "This is a small town. You can't hide anything here. Don't think there haven't been others."

And she turned on her heel and walked out of the room, her face flushed with anger.

Then Leonard began to clatter about the house with complaints.

"You're not tending to your job," he said.

He pointed to the laundry, the dishes undone, the children crying, waiting for their mother to serve their supper. Standing at the sink paring an apple, he turned around to face her, waving the knife in the air as he spoke. She could feel the beat of her heart bursting inside of her, and yet she had lost all shame.

She told herself that she would not give up Benjamin. She made no bones about it now, refusing to heed the rumors that flew over the hills from house to house.

The hills grew greener, the water ran in rivulets, sap flowed in the trees, and the air was filled with a sweet fragrance. As a tale of love long ago, the winter was past, the rains were finally over and gone, and purple lupine and orange poppies appeared in the countryside.

"There's talk," her husband said one day.

She threw off her jacket and turned to face him.

"What kind of talk?" she asked, hearing the insolence that had crept into his voice.

"You better watch it, or you'll be next. That is, if you're not already."

"What do you mean?" she said.

He stopped in the middle of drying the dishes.

"I mean that rabbi. He's not what he seems to be. He's not a man of God."

"You shouldn't say such things. It's nothing but gossip."

"One of the congregants, a woman, has complained. Seems he fooled around. There's more than one. That's what I mean. You wouldn't know anything about that, would you?"

When Sora was silent, he warned her. "Well, better not let him sweet-talk you. He'll be gone by summer. People around here will see to that."

In the midst of all this, her mother fell ill. One night her father called, telling her matter-of-factly that something had gone wrong. A cough that had lingered all winter turned into something ugly and lethal, and now, overnight, she was failing.

*Failing.*

That was the word her father had used.

Life was complicated, Sora thought. She was learning that it was never neat. Why did her mother have to die now?

"You better tell me what's been going on when you get back," Leonard said as he took her and the children to the airport, a long drive south from Napa, away from the poppy-dotted hills and across the great bridge shining in the sun.

"There's nothing."

The car lurched forward and threw her hard against the dash.

"I have a good mind to tell your father what you've been up to."

"What do you mean?" she said.

"Don't give me that. You were a slut when I married you, and you're still a slut."

"I don't know what you're talking about."

"He took you like he took those others."

His voice had risen. He looked ferocious, his face twisted in rage. The children cowered in back. They didn't understand what their father was saying, but they understood the angry tone of his voice, their mother's weeping.

She walked away without saying goodbye to Leonard, holding the children close to her.


Sora flew home to be with her parents, out of one world and into another, taking the children back to the place where they were born, although they would probably not recognize their grandmother now.

She arrived red-eyed and tired early in the morning, holding the children asleep in her arms when her father picked her up. Sora thought of Benjamin the whole time. Had there really been other women? She hadn't had time to tell him where she was going. She thought of a phone call, but she couldn't call him at home, nor did she want to write a letter that anyone could find and read.

The first day Sora went to visit the hospital. Her mother was sitting up in bed.

"I must be seeing things," her mother said. "Is it really you?"

"Yes, of course it is."

"You look different, that's all. It's the sun out there, I bet, and the fresh air. I wouldn't mind some myself. And the children?"

"They're here. I've brought them so you could see them for yourself."

"I don't think I'm going home. I don't think they'll let me out of here. I think this is it. It's over. All those years I kept thinking that all I wanted to do was to die in a soft, warm bed, and here I am."

Everything was temporary, Sora thought. Why hadn't she realized it before? But it was something her mother must have known long before she was born.

"Nonsense," Sora said. "You look well enough to me. In no time you'll be up and around."

She half believed this herself. Perhaps her father had exaggerated to bring her home again.

Her mother sighed and didn't answer.

"And Leonard?" she asked. "How is Leonard?"

"Same as ever," she answered. "But you might as well know," she blurted out before she could contain herself, "We're not getting along. I'm afraid I'm in love with someone else."

Her mother thought about this before she spoke.

"You've made your bed. You'll just have to make the best of it."

It was not what she wanted to hear—that she was stuck for life. Then her mother said something else, as an afterthought.

"Is he married?"

"Yes," she said.

"He'll leave you. One way or another it won't work out."

It turned out to be their last real conversation. Within days her mother was much worse. She slept most of the time, and when she woke up she was confused, her eyes glazed, and Sora knew then that she was preparing to leave this world.

A nurse came in with chips of ice. Sora pressed them to her mother's lips. If this is what it's like at the end, she was thinking, you might as well do everything you want to. Why did marriage have to be forever? Why couldn't you admit you'd made a mistake and move on to someone better, someone who suited you more?

But gradually her thoughts of Benjamin receded, and there was only the room in which she sat at the side of her mother's bed, with a figure who lay very still at the center, barely moving, who might as well be a stranger. She knew so little of her mother's life before her own birth. There was a shadow family and shadow cousins and aunts and uncles, and a shadow place with a strange name where her mother had grown up. And all this, these people who were only faint memories now but had occupied her mother's thoughts, would pass away with her.

Days went by without anything changing. Then, suddenly, her mother was slipping away. Every time Sora left the room she was sure it was the last time she would see her.

"Don't worry," the nurse said. "It takes longer than you would expect."

And so it had. So long that she became careless, coming and going whenever she felt like it. Returning from lingering over coffee in the dreary cafeteria downstairs one evening, she was surprised to learn her mother was actually gone.

"She died about seven minutes ago," the nurse said. "We couldn't find you in time."

"So that's it," Sora said aloud. Yes, just like that, with her last breath, everything her mother had thought and felt disappeared. But where did it go? What was the use of it all?

Now, reading of Benjamin's death, she thought the same thing. She wondered how he had died—the nitty-gritty of it, which lay beyond the article in the newspaper and would probably never be known to her.

She remembered the first sermon of his she had heard on the Days of Awe and wondered if he had thought of her over the years. His children, like her own, must be approaching middle age. How strange to think of that. And his wife? Where was Hannah now? In her mind, neither of them had aged since she'd last seen them. But perhaps that was just as well. She didn't want to think of him as an old man. That was the strange thing about the past. The way it kept coming back, each time in unexpected ways. Now she only wanted to remember the passion of that fall and winter and spring, when she had known him and felt the taste of love for the first time.

When she returned after her mother died, it was all over. Other women had come forward, each with her own story, but all of them oddly the same. She hated the satisfied look on her husband's face. Perhaps he had complained about the rabbi, too. By the end of summer, as Leonard had predicted, the rabbi was gone. Fired. The congregation had seen to that.

Sora went to see him before he left. She tried to memorize the sound of his voice, the delicate curve of his hands, so that she'd remember them later. He was paler, and his eyes were washed with sadness, the stars in his gaze that had captivated her darkened.

"Why did you do this?" was all she could think to ask. And then more sharply, her eyes growing moist, "What were you thinking of?"

She waited for a denial, for him to tell her that it was all some terrible mistake. But he didn't. Instead, he got up from his chair with an effort, as though he had aged overnight, and came around to put his hands on her shoulders so that she had to look at him without turning away.

"Do you believe everything you hear, Sora?" Then he kissed her hard on the lips. "Don't ever forget this. Don't ever forget me."

One day not long after that, as she was driving through town, she saw him walking by the side of the road, his limp grown worse, like something had broken. She thought about stopping to give him a lift, but anger washed over her love, and she passed by without even slowing down. Afterward, she had to pull over to catch her breath because she knew she would never see him again. The sight of him that day, like a bird that would never fly again, was the picture that she still carried in her mind when she read about his death.

The grass grew brittle and dry and parched again the summer he left. Her soul shriveled and closed up. But after a while she thought of what he had given her. She thought of him returning to the land where he had come from, in those wide-open spaces where he had grown up.

She didn't stay with Leonard once the children were older, even though her mother's words, "You've made your bed," kept ringing in her ears. Slowly she made the life she had always wanted, and in time she became the person Benjamin had taught her she could become. And for that she was grateful. Yes, she knew it was all because of him. No matter what else he had done, he had given her back her life. He had given her the strength to live it.

Didn't the *Shir HaShirim*, the Song of Songs, say "Love Is as Strong as Death?"

Perhaps the love she had felt for him once had entered her *neshama*, her soul. She had tasted the pleasures of the flesh that would no doubt be resurrected when the Messiah appeared in Jerusalem—a time when all desires, all that had gone wrong in your life, all that you had lost, would finally be redeemed.

# Ghosts

IT WAS THE FIRST TIME IN YEARS Nina had seen him, and his mother, Ingrid, was dying. Did he even know?

At first, she wasn't sure it was really Hugo. He was heavier, the edges of his unshaven face had taken on a bitter turn, especially around the lips, and his eyes, his mother's eyes, but more hooded and sleepy-looking, were fastened on the floor.

He was dirty, too. She recognized his jacket, navy with a red plaid lining, which Ingrid and Walter had given him for his sixteenth birthday. It was of an indeterminate color now, and across his broad shoulders it was filthy. His gray pants had lost their crease and hung in wrinkled folds over his muddy, scuffed shoes.

It was the time of night when strange-looking people came out, an assorted underworld you didn't see during the day. Nina wouldn't have been there herself if she hadn't found herself out of eggs when she fancied a late-evening omelet while her husband was out of town. Under the supermarket fluorescents, his pallor looked sickly. Perhaps it was not Hugo at all, but someone who merely looked like him.

Hugo was a name she had always loved. Slightly foreign, exotic, and very European, like his parents. It was his walk that finally decided her. With his head down and his hesitant steps, he looked, as always, as though he were walking across a field that was infested with land mines. He was definitely Hugo, the son of her friend who was dying.

Ingrid's name had originally been Irmgard, then Irma for a long time. Hadn't there been a radio program called "My Friend, Irma" about a dizzy blond, years ago? But she had changed her name to Ingrid, after the actress. The Ingrid Nina knew was no dizzy blond. She was solid and responsible, a teacher in one of the local grade schools. In fact, both of Hugo's parents had been teachers. His father taught history, and painted in his free time, working in watercolors.

Nina was always surprised at how good Walter was. A couple of his paintings were in the collections of medium-sized museums and others were often displayed at the town library. Nina would often see him puttering around the yard, with its lemon and orange bushes and tomato vines in the back and Ingrid's tree roses lining the front walkway. Or he would be making repairs to the house. It was nothing but a cottage, really, that the previous owners had increased by two bedrooms, but Walter kept making improvements until he died, after the trouble with Hugo started.

Hugo had problems—nothing that you could put your finger on, but Ingrid and Walter couldn't control him. After he turned eighteen, there was nothing they could do. He refused to get help or to take his medication. He started college nearby, and then dropped out to take a job selling the new tech gear that was suddenly popular. But that hadn't worked out either. He had been a precocious child, a math prodigy, and now he spent all his time cooped up in his room devising problems no one could solve.

"That's the law in this state," Ingrid was told. "Once a child reaches majority, your hands are tied."

Hugo finally left the quarrels with his parents behind, staying with one friend after another, at last renting a small room on the other side of town.

They had doted on the boy, a child of their later years, who arrived after they had given up on having children of their own. Ingrid was in her early forties when she became pregnant. In despair, they had adopted a girl some time before, who was already entering puberty—an orphan who had lost both her parents, friends of Ingrid and Walter's.

An orphan. What an awful, hollow sound that had, Nina thought. But when Heidi was an adult she moved north of the city and never returned to visit. She was afraid of bridges, and the only way you could come to Ingrid's was over the bridge, unless you wanted to go very far out of your way. But Heidi hadn't done that either.

Nina followed the man around the store, dismissing any last doubts that it was really Hugo. She paused out of sight to pick up bread and a carton of milk, considering. She wanted to go up to him and say, "Hugo, it's Nina. Don't you remember me?" Images of Hugo at an earlier age with his then-angelic face popped into her mind. She thought of how the past could come back, but all scrambled up, the way you saw it in dreams. Your mother's dying, she imagined saying. Don't you care? Don't you even want to see her?

He looked up, as though Nina's thought had actually leapt out of her mind and into his brain, but then stared through her without a sign of recognition. She wanted to grab him by the shoulders and shout, If you don't see her now, it will be too late. Something's eating up her stomach.

Ingrid and Walter had lived just down the street from Nina and her husband, Howard, in the late sixties. That was how Nina met her. They were always getting each other's mail because their house numbers had the same digits in a slightly different order. Usually Ingrid simply gave these items back to the postman, which was exactly what Nina did too, but one time she decided she'd just march down and bring it to Nina's herself, since it was a package, and a nice enough day. Actually, she hadn't marched at all, she'd hopped on her bike, a good-looking vintage road runner, even though Nina's house wasn't very far, and threw the package in her basket.

Nina had often seen Ingrid on that bicycle, but hadn't known until that day that she was Hugo's mother. Her own son, Josh, was friends with Hugo, although Josh thought he was a bit of a show-off and too smart for his own good. They were in the same class at school, and they often walked home together and stopped in for a snack. Nina liked that. Her daughter, Jessica, and her friends, a year younger, did the same thing. Nina wasn't working, at least not at any job where she got paid—although the housework and cooking, and taking care of the children, with her husband traveling most of the week, required all her time.

But she didn't work like Ingrid did, with a paycheck at the end of the week or month, and the expectation that she would be someplace at a certain time every day, so she was usually home. She liked listening to the children's chatter and hearing them talk about their coming tests and their teachers. She liked to bake, too, so there would always be something to eat with a glass of milk, brownies or cake or cookies that had just been taken out of the oven and were cooling on a plate, ready to pop in their mouths.

"I thought this might be something important," Ingrid said as soon as Nina opened the door. "I didn't trust the postman. I've heard too many stories."

Nina had heard them, too. There was a rash of them in the news: an entire room full of undelivered mail, a postman who had thrown all the letters away. What had he been thinking? Nina wondered. Now she was always a little surprised when the mail actually came without going astray. But a package was a different thing altogether. Only her sister sent packages. Or her mother. Something they had picked up for the children most likely. She looked at the return address and saw that she was right. It was her mother's wobbly handwriting in the upper left-hand corner. She thanked Ingrid, who introduced herself, and Nina invited her in, eager for company.

They found they liked each other. They became friends, and then best friends. They had a few things in common, even though Ingrid was older. And something else. They were both Jews, floating alone in one of the string of small towns north of Palo Alto. Nina's Josh and Jessica, and Hugo, were the only Jewish children in the town school. Ingrid taught in a nearby area, and so did Walter, where their religion wasn't as much of an issue. But the principal at the children's school made things hard for them.

Once when the children had stayed out on a religious holiday, Nina showed Ingrid a letter she had received from him:

> Wouldn't it be a fine thing if everyone stayed out for every holiday, instead of the ones that are legally mandated.

It was the words "legally mandated" that set Nina off. She went down to the school to tell the principal just what she thought of his letter. But this hadn't improved the situation. If anything, it got worse. After that, Nina was certain that tests were deliberately given on Jewish holidays, just to be sure that the children (and their parents) would be punished for their transgression.

Nina found out that Ingrid was strong and capable, and in bits and pieces learned other things as well. In her youth she had been a champion swimmer. She came from a town not far from the Rhine, where, she said, "Nothing has really changed since the Crusades." She and Walter, who had survived in their own separate ways, had come to Northern California after the war, met a few years later, and promptly married. It was a time when no one wanted to hear about the past, or what had happened.

"What good does it do?" everyone asked when the subject came up. No one wanted to hear about the dirty secrets of those years — that Jews had become victims again. And in the twentieth century yet. It was easy enough to forget. To let it go and move on with lives that had become increasingly comfortable. Almost everyone was dead, after all. How would it help them now?

But it was still fresh in Ingrid's mind. She would tell Nina about being taken on a school field trip to hear Hitler speak—

a madman, she said—or the day the school headmaster came in with two burly men to take facial measurements of all the children to ferret out Jews. Finally she was told that she wasn't welcome at school at all. Ingrid spoke about these incidents dispassionately, as though those stories had already been repeated too many times for her to feel any emotion. Almost everyone she knew was gone: friends and relatives and schoolmates.

Ingrid came from a wealthy family, a family that was able to buy their way out of the chaos, her mother calmly planning an escape while violence swirled around them. The first thing Ingrid did when she came to America was to get rid of her accent and improve her English. She didn't want anyone to know she was one of those who had survived such unspeakable times. She didn't want to be pitied or feared. Yet she was still living out her girlhood, Nina decided. Ingrid was cautious. She made friends slowly. And she liked to ride her bicycle everywhere, her strong, thick-veined hands firmly on the handlebars. She rode the bike to work and to the stores and to the post office, as though she was still in that other country where everyone got around like that.

Everything Nina knew about "that time" came from Ingrid. No statistic was as powerful as Ingrid's stories. But Nina knew something else. There was a barrier between them that would never be crossed no matter how many stories Ingrid told.

"My father owned a business," Ingrid said, after they had known each other for a while. Nina waited impatiently for her to continue. She knew almost nothing about Ingrid's life before they met.

"Women's purses," Ingrid explained. "He was an artist, but he couldn't make a living that way." And so, "he had learned to design beautiful purses that wealthy women bought. Many of these women were not Jewish, but everyone came to his shop. Then one night someone smashed the windows, or a group of people more likely. We never found out. In the morning everything was destroyed. Just like that, it was all gone."

They were sitting in Ingrid's kitchen when she said this. Nina watched her fingers flying over the dough, stretching and slapping it, beating it into submission, and thought of Ingrid's father. "Yes, they beat him up, those thugs. First they demolished his store and then they beat him up until his face was nothing but pulp. Up to that point I had respect for German courts, for German law. But I saw for myself that it was hollow. The law was only for certain people."

As Ingrid said this, Nina tried to dream herself into Ingrid's mind, the life she had before everything went wrong — the miniature baking set with which she and her sister Ursula learned to make rich yeast dough sprinkled with raisins and nuts, butter-rich pastries, apple turnovers, the Sabbath bread. Her mother's cookbook with its indecipherable recipes handwritten in elegant German script.

Being in Ingrid's house was like stepping back in time to another place. The lace curtains at the windows and a cuckoo clock over the mantle, books of famous German poets with stern portraits of the authors in the frontispiece.

"Another world," Ingrid once said. "I can hardly believe that it really existed."

In the kitchen, she went on, "The funny thing is that I can remember exactly what my father looked like," she confessed, "but I can't remember the sound of his voice. I dream about it. I can still see him the night they came to the house and took him away. My mother drove all over Germany looking for him. It was as though he had disappeared into thin air. German records were the most meticulous in the world, and yet no one knew where he was."

Nina could not imagine how Ingrid spoke about such a terrible time so easily.

After a while she simply tried to forget about the differences between them. They went bicycling together, although Nina hadn't ridden for years. They went to the park without their husbands on Ingrid's days off, taking the children and a picnic lunch. A number of times they went up to the city, and then took a ferry across the bay and went to Angel Island.

She got used to Ingrid's sharpness, her tendency to say whatever was on her mind. They had begun to speak hesitantly about their lives now, laughing about their husbands' small peculiarities, forming one of those friendships that help women keep their sanity. They exchanged news of their children, who were growing up, bewildered by their changing bodies and new emotions. It wasn't long before the years began to slide into one another.

And then one day, Nina couldn't remember anymore when the children had been younger, or even what they had looked like. Coming across a picture of Josh and Jessica, she was shocked to see how small they had been, how vulnerable, realizing with a jolt how much time had gone by. Remembering earlier events, an outing or a special occasion, a birthday, perhaps, she could barely recall just how many years had passed. Her children went off to school, took jobs, and went to live in distant cities. They were on their own now and didn't need her. Her husband was always busy with his work or traveling.

But she continued to feel a closeness to Ingrid that she couldn't explain, one that went beyond friendship. Eventually, Ingrid stopped working, and her hair, which had been a vivid black, was streaked first with silver, and then it turned white. For the first time she began to look old. Bitter complaints were voiced that Nina attributed to Ingrid's age. Now a number of years had passed, and suddenly she was dying.

Dying, Nina thought, although it seemed a made-up drama for someone like Ingrid, who was the healthiest person Nina had ever known. She was solid and well built, with ruddy coloring and a swimmer's broad shoulders. She had never been pretty, of that Nina was certain, but her good health had given her a fresh attractiveness. She never wore makeup like Nina, who had a dozen assorted lipsticks. Never tried to make herself more than what she was.

"No, thank you," Ingrid said. "All that artifice. And for what?"

Ingrid held strong opinions that were reflected in her dark eyes and penetrating gaze, as though she could see right through you.

Now that she was in the hospital, Nina went to visit her alone. Howard had begged off.

"What on earth would I say, Nina?"

Howard didn't like being in hospitals or visiting women who were barely dressed in revealing hospital gowns. Or even sitting in a chair trying to make conversation. Ingrid was really Nina's friend, after all.

"Just tell her I send my regards," Howard instructed.

And so Nina went by herself, picking up flowers at the hospital gift shop on the way, and uttering Howard's words the moment she walked in the room.

"Oh, I didn't expect *him*," Ingrid said. "It's you I want to talk to, Nina."

Ingrid was surprisingly cheerful. Nina thought that perhaps she wasn't dying, after all, that it was something she had exaggerated to make a more dramatic story. People who were dying weren't sitting up in bed talking and answering phone calls, were they?

A cousin of Ingrid's was sitting by the bed knitting. Nina had only met Charlotte a few times. She was tall and slender, impeccably dressed, an aristocrat from the old school, wearing one of the sweaters she had made herself of colorful marled yarns, which Nina found stunning. Her manners were discreet and beautiful, too. Once, after Nina had invited Charlotte to lunch, she received a note in return on thick stationery thanking her in penmanship as elegant as the brushstrokes on a Japanese painting. Now Charlotte excused herself and went out into the hallway, motioning for Nina to take her place by Ingrid's bed. There were three other patients in the room, Nina saw, in various stages of illness, a TV turned on at low volume, and by each bed one or two solemn visitors.

There was something awful about a hospital room, Nina thought. Not the usual complaints, but the outrageous exposure of being out in the open. People coming to visit, just dropping in no matter how you felt or looked, holding you hostage. Not that Ingrid looked bad, but beneath her flimsy hospital gown (she thought of Howard's comment) her breasts sagged, and her neck, suddenly naked without the subterfuge of collars and scarves, revealed just how old she had become.

Yet, in the same straightforward way she spoke about those years of her childhood, Ingrid was determined to speak about her imminent demise as though it was only a passing occurrence.

"The only thing that bothers me is the children. It doesn't matter how old they are. I still worry about them. How will I know they'll be all right?"

"But you won't know," Nina said. "And there's nothing you can do about that, Ingrid. There's nothing anyone can do."

Ingrid was silent.

"Don't you think they could have come? Heidi called, I'll say that for her. But Hugo hasn't. In fact, no one's seen him lately." Charlotte, Ingrid said, had gone to the place where he was supposed to be living and left a note taped to the door telling him that his mother was sick.

"I have," Nina nearly blurted out, but she stopped herself. It would only hurt Ingrid to know that. She regretted not talking to him, not following Hugo to see where he was staying, but she wasn't sure she wanted to know. He didn't look like someone who was working, either. Who in his right mind would employ him now, looking the way he did?

Nina wasn't sure, but she thought that Ingrid was still sending him money, depositing it in his account without even a thank you. It was just as well, she thought, that he hadn't come to visit his mother looking like that. Nonetheless, Nina felt a stab of guilt for her silence.

Why hadn't Hugo come? Even though Ingrid seemed all right, she was in the hospital, after all, and who knew what would happen now? As for Heidi, Nina had never really known what to make of her.

In earlier years, sometimes, when Walter had been busy, Nina would drive Ingrid up north of the city to see Heidi, Hugo in the back seat amusing himself with a book of Mensa puzzles, and three bicycles riding on the roof of the car. Although Ingrid had chastised Nina for the Volkswagen ("How *could* you buy a German car, Nina?"), she didn't mind riding in it to see Heidi. They had to cross the Golden Gate Bridge, of course, the same bridge that Heidi was afraid of traveling across. Had she seen a terrible accident? Had someone jumped off right in front of her, flying off the edge, like a character in a Greek myth? Or was it the memory of that fiery crash long ago when her parents had been killed?

Once they went in spring, a day with puffs of ghostly fog swirling about the bright orange railings, and the tiny boats and colorful kayaks below wrapped in gauzy cocoons, floating like miniature toys against the hazy silhouette of the city in the distance. People walked the span bundled up against the cold and blustery winds, tourists snapping pictures and small children hopping or skipping ahead of them. A tunnel appeared, and after that, an exit. The sun broke briefly through a cathedral of eucalyptus and then the sky darkened again.

She veered off, made another turn, and they climbed into the hills, first grassy slopes that twisted around and around, and then pines and firs, dense and deep and dark, shrouded in a rolling fog of silvery mist. It was a wonder that Heidi's small house, settled precariously on an incline, didn't slide down. Mudslides threatened during the rainy season, and some of the brown shingles had come off, but so far it held its own.

Over the years various men had shared the house with Heidi. None of them had what Nina would call a real job. One published small chapbooks of poetry; another tended bar in town; still a third did odd jobs for people. They all got by, mucking about whenever Ingrid and Nina came, dressed in ratty turtle-necks and jeans no matter what the season. It was cold in those hills, and at night downright frigid. The winds howled through the giant oaks and redwoods. Going there, Ingrid would be talkative with anticipation. But all Nina could think was how gloomy it was—gloomy but austerely beautiful. That day it was breathtaking, the open spaces growing green following the rains, covered with orange poppies and stalks of purple lupine. Pink and white wildflowers clung to the shoulders of the hill-sides and clusters of golden buttercups tumbled down ridges. The desolation canceled out civilization, as wild-looking as if no human had ever stopped there.

While Ingrid and Heidi sat down for a chat over a cup of tea at a painted table—the pot warmed by a cozy in the form of an old carved-wood German doll with a voluminous dress—Nina puttered among the antiques. Gathering and repairing them was what Heidi did to earn a living. Pieces she had culled spilled out of the house and onto the front porch, picked up from estates in the north country, relics that had once belonged to other people, remnants of their lives. The collection was always changing, depending on what she had found. A spinning wheel waited for a spinner in a corner of the living room; a dry sink was set up as a buffet in the dining room alongside a rustic table and four ladderback chairs; a basket for drying apples hung on the wall not far from a picture that looked like an original Gilbert Stuart, but was not.

Among all of those antiques, Heidi was wearing a brightly colored smock, her dark hair cut in a helmet style, lips painted a vivid red. She was tall and very thin—a dancer's figure. She could have been Charlotte's daughter. The nipples of her small breasts pointed beneath the softly gathered material, and her face was smooth and polished to a glossy sheen with creams she made herself.

Ingrid always brought Heidi something—a loaf of bread baked that morning or some preserves put up from one of the fruit trees in her back yard.

"It's nice of you to bring Ingrid over," Heidi said, before going straight to the kitchen to put the gifts away.

"I don't mind," Nina told her, listening to the chimes making a pleasant sound outside as the wind exhaled through the trees. "Actually I like coming. It's so different from where we live—where you grew up."

"But it was my second home. My first was in Kansas before my parents moved here. It was totally flat," she reminded Nina.

Nina tried to picture that and could not. Was it possible, even though it was true? Heidi had taken to the earth here. She seemed to have been born to it, determined to lead a simple life on the land. It was peaceful, Nina had to admit. The village, Mill Valley, was beyond the hills. Though it wasn't far away, it was hard to believe that a movie theater, shops, and places to eat were close by—even the bar where one of Heidi's live-ins had tended.

Heidi went every week or so to stock up on supplies, less during the winter rains when the roads were all but impassable. Besides the face cream, Heidi made her own candles and soap, fashioned patchwork quilts out of stray scraps, and crocheted colorful afghans and braided rugs. In the warm fall days of Indian summer when the cold rainy season was still ahead, she hung the quilts and afghans and several of the rugs over a line to sell to anyone who might be passing through.

She refused to have a television, and a phone was only a concession for emergencies. Ingrid didn't dare call her. She would write Heidi a letter and receive one in return. And Ingrid told Nina, with resignation, that Heidi did not consider herself a Jew anymore. She was on a "path of enlightenment." She belonged to a community—not a cult but a group of like-minded people who also shunned organized religion.

Nina looked for signs of this whenever she came, but there weren't any, at least none that she could see. On one of Heidi's antique tables a silver oval frame stood alone. It held a picture of her birth parents, people who looked too young to have a child at all. Her mother was merely a girl, squinting and smiling into the sun, holding a baby who must have been Heidi, her father's slightly older face somberly staring into the unknown photographer's camera.

Heidi and Ingrid were still talking. Tom, Heidi's male companion at the moment, offered to show Nina the garden. Outside she drew in the pure air. Hugo was working on Heidi's battered truck. Tom had asked him to take a look at it after he found out that Hugo was interested in cars.

Where did he learn to do that? Nina wanted to ask. But he was the kind of child who could learn anything from a book if he wanted to.

Songbirds were returning after the winter, and their voices echoed noisily around them. Squirrels and rabbits rustled through the brush. Toward the end of September, she remembered seeing a cast of red-tailed hawks soaring overhead here, wings raised slightly above a horizontal slant, their raspy voices screaming a haunting *kree-eee-ar* as they headed south.

"Do you come up here often?" Tom was asking.

"Once or twice a year I bring Ingrid and Hugo. We were waiting for the rains to stop."

"Ah, yes, the rain," he said. He took out a cigarette and offered one to Nina, which she declined. His face was deeply lined, although he couldn't have been very old, and he was tall and lanky. "Do you mind?" he asked, and smiled with a charm she hadn't noticed before. The creases disappeared then, and he was suddenly better-looking, she saw, than at first glance.

"So what do you do here?" she asked.

"I help Heidi mostly. She's fragile. Self-sufficient in many ways but fragile."

"Yes," Nina said. "I think that's true."

He showed her the vegetables he had planted as soon as the frost was over, enclosed in a fence to keep out the deer.

"It's all organic, too."

This was before the rest of the country had caught on to organic, and Nina, looking at the thin sprouts coming up, could only nod in agreement.

"No spray, no pesticides, just good old earth, water and air," he added, poking at the dirt around a fledgling plant.

Still intent on answering her question, he continued, "I read, too. We both do. There aren't many distractions here."

They walked quite a distance before he said something else.

"Heidi worries about Hugo. He doesn't talk much. He keeps things to himself. She thinks Ingrid and Walter are too old to be bringing up a boy this age."

"They've done their best. In fact, they're absolutely devoted to him."

"Yes," he said. "Of course they are. But all the same, you might talk to them. A child that age needs a longer leash."

Nina remembered that one summer Hugo had stayed with Heidi for a couple of weeks, and he'd come back a changed child. She had let him take on some of the chores, too. Nina thought it had been good for him. He'd come home tanned and healthy, full of confidence. But Ingrid and Walter had missed him, and after that he only came to visit instead of staying overnight. He'd never been to camp either, or spent the night at a friend's house. Walter and Ingrid didn't believe in that. They were from the school that believed children belonged at home.

They never took the bicycles down from the car rack that day. It began to drizzle, the sun washed out to a watery puddle, and they headed back to the house, watching a brooding mass of clouds gather. Mist sheltered the house again.

It was like a stage set, Nina thought, looking around, as though they were characters out of a story by Chekhov, their lives frozen suddenly between the past and an unknown future that lay beyond this room.

Tom brought out a fruity Merlot laced with the taste of cherries, wedges of cheese, and a tin of crackers. He played checkers with Hugo, who quickly vanquished him with a triple jump, while the women talked and sipped wine out of thin fluted glasses from another century. It was a day Nina would remember, as though there was only this moment and nothing else mattered.

If circumstances were different, if she weren't married, if Tom had not belonged to Heidi, no doubt about it, she would have made a play for him. Everything turned on the *ifs* of this world. If Ingrid had not been a Jew, she would have still been a German; if she had not met Walter, she would not have had Hugo. If Nina's package had not been delivered to Ingrid's house by mistake, she would not have met Ingrid. If Heidi's parents had not died, she wouldn't be sitting here, and neither would Ingrid or Nina.

Ingrid was quiet on the way home. Hugo stared out the window at a streak of salmon-colored sky as they reached the highway. She remembered Tom's words and thought how much they would distress Ingrid, but perhaps he was right. Ingrid and Walter were stuck in their ways. And they were often rigid, suspicious of new ideas. Even though they were teachers, they didn't understand the freedom children expected in America. And even if they had, they wouldn't have countenanced it, either in the classroom or at home. But she did not think she would ever tell them.

But there was something else that made Nina remember that day. After that spring, the trouble with Hugo started. Not noticeably at first, but gradually, so that his parents weren't aware of what was happening until it was too late.

Ingrid and Walter began having a hard time with him. There were rages. They never knew what would set him off. He had gone on to high school after that summer, but he didn't do his homework. He didn't like the teachers. He said they were down on him, jealous, because he knew more than they did.

"Bitches," he called them. "Just a bunch of goddamn bitches."

He played loud music until all hours, keeping his parents up. He refused to listen to them anymore. Once, he'd gone out while he was supposed to be sleeping in his own bed, taken his father's car and cruised around town, accidentally slamming it into a tree. The police came knocking on their door in the middle of the night to tell them what had happened, Hugo in tow.

Ingrid and Walter took him to see someone. They tried everything, but nothing helped. Ingrid showed Nina his baby pictures.

"Not a sign of what would happen," she said. "He was such a pretty baby, so good-natured."

Nina did not know what to say. Ingrid and Walter quarreled bitterly with Hugo, until he left.

It wasn't long after Hugo departed that Walter died, on an exquisite day in early fall, when the light was burnished to a soft golden glow and the Japanese maples were turning brilliant colors from the cold nights, the time of year when the first pumpkins appeared on front doorsteps. It was the kind of day, Ingrid told Nina later, when it seemed that nothing bad could ever happen.

At first, after Hugo had gone, they had been unsettled, she said, but then gradually in a few months their lives began to take on a rhythm, a lightness that they hadn't felt in a long time. Alone in the house for the first time in years, they grew closer. Walter had stopped teaching, and so had Ingrid. Walter spent his days painting at his easel and on weekends resuming the repairs that had to be done now that the days were growing shorter. Bricks had come loose from the patio he had put in himself years before, the outside vents had to be patched so the mice couldn't get in, the garden needed to be mulched and prepared for the colder weather, the winter vegetables and spring bulbs planted. A red ladder that Ingrid had given Walter for his birthday several years ago rested against the side of the house where he was replacing some shingles on the roof and clearing the gutters of leaves before the rains started.

Ingrid usually busied herself in the house at this time of year, taking out warmer clothes and extra blankets, starting the first of the fall baking. She had placed crisp apples in a basket on the kitchen counter to make an apple cake. The clear, brisk air had given her energy and purpose. Early in the morning she had decided to join Walter, the two working side by side. They were busy for hours, moving from task to task without talking, the warm sun pleasantly on their backs and arms. Now and then a skein of geese flew over them, squawking, migrating south, darkening the sky.

At noon she went back into the kitchen to make lunch and to prepare the batter for the cake, her mother's recipe, bringing back bittersweet memories of a life that had disappeared long ago. She sliced the apples and swirled them in a concentric circle over the batter in the pan and put it in the oven to bake. Within minutes the scent of her childhood almost made her dizzy, as though she were standing there in her mother's kitchen waiting for the first delicious bite with a cup of cocoa.

Then the years sped by, her life accelerating until she was standing at her own kitchen window watching Walter in his worn plaid shirt that had been washed to ocher, as though she had never really seen him before, aware suddenly in the luminous beauty of the day of his devotion and goodness. Perhaps she had loved him, after all. What was love, but a melding together until two became one, not only with their bodies, but also their minds and hearts? All at once she was grateful for their lives. She thought of the small, fragile, unheralded moments that make up a life. A stab of joy that was almost painful pierced her as she took in the splendor of the last of the summer roses, often the sweetest and most beautiful, as if they instinctively knew that the end was near. Ingrid was certain that she had never been happier.

She turned to take the cake out of the oven and placed it on the counter to cool, already thinking of how much they would enjoy it for dessert. She set the table and was just going to call Walter for lunch when she heard a shout—an inhuman sound like nothing she had ever heard before, and then her name eerily floating in the air. She looked outside to see Walter falling like a bird plunging to earth. A shiver of fear choked her as she ran to help him. He had landed on the bricks. Blood seeped from his forehead and his body had crumpled.

A sense of unreality washed over her, as if such a thing could not have happened. Later, she would go over and over it in her mind, as if going back to the beginning would make it come out another way. She called frantically for help. Neighbors who had seen him teetering and then lose his balance had come running. She never knew if he had lost his footing and slipped, or his heart had failed, heartbroken over Hugo.

Ingrid died.

Not while she was in the hospital. Not right away, but within a few months. Nina walked over every day and watched Ingrid's ruddy face growing paler. She spent her days reading or knitting or listening to Brahms violin sonatas. When she felt strong enough she liked to take care of her roses. Ingrid's bike hung in the garage now. Occasionally she would ask Nina to take it down so she could ride.

"Are you sure?" she asked.

"I was never more sure of anything in my life."

Nina took out her own bicycle, too, although she seldom used it anymore. But Ingrid tired easily, and they never went very far. No hills now. Someplace that wouldn't tax her decreasing energy. Once, she stopped suddenly to catch her breath and buried her face in her hands.

"I . . . can't . . . go . . . any . . . farther," she stumbled.

"Breathe, Ingrid. Steady now," Nina said. For the first time since she'd known her, Ingrid looked wretched and sick.

"I . . . just wanted . . . to see . . . if . . . I could still do it . . . I guess . . . I got my answer."

Charlotte came over to do the shopping and make the meals. On days when Ingrid was too ill to get out of bed, Charlotte stayed over. She busied herself in the kitchen, and ran errands that Ingrid could no longer do herself. She polished the silver and straightened the drawers, dusted the furniture and did the wash. Charlotte refused to use a dryer. She strung up a clothesline and hung out the sheets with old-fashioned clothespins. The neighbors walked by just to see it, a curiosity from another time.

As she grew weaker, Ingrid talked about the life she had known before Nina met her, her childhood in that country that Nina only knew from books and movies. Ingrid had never been religious and she wasn't now.

"It would look as if I was trying to curry favor," she argued.

She said that she had an argument with God. She had refused to enter a synagogue since the war. No wonder Heidi had decided she didn't want any part of religion.

Ingrid's eyes still held flashes of lightning, but there was a dwindling of everything else. Sometimes she started confessing things that Nina wasn't sure she wanted to hear, regrets that had stayed hidden until now. She had only married Walter because they were both refugees. She had liked him, of course, but she felt she'd had no choice. Neither of them had much family left. He had depended on her. And she had to admit, she had depended on him, too. But she had never loved him. Not then. It was only on that fateful day and after his death that she had realized how much she had grown to care for him.

There hadn't even been a wedding. Who would have given her one, after all? They had gone to City Hall, and afterward there was no honeymoon. Her life was always pared down to bare essentials. The place that she had called home did not exist anymore except in her memory. All that had been taken away from her.

"No high school reunions for me," Ingrid said.

All of her friends had either been killed or just disappeared. She had never heard from any of them again, but in her mind's eye they were as clear as if she had seen them yesterday. Their names paraded in her mind, their faces as they had been years before were imprinted permanently upon the template of her brain.

She had gone back, of course, to Germany one summer. Reparations. Everyone was doing it. She had been a guest in her own country—or at least in the country where she had been born and grown up to a certain age—offered hospitality and good will. Not many Jews had returned to her town, even the few like herself who were still alive.

"What a strange feeling," Ingrid had said to Nina. "It was like looking at ghosts, as though their souls were hovering in the air and no one saw them but me."

Even the language she spoke had changed. She quickly became aware of this from the amusement on people's faces, as though she sounded like someone who had learned German out of an old-fashioned textbook. New words had entered the dictionary. Different clothes and styles.

The house where she grew up had changed into a place she no longer recognized, with other people living there. The last time she had seen it was in the dark of night, the night when she and her brother were sent on that terrifying trip across borders. And in that moment a picture appeared from the past: the soldiers bringing the train to a stop to search for Jews trying to escape, not knowing if they would be dragged from their seats and shot.

Standing there, in her old neighborhood, Ingrid realized that nothing was left. New buildings had sprung up. The school was still there, rebuilt from the bombings, and children were playing outside. Her father's store was now another establishment, reconstructed after the war on the ruins of the bombed-out building, but there was almost no one who remembered except her.

Ingrid couldn't help thinking of those girls she had known, the silly times when they were children, running in and out of each other's houses, playing dress-up with their mothers' old clothes, chattering without a thought of the future that lay ahead of them—marriage, children, a place in a circle of familiar people she had known all her life. They were children, after all. How could they possibly have known what the future held for them?

No, they had gossiped and plotted mischief against other girls they disliked, waited impatiently to have their periods, begged their mothers for bras and makeup, and finally, slyly, modestly refused to undress in front of each other. How could their childish minds have possibly known the way all that frivolity would disappear in smoke along with their very lives?

"Yes, they're all gone," Ingrid had said to Nina as though Nina, herself, had been responsible. A fierce thread of anger consumed Ingrid and spread toward Nina and all of the other Americans she had known who could never understand what her life had been like, the memories she could never erase. What did they know about suffering, with their comfortable lives and foolish concerns? How could Nina, dreamy, impractical Nina, who had never worked a day in her life, ever understand what she had gone through?

Nina sensed that it was all Ingrid could do that day to refrain from shouting into Nina's calm, untroubled face, *What makes you think you know me? How could you know me?* But she hadn't said it, of course, because despite everything, Nina had given her friendship and the hope that she could finally be like other people, like Nina herself.

Finally, Ingrid talked about her children. Nina never asked if Heidi or Hugo had actually come to see her. As far as she knew they hadn't. She didn't want to hear the answer. It was better not to know.

Heidi, of course, had been half-grown when she came to live with them, bringing a history with her of another family and another house where she had grown up. There had never been the closeness with a daughter Ingrid hoped for. But Hugo— Hugo was her own flesh and blood. How happy she had been when at last she found out she was pregnant with him. How much she had looked forward to having a baby. Why was he so angry? What had happened to him? Why had he rejected her and Walter? No one seemed to know what was the matter. He was born when she was too old, Ingrid decided. Something had gone wrong.

"He hated hearing about the war," Ingrid said. "Sometimes I think he even hates Jews," she added, as if that explained everything.

And then one night Ingrid was back in the hospital, but for only a few days this time before she died. Nina was at home when it happened. Only Charlotte was at her bedside.

Ingrid had already given funeral instructions: She didn't want one. She had written this out with several emphatic exclamation points, but Charlotte insisted.

Howard was three thousand miles away at a meeting. Josh and Jessica couldn't make it. Nina went by herself.

It was a small gathering at the gravesite, and even that simple service might have been more than Ingrid wanted. Nina didn't know if the children would come, but to her surprise they were there. Heidi came with a man Nina had not seen before. What had happened to Tom, whom she had liked so much?

Hugo, cleaned up for the occasion, was there, too. How on earth had Charlotte found him? He was wearing a navy suit too big for him, which might have been his father's, and an angry scowl.

It was late January, a beautiful day with budding trees that promised spring, and magnolia blossoms with mauve petals as elegant and intricate as the spirals of a shell. The rain, which had been interminable the previous week, suddenly stopped, and the sun was brilliant and full and warm. Just the kind of day when Ingrid would have liked to hop on her bicycle and ride up into the hills.

It was a short ceremony: a psalm, a prayer, the soil from Israel, a few words from Charlotte about Ingrid as a young girl, and then a rabbi spoke, someone who had not known her. He was very young and nervous, stroking the straggly beard he had obviously grown to look older and wiser.

If Ingrid hadn't been dead, she and Nina would have laughed later about his studied pomposity, the words he used, the assumptions he made, calling her "a woman who had passed through the fire and come out on the other side." At the open gravesite, in those fleeting moments as Ingrid's coffin was lowered, Nina suddenly remembered something Ingrid had said.

"We're all dying, all of us, all the time—even you, Nina. Don't think you're the only one who will be saved."

It was inconceivable that Ingrid was gone, utterly gone, and that Nina would never see her again. Everything that Ingrid had felt was gone, along with her. If she knew nothing else, there was one thing Nina knew for certain. She would never have another friend like Ingrid, no matter how long she lived.

A luncheon at a restaurant had been planned. Some of Ingrid's colleagues had come, too, fellow teachers, a few scattered relatives and friends, a cousin Nina hadn't known about who flew in from a distant state, someone Charlotte must have contacted.

Nina sat at a table with some of the teachers who were praising Ingrid, part of the stilted post-burial conversation.

"She had a way with children. She was like a magnet drawing them in."

"Yes, a born teacher," one of them agreed.

In the middle of this Nina looked up and saw Hugo standing in a corner alone. She excused herself and went up to talk to him, to offer some solace, although he continued looking at the floor.

"I'm sorry about your mother. Truly sorry. She was a friend. One of the best I've ever had."

At last Hugo met Nina's gaze and the pain in his eyes answered her.

With Heidi, Nina merely touched her arm gently. "I'm sure this must be very difficult for you."

"It never gets easier," Heidi answered, and Nina knew that she was thinking of her parents.

"It's not supposed to," Nina said in a tone that sounded as if she was scolding.

Before the end of the day Nina found out that Charlotte, appointed by Ingrid to take care of her affairs after she died, had decided to sell the house, now that both Walter and Ingrid were gone.

"I can't live there, and neither Heidi nor Hugo wants to. What's the use of holding on to it?" Charlotte looked exhausted. Her eyes were rimmed with red and there were papery folds of skin beneath them. She wanted to get everything cleaned up, put the house up for sale, and be done with it.

Nina walked over to help, going through boxes, the remains of Ingrid and Walter's lives. How small everything looked. All the possessions that Ingrid had loved were taken down off the shelves and walls. The house was bare and cold. She thought of the estate sales she had seen on Saturday mornings, belongings spread about on the grass as though they were nothing more than trinkets for the curious who happened to be passing by. She hoped Charlotte wouldn't put Ingrid's things out on the lawn for everyone to see.

But Charlotte went about it more discreetly than that.

"Would you like to choose something?" she asked. "Heidi's already taken what she wants." She handed Nina Ingrid's jewelry box. Here were all the pieces Ingrid had worn since Nina had known her, and with each she could still see the way they had looked resting on Ingrid's throat, or around the tracings of blue veins on her wrist. She chose an old-fashioned pendant, delicate stones of pink petals on a gold chain, one she had often admired. She held it in her hand, feeling the weight of it. It had belonged to Ingrid's mother. She latched the chain around her neck and then went to look in the mirror. She wondered what Ingrid would have thought.

Once, when they were going out, after Walter's death, Ingrid had asked her to latch the clasp for her. She remembered the touch of Ingrid's skin, a whiff of the fragrance she put on for the occasion. How strange to wear her necklace now. She could still feel Ingrid's breath next to her own, and a shiver of recognition of how quickly those moments vanish raced through her spine.

Hugo stayed on in the house for a while, skulking around, back in his old clothes. But within a few weeks he was gone, too, and the house was up for sale. A padlock had been put on the front door and the rooms were empty. It had been painted, and new shutters framed the windows. People traipsed over the threshold and trampled the flowers in the yard on which Ingrid and Walter had lavished such care.

There would be money left from selling the house to support

Heidi and Hugo for a long time. And there was the reparations money, as well, which Ingrid had preserved for her children.

For months that stretched into years after Ingrid died, Nina saw Hugo around town in the same ragged clothes. He looked terrible. Where was he living now? He had enough money, of that she was sure. It broke her heart every time, a heaviness that was almost unbearable. Once she saw him in the grocery store again and attempted to speak to him, but he refused to answer her. He grew more ragged and unkempt, and wild-looking.

Whenever she saw him, visions of the younger, sweeter child she had known would appear. What would Ingrid think now?

You put children into the world and they travel far beyond you, so far that you can't even imagine the life they are going to live, a life that is not what you would have chosen for them, she might have said.

Nina thought of calling Charlotte, if she was still alive, but she never did. Then one day she realized she had not seen Hugo for a long time. She made inquiries, she went to the house where he had lived years ago, but he wasn't there, and no one knew where he had gone. Even Heidi had disappeared without a forwarding address, her phone disconnected. They might as well be dead, Nina thought, as if they had disappeared from the face of the earth. She never saw them again. In one way or another, she decided, Ingrid's children had been possessed by the demons that had followed her here.

Occasionally, she walked by Ingrid and Walter's house. A family with young children lived there now. Around back, the lemon and orange trees were thick with fruit, but the stalks of tomato vines had been replaced with a garish play set. The roses, though, lush and velvety red in the front, were still there, blooming, and Nina felt her heart rising. She wanted to pick one, remembering the bouquets that Ingrid brought her.

Pausing there one day, overcome, she tried to catch her breath, standing very quietly, without moving. She could see Ingrid tending the roses, bending down to pull out weeds, pressing her hands on the soil, as though she had never left. What had Ingrid said when she returned to the home in Germany that Nina could never imagine?

*There were ghosts all over the place, the haunting souls of those who were gone.*

That was what Nina felt that day—a heightened sense of clarity, an awareness of the lives of everyone she had ever loved, the laughter of youthful voices somewhere in the distance taking her back to another place. And then the realization of time's victory over them all that Ingrid had promised her.

# Grisha

ROBERT WAS EMBARRASSED by his mother's Russian name —Grisha. No one else in the world seemed to have such a strange name. He was embarrassed by the name and by her.

When he was very young, she was slender and tall, a smiling presence with flat breasts and long skirts, her dark hair cut very short and wispy when the other mothers wore it long or tied back—what he would later find out was called "rich girl's hair." And that wasn't all that embarrassed him.

By the time he was in his teens, he was conscious of her prominent ears and narrow face, her strong nose and the jutting flare of her nostrils when she was angry. Her dark brows arched above deeply set eyes the color of bittersweet chocolate that concealed what she was thinking. But he could tell when she was angry by the tremor of her voice, the set of her pale lips, the way she would close the drapes even on a rare sunny morning where they lived in a sleepy fishing village called Half Moon Bay, on the foggy coast 25 miles south of San Francisco.

They lived near the edge of an ocean, as capricious as his mother's moods—just beyond the hills, past a grove of peeling eucalyptus, fields of artichokes and pumpkin vines and Christmas tree farms, a greenhouse where he worked after school tending flowers. At night hundreds of tiny lights glowed like fireflies in the distance, reminding him of her childhood home in Dorchester. He had seen them when he returned with her to the Jewish neighborhood in Boston where she had grown up. Among the city buildings, the stars looked farther away there, and the great dome above him expanded when he sat on the stoop of the dim, dark steps that led to the bustling street, fleeing from the smell of cabbage and herring that filled the hallway of his grandparents' apartment, and the Russian herbs and potions they used for the various maladies that afflicted them.

Grisha played the violin when she was a child, a time he could never summon in his mind—to him, she had always been as she was now. Even now, occasionally, she would remove the instrument from its case and take it out as though she were cradling a baby. Robert wondered if it was the way she might have held him once. He was conscious of her thin fingers and wrists, bones like tiny doorknobs, the thin skin a map of blue veins that he'd traced with his fingers when he was very young. Sitting at her feet, transmuted by the music, he listened to the sound that he imagined lay beneath the world or beyond the sky.

Years later, when she went away, she gave him the violin for the children he would have, along with boxes of books for safekeeping. She took only her clothes, a few volumes of poetry, and healing remedies, reverting to her childhood when her mother had strung poultices around her neck or made a mustard plaster for a cough. She told him that she'd often been sick as a child because her mother hadn't had enough to eat before she was born. When she grew older, those childhood illnesses returned: weak lungs and fragile bones, a frail skeleton that seemed to barely hold her together.

She said that she'd send for her things, but she never did, so Robert was forced to carry her belongings from place to place as he moved around, a reminder of his mother, as though she were there herself. She might as well have been: she was always there in his mind, long after he married and, at last, had his own child.

He'd been young still when his father, Martin, moved out one weekend. Grisha's fits of rage, grudges, and resentments had come to fill the house, and Martin had been coming home late at night, or not at all, for weeks. As Grisha's dark moods became more frequent, there were people she no longer spoke to at all. Her brothers and sisters invoked her ire. Friends were crossed off her list with petty grievances. Robert never knew when she might explode into a fit of anger, her voice full of fury. He waited uneasily, afraid that he would be next.

He stayed because he had no choice. His father never asked if Robert would like to live with him. He had moved to Palo Alto, a few miles inland and south, a university town. He mentioned a new girlfriend that Robert had never met. He saw his father occasionally—enforced times when they would arrange to meet. He learned to be careful to change allegiances as he listened to his father's complaints. After he began to drive they met more often, at one of the many restaurants on University Avenue or on one of the nearby side streets where students gathered.

His father was not a large man, but his voice was strong and forceful, making him appear taller and more powerful than he actually was. He had penetrating eyes, a no-nonsense mouth, a direct manner that sometimes made Robert afraid he would say the wrong thing.

As they sat across from each other eating bowls of pasta, he thought that his parents seemed to exist in different worlds, a split screen. It was hard to hold both of them in his mind at the same time.

"How's your mother?" Martin began, and then before Robert could tell him, he raised his hand to stop him. "If she's still the same I don't want to know."

He talked about what he called the "real world" — his deals, the money he managed, the startups that were going to change the country in just a few years.

"TV's a drop in the bucket next to this. It's not like that fantasyland your mother lives in. You wouldn't believe the ideas that some of these kids not much older than you are coming up with."

Martin waved his fork in the air for emphasis and looked directly at Robert.

"I'll get right to the point. What are you going to do with your life?"

Robert turned it over in his mind before he answered.

"I don't know yet. I've been thinking of building…"

"Civil engineering or architecture?"

"Something like that."

His father was silent for a few minutes.

"My advice is to get out and make things happen. Don't stay in that lazy backwater like your mother, frittering your life away in some greenhouse."

When they had finished their meal, he added more advice.

"You need to think about making something of yourself." He took out his wallet and peeled a few twenties out of a thick wad of bills and leaned over the table to stuff them in Robert's shirt pocket.

"And get yourself some decent clothes. You won't get very far looking like that."

His father supported them financially. He never let Robert forget it.

The visit over, they stood for a few moments outside the restaurant in the darkening moments of the evening. Suddenly, in that parting, his father embraced him. He felt the rough stubble of his beard, the warmth of his arms around him.

"Who else is going to give you advice, ask you hard questions?" he said by way of apology. "It's because I care." It was the closest he could ever come to telling his son that he loved him.

When Robert got home, his mother's voice barely contained her anger as it rose with accusations.

"I know where you've been. You can spare me your lies."

He was overcome with guilt at the embrace his father had given him, the money that he had stuffed into his pocket.

Yet despite their quarrels, his mother and father were the two bookends of his life until he left for school, lived with a girl he loved, married another.

Robert never knew his father's parents. They were gone before he made his entrance into the world. They had lived in Chicago, along with Martin's older brother, Robert, whose name he bore, one of the early casualties of the Vietnam War.

But every year he went east to visit his maternal grandparents in Dorchester. By the time he was a child, many of the Jewish families had left for other suburbs, Brookline or Newton. Crime had encroached, and the neighborhood had changed, but his grandparents remained. He walked with his grandfather to Blue Hill Avenue and what little had survived of the world of his mother's childhood—the kosher butcher shops, fish markets with barrels of herring, shops that sold Jewish ritual practice items, G & G's deli where Grisha and her parents used to eat corned-beef on rye, the many synagogues, now vacated as their congregants moved away.

"I am not a believer," his grandfather proclaimed as he passed the few that survived.

Despite that pronouncement, his grandfather occasionally entered one of the remaining *shuls* to say a memorial prayer for those phantom souls from Kishinev.

Robert often wondered how his mother had come from people like this. They were Communists, but he wasn't certain if they had ever joined the Party. When his mother was growing up they had taken her to meetings, but after Joe McCarthy and the House Un-American Activities Committee came on the scene, they went underground with the rest of their friends. By the time he knew them, their apartment was always full of former comrades, aging immigrants from long ago, still smoking, drinking a glass of *kvass* or vodka flavored with cranberries or lemon peel, nibbling on sour cucumbers, black bread, and pickled mushrooms while they argued and shouted at one another.

Everything in his grandparents' house was old, dark, and Russian, with a brass samovar that was always being used to make endless glasses of tea, fragrant with sticks of cloves or grated ginger. Expansive meals covered the table in summer when they went to visit: cold, sweet borscht with cheese blintzes or chopped eggs with onion, or *okroshka*, a cold soup made with vegetables, potatoes, eggs, and spices he'd never tasted before. His grandparents told stories of the Revolution, the old country, a place where danger lurked around every corner, as though they had just arrived the day before. Small villages would be served up in tales of narrow escapes and Jew-baiting, the scenes where they had grown to adulthood.

"What do you suppose it was like for me then?"

He knew his mother didn't expect an answer. It was one of those late afternoons when she was calmer and her thoughts returned to an earlier time, the life she had known growing up.

"I wanted nothing of their lives," she continued. "I couldn't escape, I was too young. So I did the next best thing. I decided that I wanted to be a Zionist. I had read Bialik's poem about the slaughter and remembered that my family had lived not far from Kishinev. It moved me to tears, even though so much time had passed and the Jewish State was a reality. But it was several years before the Six-Day War, and terrible things were happening. At night my dreams were vivid, filled with scenes and people I thought I knew, or that I had met somewhere before in another life. Perhaps such a thing can actually occur.

"I begged my family until they gave in to me. We had a Polish cousin who had settled in Israel after the camps. I went for the summer to work in the fields, and I decided to remain. Life was still hard, but there was a closeness among us, a feeling that we were all in this together."

"But you didn't stay."

His voice held accusations. He was tired of hearing about his parents' regrets.

"Two girls, friends of mine, had their throats slit as they were gathering eggs. It was a time when the enemy continued to infiltrate the border. I was afraid. I came home. I always thought I would go back, but I met your father out here in California. We had both come to Berkeley to study. It was an age of turmoil in this country, too, a difficult period.

"After his brother's death, your father got caught up in the protests against the Vietnam War. We both did. We were young. We came from dissimilar backgrounds, a brash Chicago boy and a Boston girl from a leftist background with Zionism in her soul. But we were united in our opposition to the war. We thought we could build a life on that, but we found out after we married that we wanted different things out of our future."

Grisha was silent for a few moments, as scenes from that time appeared to pass before her.

"No, I never went back. I left friends I had made. A boy I might have married. Who knows what might have happened?"

He thought of that life before he had been born. The only thing that remained of Grisha's romantic Zionism was a blue and white *tzedakah* box where she'd drop stray coins every week—a little charity for Israel. That and several thin volumes of poetry and a watercolor someone in Israel had painted of her when she was still young.

After his father left, Robert and his mother had been happy at first in that house by the coast. In their yard there were apple trees and trees with lemons and oranges that they could pick for supper. During the summer, Grisha planted tomatoes and zucchini and other vegetables, whatever struck her fancy that year. Sometimes it was carrots or peppers or eggplant. Often she would set out on walks over the hills, gathering colorful lupine and poppies that dotted the newly blossoming fields in the spring, placing them in vases that she threw herself on a pottery wheel and fired in a kiln she'd built in the backyard.

Afternoons, when the dense fog that reminded him of forgotten ancient worlds finally lifted, they walked on the beach. Rocky ocean bluffs covered in red flowering currant in brilliant shades of pink, wild strawberries, rosy checkerbloom, and silvery leaves of sagebrush towered above them. They explored the tidal pools looking for tiny sculpins in swirls of sand as they hid from predators, and collected shells and bits of driftwood. Above them great blue herons swept across a cloudless sky and brown pelicans glided in staggered lines over the water. Snowy egrets, an occasional black oystercatcher, and sandpipers and sanderlings pecked along the shoreline.

These were the times he loved being with her. She looked happier then, the furrows of her brow relaxed, a smile would shower light on her face. When it rained, flecks of moisture clung to her skin, and her damp hair curled in graceful tendrils on her neck.

She baked bread that was soft and fragrant, and great batches of cookies that welcomed him home after school, when they would sit at the kitchen table drinking chocolate milk out of thick white mugs, like conspirators planning an intrigue, as though his father didn't exist.

Even then though, Grisha's body had begun to betray her. At night he would hear her coughing, trying to catch her breath, and during the day he watched her fingers curling in shapes that reminded him of the gnarled branches of the large oak that spread its branches over their house. She seemed perpetually unwell, and he spent his teenage years doing errands, bringing in groceries, helping her to endless doctor appointments. He didn't dare bring anyone home.

In the afternoons she was often still in her robe, and sometimes she took to her bed and refused to get up. He never knew what kind of mood she would be in or what she might say. He grew impatient and short-tempered with the burden of caring for her, sometimes purposely neglecting to bring her something that she had asked for or pretending that he hadn't heard her continuous complaints.

Do it yourself, he wanted to tell her.

At those moments, as if she could hear his thoughts, she sometimes looked at him with such an anguished expression that he thought she would burst into tears, which filled him with regret that he was such an ungrateful son.

Not long after a recent meeting between the two of them, his father suddenly remarried—a quickie weekend wedding in Las Vegas. It took Robert by surprise, although it shouldn't have. His parents had by then been divorced for several years. The new wife was a younger woman, the girlfriend Robert had never met.

Erica. That was her name.

Erica was pleasant and pretty, with toned, athletic arms and blond hair the color of taffy. He didn't dislike her. She invited Robert to stay overnight with them when he came to visit, and after that he would occasionally spend weekends there to get away from his mother, fabricating excuses for his absence. He was ashamed of the deceit, but would be leaving her soon enough, in the fall.

When he went off to college — at the University of Washington in Seattle — he called once a week. While the phone rang, he could see in his mind's eye her halting steps making their way breathlessly to the phone. When she spoke, he held the receiver away from his ear so that the discordance of her incessant complaints would not weigh him down.

After graduating college, Robert stayed in Seattle, keeping in touch with his mother fitfully, and always long distance. He lived for a while with a girl he loved, someone he had met at school, but every time he thought of his parents' marriage he was reluctant to commit himself.

Almost two years later he met someone else, Aviva, who lived in Seattle, where she'd grown up. He was lonely, and her family, members of the Jewish community, welcomed him warmly. She had pursued him when he was still bereft over the breakup, and he was drawn to Aviva's dark Jewish eyes and striking features, which reminded him of his mother. She brought a sense of passion to his life — her impulsiveness and volatility made him feel alive. But it was a whirlwind seduction that burned out quickly.

It was an infatuation, he realized too late. They quarreled frequently. He didn't want to repeat the constant conflict he'd experienced with his mother, but every time he thought to break it off with Aviva, he failed, and the relationship resumed. He was seduced by her touch, the lure of her body, the promise of more to come, the intense drama of being with her.

Things moved quickly, as she planned their lives. They would live in Seattle, near her parents, after they married. Everything was settled, and arrangements were made for a wedding while he was still sorting out his feelings — unable to leave her completely, hoping everything would work out after they settled down.

Grisha came to the wedding, wearing a lacy dress, not as slender as she once was. There were the first few flecks of gray in her hair, and her skin was beginning to web at the corners of her eyes and around her mouth.

After the wedding dinner at a posh Seattle hotel, the notion that his marriage might be a terrible mistake already sinking in, Grisha told him that she was leaving the country.

"I'm going back," she said, cornering him while he stood holding a cigarette in one hand and a drink in the other, a persistent dull throbbing in the middle of his forehead.

He knew right away where she meant. He looked at his dark reflection in one of those mirrors marbled with fake gilt and suddenly realized his hairline was receding, his large ears now fully exposed. No one could deny that he was his mother's son.

He observed her with dismay, remembering the way he had felt as a child when he wondered how he could have come from that body. Now he towered over her. She was shorter than in his childhood, he noticed, or perhaps it just appeared that way because he had grown to his full height.

It had been a long time since they sat across from each other at the kitchen table, and a gulf had widened between them. Gone long ago were the confidences, the secrets kept from his father, the notion that he and his mother were in this together, whatever *this* might be, and all at once, seeing her standing before him, older and frailer, he felt such sorrow that he could barely contain it.

Between the buzz in his head and that of the music surrounding him, it took awhile for the words to take shape.

"What do you mean you're going back?" He took a bitter swallow of the drink in his hand. "Why would you do that? Now? At your age? Since when?"

The music stopped suddenly: the dancers—a blur of motion a few moments before—were as still as statues. He felt everyone staring at him as his voice rose.

"Whatever made you decide that? Are you mad? What the hell will you do there?"

Out of the corner of his eye he saw his father turn around, then, his father's wife, Erica, the perpetually smiling younger woman in a glittery gown with spaghetti straps, stood near them, her mouth agape with astonishment.

"I'm going, Robert." A steely resolve weighted his mother's words. "I've already made plans." Her words contained a rebuke that he had neglected her, at the same time reminding him that he was still the child.

She had kept in touch over the years with a friend, a widow who lived in Jerusalem. The woman had invited his mother to visit, and then if things worked out, she would stay on, have her own place, and find some way to make herself useful.

"By yourself?" he asked. "Seriously?" A woman who could barely walk to the phone, he wanted to add. She waited for some sign of approval from him, but it was clear her mind was made up.

"I've been dreaming of the land again," Grisha said, "the place where all beginnings are possible, before it's too late."

Too late for what? he wanted to ask, but of course he already knew.

She was his mother, but he knew very little about her, and it was too late for that, too. He kept the thought to himself. No, he could not tell her any of this now.

A few weeks later, when he drove her to catch the flight that would take her so far away, he thought that he might never see her again. He pressed her painfully thin body lightly to his breast like a fragile bird, afraid he would crush her bones, ashamed of his behavior.

He felt her stiffen, still angry with him. She would not forgive him, at least not now.

What kind of a son was he?

Grisha wrote Robert a letter from Israel.

> I have begun traveling in the north. The countryside is beautiful here. I am walking over the flower-strewn fields and hills in Galilee where the air is pure and clear amidst the fresh scent of pine trees…

Reading this, he remembered her striding over the vast spaces of green earth stretching from their house in Half Moon Bay, still strong then in spite of her illnesses, bringing back bouquets of scarlet flowers that filled the rooms with their sweet scent.

> In the silence I feel my life taking shape as I never felt it coming together there… It's not your fault. I want you to know that…

As though she knew what he was thinking. More letters came in short, breathless rushes — one long conversation divided into minute chapters, a little bit at a time, as though she was making up her thoughts as she wrote him. She had begun to read again, all the poets she had read before, but now that she was actually in Israel, their meaning was completely transformed.

It was not only the words themselves, but also the sacred spaces between them that matter, too, like the letters of those ancient scrolls. In those unwritten pauses are centuries of longing...the years of exile, my own included, that can still be felt, the past pressing against the present, the great men who held this people together and the unknown women who would still be revealed if one listened to what was said. It is the women especially I am drawn to.

Yesterday I went to Rachel's grave (not the matriarch, but the poet) and stood overlooking the shores of Lake Kinneret and thought about my life, which seems echoed in so many of her poems. Rachel is beloved here, especially among women. She ceased using her last name. She is simply Rachel. That's enough. She was one of the Zionist pioneers who built this land, a hard life of poverty and disease, falling ill from tuberculosis, at that time, incurable. She wrote of this land that touched her so deeply, of loss and longing, of the search for love, and as a woman, the need to be understood.

Robert felt a flush of hot shame as he read. It was as if these thoughts had a life separate from that of the mother he had known. He understood now that it was written by a person he had never bothered to know deeply.

Grisha gradually felt at home in Jerusalem, where she would teach English. A place had been found for her, even at her age.

I would have been tossed on the dustbin of useless objects if I had stayed in the U.S. Here, I am teaching at a school where I am needed. I am not always well, but I am better than I have been in years.

He began saving her letters, adding another box to the ones she had left with him. Once or twice he went through those boxes, curious to see what was there besides her books, and unexpectedly uncovered the life she had left behind long ago. Among the old programs and dance cards, photographs and sheet music, the life before he knew her formed a photograph of its own, redolent with the scent of musk and dried corsages, faintly smelling of gardenias. He inhaled their odor and tried to imagine this time before he was born, traveling back to his grandparents' apartment, her university days, the boys she had dated before she chose his father.

Strangely, he was beginning to feel that he knew her better now that she had gone so far away. Suddenly, he wanted to see her and tell her that.

By then his mother had made numerous friends and new acquaintances who were in a similar position—divorcees, widows, women who had never married. Some lived in her apartment building. Others she met through work or organizations. She had made a new life for herself, and had met a man she liked. That thought reminded him that she was still a woman and not merely his mother. She wrote:

His name is Ehud. There's nothing romantic between us—not now at least. We simply like the same things—tramping about outside the city, reading poetry to each other in the evenings...attending lectures.

Her letters sounded lively, but calm, as though someone other than his mother had written them, an impostor who had come to take her place.

He was shocked to find that he was jealous, almost angry that she no longer spoke of the chronic ill health with which she'd burdened him for so many years. And he was angry that she was actually enjoying herself with a man named Ehud—a name that he was unsure how to pronounce—despite the fact that in another letter she repeated, "There is nothing romantic. We are simply friends."

He tried to picture the man, but failed. At last she sent a photograph of the two of them on one of their hiking trips. Both wore hats and sunglasses, and all he could see of the man named Ehud were the shadows that eclipsed his face. He decided that he needed to go see for himself. He felt aimless, as though he had lost, or perhaps never found, the deeper purpose of his life. Though he had a son now, and responsibilities, his marriage was unraveling. It was a good time to go.

He arrived in the winter, a Jerusalem winter, cold and rainy. She was waiting for him at Ben Gurion Airport, looking smaller than when he had last seen her, as though even her bones had shriveled. Her ears were more prominent, and her cap of sparse hair had turned completely white, which shocked him. It took him a moment to recognize her, singling her out among the other hopeful people expecting families. He saw the same surprise in her eyes. So he had aged, too.

"You're here!" she said simply.

Her pupils were moist and welcoming. As he bent down to kiss her, he knew that something in her had softened, like the earth lying hard and fallow until the rain fell, as it was falling now. The sounds of Hebrew permeated the air around him. To steady herself, his mother clutched his arm. In the other hand, he wheeled his suitcase as she guided him to a bus that would take them home, to her home. He was her son, her only child, but a stranger in a land she navigated like a native, speaking Hebrew as though she had never left — her ease amazed him.

"A miracle," she said, when he mentioned it. "It's all come back to me. The language of my dreams."

The bus, filled with passengers, ascended a winding road. The rain had stopped momentarily, and as they rose the air felt lighter. He felt himself levitating through history, passing opaque shapes that shrank into the hills and rusted vehicles abandoned on the sides of the road, silent witnesses of the War of Independence.

Grisha pointed out places to him in every direction that he could not see, as darkness descended and new drops of rain began to cloud the windows. Then, at last, he saw golden lights spread over the hilltops ahead of him, and felt the heavy beating of his heart in anticipation.

A saying that he must have heard once from Grisha thrummed through his brain: *Ten measures of beauty descended to the world, nine were taken by Jerusalem.*

It was from the Babylonian Talmud, she had told him.

"We're nearly there," his mother said, breaking into his thoughts.

"And what about Ehud?"

"You'll meet him tomorrow evening. We'll all go to a reading that I think you'll enjoy and we'll see him then."

And so the visit began.

The next day when the rain cleared, he climbed to the rooftop and saw a stunning view of the city. So this was why his mother had come. The passage of time had no meaning here: past, present, and future coalesced as one as the sweet air enclosed him in an exotic fragrance. Standing in the narrow kitchen, no bigger than a closet in her small apartment, which was in the pleasant, tree-lined Jerusalem neighborhood of Rehavia, Grisha made him a dish of eggplant and tomatoes and spices that was new to him, and delicious. They sat at a small table across from each other, and he recalled the way they had faced each other so many years before.

She continued telling him about her life, a bewildering web of engagements and people he didn't know. At first, he couldn't imagine what they would find to talk about for a week beyond these revelations. He looked around the apartment and recognized almost nothing in the sparse furniture, though there were a few things from his childhood. Old memories and forgotten grudges rose to the surface like an ancient melody. He had come to see his mother, but why? What remained between them now?

"Meet my other life," she said, when she introduced him to Ehud. The words stung. As if he was the weak "before" that was to be regretted now that the far better "after" had arrived.

"Nonsense," Ehud said, putting an affectionate arm around Robert's mother. "This is not your other life, Grisha. This is your son who has come to see you." He grasped Robert's hand warmly. "While your mother is busy with her students, I will show you my city. I am a Jerusalemite, after all."

He liked this man; he didn't tolerate any foolishness. Within a few minutes Robert was touched by the sincerity of his words, his strong features, the solid body that reminded him of roots planted in the earth, the steady gaze of his compassionate eyes that regarded Robert dispassionately, yet offered him friendship.

"Has she told you that my family has been living here for years?" the older man continued. "I am still living in the house my great-grandparents built. The stones of Jerusalem are in my veins. I brought my wife there when she was a young bride, and now that she is gone, I am still living there myself. It is where, God willing, I will die. Your mother has other things to do, Robert, but I promise you we will have a better time."

He was as good as his word, a man full of quiet, understated humor.

The next morning they walked into the Old City, bundled up against the December cold. A soft drizzle was falling while Ehud made good on his promise.

"It is the only way to see Jerusalem," Ehud said. "We will see everything, but first we must begin at the Kotel, the Wall."

They entered the Old City at the Jaffa Gate, the gate Ehud told him Israel had only gained control of in 1967. They joined the throngs of tourists, tired mothers dressed in hijabs with crying babies, Black Hats, men with skullcaps and prayer books, pious women with head coverings clutching several children, crowds of Arabs on their way to work, passing through checkpoints guarded by members of the IDF who looked too young to be in uniform. Robert's eyes passed over the apprehensive faces of the workers.

One of them felt his gaze and returned it, a human being, Robert reflected, with thoughts and feelings of his own. Their eyes fastened on each other for a moment, and then he was gone. Who was he? What was his life like? Robert would never know. How could he hate these ordinary people, flesh and blood like himself?

"We'll come back to the Tower of David," Ehud told him, as they made their way toward David Street, past the souk with stalls filled with goods to buy and Arab shopkeepers trying noisily to catch their attention with souvenirs and merchandise that beckoned with colorful allure beneath an overcast sky.

They walked slowly through the crowds, filled with numerous beggars and children holding out their tiny hands for alms, Arab boys selling street food and tourists loudly bargaining for expensive goods and souvenirs. The smell of spices wafting in the air filled the narrow alleyways on the way to the Armenian sector. As they continued to the Jewish quarter, Robert heard the sound of Arabic and Hebrew blending with occasional English phrases and a mixture of other languages he couldn't identify.

Within a short time they came to the massive upper plaza and faced the Kotel, the last remains of the Second Temple, as it had stood for centuries. Men were praying, some in Hasidic garb. Others were begging to earn some coins by saying a *mi sheberach*, a prayer for people in need of healing and divine mercy. Many were placing notes within the crevices of the wall, some just standing and embracing it with their eyes, weeping. Men and women were separated, the women as fervent as the men, intent on their thoughts and prayers, some protesting for their right to pray without the partition.

They stood silently for a few moments taking it in.

"I never fail to be moved by this sight," Ehud said. "I myself helped to liberate it in the Six-Day War as one of the paratroopers. I was still a young man. Perhaps you can imagine what it meant to me. The sound of the ancient shofar trembled in my heart. I thought of all of the generations who had come before me—and those who would come after. It felt as though they were all standing there with me, that I was a link between the two. When I touched the stones that had been forbidden to us for nineteen years I wept."

He considered that time for a few moments.

"It's said that we all stood at Sinai."

Was that really true? Robert wanted to ask. What had he ever done to deserve his faith? Neither of his parents had been observant. He remembered his own bar mitzvah, a cobbled-together affair at his father's sleek redwood and glass temple in Palo Alto, when he parroted back prayers he had learned from a tape. What meaning did that have?

"It belongs to all Jews," Ehud said, as though he knew what was passing through Robert's mind. "It's the place we have always turned to when we pray. No matter where we are, all over the world, we turn to the East, to this place that sustained us through the long years of exile.

"The medieval poet Yehudah Halevi, who wrote 'My Heart Is in the East,' said that even the lush gardens of Spain turned hollow for him after a while. He only wanted to come here to Jerusalem, and yet it's said that soon after he arrived, he was murdered. It's heartbreaking to think of it.

"I will pray with you," Ehud said. "There is always something or someone that needs our prayers. Sometimes it is ourselves who need it most of all. Perhaps you would like to leave a note here. We call it a *kvittel*—it's a centuries-old tradition, begun by leaving written requests on the graves of righteous individuals. It's believed that the divine presence rests within the Kotel."

Robert followed Ehud and stood before the stones for a few minutes, then placed his own earnest appeal in an empty cleft. He prayed to know who he was and why on earth he was here, what unique task he and he alone, above all others, had been sent to perform. Then he reached out to touch the stones, thinking of his ancestors who had stood here, too. He felt himself moving through layers of history as he remembered his grandfather, who told him that he didn't believe, but had gone to pray for the souls of those he loved who had passed on to the world after this one. He thought of the son he loved, then his own father and his father's brother, dead at eighteen in a war he didn't believe in, his whole unlived life still ahead of him. He thought of his mother, who had found a measure of happiness at last, of his marriage that hung in the balance, of the things that had gone wrong in his life. He put his hand to his face and wiped away hot tears that mingled with the light rain.

Ehud put his arm around him.

"Sometimes it is difficult to face the truth of our own lives, but face it we must."

He looked into the older man's face, which expressed concern.

"I'm grateful for everything you have done," he said. "For my mother, of course, but also for myself. I wondered what you would be like. I am glad I am here to find out."

Ehud nodded, as though he understood.

Their prayers concluded, they began walking again, as if by mutual consent.

"It is always hard to leave," Ehud said. "But you will be back."

They walked farther in silence for a moment before Ehud spoke again.

"I have come to love your mother, Robert. It began as a friendship, but now it has turned into something else. I'm happy you have come to see her for yourself. As long as I draw breath I will take care of Grisha. And perhaps you will come here, too."

"I have thought of it," he said, "but I have a son now, and I'm sure he's waiting for me to come home."

The call to prayer, one of Islam's five prayers of the day, echoed from a minaret in the distance, a haunting sound that interrupted them.

"Ah," Ehud said, "the call to the faithful, as strong in their faith as we are in ours. Once you have heard it, you will never forget. They believe it is like hearing the voice of God in your soul."

"Is it open to us?" Robert asked.

"There are problems of access. It is one of the conflicts we have with each other. There are certain times when we can visit, but not to pray. Worshipers have been killed at prayer at Al-Aksa, I regret to say, sometimes by Jews. Jerusalem is a city of three faiths, each connected to the other. Life here is complicated and often frightening. I am a man of peace, a disciple of Aaron, who loved peace. I see reality as clearly as the next man, but I am a dreamer. Nothing is achieved without dreaming of the future. Isaiah himself said it centuries ago, looking toward a time when swords would be turned into plowshares. It's a balancing act. We are still working to achieve that," he said as they walked past the many watchful soldiers with rifles.

"But we will see the Dome of the Rock, that golden structure built on the Temple Mount in 688 by a caliph as a tribute to Islam. It is not primarily a mosque, but a sacred site for Muslims. It's believed that Muhammad left the earth here and began his Night Journey traveling to heaven from this place. The Temple Mount is sacred for Jews also. It's the place where it is thought Abraham was kept from slaying his son, Isaac, and the location of the Holy of Holies of Herod's Temple."

"The mosaics are exquisite," he added, "and the interior of the dome is not to be missed."

"But first, let us stop and get something to drink. There is much more to see, a long day ahead of us, but an interesting one. Before we are done, I will take you to the Via Dolorosa, where it is believed that Jesus took his final steps, the fourteen Stations of the Cross, before he was crucified. Now is the time of the year when Christian pilgrims come to celebrate their Savior's birth. This too is part of the history of this city and the world. To understand Jerusalem you must see it all: Jews, Muslims, Christians, each with the same fervor for their religion."

The rain had subsided when they stopped at a small stand and bought two cups of Turkish coffee, taking in the day, the people, enjoying each other as though they had been companions for a long time.

How grateful Robert was to this kindly man who was allowing him to see the soul of this city he loved.

His mother could no longer stand up in front of a class for long, so now she had her students come to her, one at a time. Robert found that he had to stay out of the house, since the apartment was so small that there was barely room enough for two people, much less three.

Before he'd arrived, he had played briefly with the idea of coming here to settle, staying with his mother for a while perhaps, until he got on his feet. To test this idea, he tried to take care of little errands for her, trying out his Hebrew, consulting his phrase book until shopkeepers impatiently switched to English. He had a degree in civil engineering, but doubted that he could find work or learn the language sufficiently to make that a possibility now.

And how could he leave his son? Still, he was curious.

Forced out of the apartment, he wandered the streets, looking at the buildings and houses, even going so far as to take the bus to other cities, following the directions that Ehud had given him as he contemplated living in each place he visited. He often went to one of the many coffee shops on Azza Street in the busy neighborhood where his mother lived. More and more he realized how much he missed his son, the comfort of his daily life away from conflict and the presence of soldiers.

As he drank the strong Israeli coffee, he watched the people pass by on the streets named for the sages of the Golden Age of Spanish Jewry. The founding of Rehavia, he learned, had been inspired by the life of Rabbi Moshe ben Nachman, the brilliant Torah commentator, who, in 1263, had been commanded to defend his religion against the Catholic clergy. After winning the debate by extolling the merits of Judaism, he'd been banished from the country.

When Rabbi Nachman left Spain, he came to a desolate Jerusalem, found the remains of a house that led to new Jewish settlement, and built a synagogue. Rehavia, a garden city designed in the 1920s, named its first street for the Ramban. Many artists and

writers lived here, poets, teachers, scholars, and famous people—
Ben-Gurion himself at one time.

The visit with his mother had been smoother than he expected.
When the conversation sputtered to a stop one evening and a
pleasant silence ensued as the two of them gradually slid back
into that other time, Robert showed her photographs of Adam,
the grandson she had never met.

He didn't think he would be coming back to Jerusalem after
all, certainly not to stay. He and his wife were separated, and
the child lived with him on weekends. Being away now, so far
from the boy, he realized that he was most of all a father to this
son that he had brought into the world. His first allegiance was
to him.

When he spoke of his own father, he found that his mother's
anger and resentment still remained, flashes of the old conten-
tiousness not entirely gone.

"Why are you always on your father's side?"

"I'm not. I'm here. I've come to see you."

She considered this.

"It took you a long time."

"But I'm here," he repeated firmly.

"Yes," she said, "of course you are. I'm sorry, Robert. I'm
glad you came. I want you to know that."

She picked up the violin she had bought to replace the one
she had left with him. It was her way of making amends for
everything that had gone wrong. Her fingers were stiff at first,
halting, and then grew more limber as she began to play.

The old Russian tune by Glinka, his favorite, spoke to him
more than her words, and brought back the memory of her par-

ents, the smell of herbs and potions that permeated her childhood home, garlic stuffed in cabinets and drawers for good luck, and meals around the table in that tiny flat filled with the voices of his grandparents' comrades.

The tension between them was released, and they spent the next few days simply enjoying each other's company before he left.

The letters continued through the years they were apart.

"I should have come here years ago when I was still a young woman," his mother wrote. "Ehud has died and so have many other friends I would like to have known when we were young."

Ehud.

Dead?

Robert was stunned. He remembered him with fondness. One of the righteous of the earth.

He didn't go to visit Grisha again, nor did she ask him to come back until she wrote that she was too sick to stay there alone. By then his son was half-grown, and Grisha was only a photograph to him, the owner of those boxes that his father had carried from house to house, full of relics of a grandmother he had never met.

Robert came back to Jerusalem to bring his mother home. She was recovering in the Hadassah Medical Center on Mount Scopus, the hospital that she had helped to build with her coins. He entered her apartment with a key left with her landlady, where he would stay between visits, while he waited for her to gain the strength to travel.

Everything looked the same: the little table where they

had eaten, the bookshelves, her clothes neatly arranged in the closet, a few things left in the drawers, carefully folded, her papers labeled with instructions in case she didn't recover, the drapes closed against the bright sun. It was as though she had known he was coming and had prepared everything for him.

This was the place that had finally made her happy, the home that she had made without him. Yet within an hour of his arrival, the rooms had become airless and stifling, threatening to suffocate the life out of him. It was in the heat of summer, so finally he threw open the windows to catch a breath of fresh air as he set about packing up all the detritus of her life here.

How diminished she looked in her hospital bed. He had to keep reminding himself that this was his mother—no longer Grisha, the woman who had been given a new life. Yet she had not changed, nor had he. Only their outward forms had altered.

He took her hand and was not surprised that her fingers were weak and limp. What thoughts still churned in her mind that would soon be erased as though they had never been?

She spoke little, only directing him to take care of her things, which he told her he had already done. He had expected some maudlin scene, embarrassingly sentimental, but there was nothing like that. There was little left to say, and he took up the time by fussing over her care when the nurses were absent.

Perhaps she would die here at the hospital. Then he wouldn't have to subject her to the trip back to the States. How could she live there? He had never married again, and he worked almost every day.

The day before the end, still in the hospital, she suddenly sat up in bed.

"So, you've come after all," she said in amazement.

"But I've been here for days," he answered. "Don't you remember?"

He tried to convince her that it was true. What did she want from him? What last things could they say to each other? Love had never been easy to speak of between them. No, they had never spoken of love and he would not speak of it now. Nor would she.

He held her hand and felt the pulse of her life growing fainter and fainter. She was dying now, hour by hour. He sat there until she was gone, her soul leaving her body, diminishing until nothing was left, leaving one world and entering another, until he knew with a certainty that it was over.

Some deaths are hard, he knew, but this one seemed welcome, as though she had prepared for it for years. He sat there for a long time feeling both shock and relief.

After she died, he felt less grief than wonder at the slender threads that still remained between them, which could never be dissolved. The cord that had first bound them together would endure as long as he was alive.

Although she had never told him her wishes, he buried her in her adopted land, covering her with the soil of the earth that she had cultivated as a young girl. And he hoped that she would, at last, be completely at peace.

# Kreuzlingen

*Bertha Pappenheim's Journal*
*Bellevue Sanatorium, 15 July 1882*

I arrived in the town of Kreuzlingen some days ago. It feels as though I have been here a very long time, and yet I just realized that it has been only a little more than a week. It is hard to know what the day or time is, or even the month.

The days drift by endlessly and every day feels the same. It is cool in the morning, but grows hot and still at midday, and from the curtain at my window, the lake is a glassy mirror, without even a ripple to mar its surface. From early morning until dark, which still comes so late as the summer wears on, there are boats on the water and people waving gaily to those who are walking on the shore. When I wake up there is a mist that gradually lifts as the sun begins to rise higher in the sky. At noon there is hardly a cloud, and the crystal blue of the water is magnificent to behold. By dusk there are amber and rose-colored streaks in the sky as night settles over the lake, another breathtaking sight.

From books in the library and from the caretaker, I have learned a bit of history and geography about the region. The lake, known as Lake Constance in English — Konstanz or Bodensee in German — is shared by Austria, Switzerland and Germany and is composed of three bodies of water. The Obersee, the upper lake, narrows to form the Untersee, the lower lake, which borders on Konstanz in Germany, the name of this municipality. The connecting body of the Rhine is called the Seerhein. It is halfway between Schauffhausen and Rorschach and straddles Switzerland, and Germany. Kreuzlingen is the name used on the Swiss side.

The sanatorium itself used to be an abbey, originally called Crucelin, later Kreuzlingen Abbey, founded in 1125 by the Bishop of Konstanz. After the Thirty Years' War, following the siege of Konstanz by Swedish troops, the townspeople burned the building because they wanted to punish the monks for siding with the enemy. The sanatorium occupies the part of the old monastery that survived the fire.

The land was once heavily forested or filled with plentiful orchards and vine crops, like so many other places, until the steamboats arrived on the lake, in 1824, and the first train, in 1874, when Kreuzlingen became the capital of the district instead of Gottlieben, the same year the municipality of Egelshofen was renamed Kreuzlingen. It is now, I am told, the second largest city in the canton of Thurgau in Switzerland.

The building where I live was part of the old monastery. It was put to another use entirely until Dr. Binswanger from

Münsterlingen acquired the property and opened a private sanatorium that has become famous all over Europe. I am on the first floor now, instead of the third, as I was when I first arrived. The view is not nearly as nice, but Dr. Gerhardt gave instructions to have me moved. I spoke to him, but he was firm, and I have not pleaded my case again. I have a bedroom and a sitting room that is very comfortable, and there are ample rooms for reading, or for simply being alone, like the library, directly off the front parlor.

A glimpse into my new life here: Frau Hedwig brings in my morning tea or coffee. She is probably in her middle or late fifties, but looks older. She has a stern, unyielding face that reminds me of a knotted fist. Her hair, tied securely back with pins, is almost gray, and her dress is gray as well, with a white apron tied over it. Her expression is one of distaste for her station in life. Although she makes an effort to be pleasant, the tone of her voice is harsh and edged with anger.

"And how is Fräulein this morning?" she says, putting down the tray. This morning she has brought hot chocolate, with toast, strawberry preserves, and stewed fruit.

She speaks only German to me, whether or not I answer her. At night I lapse into English, unable to speak my own language, although I am not sure why. This makes the night nurse, Frau Elsie, angry, as well. I am sure she has complained about this to Frau Hedwig. Although they are forbidden to discuss the patients, it is apparent that they do so, even though I have objected to Dr. Gerhardt.

Otherwise, it is very comfortable here—although no one, myself included, would choose to come of her own accord.

There is no use telling Frau Hedwig that it was a difficult

night. Despite the morphine, and the chloral Frau Elsie gives me every evening, the neuralgia is no better, but I will save that to discuss with the good doctor. Before I fell asleep I had a vision of father's bedside when I fell ill. It felt so real that I wanted to reach out and touch him. I remember that I was talking to him, although he did not answer me — at least I could not hear what he had to say. At the same time, black snakes began writhing across my face, and my hands turned into snake heads. I screamed and woke up. Frau Elsie came running to see what was the matter and scolded me for such nonsense.

As though she can read my mind, Frau Hedwig reminds me in the morning, "You are to see Dr. Gerhardt directly after you have dressed and had your breakfast."

When I reply that I would rather go riding instead, she says brusquely, "You know that it is strictly forbidden until you are better."

It is my one passion here, to be allowed to ride. I must speak to the doctor when the time is right. Thankfully, I have been able to continue to take walks. The countryside is beautiful, with rolling hills and woods and abundant wildflowers. I have been as far as the next town, although there is not a great deal to see, and I am not supposed to travel that many kilometers. People come for the summer holiday, and there are some hotels on the far side of the lake and boats tethered to docks, but for now I must stay where I am.

I am allowed visitors, but I have not had any yet, not even Mutti, although I am certain that she will come before long. I am quite alone for a few moments when the caretakers are gone, without being told what to do, blessedly alone. I have the few objects that I have brought from home to keep me company: my beloved laces and dolls and china figurines, which comfort me. There is little to do here, but I have made the acquaintance of many people who come and go. In fact, I have written sketches of them. Not a few are out of their minds. Some do not know what they are doing here, whereas I know quite well, but I cannot do anything about it. Yet if I close my eyes, I can almost believe that I am in my own home and that nothing at all has changed.

*Dr. Ludwig Gerhardt*
*Bellevue Sanatorium, Kreuzlingen*
*20 July 1882*

Dear Herr Dr. Breuer,

I must apologize for not writing you sooner. Fräulein Pappenheim is now in my care, although I consult daily with my colleagues, and especially with the director and founder of our sanatorium. I was waiting to become better acquainted with her, however, before contacting you.

Far from being over her crisis, she is still exhibiting serious symptoms. I am sorry to report that she is, at present, heavily addicted to morphine and still needs chloral to help her sleep. She has, besides her hallucinations, a stubborn cough, muteness, headaches, and neuralgia pain that have proved difficult to treat. She often rises from her bed at night to roam the grounds and has to be brought forcibly back to her room. She is moderately well during the day, but I have advised her not to ride after she sustained a fall. She is an avid horsewoman, as you must know, and cuts a fine figure, but I felt it too risky, concerned that the heavy doses of medicine have compromised her alertness. In the short time she has been here she has become attached to a Trakehner chestnut mare at a nearby stable—a fine, sensitive, elegant breed—one of the smaller of its kind, approximately sixteen hands high, and has enjoyed going to feed and to help care for the animal.

She still takes great pleasure in walking, which appears to keep her in good spirits, and in the afternoon she likes to play quoits with the other patients on the front lawn. At times she will sit down at the piano and play one of Mozart's sonatas, which seems to soothe her. The other afternoon it was one I especially like, a melodious first movement, but with an adagio that is meditative and somber, expressing the essential melancholy that appears to pervade her life. Her hands as they gracefully pass over the keys are elegant and refined, indicating a sensitive nature. Strolling through the parlor and standing aside, listening, I notice that a great peace comes over her.

Yet, toward evening, she is noticeably worse, becoming agitated, as though a curtain has come down on her daytime life, and her symptoms inexplicably return by nightfall, when she abruptly begins speaking English, which presents enormous obstacles for our staff here. In your letter you wrote that the patient was sad and apprehensive in one state, sustaining hallucinations, and often behaving like a child, but remaining relatively normal in another—what amounted to two completely separate states of consciousness. We have observed the same condition here.

Let me be straightforward. I admire Fräulein Pappenheim's obvious intelligence, charm, and beauty. She has impeccable manners, grace and elegance, the hallmark of old Vienna. I must tell you that I am smitten with her, although I have kept my professional distance and decorum. She is quite flirtatious at times, and then just as quickly closes up, as though a touch or a caress, even a word, would be unwelcome.

I cannot help but feel that her emotions have been repressed, and as I look into her eyes, which often resemble dark shadows, despite their inherent alertness, I sense a deep loneliness there. I do not think that medicine will ever cure that. She feels quite abandoned since her father died. Perhaps it is not true, but she believes that he is the one person who ever truly loved her.

If she had been the favored son, she has confided, rather than her brother Wilhelm, who was born only a year after her own birth, she would have been cherished for her own gifts, and all the attention that was lavished on him would have been rightfully hers. She confessed that once her brother shook her so hard she lost her voice. This may not be true I hasten to add, but all the same, I do not think that she imagined it entirely.

We are treating her as best we can, with a combination of firmness, mild electrical shock, drugs, change of diet, and rest—and, of course, a continuation of the talking cure that you designed with Fräulein Pappenheim, which has proved of great benefit. We have not prescribed anything that might inflame her senses or stimulate her.

She speaks incessantly of her father. Her grief, at present, is all-consuming, as she sat next to him every night, watching as he lay dying. Of course, she was not merely sitting by his bedside, but was also caring for him physically, in a manner that was both extensive and intimate. Thus was Fräulein Pappenheim forced to watch his descent into complete frailty, incontinence, and finally, death. On one of those nights, she must have been pushed over the edge. I cannot help but think much of her pain could have been avoided if a night nurse had been brought in to care for him.

I conclude that she still suffers from blocked grief following the loss of a loved one, which has manifested itself in these symptoms. Occasionally, she thinks of suicide to end her suffering. We will continue to do our best to help her to regain her health and to take up her rightful place in society, to marry, and perhaps even to have children, although the possibility seems remote just now. I am also trying to reduce her morphine dosage.

I will let you know how I fare, but at present I feel that the patient will continue to manifest signs of mental imbalance, hysteria, and a wide fluctuation of moods. She often speaks of her desire to help others—an unrealistic goal in my opinion, considering that she is not even able to help herself.

Your colleague,
Dr. Ludwig Gerhardt


*Bertha Pappenheim*
*Kreuzlingen, 26 July 1882*

My Dear Cousin Anna,

I so much enjoyed my visit with you at Karlsruhe before coming here and the many activities that we shared together.

I remain haunted, however, by the sight of the Jewish women and children you showed me, who have come upon hardship, or who have been ill-treated. I commend your efforts to alleviate their suffering. It pains me that I cannot help you. I was shocked by the number of destitute women whose husbands have left them, the mothers struggling to fend for themselves, the illegitimate orphans who fill the streets—not only where you live, but almost everywhere that Jews live. And the kidnapping of Jewish women and children for prostitution fills me with a deep and abiding sorrow.

I think of them daily.

I see how much needs to be done before women can stand on an equal footing with men. Through training and education, perhaps one day they will be independent and able to care for themselves, if they need to. You spoke of Mary Wollstonecraft's book, *A Vindication of the Rights of Woman*. I should like to read it for myself.

Your discussion of women's rights reminded me of my own lack of the education that is being provided for the girls under your care. How fortunate they are. I feel that my education was lacking in everything I truly aspired to. I was brought up to be a lady, to run a house, and to take care of children—all quite useless to me now, and I expect in the future as well. There is no place for women to create lives of their own, especially in the society of Viennese Jews. Even my Jewish studies were curtailed. It is true that I learned Hebrew and biblical texts, but not in the same depth and manner as my brother Wilhelm, nor was I encouraged to do so. Nor did I have a ceremony to celebrate my completion, as he did. The education of a young woman of the upper classes is quite lacking, as though our heads are filled with the same sawdust as rag dolls.

Your great encouragement for my little tales, many written in lonely moments, has heartened me to continue. They are filled with unspoken thoughts about my life that I cannot express to anyone else. When I am composing them a wave of calm washes over me, and I feel that everything will be all right. I do not make friends easily, and I find that my stories often serve as my only companions.

Although I have been here such a short time, I have made the acquaintance of a young woman who works here as a housekeeper. She is quite lovely, with thick dark hair, blue eyes, much like my own, and a flawless complexion. She has confided in me that she is with child and that the man refuses to marry her because he is engaged to someone else. When will women move beyond such stupidity? I would like to help her, but I do not know what I can do. I am, unfortunately, still infirm myself.

Although Dr. Breuer thought me cured, I have not done well since he left off treating me. I have had a paralysis on one side of my jaw and a weakness in my body that causes lethargy. There is no one else who has been able to help me as well as he did. Just to see him walk in the room gave my spirits a jolt. One day he was taking his daughter for a ride in his carriage and invited me to come along. We went to the Prater, and it brought back so many happy memories of Father taking me. It was spring and the flowers—fields of yellow daffodils, violets, and primroses—were coming to life. For the first time in so long, I felt alive, too.

We stopped at the puppet show for a few moments, listening to the music of the carousel in the background, watching the children spin around with such abandon and gaiety that I wanted to get up and dance, as I used to do when Papa waltzed me around the room. When I was that age, I could not imagine that he would ever die. He was not ill then, but strong and handsome, the way I still want to remember him.

Please write me as soon as you are able. I shall look for your letter every day.

Your devoted cousin,
Bertha


*Recha Pappenheim*
*Vienna, 30 July 1882*

My Dearest Daughter,

I have written Dr. Ludwig Gerhardt to find out if I might come to see you, but he feels that you are not well enough yet. It is quite lonely here. Your brother is at school, and I have no one for company save our housekeeper. I have kept your bedroom just as it was when you left so that you will feel at home when you come back. Even though it is summer, I am going to close up our house in the country. There are too many memories for me to stay there, and anyway, what would I do, with Papa gone and you and Willie away? It is a bitter time in my life, but I will bear it as best I can.

I often think of my ancestor, Glückel, that good and virtuous woman that you so resemble, now gone more than a hundred years, who gave birth to fourteen children, and who whiled away the nights writing her memoirs after her husband died in order to keep away loneliness and despair.

The other evening, Dr. Breuer stopped by to see me. He promised to write your present doctor again. Perhaps he has already kept this promise. He is such a kind man. I am sorry that he felt it best to stop treating you. He says that you were cured.

"Then why has she had to go to the sanatorium in Kreuzlingen?" I asked. To that he had no answer.

Your devoted mother,
Recha


*Bertha's Journal*
*Kreuzlingen, 2 August 1882*

*"Was denken Sie?"* What are you thinking? It is the question that Dr. Gerhardt asks me every time I come to see him.

On his desk lie pages and pages of my life. I cannot read his writing. It is cryptic, in a kind of shorthand that doctors use, with squiggly flourishes. Dr. Breuer has sent copious notes on my condition, so I am told, and every time we meet, Dr. Gerhardt takes many papers from an enormous briefcase, cushions his chin in his hand, sets his glasses on the bridge of his nose, and browses through the papers while I look around the room at his diplomas and think again of the tales I have been writing, what I call my "reminiscences."

This morning I thought of the charming music box Papa gave me for my tenth birthday. Oh, what fun it was! Before Papa's illness I would wind it up and listen to the music with him, but after a few years, it disappeared. I remember that it was encased in a little red wooden chest with a glass cover over the mechanism that provided the song. Many days I would wind it up and watch the gears go round as the tune drifted through the room. Especially on rainy days, it cheered me up. I even remember the song it played, and over the years the refrain of "Good Moon, You Rise So Gently" never ceased to give me pleasure.

When Father was ill, I found myself thinking of that little music box that had given me so much joy. I went up into the attic to look for it, and was surprised to find so many things that I once loved, now unused and put away, like so much junk. I found it hidden in a corner and brought it to show him.

"I can still listen to it," he said sadly, with a slight smile on his lips, "but I cannot dance anymore."

It was not long after that that Papa died.

People and events that we loved and cherished simply evaporate, as though they have never existed. Sometimes I feel that my own life is like that, as if it has ended before it has really begun. It is difficult to think that everything we have felt and thought will simply disappear, and the people who meant so much to us will cease to exist, as well.

When I related this to Dr. Gerhardt, he listened very somberly, commenting now and then. He is pleasant enough, and quite handsome, of moderate height and weight, with large, gentle hands. Yet I do not trust him as I did Dr. Breuer. His eyes remained expectant behind his glasses as they regarded me.

I wanted to ask him, "What are *you* thinking?" But so far I have not had the courage.

When I told him the story about the music box, he simply nodded and wrote another indecipherable sentence. Suddenly he stopped and placed his fingers on the left side of my jaw.

"How does this feel?" he asked.

"It feels...," I began, "like burning embers."

He took his hand quickly away then and looked at me with barely concealed alarm.

"I'm sorry if I have hurt you. I am only trying to help."

I thought that he was the one who looked helpless, as though he had no idea what to do for me.

*Dr. Ludwig Gerhardt*
*Bellevue Sanatorium, Kreuzlingen*
*5 August 1882*

Dear Herr Dr. Breuer,

Fräulein Pappenheim has continued in my care. Far from being over her crisis, she is still exhibiting a serious neuralgia that has necessitated higher and higher doses of morphine. I am sorry to report that she has a severe addiction. As a result of prior surgery performed on the patient's left jaw, she has suffered excruciating and persistent pain. I, along with my colleagues, wanted to remove a facial nerve to stop her attacks, but unfortunately, her mother has refused.

More troublesome than that, however, is that the signs of hysteria have not abated. Her moods fluctuate wildly, ranging from depressive states during the day to playful ones in the evening, which is contrary to what she exhibited when she first came. Lately she has refused all food and we had to forcefully struggle to give her nourishment, as well as water, which she then spit out, resisting us to such a degree that we finally gave up and had to try again. She has, in addition, a picturesque way of speaking, but when she becomes agitated or is not allowed to do as she pleases, she can act like a naughty child. The other day she threw a pillow at Frau Hedwig, who was trying to help her with her toilette. Similar destructive acts are commonplace. This is coupled with a childish charm. She often acts out stories or little tales that she has written.

Only yesterday she told me a story about a lost music box. Before that it was a doll or a misplaced pince-nez—all abandoned or unloved objects. I believe that if one looks at these objects in a clinical manner, it will be apparent that this is the way she thinks of her life. I find her to be imaginative and enchanting, but often disingenuous.

Yesterday when I checked her jaw and asked, "How does it feel?" she answered, "Like burning embers."

She continues to complain of time missing, periods that she cannot remember. The talking cure of which you spoke, and about which Fräulein Pappenheim told me, has not appreciatively helped her here. I myself worked with her.

Perhaps she felt a particular affinity for you. I must tell you in all honesty that I have come to the unhappy conclusion that there is no hope for a cure, nor any hope that she will ever be able to take up her life again as it was. I merely desire to improve her enough to make it possible for her to resume some semblance of the life of a woman of her station. Despite her father's death, the family does not lack for money. They are one of the finest and wealthiest Jewish families in Vienna. If circumstances were different, she is just the type of woman I would court and marry, but, alas, I have met her under quite contrary and difficult circumstances, and I am afraid that life will not turn out to be as harmonious for either of us as it could have been.

Some of the other symptoms you mentioned—the paralysis on the extremities of her right side, hallucinations, and loss of consciousness—may not be as grave as when you first treated her. Although she is diagnosed with hysteria, at times I believe that this is more like seizures and may have a neurological basis, such as epilepsy, exacerbated by drug dependence. Otherwise, the paralyzing effect on legs and arms, dizzy spells and headaches, as well as loss of vision and hearing without apparent physical cause, are puzzling. But until we know more, I will continue with her present treatment. At the same time, I am impatient to see some improvement.

The withdrawal from chloral and morphine was to be the primary goal of the cure in Kreuzlingen, followed by a general recovery and convalescence, but when we attempted it, the patient had a severe reaction and that course was not sustained. Even so, I am afraid that Fräulein Pappenheim feels quite confined here and longs to be free. Perhaps she also believes, and rightly so, that she is a prisoner of both her body and her mind.

With every good hope for the future,
Dr. Ludwig Gerhardt

*Wilhelm Pappenheim*
*Vienna, 10 August 1882*

Dear Sister,

Our mother has asked me to write you. She looks quite anxious, with only our housekeeper to keep her company and to cook and clean for her. She would like to travel to Mainz and Frankfurt to see relatives she has not seen for some time. As there is little for her now in Vienna, she is thinking of moving to rejoin her family.

This is also to give you notice that I have inherited Father's books. Papa wanted me to have them, also his prized silver and gold goblets that he kept in the Biedermeier cabinet. Once I am settled in my new quarters, I will send for them.

I have met someone of whom I am very fond, but we have no plans to marry until I am settled in my future occupation. She looks forward to meeting you. I have told her a bit about your illness, for she will be your sister-in-law, after all, one day, and will learn for herself of your malady.

I do not know when I will see you, but I hope that you will set your mind to becoming well again so that you can be a help to our Mutter, as a daughter should.

Your loving brother,
Wilhelm

*Bertha's Journal*
*Kreuzlingen, 11 August 1882*

Why is it that Wilhelm and I have never really liked each other? Although he is younger, he has always tried to dominate me and get his way, ignoring my feelings. Now he is taking possession of what he says is rightfully his without even asking me, the books I read and understood, the very ones he has never opened, and Father's goblets, which I loved. He is simply taking them because he is the son and I am only a daughter. I cannot believe that Father simply gave them to him before he died and left nothing for me.

Wilhelm and I are still locked in a battle far worse than years ago when his toy soldiers advanced over the blankets and hills of my bed. Every time I think of the tapestry of two roosters fighting that hangs in Mutti's chamber, I see Wilhelm and myself struggling for the attention that he always wins.

Even when he shook me, Mutti took his side. "Why do you favor him?" I have always wanted to cry.

But nothing was ever done—then or now. He was only a mediocre student, but everything will go to Wilhelm simply because he is a man. I will write Mama and tell her what I think, but I know already—she will never say a word against Willie.

And yet, he is still my brother, with the same reddish-golden hair as Papa's. Except for Mutti, there remain just the two of us now, and a strange affection all the same that makes me wonder why we cannot behave better to members of our own family. Who do we really have, after all, if not each other?


*Bertha's Journal*
*Kreuzlingen, 20 August 1882*

A difficult week. I have not been able to get out of bed. I feel some paralysis on my right side and my cough and neuralgia have worsened. One eye is almost closed again. Frau Hedwig has a disapproving expression on her face. I have lapsed into English, as well.

*"Auf Deutsch, bitte!"* she says sharply, and wags a finger at me. But as soon as my head hits the pillow I cannot remember a word of it and only English fills my mind and follows me in my dreams.

I feel totally alone. Even Mutti would be a welcome relief. Dr. Gerhardt has reluctantly increased my morphine. He came to my room and sat by my bed, but it is apparent that we are at odds now. He has turned against me, citing my reluctance to cooperate with him and my refusal to get well under his care.

How impossible he is! I was suspicious of him from the beginning. He is eager to have me well for his own sake, not mine. Perhaps conflict is the essence of life, but he uses words instead of a sword to fight me. I have asked for another doctor, much to his displeasure.

As soon as I was feeling better, Dr. Gerhardt asked to see me in his office. He was stern and unyielding, but I was determined not to weaken. He immediately began speaking, waving his pipe in the air, demanding that I provide answers. To please him I forgot my misgivings, although I was sorry later. That night, in bed, I tried to recall the conversation.

"Ambiguity," my dear Fräulein," he intoned, "is at the heart of your illness. You are ambivalent about both your mother and father. You believed that your father loved you, but he belittled your dreams."

"I was only a daughter."

"And that made you angry?"

"Yes, of course."

"Do you understand that he was only trying to protect you?"

"I did not want to be protected."

"And why is that?"

"I wanted to be free. I did not want my life decided for me by someone else."

"A father wants to see his daughter safely married. It is surely because he loved you."

"Yes."

"But you were secretly angry with him?"

"Sometimes."

"And when was that?"

I felt a chill coursing through me. Dr. Gerhardt is the only one who has suspected my anger toward Papa. I suddenly began to feel frightened of him, as though he could see the secret thoughts in my mind. Although this took me by surprise, I found myself answering him once more, against my better judgment, as though he had hypnotized me into revealing things I would rather have left unspoken.

"He didn't always take me seriously. He listened to my mother, who told him what was best for me. I did not think that he was happy with her. In fact, I am not sure that he even loved her. It was an arranged marriage. My mother was only eighteen; my father was several years older. There were times that I thought he might have had other women, but he was a religious man. Papa believed in God, while I am not always sure. He prayed every morning before he left for work. He would never have left her—or us—even though she always seemed so sad. Ours was a gloomy household. Only the times I spent with Papa were happy."

"And so you tried to nurse him back to health."

"I did not succeed."

"You are not to blame for that. Your father was very sick. It was unlikely that he would ever get well."

"It was the nurse who told me what happened." As I said this, the day Papa died unspooled before me like a waking dream that plays over and over again. "I was lying in bed ill. Mutti did not even tell me so that I could say goodbye to him. I remember that it was raining. I do not know if he was covered when they took him out of the house."

"And that bothers you?"

"No matter how much I try to stop it, at night I see Papa's

face, and it is always wet with raindrops. Sometimes his face turns into a death's head. Other times a serpent crawls out of the walls of his bedroom. I know that he was put into a long black carriage and carried away. Soon the house started filling up with people, while my mother played the part of the grief-stricken widow."

"So you are angry with your mother, too?"

Yes, that's true, I thought.

"I never felt that I could tell her anything. She always stood in judgment. She did not understand why I was locked in my room writing."

When he asked if *I* knew why, he put aside his pen for a moment and waited for me to answer.

"It is my secret friend," I said at last, hoping he would understand, "the way I clear my mind. Sometimes I do not know what I think until I write it down."

And only now it became apparent what he was getting at.

"Your mother has sent me several letters. She does not like the fact that I have not let her come to see you. She is especially worried about your neuralgia, after your last letter."

"I can tell her about that, but not about the thoughts that lie close to my heart."

I imagined he would be curious as to what they were, but he merely continued, "I wrote her that we were thinking of surgery on the facial nerve that we believe is causing the pain, but she does not want us to do it. Perhaps a visit would be advisable so that she can see for herself how you are."

"I do not want to see my mother now — nor do I want to be here."

"Are you opposed to your treatment then?"

"It is not helping me."

"Because you refuse to cooperate with us. I am going to suggest, Fräulein, that perhaps you are not being absolutely truthful. Is it possible that you are exaggerating your symptoms to gain sympathy, in order to be able to do what you like?"

"That is presumptuous and cruel. I can leave of my own free will."

"I would not advise that."

"You cannot keep me here as a prisoner."

"I did not mean to suggest that. In fact, your mother has asked that Dr. Breuer resume your treatment."

"I do not wish to see him *or* my mother."

"What *do* you want? You are ill. We are trying to help you get better."

"I will help myself."

"And how will you do that?"

"I have done it already."

"And how did you accomplish this feat?"

He was angry. A rose-colored flush crept up his neck and a slight tremor of his hand betrayed him as he wrote all this down in his report.

And so it went. A barrage of questions, like bullets.

"You are a woman. Women are vulnerable and need to be protected."

"Men have not always taken care of us. We must learn to take care of ourselves."

He did not like this either.

"Very well," he said, and closed his book, as a chill set in between the two of us — a cat-and-mouse game.

Although I have begun to avoid him, he seeks me out to

resume the battle. His admiration for me has turned acid and querulous, a mutual dislike.

*Bertha's Journal*
*Kreuzlingen, 17 September 1882*

The first rain fell today, with the smell of fall arriving in the air. The fire was lit in the great room, and I wore a warm shawl for the first time here. When I came it was the height of summer. Now it is the time of endings, before winter enfolds us all in its white embrace.

Nothing has gone the way I hoped it would. I remember, once more, Papa's absence, and the soft spring rain falling the day he died. All of the people who came to the hotels are gone, and a melancholy silence settles over the water, which is covered with a gray haze. The children have gone back to their lessons and the fathers to their work.

I heard in a roundabout way that the young housekeeper has had her baby, a boy, and using the pretext of going to buy some tatting yarn I secretly visited her. Perhaps I could help in some small manner. The cook, who gave me the news, told me how to go, and I found it quickly, a small cottage just outside of town, with smoke curling from the chimney. The man has, indeed, married someone else without giving it a second thought. I am angry to think that such things keep happening, and that there is no one to help these women.

The baby is beautiful, plump and healthy—and his mother will have to give him up and go back to work as soon as he is weaned if there is no one to marry her. A widower has stepped forward who needs a wife to look after his children, and it seems that her fate is settled if she agrees. She is as confined as I am, but she has known the touch of a baby's tiny hands and his mouth on her breast. It is something I do not think I will ever experience.

I returned to my room, wet and chilled, which infuriated Frau Hedwig, who reported it at once to Dr. Gerhardt.

We continue to quarrel. "Give me the key that will help you get well," he says angrily.

"You are eating up my life with your words."

"That is why you are here — to unlock the words that will set you free."

It was a mistake to come here. It is all undone. All the good work that Dr. Breuer did with me, all the chimney sweeping that I discovered myself, getting rid of the terrible cobwebs that have cluttered my mind and made me ill, the black serpent heads that appear suddenly and hold me hostage, the paralysis and neuralgia, the frightening hallucinations — all of the other infirmities that plague me that I cannot control. Either a relationship is made with someone else or not. In this case, the initial pleasantries of Dr. Gerhardt, even his ardor, have turned sour. It is apparent that he has taken a fierce dislike to me. I have begun calling him Herr Dr. Katz, for he reminds me of nothing so much as a cat that is out to catch his prey.

My spirits are low and Papa seems so far away. I have been studying his photograph on my night table. It is strange to see the likeness of a person after they are gone and nothing of them remains but indistinct impressions in the mind. Yes, I can see Papa's face, but nothing else of him survives. All that passes through the mind of another person is hidden from us, save for their acts, or the set of their mouth, the tone of their voice, the words they speak that let us know whether there is love toward us or not. And even if there is love, we may not be disposed to return it. We are essentially alone, after all, in our isolated universes whirling around like miniature galaxies. How can I ever know another human being, even those closest to me, when I am still trying to know myself?

I tried to please Papa, but he never let me forget that I was born a girl and there was nothing at all I could do about that. Dr. Breuer is the only person with whom I have felt totally myself, without any pretense. He knew me as no one else has. Yet in the end, he, too, abandoned me. In his anger, Dr. Gerhardt let slip that Dr. Breuer is the one who referred me here—a betrayal that fills me with sorrow.


*Bertha Pappenheim*
*Kreuzlingen, 20 September 1882*

My Dear Cousin,

I am scarcely better than when I came here. My world grows smaller and smaller, even though I try to hold on to what remains of my mind. Thoughts keep churning in my head and will not leave me alone. You will be happy to know that at least I continue writing my stories, which seems to help. I am a little bit like Jane Austen, for I sit in the parlor and put ink to paper, and cover up the words when anyone comes, as though I am doing nothing of any importance. Some of the sketches that I have written are not flattering to those who surround me, despite their good intentions and busyness—or, I should say, bossiness.

In a strange way, though, I feel that I am growing stronger

and that one day this will be simply a memory in the long-ago past. I cannot believe that my life will be no more than this pain and suffering.

I have been thinking more and more about the worsening situation of Jewish women, not only here, but also in Galicia, as you described. I am alarmed to learn that white slavery continues to terrorize many young women on the streets, and that orphans have no one to care for them properly. Too many Jewish women have nowhere to turn. I have thought again how much I want to help them.

When I told my mother, she wrote back, "How can you help them, when you cannot even help yourself?"

"Who better to help them," I answered, "than someone who has suffered herself?"

I have not seen my mother since I arrived. At first Dr. Gerhardt wanted to keep her away, but now I am the one who does not want to see her. She is full of practicalities and routine, forever asking about my digestion. She would never ask, as I have, "Why are we here at this particular time on earth, and for what purpose?" With Papa, I could contemplate all kinds of questions, and he would consider them thoughtfully.

The other day Mutti wrote to ask if I would be strong enough to visit her family in December. She is thinking of moving back to Frankfurt and would like me to go with her to look at houses. Where will I be then? I honestly do not know. I would like to come and see you after I leave here. I find my visits with you a chance to leave the constant chattering of my own brain. But my eyes are still very poor and painful, and I suffer from other maladies, that alas, you know of all too well.

Before I forget, the housekeeper I mentioned in a previous

letter has had her baby. I went to see her, and could only wish that society would provide for these mothers and their children. She has nowhere to turn. Her own parents do not want to continue helping her, and consequently, she will be forced to marry a man whose wife has died, solely to take care of the house and children, as though she had no feelings or passions of her own. I understand her situation. I am nothing more than a patient here, a series of disorders that must be dealt with before I can be released from this place that has become a prison. No one considers my feelings, either—unlike Dr. Breuer, for whom I was a human being first, rather than merely a list of symptoms. I still want to believe that he had my best interests at heart.

With much love,
Bertha

*Dr. Ludwig Gerhardt*
*Bellevue Sanatorium, Kreuzlingen*
*9 October 1882*

Dear Herr Dr. Breuer,

This letter is to inform you that Fräulein Pappenheim wishes to leave the sanatorium as soon as possible. She has done nothing but complain about me, as well as rail against the hospital and the staff. She is hostile and critical of this medical establishment, because we have been unable to relieve her painful symptoms.

In a letter to her cousin she related the unpleasant effects of the morphine, which has made her physically ill and prevented her from eating. You yourself began this course, but in her mind you have been the only one who has helped her. She constantly compares the treatment here to the more satisfactory treatment under your care, even though she has stated that she does not want to resume therapy from anyone, including you. I have tried to help her with no success.

In particular, she has written her mother and cousin that she is unhappy and does not want to remain. We have tried our best, and indeed, I felt that I was making a real breakthrough with her. I have no choice but to accede to her desire. I do not think that she will have an easy time of it. In fact, I expect that she will be back before long. I am sorry that we could not do more without her cooperation, and I regret that my report could not be more satisfactory.

Cordially,
Dr. Ludwig Gerhardt


*Bertha's Journal*
*Kreuzlingen, 16 October 1882*

Snow has fallen on the distant mountains and the water is icy and perilous. A young boy drowned there last week, trying to skate across it. His friends attempted, in vain, to save him and nearly drowned themselves, and so a life has ended that had only just begun.

Our own lives are so real to us, and yet they turn out to be nothing but phantoms. Summer has gone, its warmth only a memory, and winter has already begun to set in and cover the fields. There is little to do except to write in this diary, work on puzzles in the parlor, and to read, inhabiting other lives not my own, which is a great pleasure for me. Last night I played a nocturne by Franz Liszt and was overcome by its peaceful beauty.

I have finally told Dr. Gerhardt that there is no longer any point in staying here.

"What will you do?" he asked, and then, angrily, "This is folly, pure folly. Surely you must know that." He pounded his fist on the table. "You will be back, you know. You will *have* to come back."

But I have made a decision. From now on, for good or ill, my life will belong to me. Looking at my fellow inmates, I realize I am more fortunate than they. People continue to come and go. A few have been here since before I came, and each of them has a story. I have grown fond of many of them, since this has been my home for a time. But still it feels like a stage set, as though we have all been caught in the midst of a play, acting out our parts.

Today the leaves have blown from the trees and their silhouettes against the horizon are stark and bare. In the afternoon, I walked to the stables to ride my chestnut mare for the last time. She seemed to know that I was leaving. She looked at me with unanswered questions. I held her head close, stroking her, and then I had the stable boy saddle her for one last ride. I rode her fast, far out into the countryside, until we were both worn out, and yet it left me strangely exhilarated.

The air was clear and fresh and rushed up my spine, and for a few moments I felt completely alive again, as I have not felt for some time. I have been surrounded by darkness, but I can remember light, as I remember happiness, even though it eludes me now.

I have discovered that, above all, the human spirit desires its own destiny. When the time comes, I will leave this place and follow a path that is becoming increasingly clear to me. I am certain that eventually I will find it, as the golden peacock, that mythical bird of Yiddish song, finds its way to the place for which its heart longs.

*Bertha's Journal*
*Kreuzlingen, 18 October 1882*

I received a notice today to come to Dr. Gerhardt's office immediately.

"You are free to leave, Fräulein Pappenheim," he said with a cold stare, bereft of any human feeling. "I have spoken to my colleagues and they concur that we have done all that is possible for you, despite your determination to rage at us even as we were making progress in relieving your symptoms. Perhaps you think you understand your condition better than your doctors.

"I am asking that you leave as soon as possible. Your disobedience has set an undesirable precedent here that could infect our other patients like a loathsome disease that one cannot eradicate."

He shuffled some papers on his desk, studied one, and glanced at me.

"I have spoken to your mother. She will come for you the day after tomorrow. I have thoroughly explained the situation to her, emphasizing that you are leaving against the advice of your physicians." His tone was curt and abrupt, as though he had to pay for each sentence he uttered.

He pushed a document in front of me and thrust a pen toward me as if it were a dagger.

"And what is this?"

"It explains, Fräulein Pappenheim, that you have rejected our care and that you are completely free to leave this institution. All of our efforts to help you have failed because you have refused to cooperate, accusing us of lack of insight into your nervous disorder."

"This is nothing but lies," I said, just as icily, reading it over. "I refuse to sign anything."

He snatched the paper out of my hands.

"Very well, Fräulein, have it your way. You have tried my patience and the patience of everyone who has tried to help you. You will want to come back, you will need to come back, but our doors will be closed to you." He added, with a malicious gleam in his eye, "Let me remind you that you are still addicted to narcotics, which were given to help relieve your severe facial pain and neuralgia."

His lips grew thin. He took off his spectacles and fixed his pale eyes on me in a disagreeable manner.

"I did not want it, nor any of your other treatments," I informed him just as heatedly. "And you can count on one thing: I will never come back."

And on this sour note we parted.


*Bertha's Journal*
*Karlsruhe, 29 October 1882*

From Kreuzlingen, Mutti and I made our way to Karlsruhe to spend time with our dear cousin, Anna Ettlinger.

All at once I saw the world as one who has just been born and is viewing it for the first time. As we journeyed, many of the trees were still dressed in their festive autumn garments as though headed to a ball. The sky overhead, clear with not a cloud to mar it, held the faint gold coin of the sun against its cerulean canvas, though winter beckoned in the crisp air that brushed across my cheeks. My whole being wanted to cry out, I am free! — a staccato sound that strummed through my brain in time with the clip-clopping of the horses' hooves.

Mutti and I spoke little, mainly of practical affairs. The real concern of our hearts, hidden beneath more trivial matters, hung invisibly between us, like curtains erected to keep the peace. How much remains unsaid — my sisters' deaths, and, of course, Father's passing. But there is more than that. There is the way she and Willie conspired to keep me from seeing dear Papa after I grew ill. There is Willie's shaking me so hard when I tried to enter Father's room that it rendered me mute and deaf for some time.

I have never forgiven him, or Mutti, for that. But our disagreements with one another are all put away in this moment, in an effort to be congenial.

What she thought when she saw me I could not tell. She kept it hidden and set about helping me gather my effects as Frau Hedwig hovered about trying to impress upon her the care she had given me. Perhaps she was hoping to receive some recompense for her service, bustling around to no purpose, wishing me well, with a "Fräulein" this and a "Fräulein that," chattering all the while, until at last my very ears hurt from the commotion and clatter.

As for Mutti, it was not only that she looked older, but as if the life had been drained from her. An expression of resignation had formed a veil over her face, as though she was determined to bear whatever happened until God blessedly decided to release her.

I did not look back as the carriage and driver pulled away, but nonetheless tears stung my eyes. None of the doctors had come to wish me well, and Herr Dr. Katz, as I liked to call him, was likewise nowhere to be seen. I was free, but the unknown future rose ahead of me and filled me with fear. I had to adjust to living in the world once more. As the hours of our journey wore on, and my thoughts grew more sorrowful remembering the past, the early evening darkness drifted around me like a velvety drape, enclosing me in its embrace as though to protect me against all harm.

At Karlsruhe we discussed future plans, the move from Vienna and the search for a house in Frankfurt am Main, near mother's family. But it is not just for us that life is changing rapidly. The lives of the Jewish people are being uprooted everywhere: pogroms in Russia, white slavery worsening in Galicia. Conditions in Austria and Germany are troubling as well.

Anna and I spent many days together around the fire, discussing the pressing needs of Jewish women, exchanging views on Mary Wollstonecraft's book, *A Vindication of the Rights of Woman*, talking about the needs of all women, until late at night. When Mutti had gone to bed we spoke openly of unwed mothers, the treatment of illegitimate children, of all those who are kept hidden, not only in society at large, but even more so in the Jewish community—simply swept under the rug. I could not help but think of my own situation.

"Things are changing," Anna said, wearily, at the end of one such conversation. "They must change, and we will help to make it happen." I took her words to heart. All at once, I knew the direction the future must hold for me.

*Bertha's Journal*
*Frankfurt am Main, 15 March 1889*

When I wrote those words I could not imagine how long it would be before that future would appear. My despair at the postponement grew day by day and filled me with sorrow. In fact, we were not able to move here until November of last year. I have been unable to write for some time. After my release from Bellevue Sanatorium, my life again took an unexpected turn of fate. I had several setbacks and was hospitalized on and off and our move to Frankfurt was delayed a number of years.

First, of course, was the problem of finding a home in this city, but the status of my health interfered here, too. There were good days, but also many difficult ones when my symptoms returned and I lost hope of ever growing completely well. But gradually, during my long convalescence, there were more good days than not, until I finally recovered.

I saw Josef Breuer now and then over those years, most recently, several months ago, at synagogue, on the Days of Awe before we came here. We nodded. He looked at me, as though to assess my condition, and asked, "How are you, Bertha?" A prickly sensation rode up and down my spine.

I smiled but did not answer him, as though we were nothing but strangers. We did not have to speak. Electric currents that passed between us spoke louder than any words. His wife, Mathilde, greeted me with a certain reserve, even though we had been girlhood friends. Both of us had also been friends with Sigmund Freud's wife, Martha Bernays, and I remember when Papa helped Martha after her own father died by becoming her guardian. I am certain that Josef has discussed my illness with her husband.

I have been shocked and saddened by this betrayal, even though they are colleagues. Sigmund is ambitious. I have heard they were writing a book together of case studies on hysteria, but there is little I can do if they choose to write about me. I do not know how many people in Vienna were aware of my illness besides the two of them, but I suspect that there were many.

I was often uncomfortable after returning to Vienna. I felt that everyone was staring at me and that I was marked with a stigma, not only because of my illness, but also because I am still unmarried. Even if I wanted that, who would want me? And I cannot imagine being told what to do, especially by a man—as though he could know what's best for me, better than I know myself. Thoughts of Dr. Gerhardt come now and then to my mind, especially at night when our conscious mind lies fallow, allowing the thoughts that we suppress during the day to torment us. My memories of him are painful. I am not sure what good came of my time there. I can still hear the angry plea in his voice as he shouted, "I am merely trying to help you."

I often think that I am a woman who has risen from the grave. Leaving Vienna was the tonic I needed to restore myself. This new city has made me feel alive again, as though my life can still have meaning. I have been writing once more—not only my little stories for my own amusement, but also translations and other works pertinent to women. Of course, many have been written under a male pseudonym in order to obtain publication.

During the day I have been volunteering at a soup kitchen and have seen firsthand the problems among Jewish families, particularly Jewish women. There are also a number of families who have come here from Galicia to escape conditions there: oppression and poverty, lack of education. Without knowledge of the language and skills in this country, their lives have been difficult. But these are hard times for Jews everywhere.

In my work here I have become acquainted with a woman named Sara Rabinowitsch, a social worker, whom I admire enormously and from whom I have learned a great deal. She has the education I should have liked, not only high school, but also an advanced degree from the university in social work. Observing me as I worked—and after a number of conversations as we got to know each other better—she asked me to volunteer at the Neu-Isenburg Orphanage for Girls, which is run by the Israelite Women's Association.

Since then, I have spent every day there, and have found a second home. When I look into the eyes of these little girls who are friendless in the world, I see myself at their age. I visit, read aloud to them, especially at bedtime, and listen to their thoughts and feelings, as I should have liked someone to do with me. I have begun to think that they are the children I will never have, and they are as dear to me as though they were my very own.

*Bertha Pappenheim*
*Frankfurt am Main, December 1903*

My dear Sara,

Since we returned home from Galicia, I have done nothing but dream of all that we experienced—not only the endless journeys on trains, the carriage drives in cold wind and rain, the unhygienic conditions and poor lodging, but also of the beautiful fresh-green beech and birch forests, fertile fields and good pastures glimpsed by moonlight and the small villages with their humble windows and doors lit by the hearth fires burning within.

Our brief fact-finding mission of five weeks can only do so much to offer solutions to our brethren, in light of the depth of suffering—the white slavery, the poverty, ignorance, low morality and degrading conditions. It pulls at the heartstrings to see the suffering and discouragement of our fellow Jews, especially the girls and women and their helplessness as to how to improve their lot.

(And, here, dear Sara, let me pause and once again express my gratitude to you as a traveling companion and observer. With your education, your clear vision, and level-headedness, you opened my eyes to conditions that I might have overlooked even after fifteen years of work with the poor.)

I believe that in our report to the larger Jewish community, we should make it clear that we took seriously this task that was entrusted to us, that we watched eagerly, and did not lose sight of our purpose. I am also convinced that we, as women, had more opportunity to engage informally with the people, especially women and girls, which might have been more difficult for a man.

In my perspective, as I have indicated, the problem of white slavery in Galicia cannot be separated from the general malaise in the country that has contributed to it, and which I saw for myself. First and foremost is the breakdown of Jewish life, of both families and institutions, where opportunities for work are lacking. The scarcity of educational opportunities has resulted in widespread illiteracy, especially among women, and has robbed them of their potential. Although the girls are pretty and fresh, the women age and wilt rapidly—often giving them the aspect of dull pets, leading one to question what has caused this rapid and unfortunate decline.

As you also noticed, all of the institutions lack money, and all of the defects that we found can be attributed to this. The life of women and girls in Galicia is so desolate as a result of this economic and spiritual poverty that it makes them open to sexual exploitation. I found that these girls are as ignorant of basic hygiene as they are about sexual diseases. This ignorance, in addition to their inability to read or write or to understand even the simplest geography, leads them to consent to emigration. This in turn allows them to become prey in a strange country where they do not speak the language, and coupled with their lack of basic skills, this means they can make their way only through prostitution.

Therefore, in addition to my prior suggestions, I also support training for these girls before they emigrate for a period of four to six months, with instruction in reading and writing, languages, preferably English and German, and many other skills, so that they will be self-supporting if they choose to leave the country to better themselves instead of falling into the hands of unscrupulous men who use them for their own desires and profit.

The second major problem is getting the girls off the streets at night. I suggest that evening classes be established to provide badly needed education, as well as a social environment where they can meet others and form common interests, in safe but stimulating surroundings.

A third area of concern is that girls in orphanages are released at a young age without training in a vocation. Instruction not only in household tasks is needed, but also in lucrative skills, such as horticulture, livestock and poultry breeding, artisan crafts at a superior level, nursing, and practical tailoring—skills that will ensure a good income, allowing them to compete in urban markets and keep them from being lured into prostitution in order to survive.

Finally, apprentice programs need to be established to provide qualified instruction, and through which a real interest is taken in the girls to develop their potential. These programs should also encompass their leisure hours so that they are not left to prowl the streets at night, which has led to the profound moral depravity amongst the young women of Galicia.

I will wait to hear from you to see if you are of a similar mind before continuing with further proposals. I am hopeful that our fact-finding mission will not have been in vain, and that together we will be able to effect the desperately needed changes.

Devotedly,
Bertha

*Bertha's Journal*
*Frankfurt am Main, 1904*

I can barely contain my elation at the formation of the Jüdischer Frauenbund, the League of Jewish Women in Germany. And with hard work, I hope and pray that all of my dreams for improving the lot of Jewish women in Germany will come to fruition. My election as its first president is an achievement I barely thought possible for myself, considering the prelude before I arrived in Frankfurt, but as I look back on my life, I now feel that my own pain and suffering prepared me to help others.

As my friend Martin Buber always reminds me, we are stronger when we work together.

The work of Helene Lange and others in the German Women's Association has inspired me and made me realize that we, too, as Jewish women, needed an organization that would envelope all of the smaller ones to be more effective and achieve our goals. The trust that so many have put in me after my struggles has not only given me confidence in the path that I have taken, but has also reminded me of the responsibilities that come with it—responsibilities that already weigh heavily on my shoulders. Yet I am deeply touched to be entrusted with the challenge of taking up the charge to lead us forward into a new world and a new century where women will not be passive victims, but become educated in order that they might take their place in the world alongside men—independent beings capable of directing their own lives and recognized as equal before the law and in daily life.

These are our goals: to strengthen Jewish women's rights, to fight against abuse, whether domestic or in the public arena; to help women seek gainful employment and wages commensurate with their ability; to work to combat white slavery wherever it exists: to continue to develop a safe and loving place for orphans and illegitimate children, with education and training to prepare them for the time when they will go out into the world; to help women who have turned to prostitution out of the necessity to survive; and to assist them to train for respectful work while treating them with dignity and humanity.

I pledge myself to do all that I can to help these women and girls and to change the perception of women within Jewish life and Jewish institutions. It is not only charity—which is necessary to provide funds to aid us in our work—but human goals, particularly in the realm of education and meaningful work, that will make the difference. Vocational independence is of the utmost importance. Yes, we need funds, but the task before us is far more than that. I emphasize again that we also must change our vision of Jewish women and their needs. Many Jewish women are victims, and often the perpetrators are Jewish men. How do we turn around the inequality that goes back to our holy Torah and has been carried through the centuries?

Where are the Jewish women in Jewish history? Their voices have been lost. We vanished almost without a trace after the Matriarchs. I will continue to speak the truth no matter how many men are angered.

My own experience has taught me that lesson well. I was groomed only for marriage. Unlike my brother's, my education ceased when I was still young and impressionable. From that time on, I helped my mother in the kitchen and practiced the art of embroidery and other refinements suitable to an upper-class woman, until my mind and all of my aspirations were stifled and limited, suffocating me alive.

I often believe that my illness began first in the rebellion of my mind, the desire to throw off the shackles that had bound me to a future that I did not want and for which I was unsuited. Papa's death was only the catalyst that allowed my own feelings to burst through to the surface.

No, I do not wish that for Jewish girls and women today, and I will do everything in my power to help them to rise up until they are no longer subordinate, helping them to continue lifting up their voices until they are finally heard.


*Bertha Pappenheim*
*Frankfurt am Main, 1920*

My dearest Hannah,

I could not wait to share with you the exciting news that my good friend Martin Buber came to speak at my refuge for illegitimate girls and women endangered by prostitution.

More than anyone I have ever known, Martin has a greatness of spirit and courage, although you, Hannah, are the woman who most clearly matches him in both. That is why I consider you and Martin among my most treasured friends, the ones who lift me up when I despair at how little progress we are making. I wish you had been there to hear him yourself. That a man, one so highly regarded, should come to speak to these women puts the rest of the community to shame, when so many others who consider themselves pious God-fearing men refuse to come to a home for unwed mothers and their children. I consider them pious hypocrites.

His message was to urge the Jews of Germany to pursue education as the foremost priority for those who need help to restore their lives to dignity and hope. Martin sees the divine in every human being. It is not merely words. It is what he truly believes. He spoke to them as one human being to another—not as objects, but as intimate equals. And they, recognizing the genuineness of his message, responded in kind. For Martin, being a Jew and being humane are inextricably interwoven. As I have come to know him intimately, I have been shocked to learn that his kind eyes, his compassion for others, hides the pain he suffered in his own life. When he was a very young child, his mother ran off with a Russian army official without saying goodbye. The terrible loss of learning that he would never see her again has haunted him his entire life. Few of us have been spared hurt. If we are sensitive we will recognize the suffering of others.

As Martin often says, "Man's salvation consists not in removing himself from the world but in sanctifying it with the divine." It is simply the way he lives. There are not two Martin Bubers, one who speaks eloquently for effect and another who forgets when it is convenient for him. He is a genius, but one who is fully grounded in the world of reality.

One day during a discussion we were having, he said to me, "Bertha, one must encounter another in their authentic existence, that moment when two souls meet." I could see it happening that day in the women's eyes as he spoke to them, the way shame was lifted from them and replaced by the possibility that all was not lost. As Martin explained, "God exists for man to the extent that he serves his fellow man."

He is a fountain of wisdom, but also of humanity. In my work, Martin has always advised me that when we work together for a common aim, we can achieve more than one person alone. That is what you have done, dear Hannah. You have been a helpmate to me in all that I have endeavored to achieve for our Jewish women and girls and for all those who exist on the forgotten margins of society.

I am always reminded of the story that Martin told me about going to Worms, where our great scholar Rashi had his yeshiva in the eleventh century. There is also a cathedral there that towers over the town, and Martin always said that it was a joy to see such a beautifully built structure. As you know, he has reached out to the Christian community with respect and good-will. But then there is also the Jewish graveyard that he visits, full of stones that have split into fragments; all is confusion there instead of the harmony of that other structure. And yet in spite of everything, Martin observed, we have endured. The covenant has not been terminated. Nor have we been dismissed. This is the Martin I know and love.

Thank you, Hannah, for always listening to me. You are as dear as any natural-born daughter. Meeting you has changed my life. You have helped to make possible all of the work that is so dear to my heart. We have much more to do. The needs keep multiplying with every passing year, but the fact that you are with me in all of my efforts is a great comfort and gives me the courage and endurance to continue.

With great affection,
Bertha


*Bertha Pappenheim,*
*Frankfurt am Main, 1921*

Dear Cousin Anna,

My rage knows no bounds. You may have heard about the recent uproar by the Orthodox and Hasidic Jews here. They consider our home for illegitimate children and prostitutes an immoral scandal.

I am shocked to the core. What religion or faith do they represent? It is surely not Judaism as I practice it. Where is the humanity and compassion? If it is Judaism, I want nothing to do with it.

How differently from them Martin Buber felt when he came to speak to these women. How lovingly he embraced them, only thinking how to help them and to lift them up, to improve their lives and to make them independent and capable, able to take care of themselves instead of loaning their bodies to those who only abused them.

The real immorality lies in doing nothing, in leaving people who are suffering and abused to wallow in poverty and filth without any means of bettering their lot. For all those who have no home, no one to care, I vow that we will continue to be a beacon of light.

I cannot help but wonder whether, if it were men we were helping, would these devout Jews still feel the same way? Half of us do not seem to count. This thinking is embedded in the daily prayer men recite that thanks God for not making them a woman, in the prohibition against saying *Kaddish* for their loved ones, in the way their bodies are viewed as so shameful that they must be covered up lest they drive men to temptation. Even the purity of their voices is maligned—those, too, are seen as a lure for lasciviousness. The texts themselves have been closed to us. We have not been able to write them, nor are we allowed to study them, since they have been forbidden to women.

I often think that if there is any justice in the next life, women will make the laws and men will bear the children.

When I spoke publicly at the first Jüdischer Frauenbund delegate assembly and said, "Under Jewish law a woman is not an individual, not a personality; she is judged and assessed only as a sexual being," it was met with outrage. And there remains our battle—to secure equal rights for women and to change the laws for a new century. I went on to criticize sexual enslavement in women and the neglect of illegitimate Jewish orphans, the lack of equal rights in Jewish institutions and of living wages for women, and this prompted a hostile reaction as well.

It will be a long and difficult battle, but we must take up arms and fight it. We progressive women are criticized for upsetting the so-called God-given order. I have had to live with the knowledge that my own parents would have preferred a male child instead of a girl. Women have been burdened with that knowledge since birth. Is it any wonder that we fall by the wayside, when even our own religion does not accept us fully and devalues the importance of our lives?

We will never give up. When we are gone, other women will take up the cause and enlightened men will be with us, too. So be forewarned. I have made translations from the Hebrew of Scripture and other literature to educate young women who have been denied our texts, with the aim of giving them what has been withheld from them: their rights and their history, the holy language that belongs to them as their birthright. I do not expect their publication to be met with public approval.

It saddens and troubles me that even liberal and emancipated Jews have continued to advocate a patriarchal and traditional attitude toward women's rights.

Shimon, the *Tzadik,* the righteous one, from the last of the men of the Great Assembly would say, "The world stands on three things: Torah, worship, and deeds of loving kindness." Then why not for women? We are living in the twentieth century. Our voices will not be silenced no matter how much you assail us.

Bertha

*Bertha Pappenheim, Frankfurt am Main,*
*Neu-Isenburg Orphanage for Girls*
*16 April 1935*

Dear Frau Schmidt,

I am writing to inform you of a recent troubling incident. One of our residents, a mentally retarded girl, made a remark against Adolf Hitler, calling him a criminal, a raving lunatic who is trying to destroy the Jews. This comment was reported to the police by one of our Aryan day workers. I summarily received a notice to appear at the police station, and have settled it at least temporarily by supplying the necessary information in writing. I have heard nothing further.

I am deeply troubled by this and while I do not want to alarm you, if we are to continue to help our girls and women and avoid further such incidents, we must exercise good judgment in what we say when others are about. In this hate-filled atmosphere, it is clear that Hitler seeks to frighten us into submission. I believe that it was a warning. Now that evil has been unleashed, he seeks to take advantage of the rising, baseless hatred against the Jews by declaring war on ordinary law-abiding citizens and using them as scapegoats for the economic woes of the German people.

Hitler is obviously creating this nationalistic fervor to get rid of all so-called outsiders, anyone who is considered marginal, including Jehovah's Witnesses, who have already been banned; the mentally and physically disabled, who have been disappearing; political opponents; homosexuals and prostitutes; orphans who have no protection whatsoever; and any foreign influences that would interfere with pure Aryan blood, which includes not only the Jews of Germany, but also the Jews of Galicia whom we are helping.

I have personally brought many Jewish orphans, victims of pogroms, from Russia to safety in Germany throughout the years. However, the Weimar Republic is a thing of the past. Madness has overtaken the country. The decency of good German citizens has been swept away by a madman. And Germany, once a country known for its literature and the judiciousness of its courts, has become a distorted image of its former self that defies any rational explanation.

We need to protect our charges at all costs. In a time when law has ceased to exist, we must take all precautions as we look to the future. I want to believe that conditions cannot get much worse, but each day brings some new outrageous and unthinkable law. Perhaps we will have to think about getting these children out of the country. I have decided that I will bring a group of girls from the orphanage to safety by traveling with them to Great Britain. Even at the risk of our own lives, we must protect our innocent charges from the rampant flames of evil that are enveloping our country.

Bertha Pappenheim,
Head of School


*Bertha's Journal*
*Frankfurt am Main, January 1936*

You are my dear companion, the repository of my innermost thoughts, the secrets that I speak about to no one except you.

And even then I succumb only late at night, when fatigue and weariness conspire to break down the inhibitions that guard us during the day, restraining us from allowing others to see our vulnerability.

My health has been failing of late, and my looming mortality, combined with the disturbing and frightening tenor of the times, has so deeply saddened me, especially for the future, that all I am left with is the bald and often unpleasant truth of my life: that nothing is as I had hoped it would be. In spite of everything that I have accomplished, when all is said and done and the last chapter is written, does it really matter? And will anyone remember me?

Yes, I have done some good, much good—in fact, more than I ever thought possible—but I have also suffered greatly and overcome more than most people know in a lifetime. The truth is that my life has been an inner and outer struggle that others have never seen, even my closest friends who have sustained me.

I despise pity. I have tried not to pity those whom I have helped. Pity is humiliating and helps no one. Perhaps I have been idealistic, but I have tried to assist others to realize their own humanity and to take charge of their own lives, especially women and girls, who have so desperately needed it during this difficult time. It is what I have done, what I determined I must do, and what I have continued to live for—to practice my faith as it is written in our sacred literature, to protect the widow, the orphan, the stranger, because we were strangers in the land of Egypt. Does any other religion have that as their credo, their reason for existence?

And yet, in the dark of night, what I have lost weighs on me like a stone that sinks beneath the surface of the water: my dear sisters, one I knew and one who perished before I was born, whose memory shadowed my own life; Papa, of course, whose death still lies heavy on my heart (it was never the same with Mutti); and Dr. Josef Breuer—whom I believe I loved, and whose many betrayals remain the cause of torment. I believe in my heart of hearts that he was strongly drawn to me, too, which frightened him into fleeing and sending me to Kreuzlingen. I wanted to bear his child, but alas it was only a phantom, instead of reality.

I have read the book he wrote with Sigmund Freud, and felt the depths of hurt—as though my entire life was nothing but a case history, and I was not a human being but a list of symptoms to be extinguished. Sigmund never treated me. He knew me only slightly, through my friendship with Martha, and only wanted to aggrandize himself. I feel as though something precious was stolen from me that can never be put right. Yet I am occasionally comforted by the suffering of Hagar, Abraham's Egyptian concubine, who was saved by the compassion of God. Perhaps the lesson is that I must have compassion for myself and not wait for God, who seems invisible in our lives now.

My heart has been open for others, but never for myself. Loneliness has been my constant companion. I often feel that I am not necessary to anyone. Why is that? Does everyone feel like this? I wrote a poem expressing the wish that it could have been different. Some Jews believe in an afterlife, but for me this life is all there is, and we must make the best of it. Our hopes, our passions, our regrets, whether they have been fulfilled or not, are all we have, and we must somehow make peace with them before we die.

This poem is the elegy that keeps running through my mind and will not leave me alone—the time in our lives when all is swept away as though it has never been, the veil stripped from all pretense.

*Mir ward die Liebe nicht*
(Love did not come to me)

Love did not come to me—
So I vegetate like a plant,
In a cellar, without light.

Love did not come to me—
So I resound like a violin,
Whose bow has been broken.

Love did not come to me—
So I immerse myself in work,
Living myself sore from duty.

Love did not come to me—
So I gladly think of death.


## AFTERWORD

Bertha Pappenheim, ill with cancer, underwent surgery for a tumor in July of 1935, after being interrogated by the Gestapo, and died on May 28, 1936, at the age of 77 at her beloved home for orphans and unwed mothers, Neu-Isenburg.

At her request, Bertha was buried next to her mother, Recha Goldschmidt Pappenheim, at the old Jewish cemetery, Rat-Beil-Strasse, in Frankfurt, the city where Bertha emerged as a feminist and leader of Jewish women and a founder and the first president of the Jüdischer Frauenbund (the League of Jewish Women) in 1904.

A pioneering social worker for women and children, she championed the cause of Jewish orphans, especially those who were illegitimate, as well as unwed mothers, prostitutes, and all those women and girls who existed on the periphery of society. She was a lone voice for change and put her words into action by caring for them and establishing programs to enable them to become independent.

Her courage is legendary. She spoke out against abuses within society on behalf of those who were not able to speak out for themselves, and she traveled to other countries to rescue orphans who were victims of pogroms. She instituted measures to combat sex trafficking, and worked to obtain help for the distressing conditions of the Jews in Galicia, particularly Jewish women and girls, by conducting a fact-finding trip to assess the situation for herself.

As the Nazis stripped Jews of all their rights as citizens, she personally took many of the orphans at Neu-Isenburg to safety in Great Britain. She fought for education for women, for good jobs with meaningful employment and pay, and against the discrimination of Jewish law that for centuries had penalized women and made them subordinate to men. To allow women access to the sacred books, Bertha Pappenheim translated many texts from Yiddish into German, including the memoir of her famous relative Glückel (Glickl) of Hameln, whom she admired for her unusual intellectual gifts. Glückel was a woman deeply rooted in her times (1646–1724)—true to her faith, her people, true to her family, and true to herself—demonstrating independence and pluck when she was left with twelve children to care for after her husband's death.

Bertha Pappenheim wrote numerous papers on feminism, including an indictment of her own constrained girlhood in an article entitled "On the Education of Young Women of the Upper Classes." She also wrote plays, poetry, prayers, and two volumes of short stories.

Perhaps the most difficult crisis she faced was the psychotic breakdown she experienced as a young woman while she was caring for her beloved father during his last illness. It dramatically affected her physical and mental health for many years. In view of that, her recovery and accomplishments are all the more extraordinary.

Her symptoms included hallucinations, disassociation from reality (Multiple Personality Disorder), speaking only English and forgetting her native German, paralysis of limbs, aversion to food and water, lethargy followed by excitably, the feeling that black snakes were crawling across her face and that her hands had turned to snake heads, and other distressing maladies that rendered her unable to function.

Bertha's parents called in Josef Breuer, a prominent physician in Vienna, who treated many of the well-to-do Jewish families in the city. Breuer decided she had a case of "hysteria," a condition that was often cited by male physicians to describe the emotional instability of women, caused by a trauma. Breuer at first treated her with hypnosis and then Bertha herself began what she called "chimney-sweeping" or the "talking cure," culled first from her private theater of tales and then merely whatever came into her mind—what Breuer called later "profoundly melancholic fantasies," and what Freud termed "free association."

This "talking-cure" formed the foundation of psychoanalysis. Through these tales and reminiscences, Bertha was at least temporarily relieved of some of her symptoms. Meanwhile Breuer began to withdraw from her to resist the growing intimacy of their relationship, and to save his marriage. (Breuer's wife became jealous of the time he was spending with Bertha, as well as his patient's growing romantic interest in him.) Freud, who never saw her as a patient, later called Bertha's reaction transference.

At one point during her treatment, Josef Breuer told Freud that she was deranged and that he hoped she would die to end her suffering. Freud remarked to Carl Jung, possibly in an effort to downplay Breuer's role in the discovery of psychoanalysis and inflate his own, that all her old symptoms returned after Breuer had given up the case.

"So the famous first case he treated together with Breuer and which was vastly praised as an outstanding therapeutic success," Jung said in a private seminar, "was nothing of the sort."

Nevertheless, Breuer maintained in *Studies on Hysteria*—the book he wrote with Sigmund Freud, where Bertha was known only as Anna O.—that he had cured her. This despite the fact that after giving up the case he sent her first to a clinic in Inzersdorf and then to Bellevue Sanatorium, in Kreuzlingen on Lake Konstanz.

Her stay at Kreuzlingen may have been a turning point for Bertha in redirecting her life and regaining her health, even though she disliked her treatments as well as her confinement, and fought to leave. After she returned to Vienna, however, several years of convalescence elapsed before she moved to Frankfurt with her mother and began the second part of her life. Even her closest friends and relatives in Frankfurt were unaware of her illness. Her identity as Anna O. was kept secret until 1953, when Ernest Jones published *The Life and Work of Sigmund Freud*.

It is not known whether Bertha actually read *Studies on Hysteria*. However, she maintained a lifelong aversion to psychoanalysis and was against such treatment for any of the girls or women in her care.

On November 10, 1938, one day after Kristallnacht, the main building of the Neu-Isenburg Home for Girls was set on fire and the other buildings damaged. On the last day of March 1942, the Gestapo took over the home and those who remained were deported to Theresienstadt.

Hannah Karminski, the woman who was like a daughter to Bertha, cared for her during her illness and continued her work after her death, refusing to leave Germany to save her life. On December 9, 1942, Hannah was sent to Auschwitz-Birkenau, where she was murdered on June 4, 1943.

In 1954, the West German government issued a postage stamp in honor of Bertha Pappenheim's contributions to the field of social work. A museum in her honor is located in Frankfurt at the former site of the Neu-Isenburg School for Girls.

# Homecoming

THE VIEW FROM ELEANOR'S SMALL ROOM compensated for staying at this plain hotel, once owned by the Communist Party, with its worn carpets and austere furniture, even though her husband, had he still been alive, would have wanted more spacious and pleasant accommodations.

She could see the famous castle, an immense fortress whose spires were illuminated at dusk with a golden light. Just beneath, the lamps on the bridge and the silent statues of past occupants were lit under the darkening crown of stars exploding over the city.

Prague, a poignant return to the city with her husband Edward after he retired from the university. They had been planning a journey to Prague for over a year, a kind of homecoming for Edward, who had left when he was still a boy yet retained vivid memories of his birthplace. For months he had spread out maps on the dining room table and pointed to one landmark after another, calling up the past.

"Here's where our apartment was," he said. "We used to live in the old city, the Josefov district, but this apartment was in a better section of Praha after my father's business became more prosperous.

"That is, until the Nazis took it over," he added. It faced other apartment buildings, and within that narrow corridor was a place where the children gathered to play." He closed his eyes for a moment as the memory was called up from a distant time. "I even remember their names—Jan, Max, Petr—my three best friends. Their faces are still as clear as day. I'm not sure any of them made it through."

Edward himself had, of course, one of the few. His family had enough money to pay off an official, handsomely, and escaped just in time. The memories were never easy, but Edward had gone on to thrive, to come to America, finish school, and attain a position at Stanford, one of the finest universities in the country, teaching European history. They lived on the sprawling campus in one of the comfortable homes set aside for faculty.

Yet one could study forever, he was fond of telling people, and still not understand what happened or why. It came from the dark shadow of what it meant to be human. Perhaps it was yet another manifestation of the human condition that consistently erupted, both individually and collectively: violent, xenophobic, demonic.

Then, just when they were getting ready to leave for Prague, Edward developed something that was equally incomprehensible, a disease that spread rapidly through his body, beginning with a pain in his stomach, then invading one organ after another, as though it was an echo of the evil that had spread in his childhood.

"I hope you'll go," he urged. "It's a beautiful city, barely damaged during the war." He had grown so weak and fatigued that he broke off from saying more.

"You'll get well," she said, trying to encourage him.

He shook his head.

"No, Eleanor." In bed, dressed in a flimsy hospital gown, he looked smaller than he had in his busy life. He had been tall, slender, impressive, with a distinguished face now grown gaunt, his nose sharper in that thin face. His pale blue eyes, once bright and clear, now looked washed out and dull. In that other time, he had been so fair that he'd passed easily as a gentile during the Nazi occupation, able to ride his bike all over the city without being stopped.

"We have to face reality," he said with his usual candor.

Then, strangely, with medication and treatments, Edward actually began to feel better. And for a while, there was a cautious measure of hope again. He took the maps out of the drawer where they had languished and began to make lists of places he wanted to see, starting with the castle, of course, which had loomed so large and frightening when he was a child.

"Kafka must have felt the same way," he often said, and yet he looked forward to walking over the bridge and ascending the hill to the fortress.

She was relieved. Possibility came back once more into their lives, and they made plans and took day trips over to the coast to enjoy the fresh ocean breezes. Edward was even well enough to do some hiking. And they went to concerts and the opera and museums in San Francisco. Their sons, Michael and Matthew, who had phoned nearly every day when their father was in the hospital, resumed their normal lives. A window of health had opened, encouraging them to imagine a future.

But then, after a few months, just when the whole family had breathed a sigh of relief, Edward was back in the hospital again. The doctor, a woman with an Indian name and the coloring and features of her country, spoke to them, her eyes glistening slightly.

"I'm sorry, there's nothing more that can be done except to make your husband comfortable."

How very cruel this seemed after all their planning. It didn't seem possible that nothing could be done. Edward was, after all, being treated at a world-renowned university medical center — a vast complex with state-of-the-art equipment, where brilliant doctors did cutting-edge research.

But after that moment everything happened quickly. And then it was over.

Eleanor sat with him all day holding his cold hand until he took a deep breath, but then . . . not another.

Edward was gone.

For a year, Eleanor was in shock, putting up a good front, busy taking care of everything, replaying the couple of months before Edward had died, remembering the first time she had seen him: dazzlingly assured, finishing up his doctorate and just beginning his teaching career, while she was still an undergraduate.

He could have had so many women. And yet he pursued her. An image from the past played out on the screen in her mind. After they had gone out a few times, she wondered why. What did he see in her? As though she had uttered the question out loud, he answered, "Your beautiful hands," with such complete seriousness that Eleanor believed him.

Even when they were first married, she wasn't surprised that Edward wanted to go back to Prague. But the Communists had stayed after the Nazis left, and it became impossible. He followed developments closely, with the expectation that events would surely improve after the Prague Spring, but then the Soviets crushed the uprising.

"How terrible," Edward said, saddened at the spectacle of students immolating themselves in protest.

Czechoslovakia had remained a closed country until the fall of Communism and the Velvet Revolution, the beginning of privatization after so many years of deprivation. Then returning to the city became a possibility.

And with that possibility, the memories of the time before the war came rushing back to him: the trips to the zoo and visits to the park to see the famous puppet comedy duo, Spejbl and Hurvinek, until the Nazis came and his father's business—importing Italian fabric—was shut down. It was summer, and their trips to Karlsbad were forbidden. Nor could they go to their summer home outside the city.

Before that, Edward had never wanted to dwell on it. He had even Anglicized his first name—Evzen—when he was young. "It means noble birth," he once said, half joking.

When he was ill, he said, "I've had far more of life than I ever thought I would. My friends never got the chance I did, nor did most of my cousins and aunts and uncles."

Eleanor knew that his words rang true. He had lived a lifetime after his friends died. But that didn't make his illness any easier to bear. Wasn't it only human nature to want to stay alive as long as one could?

———

In the year after Edward's death, she forced herself to take part in all the activities they had shared together. She imagined him beside her, and still tried to enjoy the things from which together they had taken so much joy.

She continued working as a finance officer for a large company as well, overseeing a vast number of clients, edging closer to retirement. But on weekends she went for long walks alone, and to the theater, which had been Edward's love, or to the symphony with friends. Michael was nearby, although her daughter-in-law, Emily, was quite willing to leave her alone with Edward's memory unless it was a major holiday, when duty demanded that she make plans that included Eleanor. Matthew had chosen to live in the East and work as a legal aid attorney instead of working for the prestigious law firm that had wanted to hire him.

The first time she was alone on Mother's Day, Michael invited her to go out for brunch while Emily was across the bay visiting her own mother with the twins. Although she always assured him no gift was necessary, he gave her a laptop, proudly pointing out its features.

"You can go anywhere in the world with this and still be in touch."

"In touch with what?" Eleanor asked.

What was so important about being in touch? Her first thought was that the computer could not reach Edward, silently beyond her.

Michael's face darkened. He looked at her sharply.

"With me, with your grandchildren, with anyone." He bit into a blueberry muffin, and the juice left a blue rim around his lips.

"You're bleeding blueberries," Eleanor said, irritation creeping into her voice.

He dabbed at his mouth with his napkin. She remembered him as a chubby baby, spooning too much food into his mouth, eagerly eating every last crumb, utterly dependent on her. Now the tables were turned.

"Is this what's called an intervention?" she asked, because it had just occurred to her.

"Call it whatever you like," Michael answered. "It's been a year since Dad died. Don't think that Matt and I haven't felt grief too. The point is," he said, pausing to take another bite, "it's time to move on."

*Move on.* Those were the words she was beginning to hear over and over again.

In this country there was no time for grief or grieving. She looked around the restaurant. It wasn't only the cellphones, which made her wonder what on earth there was to talk about so early on a Sunday morning in May. It was also the impatience that was reflected on almost every face. No sooner had the thought passed than Michael whipped out his own phone, checked his messages, and closed it firmly without looking at her.

"Matt and I have discussed it. We think it would be good for you to get out of this rut. Whatever happened to the trip you and Dad were supposed to take to Prague?"

"Oh, that," she said, stunned for a moment that she had been an object of discussion between her sons. She didn't want to go now. It would be a terrible mistake. But Michael pressed forward, oblivious, as always, to her discomfort.

"How long did Dad actually live there before the war?"

"Your father was still a child, not even twelve when his

family left Prague. But he had vivid memories nonetheless. He wanted to show me the places where he grew up." Then she corrected herself, "Where he *would* have enjoyed, growing up, if things had turned out differently."

"That was a long time ago."

"Not for him. It was as though it had just happened."

"Going anyplace at all would be better than staying here and doing exactly the same things you did with Dad. It's not healthy."

"Healthy," she repeated as though she were uttering an obscenity.

"I just don't get it, Mom. Dad is gone. Why do you want to hang on to the past?"

"The past was good," she said.

Michael didn't answer. She didn't tell him that going to Prague would also be a continuation of her life with Edward. It would have defeated her son's purpose.

She thought about it. Yes, she would go, she decided, but it wasn't until a few weeks after she had made the arrangements that she told him.

Eleanor landed at Prague-Ruzyně International Airport, recently renamed in honor of Václav Havel, the hero of the Velvet Revolution, making it possible for her to finally visit the dense mass of houses and buildings, greenery and churches, and the silver ribbon of water that separated the two parts of the city.

The plane ride was uneventful, but she hadn't been able to sleep for very long, too conscious of the noisy couple, unmistakably Americans, seated across the aisle from her. They called constantly for the stewardess, who addressed their shrill demands with a steady calm that Eleanor envied while feeling embarrassed at her compatriots' behavior.

Unfamiliar languages drifted around her—mostly Czech, she assumed, but with a few conversations in German and Russian. People were no different, though, no matter what their language. When the lights went out, they pulled blankets over themselves and closed their eyes, looking as vulnerable as she felt herself, like overgrown children who needed tucking in.

She smiled at a trio of little girls, who were excited at first and then became cranky at the length of the journey, while their weary mother tried to soothe them.

She curled up finally, alongside the young stranger in the next seat. Although an armrest separated them, she could feel the pulse of his body, the odor of his hair, an unfamiliar scent, hear the soft, muffled sleep sounds echoing from his throat.

Dare she take hold of the hairy back of his hand and tell him, my husband's dead, he's gone from this planet, and I don't know how I'm going to go on?

As though she had actually spoken, her seatmate, who had slept from the time he boarded the plane, roused for a moment, at last acknowledging her presence. She could not help wondering about this solitary stranger. Who was he? And where was he going? She retrieved her phrase book from her purse, tentatively trying out her Czech.

*"Jak se máte?"*

His sleepy eyes looked startled for a moment, then he smiled. Perhaps he was laughing at her crude attempts.

*"Mám se dobře, děkuji."*

The simplest of human exchanges, almost comically elementary: *How are you? I'm fine, thank you.*

She couldn't understand anything else he said, but she thought of Edward. Although with his parents and family he had spoken German, Czech was the language he used in the world until he left the country. Perhaps she would try to take learning it more seriously, but how many people taught Czech? She could stay here for months, a year. What did it matter?

There was nothing to tie her down anymore. Yes, her job, but a leave could be arranged for a time. She didn't need to work. The boys were on their own. Even Michael and Matthew had become only voices on the telephone, checking in with her on holidays and weekends when they remembered. The two boys seemed remote, their birth and upbringing part of another life that had nothing to do with her now.

The tour she was booked on was to start at the hotel with a kickoff reception and dinner. She and Edward had gone on similar tours before, and at some point decided they never wanted to take one again—the enforced sociability with people they would never see in the future, the long bus rides, the guide droning on interminably, the rising at dawn to move to the rhythm of someone else's schedule had left them weary. But now, traveling by herself—a woman of her age, alone in a country where she didn't know the language—didn't seem to be an option, either.

Before she left, her sons were full of advice.

"Get right out in the sun," Matthew had cautioned. "That way the jet lag won't hit you so hard."

He was a seasoned traveler, seeing the world before he had settled down to save it, and his words had the ring of experience and authority. But she was so tired that as soon as she had been shown to her room, she pulled back the thin spread and slipped into the cool sheets. When she woke up, several hours had passed. She rose reluctantly and washed her face to refresh herself. When she looked at herself in the mirror, it was clear how much she had aged since Edward's death, though she had been almost a decade younger than her husband.

Her hair, which had remained salt-and-pepper for a long time, was turning white, while fatigue and grief had planted creases on either side of her nose down to her mouth. But it was her expression that had changed too, and that troubled her the most. It was the same expression she had noticed in the elderly when she was a child—an absence of joy in her eyes, the resigned set of her jaw.

I am through with life, it said.

She remembered Michael's final words:

"Meet new people. Move out of your comfort zone."

"What's wrong with being comfortable?" she wanted to ask.

But now, unless she sent him a message on the laptop, which Michael had insisted she bring, she was only talking to herself. Feeling like a disobedient child, she slipped it into a drawer. What could he do from thousands of miles away except scold her?

Already late for the tour's reception, she washed up and put on some makeup. She selected one of the few new outfits she had purchased, regretting the dull, uninspired clothes that now seemed too heavy for the weather. The city was in the grip of a heat wave, and she knew at once, even before she put it on, that the dress and accompanying jacket would be hot and uncomfortable.

"Oh, Mrs. Weiss, we've been worried about you."

The woman was on the far side of fifty, judging from her appearance, but she wore a bright fuchsia blouse with matching lipstick and glittery eye shadow.

"We were about to check to see if you'd arrived. Actually, you haven't missed much. We're just getting started. They do insist that you wear some sort of identification," she added, taking a pen to fill out a nametag in bold red letters. "Some of the participants' balk about that, but we're all strangers here, and it helps people to get acquainted."

"Eleanor," she said, spelling her name. "So many people get it wrong today."

She fastened the nametag firmly on her jacket and stood on the outskirts of the voices, feeling lost. Bolstering herself with a glass of sherry and some appetizers offered by a waiter whose straight black hair was cut like a medieval serf's, she scanned the group. There weren't more than twenty-five people, mainly couples, who appeared to have blended into each other. Had she and Edward looked like that too?

She saw only one man by himself, looking awkwardly out of place, and a few women like herself: gray-haired, colorless, with lumpy figures. Widows, of course—they had it written all over them.

"The Three Harpies," she decided to call them, and then she corrected herself as she realized that, of course, there were four. She'd always pitied the widows on these trips. If Edward were here, she thought, they would have discussed these observations later.

On the other side of the room, she sighted the American couple from the plane, the husband and wife she had hoped never to see again. To avoid them, she was forced to plunge into a chattering cluster of people. She felt a rush of anger that she had let Michael push her into this bewildering sea of strangers.

"Are you alone?" one of the women asked. Her name, Connie, was written in the same large red letters as Eleanor's. A name, like her own, that belonged to another age.

It was the question she had been dreading.

"I lost my husband last year," Eleanor heard herself saying, even though she hated that expression, as though Edward, his mind still clear and intact, had wandered off somewhere and not been found.

"Well, there are always plenty of widows to keep you company," Connie sympathized, not unkindly, although the words hurt and drove home a truth Eleanor expected to hear over and over again. It was only the first day, she thought. They would be in Prague a week.

She was left on her own to get through dinner. People had already saved seats, and she was forced to sit with the three widows, their histories varying only slightly, even their names sounding interchangeable. Now she was part of that great, dreary group of the unattached.

Her first attempts at conversation were thankfully cut short as the tour director, a short, broad-chested man, no longer trim through the midsection, with gray hair tufting around the edges of his scalp and an expression of serious intent, got up to welcome everyone.

"This is an opportunity to get to know your fellow travelers in one of the most beautiful cities in Europe," he urged, before launching into a history of Prague and recounting the Nazi era, when all of the Jews were deported. They were all Jews, after all, from every corner of the U.S., part of an organization that sought to offer their members an opportunity to trace their European roots.

Eleanor wanted to tell him that at least a few had escaped. She recalled anecdotes that Edward had related, especially about the boat that brought his family to safety, the last one that actually made it, she thought gratefully. The names of many of those who hadn't been so fortunate were inscribed on the wall of the Pinkas Synagogue, lives once full of promise that had ended too soon once the Germans had entered the city.

The tale of so much misery threatened to overwhelm her. Why *had* she come to the home Edward had left so many years ago? She couldn't blame it all on Michael. Perhaps she hoped to find a remnant of something Edward had loved before he knew her. But without him, however beautiful, the city already seemed hollow and empty. If only they could have come when they were newly married, discovering it anew and putting the dark memories behind them together.

On the bus the next morning, her mood lightened briefly until she realized that the seating was assigned according to a plan that the tour director determined, which placed her beside the only single man. She had no choice except to take the seat next to him, aware that he shifted slightly away from her. Even though she had met him the night before, his name escaped her. He smiled softly and wished her a good morning with formal courtesy, an edge of melancholy in his voice, as though he'd known many mornings that were not good. His words were heavy with the inflections of another language as he tipped the brim of his straw boater in her direction, a hat that looked out of place next to the other men's baseball caps advertising various sports teams above the brim, vaguely juvenile on all those gray heads.

She noticed that he wore no wedding band. Her own ring had been transferred to her right hand, and now the naked left finger where it had made its home announced the formerly married. She didn't want to hear this man's sad story, the one she assumed he had. She didn't want to hear anyone's sad story. In a group like this, even the people who looked perfectly happy concealed secrets that amazed her as they were revealed: deaths of children, terrible illnesses, unspeakable tragedies.

She was not happy to be sitting next to the only single man on the tour. It wasn't that he was unclean or offensive in any way. No, he was nicely dressed, wearing well-creased pants and a pale blue sport shirt that matched his eyes, eyes as blue as Edward's. Yet she was not in the least attracted to him. She couldn't even imagine companionship now. It invariably led to more intimacy than she wanted.

Even though the guide was telling everyone that the city had more than its share of pollution, brilliant sunlight bathed its inhabitants with a luminous glow as the bus crossed the Charles Bridge, already filled with artists, musicians, and souvenir vendors. White swans glided by below on the river, and boats traveled in each direction. She hadn't been able to appreciate the beauty of Prague the day before. The people hurrying by, intent on their own thoughts and business, oblivious to their surroundings, however, were no different from men or women anywhere, a throng of individuals, most of them not even born when Edward was a child.

The trip was to include the part of the city where the Jews had lived. The bus moved past Old Town Hall as the Orloj came into view, an elaborate astronomical clock with multiple dials and glittering gold hands, displaying the course of the heavens. Then the bells tolled, the windows flew open, and mechanical apostles, led by Jesus, appeared, while the skeleton figure of Death and sinners paraded in a circle. It was an obvious warning, she thought, to be cognizant of the wages of sin.

But just then, incongruously, in the growing heat of the day, the chattering on the bus stopped, replaced by stunned silence as a group of skinheads sauntered by, wearing leather vests in spite of the heat, bare flesh liberally tattooed and decorated with metal chains, a reminder that the past would never stay buried, but had made its way into the future. Around her there was outraged shouting and the shaking of fists. The skinheads turned for a moment and raised their fingers in a vulgar gesture.

"Brutes," her seatmate said, with a rage that Eleanor did not expect.

Before she could think of an answer, they moved on to New Town, passing Wenceslas Square, which was not really square at all, but a massive rectangle that could hold thousands of people. The real angel of death had been here frequently. Hadn't Edward spoken of the mass demonstrations filled with storm troopers and swastikas, the burning of books and looting of Jewish stores that had convinced his family to flee Prague?

In the Jewish quarter, they disembarked at the Altneushul, the oldest synagogue in Europe. Inside, it was cool and white and still, a sanctuary from the world outside, although Eleanor had heard that in the Communist era it, too, had been filled with spies and informers.

The men were allowed to stay downstairs. Offended, the women were sent up a narrow staircase to peer through slits in the wall at the men below, as women were permitted in the sanctuary only on their wedding day. A few Orthodox women with long skirts and hats, oblivious to their presence, prayed with a fervor that Eleanor envied, here in this windowless storage room with its few tattered books and stale, musty smell. She moved from one window to the next, trying to get a view below. Beneath them, the men were engrossed in the service, and beneath that, in the cellar, perhaps, the Golem that Rabbi Loew purportedly brought to life in the sixteenth century might still be lying, ready to do battle with the antisemites they had seen today.

Her seatmate, Emmanuel (for she had looked for his name on the seating chart as they left the bus), had removed his hat and now wore a prayer cap perched on his head, and a white shawl with black stripes that cascaded over his shoulders for worship, enveloping him in an aura of piety, unlike the other men, whose baseball caps were still on their heads.

The tour guide was motioning the women to descend from that dark alcove to walk to the centuries-old cemetery. Outside, a few drops of rain began to fall, breaking the heat.

Emmanuel was wearing his straw hat again, its flat top giving him an unexpectedly jaunty air, the skullcap and prayer shawl hidden in a small velvet bag with a Lion of Judah embroidered on the outside. He fell in step beside her as they walked to the graves. Long, long ago, mourners had once grieved for these people, but now the crooked tombstones, bulging twelve layers deep, green with age, marked lives that had already been forgotten for hundreds of years.

"Have you been here before?" Eleanor asked.

"Only once. I am from Budapest."

"Budapest," she said. "I'm not going there."

"A pity," he replied. "The Great Synagogue itself is worth the trip."

They ate lunch, a simple meal of stew, dumplings, and apple strudel, in the dining room of a small place of worship where the young Franz Kafka, browbeaten by his father, had gone through the ritual of bar mitzvah, his future already set in motion. How strange to see the past through the eyes of the present, already knowing the outcome.

Over the past few days the rain had cooled the oppressive air, but the hotel room was still suffocating, even with the windows opened. The thin curtains fluttered softly against the panes. Some of the bustle of the city had died down.

Eleanor thought of Michael on the other side of the world. Guilt gnawed at her. She opened the drawer and removed the laptop. Opened, the blank face glared, an angry lover, insulted at being abandoned, prompting her to leave its reproach amid the stifling silence of the room.

Afraid she would get disoriented if she went out, she wrote down the name and address of the hotel and put the note in her pocket. Although many people had left the city for their suburban homes, the shops were still open on Karlova Street, and she strolled in and out of them, among the other tourists, some of whom she recognized from her own tour. She browsed through heavy, leaded vases and porcelain dishes, making her way over to the edge of the Jewish quarter to Parizska Street, amid the boulevard's fashionable boutiques and restaurants.

At one store, a particularly attractive blouse in the window caught her eye. She went in and asked in English how much it cost. The clerk, a young girl no more than eighteen, replied "Of course, madam," and gave her the price, urging her to try it on as she lifted it deftly off the mannequin and held it up.

"The green matches your eyes, madam. Would you like me to wrap it up for you?" she asked boldly when Eleanor hesitated.

"I'll think about it," she said, calculating the amount in dollars and deciding it was too pricey, at the same time envisioning how much better it would look on her than anything she had brought.

On the way back to the hotel, she stopped at an outdoor café and ordered a glass of wine. She had just settled in with a guidebook when she saw Emmanuel at another table. Perhaps she would have decided against stopping if she had known that he was there too, reluctant to encourage more than a polite friendship between them. He was not wearing a hat, and she realized that his hair was sparser than she'd thought. His bald crown shone beneath the light, illuminating his face as he recognized her, his despair of a few days ago gone.

When she was ready to leave, she nodded courteously. He must have been waiting for her and rose to ask if she wanted company.

She didn't dissuade him, afraid she would take a wrong turn, suddenly aware that darkness had gathered around her.

"I'm afraid I'm not used to being alone," she said, as they began walking together. "My husband and I were to take this trip together."

"He is ill?"

"Was," she corrected. "He was ill. He passed away a year ago."

Another expression she disliked. Passed away to what? Walking side by side in the dark, instead of facing each other in the bright light, it was easier to talk. Edward had been much taller than Eleanor, his long legs always far ahead of hers, but Emmanuel's strides equaled her own. She thought that he would reveal some sorrow of his, but he merely offered her a well-known proverb.

"Man makes plans and God laughs."

"Yes," she reflected. "Sometimes I think that too."

In the pleasant evening, couples strolled down the street, some with children in tow who skipped and called to each other while parents spoke quietly. On summer evenings, she and Edward had often gone out for such strolls around the university. It was the time when they spoke about the events of the day, the children, the direction their lives were taking, Edward's work.

Their marriage had been about him, after all, his comfort, his vocation, his needs. Still, Edward had also been a shelter between herself and the world. How forlorn she felt now in the midst of all these people she didn't know.

When they arrived at the hotel and said goodnight, she held out her hand, lest Emmanuel think that she desired any further company. Unexpectedly, he brought it to his lips. She pulled back instinctively, creating an awkward moment that she replayed in her mind as she went to her room.

She was unable to concentrate at first on writing about the events of the day. It had been Eleanor's custom on trips to record places of interest, people she had met, experiences—a practice that Edward had thought useless. Did she ever review these writings? They both knew the answer to that. Eleanor had a shelf of these journals chronicling trips she had taken. No, it was true, she had never gone back to reread them, but the effort gave her enjoyment.

Now what she wrote on her computer was directed to him:

My dearest husband, I am here at last in your beloved Prague. I have been imagining you as a small child riding your bicycle about town, going to school, with your parents, enjoying outings. I seem to see you in every place I go, but without you, it is lonely. Today, we visited the Old–New synagogue, a place you always talked about, but I seem to recall that your family attended another house of worship entirely.

Suddenly she stopped. Perhaps Edward had been right. What good did it do? And yet, adrift in a world in which she no longer felt at home, the writing kept her feeling closer to him.

She closed the laptop and prepared for bed. The sky was clouded, which meant more rain, but the air was fresh. Before she fell asleep, she saw Emmanuel, his eyes alive and desirous, radiating pleasure in her presence.

The heat returned, but in the afternoon dark clouds tinged with lavender floated over the city, and it began to shower. The couples on the tour had already formed cliques, like high school students. The women talked about their children and grandchildren; the men continued their stories of golf and fishing and baseball — big red-faced American men who had never quite grown up. The three harpies simply nodded coolly in her direction. The couple she had loathed on the plane, the whiny wife, the complaining husband, were oddly quieter, perhaps aware that everyone was avoiding them.

Emmanuel dined alone or with the guide. He and Eleanor spoke only a little, but in spite of her determination to keep him at a distance, she felt a gradual but growing intimacy between them, his presence unexpectedly welcome as they rode every day about the city, or in the few words they exchanged, his English often awkward, as though he had never truly made the adjustment to another language. What did she really know about him? Only that he had been a chemist at one time and a teacher. During the war he had worked as a translator, marrying a childhood sweetheart from Budapest, a schoolmate, the daughter of friends of his parents.

"My wife, the same as your husband, as though she never was."

"I'm sorry," she said.

"Everyone else is gone. In other words kaput. They perished. There are no school reunions, no family except for a sister in south Florida. A desert," he said. "The rest up in smoke. People are tired of hearing about it. What more can be said? It has become a cliché, evoking false emotions. Nothing left, not here, not in Budapest. Unlike you and your husband, we never had children."

She thought of her own children.

"It doesn't help," she said.

She reached into her purse and took out the photographs of Michael and Matthew, shocked at how young they looked. When had they grown into people she no longer knew?

He stared at the photographs for a long time.

"They look like you, although of course I never knew your husband."

When they occasionally sat at the same table, Emmanuel

helped her interpret the menus. She found out that his family had lived in Budapest for centuries. He spoke of the city again.

"Perhaps you will change your mind," he said. "It is a beautiful place too, with many interesting sights." It was the day they went to the museum that the Nazis had proposed calling a "Museum of an Extinct Race," containing the possessions that had been left behind by their victims.

Perhaps it was the afternoon heat that was seeping into the building, or emotions that had finally caught up with her regarding Edward's absence, and how closely he had evaded the fate that she saw here, that made her feel ill. Might there be things that had belonged to members of Edward's family, or to all those relatives who had disappeared? The decorated hutches and cupboards reminded her of unseen hands that had once used these objects.

But it was the contents of the drawers that shocked and sickened her: drawers of discarded eyeglasses and shoes and clothes and children's rattles and stuffed animals and dolls, but most of all, the baby shoes, no bigger than a man's thumb that had never held the tiny feet for which they were intended.

"I'm not feeling well," she murmured. She felt Emmanuel glance at her anxiously. The room appeared to be enveloped in a haze; the light dimmed, and nausea caught at her throat and threatened to spill out.

"Are you all right?"

"Yes," she said, determined to be independent, to take care of herself. A cold sweat moved down her spine while her legs threatened to sink beneath her. "I'll take a taxi back to the hotel."

In her room she closed the shades, undressed, slid under the covers, and slept for hours. When she awoke, the last rays of light were slipping through the bottom of the blinds. Still in bed, she heard knocking at the door; she pulled on a robe to answer it. Emmanuel was holding a bowl of steaming chicken soup on a tray.

"Why did you come?" she asked through a small crack of illumination from the hallway that entered the room.

"I was worried."

"I'm not hungry," Eleanor said.

He nudged open the door with the tip of his shoe.

"You must take some nourishment," he insisted.

She grew silent, too weak to protest as he made his way into the room and set down the tray. She retreated to the bed, feeling like a small child with her bare feet dangling over the edge and her misshapen toes showing, her face drained, she was sure, of color. A woman growing older, clutching a robe over her sunken breasts, taking food from a stranger.

"This is very kind of you," she said as she began to eat, feeling strength enter her body.

"Eat," he said again when she stopped, and he stood over her while she finished the soup. "I'll be back later to see how you are."

"How can I thank you?" Eleanor asked, but he silenced her with a wave of his hand and was gone. She had showered and dressed by the time he came back, asking how she was feeling.

"Still unsteady," she might have told him, but, touched by his concern, she responded with a lightness that she hoped was reassuring.

"I'll be fine," not at all certain that she would be.

They were on their own for dinner. Though the thought of

food made her feel queasy again, she didn't have the heart to refuse when he asked her to join him.

They ate in a small restaurant near the hotel. She didn't trust herself to try much more than chilled blueberries and cucumbers in sour cream to settle her stomach. She remembered Michael eating blueberries on Mother's Day, a memory that had faded away, as though it had been years ago instead of months.

"Your wife?" she asked, nibbling on a piece of bread. "What was her name?"

"Anika," he said. "Agnes in English. We found each other after the war."

He drew a wrinkled picture from his wallet. His nails were pared and well-groomed, she noticed, and his hands, smaller than Edward's, were soft and white

"I like Anika better," she said.

"So did she."

He handed her the picture. She held it in her palm for a long time. They must have been newly married then. They both looked so young and happy that it brought tears to her eyes. Emmanuel's wife was slender and lovely, with a crown of dark curly hair. His arm circled her waist.

"She's beautiful," Eleanor said. And then, as if it had just occurred to her, she asked, "What are we supposed to do with the past?"

"We can do nothing about the past but remember it and continue to live," he said simply.

In the remaining days of the week, they visited Karlsbad, the place where Edward had spent so many happy vacations. Yet the spa, filled with travelers taking the waters and vacation-goers intent on having a good time, gave her no joy.

On the final day, they went at last to Terezín, where so many members of Edward's family had been taken, where Edward himself would have been, and where he would have either died or been sent on the train that ran through this camp, known in German as Theresienstadt, to another one at Oświęcim, which became infamous as Auschwitz.

They had driven more than an hour away from the city and its distractions. The countryside was flat and fertile, filled with fields and gardens, and interspersed with cottages. It was raining again and, through the watery downpour that blurred the view, she witnessed the ordinary daily lives of people, as if what had happened never entered their minds. At last the rain stopped, and the sun came out, inappropriately, Eleanor thought. It should never shine here. Never.

In spite of the sun, the drab, ruined buildings with broken windows and crumbling stucco walls held another story, one that was devoid of joy, as though what had happened here years ago could never be forgotten. Old men, who were still youths then, moved slowly down the street, as if weighted with mem-ories that would not leave them alone. An elderly woman lean-ing on a cane went into one of the squalid stores to complete an errand. And then, in the midst of this dreary scene, a young mother wheeled her blond, blue-eyed baby across the street, as if to say, "Don't you know? Life goes on."

"How can you?" she wanted to ask, but she knew that the young mother would have just looked bewildered. How could you stop life from continuing?

"There are photographs of frightened Hungarian girls walking to the gas chambers," Emmanuel had said the night before over dinner, "the expression on their young, beautiful faces asking, 'How did this happen to me?' They were my sisters, my cousins, my friends."

Although it was summer in this desolate, melancholy place, it was not hard to imagine the cold and bitterness of another season. Even on a day like today, the wind blew fiercely. The normally talkative men were silent, and the women, too, had ceased their chatter, peering out at the countryside.

There was the sight they had hoped to avoid as they got off the bus: the fortress just outside the walls, which had originally been a garrison, then a prison, and finally a transit camp for Jews. Within the walls were isolation cells, rooms for starvation, and worse. Outside, in the vast cemetery, thousands of political prisoners were buried. Beyond that were the mass graves, each containing human beings wrenched from their lives to expire in what was supposed to be a model camp. But worst of all, she thought, were those who had no graves, who had been sent away on the trains to die elsewhere.

No, it was too terrible for memory, or for anyone to bear. She had left death and despair at home to find it magnified a thousand times here.

The rain was coming down again, more heavily now as the sun hid behind dark clouds, and she sought refuge in the small museum where the children's drawings were posted, along with their names and ages and whether they had survived.

She didn't want to look, but she was attracted to them all the same, imagining the children who had drawn them. Edward's drawings might have been here too. He could have been one of the 30,000 rumored to have turned the nearby Eger River red.

But she never would have known, of course, because she would not have known him. He would have been simply one of these faceless names, the last traces of murdered children.

As they filed out of the museum, Emmanuel walked at her side.

"I leave for Budapest tomorrow," he said. "Will you come?"

He was waiting for her answer, and, in the silence between them, she thought she would say yes.

# How I Found My Life

THERE WAS A LOT I WAS UNPREPARED FOR when I went off to college, to a state school for women in Texas. I decided that going to a women's college appealed to me. I was shy and uncertain around boys. The thought of being with girls gave me courage; I imagined a place where I wouldn't mind voicing my opinions and would be able to hold my own without the interference of boys my age, who always thought they knew more than the girls and were quick to put us down. When the brochure came in the mail, I knew it was the right place for me.

I had already been offered a scholarship at a well-known college in Pennsylvania, Bryn Mawr, a gentrified school for genteel young women, when a sudden urge to discover the world overtook my good sense, and I decided to go to a school I had never seen and knew nothing about. The brochure that came in the mail was one of those enticing folders with prettified pictures of students, all girls, happily lolling about on the grass in the balmy sunshine, while the text extolled the virtues of the college. Whoever put it together was a genius, because the minute I saw it, I changed my mind, and knew that *there* was exactly where I wanted to go. I tossed away the Bryn Mawr scholarship and told my parents I was going to Texas.

At first, bewildered, they put up a fight. Who knew what I'd find there? Texas was a wilderness they knew nothing about—or knew about only from the B-movie westerns they saw. But after a few days, they unexpectedly relented. The school was far cheaper than the one I'd planned to attend, and, even without the scholarship I was giving up, my surprising choice would save them a great deal of money. But much more than that, I think, they were simply tired—tired of the children they had brought into the world, tired of fighting our demands for anything that appeared in our heads as we grew older and more insistent, tired of taking care of us.

Their lives were humdrum—or they seemed so to me at the time—and I was desperate to escape their dreary fate. My father taught high school history; my mother was a housewife, which is what most mothers were then. I was the last child, and they were worn down with parenthood. I didn't know that at the time, of course. It was years before I realized how they felt, when I had been through it myself, which is the only way we seem to really learn anything. Now I understand how eager they were to do all the things they'd put off for years before the inevitable end that approached ever more rapidly toward them with each passing year. They'd married young, and even then they weren't that old, but they looked old, as most parents did back then, before they began dressing and sounding like their own children.

During the summer before I left home, I would often catch

my usually energetic mother simply sitting and staring into space for hours, sipping her coffee and smoking a cigarette down to a stub, without even being aware that it was about to start burning her flesh. I don't remember ever having a real conversation with her until years after that, when I was an adult.

Parents were different then. They did not expect to be pals with their children, nor would they have wanted that any more than the children did. My father was easier to talk to than my mother when I was a child; he didn't lecture me as much. But my memories of him are dim, and few. I do remember coming home from a Halloween carnival once, walking through a silent, frosty night with him, hand in hand.

A few nights before I was to leave, my father spent a long time packing my clothes in a steamer trunk. It was the same trunk that had gone with him to Harvard from a small town in Pennsylvania. There were small dents where it had been damaged by that trip, and when my sisters went off to school. The trunk smelled musty. It had been stored up in the attic and exuded the essence of lives lived years before my own. It had drawers, much like a miniature doll trunk I had as a child, places to hang up skirts and blouses, and pockets for shoes and belts. My mother had carefully ironed all my clothes, and now she gave me strict instructions about unpacking.

"Be sure to take everything out the minute you get there and put it away," she said, even though we both knew that once I was out of her sight, I would do no such thing.

"You don't have to keep telling her over and over again, Bess. She's a smart girl," my father said.

As he spoke his face was illuminated by a single yellow bulb in the garage that cast a dull glow on him and accentuated the signs that had come with age. I remembered him telling me that he'd never gone home again after he left for school, even though his mother pleaded with him.

Now he bent solemnly over his task, focused on it, the way he did everything.

"Waste not, want not," he often said.

There was little money when he was growing up. The same was true for my mother. In fact, she still had her original dishes and bedding, feather comforters and pillows her sister made for her before she was married. She would never spend money on anything new when what she had was still serviceable.

Even so, my mother had purchased some new outfits for my first year, and now she walked back across the yard to get the remainder. As soon as she entered the house, my father turned to me.

"You're sure this is what you want, Joanna? Because it's not too late, you know. It's never too late to change your mind. I just wanted you to know that." He was wearing a familiar gray cardigan that had lost its shape and now hung awkwardly on his slight frame. I looked at his face. It was drained of color, and, in the way his jaw had gone slack, I realized that he was afraid he would never see me again.

I was suddenly frightened too, as night closed in. Early in the morning I would board a train for an unknown place I had seen only in a photograph.

"Yes," I said, "I'm sure," but the unsteadiness in my voice, an octave too high, betrayed me.

He hesitated. Perhaps in that second he could have talked me out of it, but he turned back to continue his task.

"Well, then," he said and touched me lightly on my arm. "I guess that settles it."

I was eighteen, and I thought in dramatic terms, as adolescents do. I knew that, like my father, I would never really come home again. My parents would still be my parents, but I would enter a different realm entirely, where more important events would take place.

As the train pulled away from the station the next morning, my eyes stung with unexpected tears after that final glimpse of them standing mutely together on the platform with their crestfallen faces.

Sitting up all night, I tried to sleep, with my head resting against the back of the seat, bobbing with the motion of the train. My neck was stiff when I awoke. I was only faintly aware of the place that I had left behind, as though leaving had happened not just hours, but years before. I felt that I was traveling to the ends of the earth.

I washed in a small lavatory with only a basin and a toilet, where I could barely turn around. Somehow, in that tiny space, I also managed to change my clothes, a white blouse and a black skirt I didn't like — my mother's idea.

Several times a day a porter came through the cars, collecting tickets, tending to passengers, and announcing the time the dining car would be open. The porters changed as I traveled from one place to another, some getting off, others coming on board.

I couldn't help but wonder what their lives were like. One of them asked me a question.

"You from around here?"

"No," I told him.

"Where you bound for, all by yourself?"

"I'm going to college in Texas. To the state college for women."

"Good for you; I wish I could've gone to college. You one lucky girl," he added as he gazed curiously at the book I was reading.

I heard in his voice the sadness over the opportunities that hadn't been his to take—and envy that I, a girl, and a young one at that, had been given the chance that he had not. In spite of that, he flashed me a broad smile.

"That mighty fine," he said, as though he really meant it and harbored me no ill will.

After a couple of days the train headed toward north Texas, and a string of small towns I had never heard of filled with people I didn't know, Gordonville, Grayson, Pilot Point. But looking out the window as they passed by, one after another, as bleak winds whipped across the monotonous flat scrub and plains, I could tell there was a toughness to this country that would test anyone who lived here, stripping out the softness and leaving the hard core beneath. The light was fading, creeping over the land and enclosing it like a giant fist, chasing away the sultry summer days.

Sooner than I anticipated I arrived at my destination, a town not much different from the others, known for its wild rodeos and deadly tornadoes. My trunk was hoisted down from the baggage car, and a truck was waiting to pick me up, along with several other students, and to take us to the campus.

The driver tipped his ten-gallon hat.

"Howdy there," he said, and we piled in the back.

It was a dull, sunless day, not at all what I expected, nothing like the day that was pictured on the brochure. But I was here, and there was no going back the way I'd come.

Of the two girls who had arrived, one was dark-haired, glum, and sure of herself, a city girl, and the other was a petite blond with frightened eyes, who already looked homesick. I soon found out their names: Terry came all the way from New York. She spoke with an unpleasant edge to her words and her large eyes, black as pitch, appeared to pop out of their sockets. Connie came from a small town in Arkansas and had never been on a train before. Her pretty lower lip trembled as she said this, as though any minute she would burst into tears and ask to return to the station so that she could go home again.

I saw at once that the town was dreary, not a real college town but a dusty backwater, with twenties-era stores and bald mannequins staring blankly out the windows at empty streets.

The campus itself was a bit better: two-story brick buildings and dorms with graceful columns that were handsome enough. But they looked neglected, as though a college for women wasn't worth the trouble. Families who lived closer to campus carried their daughters' belongings—bedding, lamps, even stuffed animals they couldn't bear to do without. I both envied and pitied those girls—because they were taken care of, because they weren't yet free of their parents.

Many of the girls wore the colorful, tiered skirts and peasant blouses they were used to wearing at home. Others, who had grown up on ranches, dressed in boots and jeans and western-style shirts. I didn't look anything like those Texas girls, and my old-fashioned name suggested someone who had just arrived from the old country.

By the time I found my room, my roommate was already waiting for me.

We had exchanged letters and snapshots. Her name was Billy Jo Jordan, and she was Texas tall, with a slender, muscular figure, a long, elegant neck, broad shoulders, and high breasts. Billy Jo was from Dallas, not far away.

It was clear from the beginning that we were ill-matched. She already had a boyfriend and announced that she would be going home every weekend. It was just as well. I discovered that she liked to stay up late, smoking and listening to country music. She wrote her boyfriend nearly every night, which took up her entire evening, or had her friends pile into the room while I was trying to study. I rarely saw her open a book. In the evening, before she got into bed, she walked around naked, which shocked and embarrassed me.

I soon found out that almost everyone had come here because they were only biding their time. It was a space in their lives that had to be filled, and this was the perfect place, where few demands would be made of them. They came from all over: the Gulf Coast, the Panhandle, even border towns, and all those forgotten places that dotted the state. On weekends and holidays I often went home with one of them, catching glimpses into other lives.

Some lived in shacks without running water and electricity —scholarship girls, who worked to pay their way through school, planning to go back as soon as they graduated and teach in the one-room schoolhouses of those towns. Others came from families that had become wealthy through a stroke of luck, oil, or sprawling ranches.

Maggie Holmes was one of the latter. She invited me to visit not long after I arrived. She was from Hereford, Deaf Smith County, in the Texas Panhandle, a town named after the many cattle raised in the area. It was once called the Windmill City; over four hundred windmills had been erected to pump the underground water that had been discovered just after the war. Her father was a prosperous farmer who had cashed in, leasing his water rights during those boom days, no longer at the mercy of the Great Plains weather.

"So this is the girl Maggie drug home from school," he said when he met me.

Maggie resembled him — big-boned and strong, with a chiseled face, a girl who looked like someone accustomed to hard work. It was the way I imagined her father appeared before he became weathered and stooped. Her mother was short and plump, with a round, red face, who spent her days in the kitchen cooking for the family and ranch hands. Maggie encouraged me to try her mother's specialties — rabbit chili, tortillas with a thin layer of beans, Texas corn chowder with salt pork, and plates of food that had no name, at least none that I recognized — which would miraculously appear on the long, wooden table. Maggie's father, reaching for a second helping, took the opportunity to rant that girls needn't go to school for what they were going to spend their lives doing.

"Don't pay attention to him," Maggie said more than once when we were alone. In the evenings the boy she was keeping company with came over, and we sat and talked on the front porch, although Maggie and I did most of the talking.

"I'm not in love with Wayne," she told me after he left, "but he's like most of the boys around here, good and decent and hardworking." After a pause, as though trying to convince herself, she added, "I could do worse."

We sat so close that I could see the summer freckles spread across her nose and cheeks as I tried to form an image of her in that far-off future—a life of hard work and a half-dozen children with a husband like Wayne, who would grow into a taciturn old man. I heard in her words the sense of fate that many of the girls expressed—the idea that it wasn't really up to them to decide these things, but to finally bow to their parents' wishes and accept a life that had been preordained for them: marry a local boy, and end up like their mothers.

Look, you don't have to do this, I wanted to tell her, but I never got up the courage. What good would it do? Her life was already sealed, as if someone had already presented it to her in a box. I wasn't surprised when Maggie, like my roommate and many other girls, went home for good before the semester ended. I never saw any of them again.

Yet even as I looked down on the boys they had settled for and the lives they had chosen, I couldn't help envying the way girls like Maggie were wedded to the land and knew their place in the world, as I did not. My people were eternal strangers, wandering first through one country and then another, never truly welcome anywhere. My parents had all but abandoned the religion of their childhood. We were Jews, but they had shrugged off the restrictions of the past and considered themselves Americans, even though they hadn't severed their ties as much as they liked to think they had.

Feelings and memories remained of pious families on both sides, although neither of my parents could see that it had done them much good. Even so, I wondered what they would have thought if they had seen me eating salt pork and going to the Methodist church on Sunday, which Maggie told me was one step up from the Baptists.

Who was I then? I felt like an impostor, still searching for my life, the one that would belong entirely to me. When Maggie asked, I told her that I didn't have a religion, which seemed unbelievable to her. It was what I told everyone. But I didn't mention any of this in my letters home. Instead I wrote about the interesting people I was meeting and the excellent teachers who taught my classes.

It was easier to lie in letters. The truth was that many of the professors couldn't get jobs anywhere else, and with a few exceptions—English and biology, taught by women born and raised in Texas—most of them had landed there out of desperation.

The English teacher, Miss Wright, had unfortunate teeth, while the biology professor wore no-nonsense clothes and scorned makeup, as if she was trying to look as unattractive as possible. Neither was married. Married men did not like to have working wives. It was a poor reflection on them, and it meant that they weren't going to come home and have their dinner on time—or perhaps no dinner at all. They didn't want to suffer a dirty house and meals that were not well-prepared and tasty, nor did they want to take on any women's work— ferrying children to doctors' appointments or taking care of them when they were ill. Their job was to support the family, and they felt that this was sufficient.

We didn't know then, on the cusp of that new age, how much everything would change. We didn't know that our daughters would go out into the world and expect to be taken seriously, and that our virginity, which we had been told to protect above all else, wouldn't matter very much in that distant future where our daughters would hold jobs, hire housekeepers and nannies, and get their food not from slaving over a hot oven all day, but at the takeout counter at the grocery store.

One of the professors had arrived from Harvard. No one knew precisely why David Webster had left, although various rumors kept circulating. It was known that his reputation had been tarnished and that he fled in disgrace. Otherwise, everyone knew, he would never come to a place like this. He had not only a master's, like everyone else, but also a doctorate in mathematics. Yet he was given the lowliest courses to teach, math for those of us, like myself, who never wanted to open a math book again.

Professor Webster was slight for a man, with curly hair, a round face, sensual lips, and long, delicate fingers that scribbled proofs on the blackboard. We were all in love with him, with his shabby corduroy jacket, the pipe he smoked, the way he lifted his eyebrows when he was thinking. We listened to him speak with his strange Boston accent, dropping off the ends of words and sounding his *A*'s in incomprehensible, broad strokes. He didn't seem like an ordinary mortal. He looked at us with eyes that blazed a shade of dark amber when he lectured us.

"Mathematics is the poetry of ideas, ladies. It is sublimely pure, as artistic and beautiful as a composition by Mozart." Or, on a beautiful, sunny day, as his gaze roamed the fields outside the window: "Open your eyes, girls, and look around you. Math is the language of nature." Occasionally he would bring in a perfect flower and hold it up, telling us about the Fibonacci sequence of numbers that was reflected in the golden spiral of the flower's petals and seed heads.

Of all the people at that school, he was the one who pointed the way to the world of ideas I longed to enter. I often stayed after class just to talk to him, and sometimes, with our faces bent over the problems he was helping me solve, showing me shortcuts, I felt an energy pass between us that was almost palpable. At those times, I thought he might kiss me, but he never did.

On one of these occasions, when I had solved a particularly difficult equation myself, he asked why I had come here.

"You're head and shoulders above this rabble," he said, tapping his pipe on the desk for emphasis. "You need to take yourself more seriously, Joanna. You won't find what you're looking for here."

His advice played over and over again in my mind. I felt that he had seen right through me, that he knew the hidden spaces of my soul, my longing to find my place in the world. He understood me because he was searching for the same thing himself. Unlike the Texas boys I was meeting, brash and immature, rough around the edges and trying to sweet-talk me into the back seats of cars, David Webster was suave, interesting, and brilliant.

On the weekends, sometimes a group of us would meet those boys at the edge of town, where we could dance on the sawdust floor to a jukebox and twine our arms around them, pressing our lips so hard against theirs that they were swollen the next day. The boys were raw-boned giants with thick, ropey muscles and faces that were going to age fast in the hot Texas sun. I already knew that none of them would be a boy I'd want to marry.

Terry, the dark-haired New Yorker I'd met my first day, never came with us on those nights. She liked to hang around with a group of girls who smoked and drank and stayed up late, but no one knew exactly what they did in those wee hours of the morning. She didn't have a good word to say about anyone, especially men. I soon found out that she had a loud, foul mouth. She said whatever she wanted to and let the words tumble around her.

"Why do you think he lost his job?" she asked, catching me as I left math class. She waited a moment before telling me with a malicious smile, "I heard Webster likes men. You know what that means, don't you?"

"What?"

"He's a faggot, silly. Do I have to spell it out for you?"

The word made me feel physically ill. *Faggot.* It confused and excited me at the same time.

"He likes to fuck men," she continued with unrestrained glee. "That's why he's here. Don't you know that's the reason Harvard didn't want him?"

*Faggot. Fuck.*

Unpleasant words that stuck in my throat. I liked David Webster. I didn't want to think about what faggots did with each other. In spite of what Terry said, I had a crush on him. I liked the way he taught, the way he made vague numbers easier to understand. For the first time I became interested in those numbers, in seeing what I could do with them, how they would help me translate the world into a form I could comprehend.

After Billy Jo Jordan went home, I had the room to myself. Stripped of all the things she had brought and the commotion of girls camping out until all hours of the night, the silent space settled around me. I began to apply myself to my studies. Every night I got a couple of Cokes from the vending machine and began to work. I bought a pack of Camels, thinking the smoke would spur me on, but I hated the taste of tobacco in my mouth and finally threw the cigarettes in the trash at the end of the hallway. Sitting at my desk, I would think about my life and wonder at how differently it was turning out from what I had expected.

The weather grew colder. I didn't know that Texas would be so cold. In the early morning, when I walked to class, my hands grew so red and stiff I could barely hold a pencil. Finally, I walked into town to buy some gloves.

I had only been there a couple of times. The sky was bleak and unfriendly; all the warmth was sucked out of the day. Above me the flutter of silvery wings rose and descended in the air as a flight of birds lifted off for sunnier climates. A sudden longing to follow them overcame me and settled in the pit of my stomach.

The town was desolate, smaller than many of the places I had glimpsed from the train. Besides the drugstore where I had been for a soda, there were a few restaurants—the hotel with its respectable dining room, where parents who visited their daughters took them to Sunday dinner for fried chicken, mashed potatoes, and creamy gravy; the Wrangler across the street, with ten-gallon types who came in their battered pickup trucks with mangy dogs in the back; and a Chinese restaurant that served pork chops and chop suey. There was one in every western town, holdovers from the days of railroad building when hundreds and then thousands of Chinese workers were brought over. Many never went back; their descendants stayed and started families and, eventually, all those chow mein joints that catered to American tastes.

I headed for the Western Apparel and Dry Goods store, which only had bald mannequins in the window when I first passed through town. Now those heads wore hats, and gloves were scattered like colorful leaves in the window. I pushed open the door, and a bell rang. A girl was sorting out boxes, putting boots away, and the pungent smell of new leather filled the room. It was dark inside, but once my eyes adjusted, I saw a baby sleeping in a drawer on the counter. I thought of Maggie Holmes. It would be a long time before I would be ready for that.

"It's cold," I said and held out my hands, which were turning blue.

"It's always cold this time of year. You from that fancy school?"

"It's not that fancy."

"I never seen you before, that's all. So where you from?"

I told her the East and she made a low, chortling sound. "Then why'd you come all the way here?"

"I dunno. I ask myself the same thing. Anyhow, it's too complicated to explain."

"Isn't everything?" I knew she meant the baby when she nodded her head in that direction, and from the way she said it, I also knew she didn't have a husband.

She searched in a cardboard box for a pair of gloves and tossed them on the counter. I picked them up and drew them carefully over my fingers. They were so warm I didn't want to take them off. I flexed my hands to see if there was any give. Real leather covered the palms. "Nice," I said.

"You won't be needing to buy new ones for a long time."

"Can you cut off the tags?" I noticed that the baby was opening his eyes. I think it was a boy, a fat-faced baby that looked like her. In a few minutes he would be crying, and I wanted to be out of there. She took scissors from a drawer and, bending over, until our faces almost touched, took the ticket off. I could smell her hair and the leaky scent of milk from her large breasts.

"I never been out of Texas," she said as I left, and her voice was friendlier now as she picked up the baby, who had begun to wail.

I had a few coins left in my pocket, so I went into the drug-store and ordered a hot chocolate at the counter before the long walk back to school. A couple of men were bantering with the waitress. She poured hot water out of a faucet into a cup, mixed it with chocolate powder, and sullenly dumped a marsh-mallow in the center without saying a word. It was clear she didn't like me. I was an outsider, after all, and suddenly a wave of sorrow shivered through me for all those ancestors, strangers in strange lands. But I was already picturing the evening ahead of me. I had a math exam the next day, and I wanted to do well. I wanted David Webster to be proud of me.

Life settled into a routine. The old world I had known fell away, and the dreams of home grew further and further apart, and then stopped. I was getting good grades. I made new friends. I actually learned the Texas two-step, along with the Texas songs we sang with gusto in assemblies. It wasn't as easy as it looked. The trick was to glide through the steps and turns instead of picking up your feet, which at first I invariably did, making it obvious that I came from somewhere else. This was decades ago, before the big-box stores and homogenized accents and TV all over the place. Texas was still another country, with a special jargon and songs and food.

For Christmas vacation I went home with a girl from San Antonio, Rita Sanchez. The day after we arrived, her mother woke us up early and put us to work. She was a woman who did not waste time or suffer any sloth. We trimmed the tree in the morning and spent the afternoon cutting designs out of paper bags, putting sand in the bottom to hold candles. Just before dusk fell, we lined the walkway of her house with these *luminarias* that glowed warmly to welcome visitors. Between these two tasks we made Christmas cookies with a globe of jelly in the center, dusting powdered sugar on the top, so they looked like miniature flowers, and then we kept baking cookies in all shapes and sizes following recipes from a spattered cookbook until Mrs. Sanchez finally stopped.

"I think that will do it."

"Mind if I take a few?" Mr. Sanchez kept coming in to swipe them.

His mustache was dusted with sugar. He was very handsome, with a flirtatious swagger. Looking at Rita's parents, I could not imagine two people more different from each other.

"They fight a lot," she told me. "My father's always got someone on the side." While I was there I didn't hear any fighting. Instead there was almost an eerie calm, in deference, I suppose, to the holiday and my presence.

Mrs. Sanchez was making a Christmas log, frosted with thick chocolate and green piping that represented holly, with red berries on the top.

"Perfect," she said when she was finished. "Per*fec*to."

She had a birdlike face and very sharp brown eyes, a little bit like the chocolate frosting. I thought of my own parents. Christmas was simply another day in my family, though sometimes we would drive around the neighborhood to look at the lights that decorated the houses.

On Christmas Eve, the Sanchez family marched in Las Posadas, a procession re-creating the pilgrimage that Mary and Joseph took from Nazareth to Bethlehem on a winter night nearly two thousand years before. Rita was Mary and her younger brother was Joseph. I played a shepherd. My flock consisted of the family dogs, trailing curiously and obediently after me, with a vigilant eye out for my staff.

I wondered what the townspeople would have thought if they had known that I was really a Jew? I knew that Jews had been in Texas before the Alamo, had herded cattle on the Chisholm Trail, and fought in the Confederate Army, but that night I felt that I was the only Jew who'd ever been in Texas.

At each house, we went up the front walk, dressed as travelers from centuries ago, and knocked at the door. Joseph asked, "Is there room at the inn for my wife, who is about to give birth?" After her brother said this, Rita held her stomach and pleaded for a place to stay. She looked much more the Jew than I did. She was vividly dark, with curly hair, a nose that arched at the brow, and olive skin, as though centuries ago, her family had been *conversos* who tried to escape the Inquisition by coming to the New World. As if to quiet any doubts, she always wore a gold cross around her neck, incongruous that evening. No matter how desperate her appeals, each door was slammed in her face.

Of course this had all been planned in advance. It was only a play, but my eyes brimmed with tears. I did not even know why I was crying, except that I, alone, knew that the child who was about to be born was not the Messiah as they believed, but an ordinary man like everyone else.

It was a perfectly still, cold night. I looked for the brightest star. But here the whole splendid dome above me was filled with stars, frosty bits of chips like glass. We were led only by the glow of those stars, the moon, and the flickering candles that lit the street. Perhaps, I thought, I truly was in Bethlehem, making my way through history, as the people I'd come from had, long, long ago, beneath that starry splendor, to this place where I would finally belong. It seemed to me that I was no longer on a street in a town that was in a state and a country, but was instead moving back to that ancient land before the long exile.

What was I doing here? For the first time I realized there was a lie between myself and the world. I wasn't the person I pretended to be, and this troubled me.

When I came back from Christmas break, I found out that David Webster was gone.

He never returned, and no one knew what had happened to him, but I imagined him living in an English country cottage with hollyhocks growing in the back and perhaps some of Walt Whitman's fragrant lilacs blooming in the dooryard. That was as far as I got. All the time he had been here, he must have been plotting his escape without my knowing. It made me realize how little I knew other people, the thoughts that spiraled around their minds and settled into their hearts, the secrets that they kept to themselves—and the realization that I was no different.

Someone else came and took over his classes, a pudgy man with thick fingers and a big belly who wore a ridiculous French beret.

"So what do you think happened to him?" Terry asked, entering my room without asking and sitting on the edge of my bed.

We both knew who she meant.

"I'm not sure."

"They must have found out he was a faggot," she said.

"Hey, lay off, will you?"

It took me a long time, but I was learning to give it back to her. She liked the give and take of combat.

I knew why David Webster had left. He needed to find a place where he could be himself, without pretense or deceit. And at once I understood that Terry hated him—or anyone— who reflected the vulnerability that she despised in herself.

"No one can keep a secret forever," she said slyly.

It made me wonder what mischief she had set in motion. Terry reached in her pocket and took out a cigarette from a crumpled pack of Lucky Strikes and lit it.

"Figure it out," she said when she saw my expression.

She blew out the match, got up, and tossed it on my desk, still smoldering.

A few weeks later I received a letter from the dean. She said it had come to her attention that I was not attending any religious services. She emphasized that this was an important part of my education. She had looked up the forms I had filled out when I entered. It just so happened, the letter said, that two other girls of my persuasion had been found. We were now to be required to get together and hold services. One of the girls was a teaching assistant, a grad student on loan from a neighboring school who would lead us. She had an apartment nearby, with a soft sofa and toss pillows, a passageway that served as a kitchen, and a pull-down bed known as a Murphy. It was in this small place that we first met.

Her name was Chana Stern. She had beautiful red hair that she wore tied back from her face and cinnamon-colored freckles spun over her pale skin. She was not pretty, but striking, with hazel eyes, a sharp nose, weak chin, and an expression of disdain. Her body was hard and tough. She invited me in. The other girl had already arrived. A small table held two candlesticks and a twisted bread covered with a colorful cloth.

Chana asked if one of us would like to light the candles, but neither of us knew how. She reflected on this, tightened her lips, and did it herself, circling her hands toward her to draw in the light, and then blessing the warm loaf, which we passed around, following her lead, and broke off in thick chunks until it melted on our tongues. Then she uttered some more words in a language that I couldn't understand, sipped the wine, and invited us to take some of the salads she had prepared while we told her something about ourselves. She said this in a voice that was heavily accented, used to giving commands and taking charge.

When we were silent she asked suspiciously, her eyes growing dark and narrow,

"Aren't you Jews?"

We nodded, embarrassed.

"Ah," she said, "of course, *American* Jews," and the way she stressed "American" left no doubt as to how she felt about us. "I thought so," she added curtly. "Then we will skip the service. We will simply get acquainted. I will tell you about myself. I will tell you why I am here in this forsaken place where there are only three Jews, with only one who knows enough to light the Sabbath candles."

She had been born in Palestine before the creation of the State of Israel and later fought in the War of Independence alongside men who had died next to her.

"Do you know what that was like?" she asked sharply. "I was sixteen years old, but I saw things that no child should ever see. I was too young to feel fear. I only knew that we had to win. Where else would we go? What happened during the war showed how much the world wants us.

"I learned something else too; I learned that women do not have to depend on men. We can be strong. We can do what we want. I will go back to my country. That is why I am here in this town in the middle of nowhere, completing my studies.

"But what will happen to you girls?" she asked, clearly bewildered about our futures. "What will happen to *you*?" she repeated with unexpected concern as her eyes fastened on me. "How will you find your life?"

Her directness startled me.

When I didn't answer, she went on.

"Then you must find out. That is your task. To find your own life and not someone else's."

We finished our dinner, and Chana Stern stood up. It was her way of dismissing us.

"I will tell the dean that we have met. I will also tell her that we will not be meeting again. What is the point of this, after all?"

Winter was already turning into spring; the trees were fragrant with magnolia buds, and the evening was warm, but I felt chilled to the bone, as though this woman had seen the turmoil that was inside of me.

Something unexpected happened after that. As though I had a sign posted on my forehead, or wore a yellow star, students I didn't know started dropping by to see what I looked like.

They had heard that I was a Jew. They had never seen one before, they explained apologetically. What did they imagine I would look like? Did they see a human being or some strange, alien creature? My hair was the color of corn silk, my eyes were pale blue, and my skin was so fair I couldn't go out in the sun without burning. My feelings, too, were no different from theirs—or the things I yearned for—but I did not know how to tell them this.

Before long, that spring, by an odd coincidence, my wisdom teeth erupted through sore angry gums that thrust me into misery, like a punishment. I stopped answering those curious knocks at the door. I didn't want to face the awkward stares or the things people said.

There is beauty and power in knowledge, an eloquence that is as elegant as the mathematical formulas that David Webster used to dazzle our young minds on the brink of womanhood.

Eventually, people stopped coming to my door to satisfy their curiosity. I hardly noticed. Something inside of me was changing too. A passage was opening, and I was entering a place I had never been before. It was the recognition that I was among people who knew who they were and what their life was about, and I wanted the same thing for myself. Looking out at the vast Texas prairies and open spaces, I began to see myself in a different light. I had direction. I had a history as surely as anyone here. I had a place in the world, if only I allowed myself to return to it.

Before summer, I traveled home the way I had come, knowing that I would not return. The fields I saw through the train window were covered with acres of flowers, Indian paintbrush and lupine and blooms of prickly pear cactus. I had been this way before, but now I saw it with altered eyes. In that year I had become a woman, with a woman's self-assuredness.

I thought about my parents. It seemed such a long time ago that I had seen them. They would be more or less the way I had left them, I thought, but I wasn't the same. They would know that something about me was different, but they wouldn't know what it was. And I wouldn't tell them.

I began to see my life as something that belonged to me. I could mold it any way I wanted to. I could be who I wanted to be. The world was studded with possibilities, not as numerous as the constellations that covered the vault of the Texas sky, but there all the same.

I hadn't found what I was searching for in Texas that year, but I began to realize that it would be waiting for me somewhere else. It was the beginning of my education. I had been a stranger in a strange land, like my forebears, and it had forced me to confront myself. Perhaps it was my own *Mitzrayim*, the name of the ancient Egypt of the Exodus, a place of narrow straits that had held me captive, so that when I left, I would find my true being, the person that I was destined to become.

# Why Are You Afraid?

ONLY DAYS BEFORE THE TRAGEDY, Elizabeth Gordon had looked out at the sea through the palm trees and at the bare, jagged mountains in the distance. The water was still and serene, a vivid shade of blue that reflected the cloudless sky. She might almost be framing a painting for the boutique gallery she owned back in San Francisco.

The place was a real find, an undiscovered paradise. It was part of territory occupied by Israel after the Six-Day War in 1967, and the last piece of land to be returned to Egypt when Israel finished pulling out of the Sinai, in accord with a ruling decided by an International Commission in 1989. Elizabeth and her husband, Paul, had planned to stay in nearby Eilat, at the southern point of Israel, with its dazzling coral reefs, but no rooms were available, and so they had come here, even though Elizabeth had been afraid.

Threats of terror were in the news and the hotels were empty, but Paul had turned to her and asked, "Why are you always afraid of everything, Lizzie?"

She just was, she thought. She spent her life seeing dangers that everyone else laughed at.

"It's daaan-ger-ous," her son Avi had begun saying, drawing out the word slowly in a low, threatening voice, mocking her, when she asked him not to do something that frightened her. Whatever it was, she always knew of something that had happened, a bad ending that could have been avoided.

"You're teaching our children fear," Paul said. "Sure, there's unrest," he continued matter-of-factly. "Political factions, religious coercion, tribal hostilities—simply put, bad people. There's no way to avoid it today."

I haven't always been like this, Elizabeth wanted to tell him. Years ago nothing frightened her. In fact, she had often been foolishly adventurous, ready to try anything, but life had taught her to be cautious or she might regret it.

"The world," she began.

"Is the same it's always been," he interrupted. "It just seems worse because we know about it, every damn single thing that happens."

Paul had been right, she thought. This was a much-needed rest before they returned home, picked up the children, and resumed the busy thread of their lives. And the coral reefs where he had looked forward to diving were dazzling here, too. In fact, it was one of the most breathtakingly beautiful places she had ever seen.

Taking another sip of crimson-colored *karkade* made from hibiscus leaves, she decided it must be at least 120 degrees, even in the shade. She'd taken the precaution of covering most of her face with wet towels and putting plenty of sun lotion on the rest of her body, but now that, too, was covered.

Paul lay on an adjoining chair. He had been diving the coral reefs earlier in the morning. Now and then he'd get up suddenly and plunge into the pool, where a group of young men were tossing a ball back and forth, speaking quickly and excitedly in Arabic.

Although there were few people, the serving boys went back and forth with frosty drinks on silver trays that winked beneath the sun, also offering delicious tidbits, stuffed dates, hummus with pita, or some other Middle Eastern delicacy that she would try to re-create once she got home.

Their handsome, healthy faces and nut-brown skin seemed to come from some ancient papyrus recently unearthed, images with hieroglyphic captions that might have said, Young Egyptian Boys at Play. In another time, she realized sadly, they would be in the army, fighting Israeli boys across the boundary that separated their countries.

She had learned their names. One, bolder than the rest, smiled, revealing well-shaped white teeth. He picked up a blue lotus from his tray and presented it to her with a bow.

"For you, madam."

"But why?"

"Because you are beautiful, madam."

She smiled in spite of herself. He was so sweet and young.

"Thank you, Husani. It's lovely," she said, looking at the pointed leaves and bringing the intense fragrance closer to inhale deeply. "It is very kind of you."

"You are welcome, madam. Thank you, madam."

She didn't consider herself beautiful. Oh, maybe when she

was very young, but such a long time ago. Attractive, yes, a word that could encompass so much. Yet he flattered her. It didn't have to be true.

"Madam, may I ask you a personal question?"

Husani's face was suddenly serious.

"Yes, of course," she encouraged. "You may ask me anything at all."

"Why are you afraid of the sun?"

The question was so unexpected it startled her, and then she almost laughed out loud. Couldn't he see for himself how fair she was? Her skin was almost pure white, and her dark sunglasses protected her pale blue eyes. Even her hair, which was naturally blond, shielded now under an enormous sun hat, was almost platinum, and looked pink where the part divided it if she got too much exposure.

She and Paul were both fair, she thought, but she was lighter by far.

"I burn," she told Husani.

"Burn?"

"The sun is too strong for my skin. I'm not as used to it as you are."

"Ah," he said, and the stunning smile returned.

"But surely you must be afraid of something too," she went on.

The smile disappeared.

"Sometimes, yes, but only of people."

"People?"

"Yes, the bad ones."

"Well, of course," she said, in what she hoped was a comforting tone, "there are always those, aren't there?"

Her eyes lifted to the large rocks that rose on the side of the hotel, where the Bedouins had sat every day since they'd arrived. Only three today, but often there were as many as thirty. She had no binoculars, but they appeared to be smoking long pipes.

They did nothing, it seemed, but sit there and stare at the hotel. No matter where she was, or when she looked up, they were still in the same place, like birds perched for flight. She was certain that they never slept like normal people. At night, in the silence of the desert evenings, she could still feel them waiting. Perhaps they rotated their endless watch—some left to sleep, and others took their places.

"What do you suppose they want?" she asked Paul.

"Why ruin the last few days of our vacation thinking about it?"

For her husband, there were no secrets, no hidden mysteries. In his work as a litigator for a large law firm, reason reigned instead of emotions. She hadn't said any more about it, but still she looked up from time to time, distressed to see them still there.

She turned back. I would rather be afraid of the sun than of people, she was going to say, but he had already moved on to another couple, the only other Americans here, who appeared to be on their honeymoon.

They had seen this young couple at breakfast or dinner but never during the day, when they disappeared to their room, perhaps, or went diving or snorkeling to explore the coral reefs. She had heard the fish were beautiful here, strange and exotic species with equally strange names. The couple was athletic-looking: tall, slender, and muscular. When the young woman—though she seemed hardly more than a girl — rose to take a swim, all eyes were on her slim body, her flat stomach and slender hips. Elizabeth couldn't take her eyes off her, and she noticed that Paul, too, followed her graceful dive from the high board, her well-paced strokes.

The young people kept to themselves and only spoke to each other, out of shyness or perhaps reserve, or even the self-consciousness of being newlyweds, which reminded Elizabeth of her own long-ago honeymoon.

Elizabeth and Paul had been married for twenty years and had two children: Avi was 12 and his older sister Abby, who was 14. Both were at summer camp, and Paul insisted that it would be foolish not to take advantage of the chance for a little R&R in Israel.

"We can see where all our donations and fund-raising have gone over the years," Paul told her. He didn't add that it would also be a chance to rekindle their marriage, even though Elizabeth knew they were both hoping for that outcome.

Paul made the arrangements, and she had gone along with it — eventually, even with a last-minute change to conclude the trip in Egypt.

She was afraid to be in this part of the world, even though bad things could happen at home too, and often did. The world itself frightened her now, she had wanted to tell him. Everything seemed so unpredictable.

"You won't be sorry, Lizzie," Paul promised, and she had to admit that first day, it really was even lovelier than the pictures.

As they'd walked to the bus that would take them over the

border to the hotel, they had to chase away the Egyptian touts who wanted to carry their luggage a short distance.

"*La shukran,*" no thank you, "*la shukran…*"

Before they were permitted to get on the bus, they were ushered into a government station where their passports were examined. Three officials sat at a long table, although they were the only people there.

"Israeli?" one of them asked Elizabeth and Paul before they took out their passports.

"No, American," Elizabeth said quickly. The man looked up and smiled at her. She had cut her hair before coming, a mistake. It didn't match the image on her passport.

"So you have changed your hairstyle, madam?" he asked.

"I cut it short for the heat."

"You also like to travel, I see," he observed, riffling through the pages of their documents before he told them to open their luggage.

Paul's suitcase was neat, more methodically packed than hers, and yet it felt like a violation of their privacy to have the contents laid out on the table in front of them.

"A precaution," one of the men said, who had the task of going through them. "And what is that, madam?" he asked as he examined Elizabeth's belongings.

When she told them him that she used the little machine occasionally for sensitive lungs, he had not understood.

"I'm afraid, madam, that I must ask you to leave it here until you are on the way home. When you return, you may have it back."

She ignored him and took out the parts, the mask, and mouthpiece and demonstrated it.

"Ah, so, my mother also," he said after a few moments, and made exaggerated sounds of breathing, his English failing him before he beat his chest to show that he, himself, at least, was hale and hearty. "I no have."

He smiled and shook her hand, said something to his colleagues, who waved her through the formalities, along with Paul.

It was July and hot—the sun burned her skin right through her clothes. The prior week in Israel, they had gone to see all of the obligatory sights, littered along the way with destroyed tanks from other wars, left where they had met their fate.

It wasn't their first trip to Israel. Once, years ago, before the children were born, they'd been introduced to numerous officials and gone to one of the towns in the northernmost part of the nation, which was filled with immigrants—a dusty, ragged town, the victim of numerous attacks. Another time they'd been taken to the Ben Gurion Airport, near Tel Aviv, at two o'clock in the morning, to watch a jumbo jet come in with those same immigrants who were to be resettled there. Tears had welled in Elizabeth's eyes. She didn't want to be moved by mere sentimentality, but as the passengers, Russian Jews, embarked into freedom, blinking in the sudden glare after the long flight, she couldn't help weeping.

On their travels around the country on that trip, Elizabeth had once become lost in an Arab town. The guide found her and scolded her for her carelessness. She was afraid most of the time, looking over her shoulder. Bombs exploded without warning, and stabbings, she knew, happened almost every day. More than once, when she and Paul were out by themselves, strangers had come upon them so stealthily, begging for alms, that she hadn't even heard them. But it was the cab drivers that frightened her the most. Several times they'd had unpleasant encounters that left her shaken. One, especially, had stayed in her mind after they had hailed a driver and asked to return to their hotel.

"I want to show you Bethlehem," he had said, but he pronounced it like a native. "Beit-lehem," each syllable said distinctly.

"No," Paul responded, "not this time."

"Why you don't want to go?" he asked belligerently, as though their decision was a personal insult.

"Not today."

"Why you afraid?" he asked again.

"We have other plans," Paul said calmly.

Elizabeth glanced nervously at the locks on the door while the driver pounded his fist on the steering wheel, rage exploding on his face.

"Why you don't want to go?" he demanded once more. "Pretty place. Religious. Good place, I promise. Twenty dollars, American money, I take you. Is deal?"

Perhaps they would be kidnapped and murdered, Elizabeth thought. They had told no one where they were going. They had wanted to be alone, away from the relentless pressure of conversation and sightseeing. Perhaps because they were so fair, he didn't take them for Jews, and thought they were just being obstinate.

"I have a headache," Elizabeth said at last, putting one hand to her brow. "I don't feel well," which was not a lie.

Her voice sounded stilted and frightened, as though she was speaking English for the first time. In the afternoons, her head did indeed ache, and her eyes, after the hot, bright sun all day, needed a rest. Every afternoon she wanted to crawl beneath the cool sheets, with the wish that she could stay there for the rest of the visit and not have to see one more sight.

The man looked at her to see if she was telling the truth. She knew that her face must have looked as pale and clammy as she felt, because he sighed.

"Okay, lady, I take you back," he said, more quietly. "Next time you go to Bethlehem. You not be sorry."

Now they were older and things in Israel had changed, becoming even more complex and difficult.

Before they left Israel on this trip, they had visited the South African branch of Paul's family. After World War II, half of his family had come to the U.S. and half had gone to Johannesburg. Then, eventually, the South African branch came here to Israel.

Elizabeth had learned not to talk with them about politics—or religion. Good rules at home, but even more so in this country. Paul's Aunt Haya was driving them back to their hotel in Jerusalem, along a dangerous road—but she drove it all the time to work and back. Two women had been killed on that highway recently. Haya was used to having stones thrown at her car, people shouting, calling her names.

"What does it matter?" she said.

Nothing frightened her. She had become like a Sabra, a Jew born in Israel and named after the desert pear that's prickly on the outside and sweet on the inside.

Elizabeth found Haya difficult. She chain-smoked, and her language was straight to the point. Listening to Haya's hair-raising stories, Elizabeth felt she would not come out well in a test of courage. But, of course, she already knew that. She was even afraid to disagree with her.

"And where is the Hebrew?" Haya asked impatiently at the restaurant, picking up a menu to order, then tossing it aside after a few moments. "Do I have to break my teeth on English in the middle of Jerusalem?" She stamped out her cigarette in a saucer, angrily resuming her conversation. "They're trying to push us into the sea. They won't be satisfied until we are all dead." Her voice had risen, and she looked straight at Elizabeth. "We would not have this restaurant...We would not have this city...Tell me what would we have? We must fight for everything. We have no other choice."

When they left to come south, Elizabeth noticed the tanks and pointed guns protecting the plane as it left the runway. After they landed, their luggage and passports inspected, they rode a bus to the hotel, and for the first time, she understood what an oasis in the desert really meant. Of course, this was a man-made one, but it was a beautiful place.

As soon as they checked in, one of the young men behind the desk welcomed them, trying out his English as he described the amenities.

"We have dinner at six and eight, two seatings, an exercise room, the pool, of course, and a fabulous disco."

They dressed for dinner the first night and found only the pair of newlyweds, a large, noisy family, and a scattering of other guests. Elizabeth wore a peacock–blue sleeveless dress, Paul a white jacket and light, tan pants. Their server was named Ngozi, Elizabeth noted, as she glanced at his nameplate. She asked him what it meant.

"Blessed," he said, with a slight bow.

"Your parents named you well."

"Thank you, madam. Perhaps you will come to my father's house in Cairo one day. He will be honored."

"That would be lovely," she said, and tried to picture his father's house in her mind, the white blinds shut against the glare of the sun, the cool, dark rooms inside.

"And what does your father do there, Ngozi?"

"He is professor of English at university. He speak very good English, not like me. I try to learn, too. I learn in school, but not speak well."

"No, no," she insisted. "It is very good, indeed. Much better than my Arabic," she added with a smile.

"Thank you, madam," he said.

"What should we have, Ngozi?" she asked, so that he could enjoy helping them.

He chose well. White bean salad with tomato basil vinaigrette, Egyptian lamb and eggplant, and pineapple rice for dessert, with a surprise that he brought them after they were finished — cups of espresso and wedges of Egyptian chocolate cake.

There was a surfeit of servers. As soon as they took a piece of the delicious onion bread, the basket was whisked away to be replenished. Another boy brought flower-shaped pats of butter, and someone else filled their water glasses, while a wine steward poured more wine.

After dinner, Ngozi bowed again as they left.

"Madam, Sir, I will see you in the morning." His face was so hopeful, so eager, that Elizabeth already knew that she would miss him when they left.

Except for the young American couple, with whom they had

only exchanged smiles and a few words of greeting, none of the other guests spoke English. There was nothing to do after dinner but walk around the hotel, and there were so few people it was beginning to feel uncomfortable, reminding Elizabeth and Paul of a stunning art museum that was devoid of pictures. Tourism had declined, they'd been told, after the borders changed, and now attacks against tourists had kept even more away.

The disco, when they peered in, was deserted, except for the noisy family they'd seen at dinner, whose children tried to catch the elusive motes of a disco ball that spun dazzling lights around the floor. The honeymooners strolled by, looked in as well, and continued on their way without speaking.

The young woman had tucked a flower behind her ear, perhaps the same kind of flower that Husani had given Elizabeth, accompanied by the same compliment. If he had, then he was right. She was beautiful, wearing an elegant sundress that set off her tan, her long, dark hair cascading down her back rather than twisted into a bun as she wore it for swimming.

Elizabeth felt a twinge of envy for this couple just starting out. Everything was fresh and new for them, without the differences that inevitably crept into a longer marriage like her own.

Next to the disco, on the balcony facing the beach at the northern tip of the Red Sea, the Gulf of Aqaba, she realized that she would be able to see four countries at once from the water: Egypt and Israel to her left, Jordan, on the opposite shore, and Saudi Arabia in the distance. Ferries left daily from here to Jordan, a land like this one, filled with thousands, or millions, of people Elizabeth and Paul didn't know, and to whom their lives meant nothing.

"How far away?" she asked, hoping her husband would know.

"I heard someone say a few miles."

"A few miles! You could almost swim there."

They walked the length of the terrace to the side overlooking the pool. At night, the bright sunlight gone, even the water looked sinister, with dark fronds overhead that swept their shadows across it as if they bore seeds of evil and might explode at any moment. Something shifted in the night air. Above them, the moon shone brightly in the sky, revealing the sitting figures of the Bedouins.

"They're still there," Elizabeth said, as if they should be gone because she wanted them to be. "But what on earth are they *doing*? They seem to be waiting for something."

Even later, when they made love, she looked up through the slits in the blinds to see if they were there. Each night, before she went to sleep, she would throw open the shutters to determine if they had finally left, a kind of game she played.

She thought of Paul's intrepid Aunt Haya. How dismissive she would be of Elizabeth if she found out that she was afraid of such a harmless, silent presence.

In the morning, she asked Husani if he knew anything about them.

"They sit on ancient caravan route of their fathers," he said simply.

The news calmed her. Of course, it made perfect sense. Territorial rights thousands of years old. They were protecting ancestral land that the hotel had appropriated.

She and Paul had talked of leaving, but now an airline strike began overnight, so they decided to stay a bit longer, settling into contented, lazy days of swimming and relaxing, each day blending into the next. It was summer, after all. The children, thank God, were still at camp.

Occasionally they took guided car trips in the surrounding area, exploring the bays and lagoons and coastline. They visited a tiny inlet where a fortress still stood, built by Crusaders to exact ransom from passing pilgrims and occupied a few years later by a sultan. They were taken to colorful canyons in the desert, walls streaked with stunning shades of gold, magenta, purple; they crossed vast stretches of endless barren land that dwarfed everything else. And stood in awe before an ancient monastery set into the granite rock of rugged mountains, which contained a room holding the skulls of departed monks.

A few Egyptian guests passed through the hotel, the women in their *niqabs* and *khimars*, the men, wearing white robes and checkered head scarves. There were small dramas and even some changes. Ngozi left for a day or two to see his father, who was ill, and Elizabeth could hardly wait for him to return. Husani's job had been changed to handing out towels to the few swimmers at the pool. How young he was, she thought, and yet he took his tasks seriously, with an ever-present smile. She could not imagine such a life for her own son, who was the same age.

A couple arrived with a baby named Mohammad and an entourage of grandparents and other assorted relatives, fussing over the infant, no different from families anywhere.

The honeymoon couple, whose names they had discovered were Tom and Melissa, now brought out thick books to study. Elizabeth tried to piece together their lives from fragments. They resembled the children of many of her friends, obviously married while they were still in school. People she would never see again, and yet they had become as real to her as her own family.

Ngozi, who'd come back from Cairo with good news about his father, was waiting for them to come down to breakfast. But they took only a roll and coffee, and picked up a lunch they had ordered from the kitchen to eat on the beach later. They were eager to do some snorkeling among the coral reefs close to shore before they left.

Tom and Melissa, who'd spent most of their days up to now diving, must have decided to lounge on the beach. They were still immersed in their studies, sitting apart from everyone else, engrossed in a world of their own making. Even though Elizabeth had barely spoken with them, their familiar faces and steady calm pleased her as she sank into the warmth and beauty of the day.

Boats were scattered haphazardly on the horizon, scuba divers geared up for action, and swimmers with their snorkeling antennae flecked the open expanse of the water. The day beckoned to them, unfolding exquisitely like an offering from the gods who had once reigned here. The blue of the sky was reflected in the water, serenely transparent and as clear as glass, a dramatic contrast to the stark mountains and desert. The coral reefs were ancient, Elizabeth had read, at least five thousand years old, longer than all the peoples who had passed this way. They had been here at least two thousand years before Moses found his way to Mount Sinai.

Finning over the reefs, Elizabeth saw that beneath the placid surface a whole universe existed, invisible to the earth-bound eye—a world of predators and power, of victims and survivors. Brilliant colors, odd, undulating shapes, protective camouflage: she tried to match them to their exotic names, but mostly failed. She was a stranger here, yet they ignored her as she swept past them, pleasant hosts who, as long as she didn't disturb anything, were happy to let her look around for a while.

Paul's shadowy form swam nearby, an aquatic being now beneath the water, wearing those ridiculous-looking antennae and mask, and fins, disguised like other inhabitants of this unfamiliar place. The masked man, she thought. He might have been a stranger for all she knew. You could live with someone a long time and still not know everything about him.

Had this vacation changed anything in their marriage? Or would they return the same people they had been before? Tomorrow was their last day to cram in some sightseeing. A bird sanctuary, an animal park, some caves and other sites they had not seen. Home seemed far away, like a distant mirage. Away from everything familiar, sometimes you could see your own life more clearly. In those watery depths everything floated away until there was nothing but a gentle peace washing over her. But she knew it was a peace that could be deceptive. There was a whole world seething beneath it.

Before she went to sleep that night, she stepped out on the balcony and looked up for the customary figures. She felt first puzzlement, and then disbelief.

"You won't believe this..."

"What's that?" Paul asked.

"Those people..."

"Which ones?"

"The ones who have been sitting on the rock since we arrived."

"What about them?"

"They're gone—just like that. What do you suppose..."

"They probably got tired of having you stare at them every day."

"Oh, Paul!"

"Either that or they found something better to do with their time."

Something was wrong. She felt it. Why would the men have left of their own will? After the strenuous activity of the day, Paul was already asleep, but she lay awake for a long time thinking about their disappearance.

Then, as she sank into her dreams, the brooding figures swept down on them to take back their land.


The next morning, there were already other tourists on the bus when the driver pulled up to their hotel. Tom and Melissa were waiting, as quiet as ever. Instead of merely nodding as before, Melissa smiled, and Elizabeth smiled back, hoping that at last she would open up and chat for a few minutes, but they quickly boarded the vehicle once the driver got out and took their tickets.

Melissa looked to be no older than her early twenties, Elizabeth thought, especially this morning, without any makeup, wearing a white T-shirt and khaki shorts, her long hair, still wet, done in a single braid that cascaded down her back. Tom was checking his guidebook, absorbed in reading, wearing a matching outfit. Perhaps they would still be here after Paul and Elizabeth left, in no rush to return to school and a routine.

Another couple, about Paul and Elizabeth's age, who arrived recently, ran out just as the driver was ready to pull away, afraid they would be left behind. The woman was wearing a black dress, despite the heat, and had a black purse slung over her shoulder; the man carried a pair of binoculars around his neck. Surely not Americans, Elizabeth thought, which was confirmed as soon as they spoke.

The other passengers, at the back of the bus, were a large family group who spoke animatedly among themselves in an unfamiliar language, and a well-dressed couple who sat sedately in their seats looking out the window, talking in low voices barely above a whisper.

Tom and Melissa took two front seats, Paul and Elizabeth sat just behind them, and the new couple took the ones just behind the driver. Elizabeth could smell the scent of Melissa's hair drifting around her, the fragrance of gardenias in the shampoo and soap she must have used at the hotel. A few empty seats remained. The bus driver said something she couldn't understand, uncertain if it was Arabic or English. She heard a low murmur from the passengers in the back as they got underway, incomprehensible words from somewhere across the globe. Elizabeth felt comforted by the presence of these strangers, all of them intent on the same purpose — merely to enjoy the day and to learn something about the country where they were staying.

Paul took out his camera.

"I'm not missing these shots," he said, adjusting the settings and pointing the lens out the window as the bus rolled along unfamiliar roads, past craggy rocks, and the arid soil of an endless desert far from the water. Perhaps it was the early hour, but the roads were nearly deserted apart from a few vans of families, belongings tied to the roof of their vehicles and curious children waving to them from the back seats.

They also saw Bedouins, methodically making their way across the land, some on camels, others walking with sticks. The immensity of the desert was overwhelming. Its raw enormity dwarfed everything else, the ancient rocks and rugged stones that like the oceans had existed thousands and even millions of years ago and still endured.

Elizabeth began to feel vulnerable again, out here in the midst of nowhere, an interloper who had wandered here by mistake. One could understand the search for a protector in all of that vastness. The desert seemed devoid of creatures, but within these rocks and underground, surely some were staring back at them, though many might be nocturnal. At night, lightless except for the moon and stars, people must have felt that grandeur, mixed with a longing for comfort so sharp that it was painful.

The road stretched ahead of them, seemingly endless and silent until a number of motorcycles passed by them with a roar of their engines. One had a sidecar and a passenger: all were driven by bearded young men wearing dark glasses.

The ride seemed interminable, but after an hour the driver turned off the road and drove onto a path that made its way through the rocks, the bus bumping along on the dirt. At last he came to a stop and stood, announcing their arrival and pointing to where they would have to walk a few yards to reach their destination, a place with no name and nothing but silence.

Paul put away his camera, eager to view the sanctuary, and waited in the aisle while Tom stood aside so that Melissa could get off first. Then, just as they were descending the steep steps, Paul moving ahead to help Elizabeth, the motorcycle with the sidecar she had seen before pulled up with a screech of tires.

A bearded young man in sunglasses jumped out, and looking straight at them as they descended, pulled a semi-automatic rifle from the sidecar.

"No!" Paul cried.

But then there was an awful accelerating pop-pop-pop and a line of sand puffing up as the man sprayed a volley of shots.

Tom and Melissa, still in front, were the first to be hit, falling down to the ground without a sound.

Paul began to run toward the man with his hands up, in supplication.

"Stop...Stop!" he yelled, his words cut off as he was shot in the leg and fell next to Melissa and Tom, their beautiful young bodies torn with bullets, white T-shirts turning crimson, blood seeping into the dirt.

"Oh, God! No!"

Melissa's beautiful face, her smooth, tanned skin, was mutilated beyond recognition.

"Stop! Please stop!" Elizabeth pleaded. "Why are you hurting us? What have we done?"

Deaf to her appeal, the man lifted the weapon and began firing again, shattering the windows of the bus. The driver, who shouted at the killers in a language the men seemed to understand, was caught by another round, and fell down the steps at their feet.

The two assailants spoke rapidly to each other, mimicking the rapid-fire sound of the gunfire, and then laughed, a terrible laugh like a voice from the gates of hell. Then the angry young man raised his rifle, shot out the bus's tires to make sure there would be no escape, and for good measure let loose another volley at the screaming, terrified passengers before the motorcycle sped away as abruptly as it had come.

It had happened so fast Elizabeth hadn't had time to be frightened. But in the aftermath, she was shaking and weak, retching into the earth and trying to catch her breath.

Paul's face was contorted in pain as she went to help him. He had a gaping hole in his thigh, oozing blood.

The only sounds were moaning and sobbing. The driver lay on the steps where he had been shot, groping for his phone to call for help. Elizabeth tore off her blouse and tied it around Paul's leg, just above the wound, knotting it as tightly as she could to make a feeble tourniquet—enough, she hoped, to stop her husband's bleeding

Then she ran over and knelt beside Melissa's and Tom's horribly maimed bodies, two children far from home. Her grief ran so deep she would have given her own life to save them.

Elizabeth spent the night at the hospital with Paul, but neither of them slept.

There was nothing to say. They lay silently in the dark. Paul's leg had been treated by a kindly young doctor. "Good job with the tourniquet," he said, smiling at them.

It would be a while before Paul could walk. For now, he would have to use crutches. They arrived home—at the hotel that had become their home—the next day, after meeting with the police. Elizabeth learned with sorrow that the couple who had been afraid they would be left behind, just reaching the tour bus before it pulled away, were also among the dead.

The police took Paul and Elizabeth's names and address in case they were needed for further questioning. The bodies of the two young people were to be shipped to that nameless place where they had come from to parents who would wonder how such an unspeakable thing could have happened. Perhaps they would want to contact Paul and Elizabeth. Perhaps not. Maybe they didn't want to hear the terrible details.

'We'll go home, Lizzie," Paul said. "We're all right. Home to our children and our lives. In time we'll even forget. My leg will heal. All this will be just a remote memory, as though it happened to someone else."

But he was wrong that she would ever forget, and he probably knew it, Elizabeth thought. Perhaps the grief would become dimmer with time, but she was certain that the memory of Tom and Melissa's deaths would never leave them, no matter how long they lived.

The morning after they returned to the hotel, when she woke up she pulled on a robe to open the veranda doors. It seemed as though the distress of what had happened would be washed away in the brilliant sunshine. At such an early hour, the water was stunning, a primeval force that renewed itself each day, regardless of what had happened on land.

Another young couple sat huddled together at the pool. More people were out on the water, diving to explore the reefs, oblivious to any danger. Others sat on the beach. Everyone knew about what had happened, but the tragedy had happened to someone else, people they didn't know. How many times had she turned the page after reading of another catastrophe in the world because it had nothing to do with her?

Then she saw them. They were back, as though they had never been gone. Could she have been imagining it, then? But no, she was certain that they had not been there a few days before.

"They're here," she said.

"Who?" Paul said irritably, his voice still groggy with sleep.

"The Bedouins," she said.

"Damn it, Lizzie. What does it matter now?"

"It just does."

He got out of bed with effort, to see for himself, making his way painfully to the open doors. He stepped outside and looked at the figures with their white *kaffiyehs* and long, flowing robes.

"Ask them, for God's sake, Lizzie. Ask them where they've been."

"I'm not sure anyone knows," she said quietly.

"Have they found out who was responsible?" Paul demanded of Ngozi when they went down to breakfast. "Was it the Beduoins?"

"Ah, no, sir. They were questioned, of course, but this seems to be another group—those who also wish to discourage tourists from coming."

"The honeymoon couple that stayed here was murdered in the attack," Elizabeth said, trying to keep her voice steady.

"I'm sorry, madam. Perhaps we will know more at a later time. It is over now. The guilty parties will be found and dealt with by the government."

"How can you be so sure?" Elizabeth asked, aware of how quickly grief could turn to the anger surging through her, ready to erupt, but his face was impassive.

She wanted to know. It could have been them, she thought, aware of how close they had come to being killed themselves.

They would leave, but this place would remain in her memory, jogged loose when she remembered Tom and Melissa, and the brooding figures sitting on the cliffs above them.

Paul would never acknowledge the irrational forces that could take over the world, overpowering logic, until it was too late. But Elizabeth knew that there was always reason to be afraid, that the graceful palms and quiet were all an illusion, like the peaceful life of the fish under the sea.

How terrible to be murdered, butchered by people who knew nothing about you, really, but were themselves the unwitting prisoners of ancient and intractable forces. How helpless we are to resist the finality of our own inevitable death, which might come when we least expect it, on a brilliant, sunny day like any other day, taking you by surprise with its fierceness and its finality.

# Miracles: A Novella

LIFE IS FULL OF MIRACLES, Sonya thought.

Her own life was an example. She had come to America, not once but twice. The first time she had been the oldest of three children, traveling from a village near Kiev with her family. Times were hard and getting worse, which made it more difficult for the Jews, who suffered even in good times. Many were leaving. The town was as empty as a glass of water that had been spilled, until there was barely a drop to drink. Every evening through the long, dark winter her father, Yankel Danelovich, sat silently brooding with a glass of tea as he drew up plans, muttering, "Why stay here and die like a dog?"

"What will happen to the children?" her mother cried, peering out into the darkness. "God forbid if we meet a robber on the road or worse."

Sonya's mother, Tirzah, had weak lungs. She was deathly pale, more so after she gave birth a few years ago. There were times when she had to stay all day in bed.

"I suppose you want us to wait until we're eating black dirt in our graves. Is that what you want?" her father asked. "Don't you see? They're forcing us to leave. Half the village is already gone. There is no choice anymore." Yankel Danelovich's face grew flushed. "I've made the decision. We'll travel to Warsaw, then board a train to Gdańsk. It will be easier. There are not too many who leave from there."

"And the border?" Tirzah questioned, suspicious of his easy confidence.

"I have figured that out, too," he said. "The agents are crooked. They take advantage of others and rob them blind, but a bribe will get us over. We'll go in the spring. Once a decision is made, there is no turning back."

Sonya's father was a simple man, a blacksmith, but used to taking charge, known for his strength and for dancing the *kazatsky* at weddings. He had a voice that rocked the room when he spoke. His footsteps pounded on the floors and his snoring could wake the dead. He liked a glass of schnapps, a good joke, and having his feet rubbed after he took off his boots.

Sonya's mother knew there was no arguing with him when he had made up his mind. She sold her wedding jewelry and her brass samovar that stood at the table's edge steaming a tuneful melody, so that when company came tea could be served with almond cookies. Also the household furnishings, until they were living surrounded by four walls and little else.

Yankel's shop would have to be sold as well. Besides shoes for horses, he made parts for harnesses, stirrups for their riders, and fittings for carts and wagons. Tools were also forged: knives, weapons, locks, keys, and hinges. A fire raged there, winter or summer, changing according to what he was fashioning. He fanned the fire with a large bellows as red and yellow shards of flame and black soot licked the air. Yankel's face glowed from the flames, his beard a fiery tangle of crimson. To Sonya it looked like the fires of hell.

One night he woke them from their beds and said roughly, "Get up. It's time."

The wagon and horses were ready. Tirzah Danelovich placed feather beds on the straw, a few photographs and other possessions, baskets of food that would see them through until they got to the next stop, a couple nights' journey, where they would stay with their uncle, Yankel's brother.

It was several years before the Revolution. They left behind a wooden house with a straw thatched roof, chickens pecking in the dirt, neighbors gossiping, and relatives as poor and beleaguered as themselves, who pleaded with Yankel Danelovich not to leave them behind.

Sonya shivered. The night reminded her of a dream, one in which she felt as though she was walking on air. The moon cast luminescent pools of light like pearls on the ground. There was a scent of pine needles. She breathed deeply. Perhaps she would never smell them again.

"Where are we going?" the youngest, little Isaac, cried sleepily.

"Off to America!" his father exclaimed.

"When will we be there?"

"God willing in a few weeks."

"Why not tomorrow?"

"Get in!"

Yankel said this so loudly that the child started crying again and Sonya had to comfort him.

"It's over the sea, Isaac," she explained. "We will sail on the water for many days," although she only half believed it herself. "But first we have to travel on by wagon and then by train to the boat. That's why it will be so long."

"I'm afraid," he said.

She didn't tell him that she was, too.

"*Sha!*" Tirzah Danelovich said. "You're frightening the children."

Yankel ignored her, stared straight ahead and slapped his whip. The horses stamped their hooves and snorted, and soon the house where she was born was behind them—the ground where Sonya had walked barefoot, the flowers that were just beginning to bloom, the horse-chestnut trees blossoming, sweetly scented candles of white bouquets that she would knock down with sticks if no one was looking, stuffing the nut holes with matches to fashion miniature animals. The storks had come back to build nests. And next door, the neighbor child she had often taken care of, Nadija, with a weak heart and lame besides.

Yes, perhaps the world itself was only an illusion and they were all apparitions that would soon disappear. She pinched her flesh until it hurt so that she could be certain she was alive as they rocked past the cemetery where only the dead lay, the tombstones in the form of tree trunks whose branches had been severed, the two synagogues, the small shops where they had purchased bags of flour and fabric to make a dress for her sister Basha and pants and a jacket for her brother.

The little ones fell asleep, and in the soft murmuring of the night the stars spread over the sky like so many glittering jewels against a background that was deep and black, as though she could fall into the vast sea above them. The tips of the trees kissed each other, shielding the family from harm, forming a canopy of leafy branches, the wind at her back singing her name — *Sonya! Sonya! Don't leave!*

But she had. They all had.

The towns they passed through looked alike: the muddy streets after the thaw and rain, bits of snow clinging to the hillsides and dirty chunks melting in the streams. They passed by cows grazing in pastures, flocks of sheep, children playing in yards or going out to their chores, waving.

Every so often her father stopped the wagon by the flowing water to let the horses rest and the children play.

Sonya lifted her skirt and went wading.

"Watch the current," she warned as her sister Basha followed her. "It will pull you in if you're not careful. The cold water will make you gasp and your clothes will drag you down."

Basha waded timorously into the water.

'It's too cold," she cried at once. She was timid and shy. She had to be prodded to do anything new.

"Don't say I didn't warn you," Sonya told her.

At times Basha resembled a porcelain doll with her blond ringlets and rosebud lips. Every few minutes she would ask Sonya to tell her a story. So Sonya made them up as she went along, taking the parts of each character, imitating the sounds of people and animals.

The icy cold made her feel alive. She wiggled her toes so that they looked like tiny fish swimming. Her body was sore from the constant jostling of the wagon. She filled a cup with water and passed it around to the younger children and then settled them for naps before lying down herself in the hot sun that entered her body like food and drink.

Later her mother drew out baskets from the wagon and spread black bread, herring, and onions on a cloth. They ate hungrily while their father tended to the horses and lay in the grass, soon fast asleep, his chest moving up and down, his lips muttering something unintelligible. Suddenly he awoke, stumbled to his feet, and rubbed his eyes.

"Do you think we have all day? We have to press on ahead before nightfall. Don't you know they're expecting us?"

At their uncle's house they would sleep in real beds and eat a pudding with noodles and raisins. An outhouse instead of squatting in the woods with the grass tickling their bottoms. The boys had it easier, Sonya thought. Only a few weeks ago she had started her first period.

She had brought cloths, but where would she wash them? Where would they wash anything? She was self-conscious now, as though just by looking at her everyone knew. Thumbprints appeared beneath her eyes and her stomach hurt before the blood flowed, as though she had eaten rotten fruit.

She had a cousin here, Irina. She was taller than Sonya, but otherwise it was like looking in a mirror. Her hair was dark, as black and glossy as her own, but her skin was lighter so that in summer freckles dotted her nose. Her green eyes caught the flecks of golden light that shone from the lamp.

"What will you find in America?" Irina asked.

"I'm not sure."

"What will you do there?"

"Something useful. I want to help people."

"And how will you do that?"

"Perhaps I will become a nurse," Sonya said. "I have been thinking about it. I helped Mama when little Isaac was born. I have been taking care of a neighbor's child who is lame."

She remembered the way Nadija had clung to her, weeping when Sonya told her she was leaving.

"You're clever," her cousin said. "I envy you. There is nothing here, but I have to stay all the same."

While the mothers were busy with the younger children, the fathers sat at the table talking. Their uncle, Pinchas, was tall and lean and thoughtful, as if her father and his brother had come from separate families.

He reflected on the wisdom of the journey. "And what will you find?" Pinchas asked. "You'll never see any of us again," he went on without waiting for an answer. "You will lose your family and your faith. You'll disappear into the abyss — like all the others," he added.

He drew on his pipe and considered the matter, speaking clearly and deliberately as he continued.

"We will stay here. Either way we are in exile. Yes, they hate us, but at least we can pray, and perhaps God will hear our prayers one day and take us to the land of our fathers. In time, after the peasants have their fun with us, this pogrom will blow over. But who knows what lies ahead in this strange place where you are going?"

His face had become more animated, his speech faster the longer he spoke.

"I have a job," Yankel said.

"And is there a need for a blacksmith in America?"

"I will work in a factory." Yankel replied with satisfaction. "I will no longer be a blacksmith."

"As you wish," his brother said. "You have children, responsibilities. There is no shirking that wherever you are."

"That's true. Of course it's true," he said. Then, as he contemplated the import of his words, his face grew dark. "What are you suggesting? That I would desert my own family?"

They were like Jacob and Esau, Sonya thought. Whenever they saw each other, angry words flew back and forth.

"I am not suggesting anything of the sort," his brother said matter-of-factly. "I am simply mentioning it." He fell silent, tapping his pipe on the table. Then he said, "Many people believe that there is still a place for us here."

"A leopard doesn't change its spots," Yankel replied at last. "We will go."

"Yes," Pinchas agreed, "sometimes that is true, "but I will hope for the best. I refuse to run like a scared chicken."

"That is where we differ," Yankel retorted. His temper flared as if the bellows in his shop had roused it from embers.

When Yankel and his family left, though, the brothers threw their arms around each other. It didn't matter who was right, Sonya thought. One thing was certain. They would never see each other again.

Tension rippled through the air. Sonya listened intently to the murmuring voices in the front of the wagon.

"We'll stop on this side of the border tonight at an inn where I'll sell the horses and wagon. Then someone will take us to the other side before we cross into Poland. Then on to Lublin and finally to Warsaw."

"And how will we do that," her mother asked cautiously, "without a passport?"

"I have a name," her father said.

"A name?" Tirzah repeated. "And just who is this name?"

"Why do you always have to question everything?"

Her mother was silent. She had wrapped another shawl around herself. She was always cold. Her mouth was set in a thin line. Her shoulders sank as though the weight of the whole world was pulling her down. She had been sick during the winter. Consumption beat at her lungs and made her breath short.

Yankel had fitted a tarp over the wagon of burlap sacks and Sonya snuggled down on the featherbed beneath them to keep warm.

"Are we there yet?" little Isaac asked every few minutes.

"Go back to sleep," Sonya told him. "I'll wake you when it's time."

Basha, quiet as always, kept to herself. They were passing other families more frequently now, all headed in the same direction. Children peered over the edge of the wagons and stared at them. Sometimes they waved or called in greeting, made faces or stuck out their tongues, bored with traveling.

At last, when she thought that she could no longer endure the bouncing of the wagon or the rain, lights appeared in the distance and gradually grew larger. Sonya felt a thrill of excitement. Smoke curled from the chimney of a wooden building. A muddy yard was filled with wagons and people, all talking at once.

Her father stayed in the yard taking care of the horses. Inside the inn, a fire glowed and threw its warmth around the room. Children wandered everywhere, crying for attention and something to eat. Conversations animated the air. Plans and routes were shared, as well as experiences on the road.

"Once you get on the train at Warsaw you're on your way," one man was saying.

"At Hamburg they have dormitories and dining halls with kosher food," said another.

"And a place where you have to stay before you get on the ship to make sure that you're not sick."

"If you're sick they send you back."

"Who decides?" a woman asked. She was spooning food into a baby's mouth. The child reminded Sonya of a bird plucking worms out of its mother's beak.

"Who do you think?" the man retorted. "They have nurses and doctors there. If you cough they think you've got the lung disease and the game is up. They won't take you on the ship. You think they want to deliver dead bodies? Or worse yet, have to throw them overboard?"

"The trip is hard even for the healthy. One year there was a measles epidemic and many died, not only children."

Sonya heard her father's heavy footsteps entering the room. He had sold the horses and wagon, and counted out the money carefully for their food, putting the rest away. So they were really going, cut adrift even from those steady, loyal beasts.

Sonya kept spooning thick soup with vegetables into her mouth and chewing slices of crusty bread.

"Hungry," little Isaac said.

Basha gobbled up the food, as if afraid it would disappear and she would be famished again, her belly aching with hunger.

"More," they cried.

Sonya spooned some of her own soup into their bowls. The men continued talking animatedly until the children, unable to hold their eyes open any longer, fell asleep on the hard benches next to her. They were talking about the borders.

"You need someone to take you across. More cash for a bribe, or you could be stuck unless you wanted to chance it yourself."

"Do you think I'm crazy? Who would risk it? Anything could happen. You might wind up losing everything and having to return where you came from, poorer than before."

One of the men, not young, with a deeply lined face, got up and strummed a balalaika softly, then began singing a mournful song about a poor orphan boy who had lost his parents and sister and was alone in the world. It was like a party, Sonya thought, but a sad one. Yes, a party made up of strangers who had not known each other even hours before but joined together in a few minutes—all Jews, who would make a leap together into an unknown world where they knew almost no one.

The women began weeping as they thought of loved ones who would be left behind. Sonya's mother brushed tears from her eyes, grieving for her widowed sister with eight children, nearly penniless, who would have to fend for herself now. Who knew where they were going? Or how long it would be? Across an ocean? They couldn't fathom such a thing. They had only traveled a few *verst* in their whole lives. Some said the trip was days—others, that it took weeks.

"A fearful voyage," a man shouted and downed the last drops of a pint of liquor. "A voyage from hell!"

Sonya had heard enough. She went to help with the children. The men slept in one place, the women and little ones in another. Before it grew light they would continue on their way.

———

When she awoke it was still dark and cold. She shivered with foreboding as she and her mother gathered up Basha and little Isaac and took some hard rolls to eat later. Someone was talking to her father, asking to see his papers. A man on horseback with a gun was telling them to go ahead. He looked at Sonya. She shrank back, frightened.

"Don't be slow about it either," he said, and turned around to stare at her again. She felt herself blushing in the dark.

They all got into another wagon with a stranger who would take them over the border at Chelm. She covered the children with a blanket as they came closer. There were voices again, questions, the rustle of the trees, the click of rifles. And then she heard a voice.

"All clear."

"You see, what did I tell you?" Yankel exclaimed.

By the time the sun rose they were on their way to Lublin and then on to Warsaw, where tracks went in every direction carrying trains billowing steam, noisy beasts out of a fairytale, reminding Sonya of dragons breathing fire and black smoke.

"A ticket to Gdańsk," her father said at the station, where hundreds of passengers rushed chaotically here and there.

"So you're going to America with all the rest?"

"What's it to you?"

"The train will take you all day," he said, "longer than a team of horses."

"Too late to turn back now," Yankel said and slapped the money on the counter. "Even if I wanted to."

"And now you got the tickets as well," the man said, counting out the money he received and sliding them beneath the wire cage that separated them. "Don't think it's that easy. You still have to get your papers in order before they let you on the ship. They'll check you from your arse to your eyeballs before that'll happen."

It took them all day and more to get there. A miracle, Sonya thought, as fields and rivers sped by, roads and woods and meadows and hills taking flight like silvery birds, as though they were flying through the sky. It seemed that they had been gone for a year instead of a couple of days. How strange not to be anywhere at all, but simply traveling from one place to another without a home, not knowing where they would spend the night or who would be there.

Her father had already struck up a conversation with a man going to Gdańsk. The man was heading to a place in America called Po Kip See, the strangest name that Sonya had ever heard. Would all the names in America sound like that?

"It's Indian. Not Indians like the people in India," the man explained, "but the savages in America who roam around the country, scalping people if they have a mind to.

"And where is that?" Yankel asked, alarmed.

"In the wild west. If you want to go to America you have to know something. Otherwise people will take you for a greenhorn and steal the shirt right off your back while they're shaking your hand."

He had a sister in Po Kip See who had sent him the money for passage and was waiting for him to come any day now. He held up a book that he was using to study English.

I can say, "My name is Lazar Fierbush."

Sonya repeated it to herself slowly.

"My . . . name . . . is . . . Lazar Fierbush."

How strange the words sounded. How could anyone speak a language like that? Why hadn't she been told that no one would be able to understand a word she uttered?

Lazar Fierbush kept talking. His wife was dead and his children didn't want him. He woke up one day and decided to go to America. It was as simple as that.

In Gdańsk, the women gathered in groups and took out their needlework, speaking with people they would never see again, trading stories as though they had known them all their lives, exchanging recipes they had once cooked in their own kitchens—plum dumplings, stuffed goose neck, apple strudel, their eyes moist with memory.

The men played cards. The families stayed near the water at the edge of the world, staring out at the waves, watching the ships docked at the port while they waited their turn to depart, a day in April after the Feast of Unleavened Bread, the past behind them, the future beckoning, waiting to take a voyage to another, unknown world.

The day they boarded the boat, the sky was black and a storm was brewing. Sonya felt that she was stepping into the mouth of a gigantic whale. Perhaps it was like the whale that swallowed Jonah. Would it truly ferry them across that vast ocean? How could the water stretch from one side of the world to another? The surface was calm, but she had heard men say that once you were away from land, storms raged and lashed the ship so hard they thought it was going to split in two. And who knew what would happen then? They were at the mercy of the unknown.

Sonya took Basha's hand when she hung back, although she was trembling herself. Her mother carried little Isaac. Her father hoisted their bundles and belongings. In the belly of the ship, as dark and damp as a dungeon, they would sleep on hard pallets arranged in bunks, surrounded by hundreds of other people.

Her mother began to cry again, though softly.

"A coffin of water," Tirzah wept, "instead of black dirt."

"Quiet, woman," Yankel shouted so loudly that everyone turned and stared at him. "There's no turning back."

Sonya rooted in their bundles to find something to shield them from the other families, who were also hanging shawls and scarves to mark off their space, wrangling more room from the family next to them. She carved out a place, found out the times that food would be served, and took charge of the children.

Her mother would only eat bread, herring, and tea, afraid of eating forbidden food, but Yankel scoffed at her.

"Do you think God wants us to starve?"

A barrel of herring was on deck if they wanted it, but the soup was watered down, with mealy potatoes, and gruel that Sonya could barely swallow. Once the ship was out on the sea, tossing them around like playthings, however, Isaac and Basha lost their appetite and took to their beds. Her father moaned, trying to drown his woes in drink. In days Tirzah had grown yellow and wizened.

Ten of the men formed a *minyan*, but only a few were able to join in prayer after the first few days. Even the hearty Hasidim in their black coats had taken to their beds.

The stench of flatulence, waste and vomit, the pails of one or the other, the unwashed bodies, the threat of death and destruction that hovered over them as they traveled to this golden land, the endless sea and storms all made Sonya feel ill, but she was the only one in her family who hadn't completely succumbed. The stink was unbearable. She thought she would die if she didn't get away for a few minutes from the constant chatter and clatter, the woman next to her who kept complaining.

"Watch your step, young lady. I've got my eye on you."

Sometimes she would go up on the deck to get a breath of fresh air, letting the mist spray her face. She looked for whales, a spout of water thrust into the air, to relieve the tedium. Occasionally seabirds flew overhead, alabaster forms silhouetted against a mass of leaden gray clouds that took on a patina of gloom. Surely there must be land nearby.

"Steady now," one of the black-hatted men said when she slid on a puddle. She had seen him pacing back and forth. He always carried a book behind his back as he walked, although of course he couldn't read it in all that chaos.

"Do you think we will ever see land?" Sonya asked.

"If God wills it," was the answer.

"And if he doesn't, what then? Do you really think that God will save you?"

Did everything happen because of God's plan? She didn't think so.

No reply.

During the black of night, when darkness swept over the world in the tomb where they lay as though they were only incidental, was God really watching to protect them from harm? Or was it another joke that was passed from generation to generation? Was God a jokester who played tricks on the unwary?

Unable to sleep she would sneak to an upper deck and stand perfectly still, listening to the thundering of the waves beneath a sky that was as dark as coal, nights when even the moon was obscured. Once, as she peered into the watery abyss that must surely contain the answer to a mystery if only she could unlock it, a small body in a white shroud was brought to the railing and slipped over the side.

Before long, almost everyone was not just seasick but truly ill: by turns, her mother who lay shivering like death itself, her father in a drunken stupor, her sister Basha. And little Isaac.

She took care of them all, but looking at Isaac, his fierce little face and stubble of a nose, his tiny body burning up, she was frightened. If anything happened to him, she couldn't bear it. They were all lost, she thought, tears welling. They had lost their moorings in this hellhole. How long since they had left home? She couldn't tell. One day blurred into another, each one worse than the one before.

As though he could hear her thoughts, Isaac opened his eyes. "Are we there?" he asked.

"Not yet," Sonya said. "But if you close your eyes, perhaps we will be there sooner."

She pressed cool cloths to his forehead to beat back his fever and demanded broth from the kitchen for him to sip. She kept him clean and fetched water to bathe him, and when nothing helped, she sought out the doctor, the only doctor for all of these suffering people, and begged him to come look at her little brother, imploring him with words he didn't comprehend.

"I'll come when I'm able," he said curtly in that language she couldn't understand.

When he turned away, she insisted, tugging at his sleeve.

"No, now. Otherwise, it will be too late."

He must have understood.

"Very well."

He followed her into that hellhole with resignation. He was thin and tall with a bony Adam's apple and yellow skin, his eyes shot with blood as though he'd had no rest in days.

"Who taught you to care for the sick?" he asked, looking at the child, the figures of her sister huddled under the meager covers, her mother and father. And then, after a moment of silence, taking in the scene, he observed dryly, "It looks as though you will have to take care of your whole family." And then he added, "You're a clever girl, hale and hearty. There will be a place for you in America."

She knew that he was praising her by his slight smile, his weary eyes that looked into her own soul with sympathy for her plight.

He took out his stethoscope and listened to little Isaac's heart, tapped on his chest and back, peered into his mouth with a long stick, though the child tried to prevent that by clamping his teeth tightly together so that the doctor had to pry it open.

"I'll give him something to bring his fever down."

He did, and it worked.

Sonya sat by Isaac's bed by day and got up to check on him at night, until he gradually got better and Sonya was able to start scolding him again.

"Why do you ask so many questions? Why can't you be quiet like your sister?"

He was everywhere, rummaging through other peoples' belongings, taking food they had hidden until they were ready to thrash him.

Tempers grew short. Quarrels broke out. Two men got into a fistfight over a tin of tobacco one had stolen from the other.

She counted every day, waiting through the long nights for the sun to come up.

"How many days?" she asked of the sailors, who were always polishing the railings and washing the deck, holding up her fingers. They laughed and told her, but she could never make out their answers. Everything was hard. Keeping clean was a chore. There were lines for washing themselves and lines for washing their clothes, and longer lines for the food that had become even more meager. A storm broke out, with bursts of thunder and lightning strikes, terrifying everyone. The ship heaved from side to side. Weeping, people got out their prayer books to implore God not to abandon them.

"We are in the wilderness," one cried angrily. "Tell me, how long must we wander?"

One of the men began playing a concertina to relieve the misery. People came on deck to dance. In spite of the despair, their faces appeared younger, hope rose in them again. Even the old men joined in.

"God willing," a woman said, "I am still alive."

They would have surely killed each other if they had been forced to stay together any longer, if someone hadn't finally sighted land. Buoyed by the news, the sick got up from their beds as though they had been resurrected from the dead.

"Where are we?" Tirzah said.

"We're almost there," Sonya replied

Her mother looked at her in confusion. In only a few weeks, their roles had reversed. Tirzah was weak, her clothes hung on her like those of the scarecrow they'd stood in the garden to frighten the birds away.

"It's the end of me," Tirzah wailed.

"No, a miracle," Sonya told her. "We have come safely across the sea to land."

"And where is that?"

"We have reached the Promised Land."

"Perhaps it is only an island," one of the men said, over-hearing her.

Sonya thought of Lazar Fierbush. Where was he now? She had looked for him on the ship, no doubt already saying, "My name is Lazar Fierbush." She tried to hold on to the words he had taught her a little longer, while practicing some of the other words she'd picked up from passengers and the sailors on the ship.

And then another miracle. As the shore grew closer, they saw a huge statue of a woman who held a torch. Then they reached a place where the ship dropped anchor. They would take ferries to the island. More water. The Hudson River, someone said.

People wept, hanging on to the railing. What would happen now?

One of the men took it upon himself to tell those around him that the worst was yet to come. They would have to wait hours in another hell—without food or water, or a place to relieve themselves. Then more disinfectant, more questions and examinations, before they would be free.

"Watch they don't put chalk on your back," he warned.

"Why would they do that?" a woman asked. Her belly was so large she was weaving from side to side. It looked as though her baby might be born right there while they were waiting.

"To separate those who will be sent back," he said.

People were carrying their possessions onto the boats, jostling to move to the front.

Yankel had bounded ahead. Sonya lifted Isaac with one arm and held on to her sister with the other. Her mother trailed behind her.

A terrible swell of humanity was fighting to secure a place for themselves, but there was no place. They would have to wait their turn. Even though the sun was warm, a wind flared up and left them shivering. Mothers began to weep, as children grew faint. Were they to die here, then, within sight of the land, like Moses, who had completed the journey, but could only see it from afar?

"We are nothing but cattle," one man shouted. "God have pity on us."

Confusion reigned, but beyond them, past the frantic crowds, Sonya looked up. She had never seen such tall buildings, the skyline undulating like glittering palaces floating in the sky.

Patience, she thought. It will soon be over.

Finally Sonya and her family got on a ferry and reached land. No one could understand the uniformed men who shouted instructions as they made their way ashore. They waited in line again for a doctor to examine them. A hard look, and then their eyelids painfully pulled up and over a metal buttonhook. A cursory glance at the children to make certain they weren't sick. A closer look at the parents. A doctor hesitated when he saw Tirzah.

"Are you sick?" he asked.

"She is tired," Sonya replied quickly. "She wouldn't eat the food. It wasn't kosher. She has grown weak." How strange her words sounded when they were translated.

"And what is your name?"

"My name is Sonya Danelovich. I am her daughter."

"Ah, so you speak English! A clever girl! He looked at Tir-zah again. "Your daughter says that you are weak because you haven't eaten. You must take care of yourself." He added firmly, exaggerating his words in a loud voice when she didn't understand, "Listen to your daughter!"

An examiner was questioning Yankel, but he wasn't sure of the answers,

His face turned red. He became flustered. He turned to his wife, who did not comprehend either.

"Where will you live?"

"How will you earn a living?"

"How old are your children?"

Sonya answered for him. When it was over, they were given permission to leave. Down the left staircase was freedom. They never looked back.

It was a miracle! She would never forget that moment of dizzy elation, her wobbly sea legs getting used to land once more. It was like being born again and emerging into another life.

Once they were off the ferry that took them into the city, away from the endless water, another world appeared: horses and wagons, automobiles and trolleys, a cacophony of sounds and light, elegant gowns of all colors in the windows, people dressed in fine clothes on the streets.

The rhythm of the city was nothing like Kiev. She could feel its pulse like that of a live being, ready to pounce. A warm day, the beginning of summer, but in the shade a cool breeze flut-tered over her that felt delicious. To think that all this existed and their little village, too, which must be sleeping now on the other side of the world.

She caught her image in a store window, a babushka tied under her chin, a pale face that had lost its healthy color, her old-fashioned shirtwaist and shoes. People stared at her. They stared at all of her family. They must have looked like rag pickers carrying bundles and baskets down the busy streets. The sound of English was all around her. Even though she couldn't understand all the words, she tried to pull them apart like a beast looking for food, seeking to find a morsel she could savor.

In a flash she remembered the trees and woods, the scent of pine and streams, even the chickens and horses, the easy familiarity of everything she knew, as though it was a place that had existed only in her imagination. Here there was a purpose, the sense that people knew where they were going and what they had to do. No vegetable gardens, but markets of colorful vegetables and fruits. She would miss looking at the stars and the sky shining at night, the different shapes of the moon. She could barely see the sky here. It was all walls and pavement, no dirt paths, and trees were scarce. Yet the breadth and width of it made her breathless with excitement. Rows of brick buildings that all looked alike, peddlers and pushcarts of all kinds, things to buy that she hadn't known existed. And when night fell, instead of bringing darkness, light shone from windows and streetlights all the time.

A new world. A miracle!


They found their way to a *landsman* named Rose Bender on Cherry Street who took in boarders, families who'd just arrived. She lived in a crowded apartment several flights up narrow dark stairs, in one of the large buildings that lined the street.

"This will be your home," Rose said. "I can't offer you much except three small rooms and a kitchen where you can prepare your meals. I'll help you get settled. I myself come from Odessa."

In the small apartment, Yankel looked like a giant with no place to go. He gazed around at the new surroundings in a daze. They all did, as if they had suddenly walked into a lion's den. Tirzah was as white as the lace curtains that hung at the windows. Basha and little Isaac explored, opening and shutting drawers, looking out the single window at the horses clopping down the street, the endless streams of people in a city where they knew no one except this woman who was setting out something for them to eat. The little town near Kiev seemed very far away.

Sonya offered to help their new landlady.

"What a comfort you will be to your mother," Rose Bender said to her. And then, remembering her own arrival, she added, "At first everything will be strange. And sometimes it stays that way for a long time. For many people that feeling never goes away. It is easier when you are younger."

"Come," she said more cheerfully, "Sit down and tell me about yourselves. "Where are you from? What has brought you here?"

Rose was thin and slight, but wiry and energetic, with features that looked crowded in her small face. She had curly hair of faded blond swept on top of her head. Wisps were always coming loose and pins falling out as she worked. Rose was a seamstress, up early in the morning and the last one to go to bed at night. Her bony hands with their thick blue veins visible beneath the surface were always moving. She was everyplace at once. She loved to talk. She had an opinion about everything. Rose didn't have a husband, at least no one ever saw him, only a grown daughter who came around now and then.

Rose sewed day and night. She sewed for ordinary Jews, but she was proudest of her costumes for the Yiddish theater. She had acted years ago, and now fellow actors came whenever they needed costumes for a new play. They all wanted something colorful, even flamboyant, that would make them stand out.

"The competition! The fights and quarrels! The affairs and romances! The scandals," Rose exclaimed when Sonya knew her better. "The things they say about each other! They should burn in Gehenna!"

She sewed furiously while she spoke.

"Each group has its *patriotn*, fans that follow their idols from theater to theater and purposely buy tickets to their opponents' plays to heckle and rattle them.

"New York may be a big city, but here among we Jews it is still a small town, a little *shtetl* in the middle of the modern world. Jews are the same wherever they are. One needs to know these people to believe it! That handsome man, Boris Thomashefsky with his beautiful eyes that set all the girls swooning. His wife Bessie, who has had to put up with all his women! The great actor Jacob Adler, and Adler's wife, the beautiful Sara, who was once married to Maurice Heine. I was in love with him, too, but so is every woman," she confided. "I fell for his handsome face and melancholy eyes. Whenever he looked at me, I melted. He took me when I was young and pretty, and then left me! What a scoundrel! He is called the *Nesher Hagadol*, the Great Eagle, because of his name, but he should be called the great carouser!"

Rose stopped to rethread her machine. Look at this," she said, holding up the material. "I'm making a new costume for Jacob even as we speak. You'll meet him one day, or better yet see him perform."

Then Rose became serious again.

"This country is our last hope. We settle where we can to live out our lives with all of our pent-up yearning to be accepted for who we are."

Sonya was silent, unsure of what to say.

Bolts of bright fabric stood around Rose like soldiers guarding a fortress. Needles, bobbins, and scissors littered the tabletops, while scraps of braid and ribbon lay scattered like colorful leaves blown about the apartment. It seemed as though Rose never slept. People were always passing through, trying on clothes. Mannequins lurked in corners, silent ghosts covered in muslin, waiting for the stars they stood in for.

"It's easier," Rose explained. "I can do the fittings without them."

"Look at Boris's form. Did you ever see such shapely legs? Every costume has to show them off." She held up a satin cloak with sequins and spangles, "The gaudier, the better."

As if on cue, Boris thundered up the stairs and asked for another costume that was still flashier. It was his size that Sonya noticed first: his height, the bulk of him, the way he took up space in the room and dominated it. And after that his eyes, warm and lively, fastening on her.

"And who is this pretty girl?" he demanded, looking straight at Sonya.

"She is not for you, Boris," Rose said. "She's still a child, just arrived with her family. She barely knows a word of English."

"So, a greenhorn, but a pretty one. Her name should be Shayna. That is what I will call her. A *shayna maidel*."

He looked her over while Sonya blushed.

"She's not such a child, Rose. In fact, we could use her in this production. There is a place for her if she wants to come by the theater. And she doesn't need to know a word of English."

"She's helping me, Boris."

"Yes, during the day. But surely at night she is free."

"You're a rascal."

"She can speak for herself, can't she?"

"She needs someone to speak *for* her," Rose said firmly. "Her mother is not well. This child has had to become the mother, like so many others here. Her father is out looking for work. So wait. I'll talk to her and let you know."

"Don't wait too long. We start rehearsals next week. She'll feel right at home. The play is about a Russian Jew in America."

Something about the way Boris looked at her made her uncomfortable, his penetrating glance grazed her breasts, admiring her face. After he left, it was as though Rose could read her thoughts.

"You're too young for Boris. He looks at all women that way. Boris is a star, a man of great appetites. Stay away from him. His wife ran away from home when she was fourteen to join him. He loves wine, women, and song. Jacob is an artist, but Boris is a master of musical interludes, of knowing exactly what the audience wants. The first time I saw him he was naked to the waist, his legs in golden tights."

Rose kept stitching away as she spoke.

"Boris doesn't mind *shund*, what we call trash, but good trash, to keep people amused. A song, a dance, a tumble, and plenty of women. But good theater, too, when he wants to offer it. When you see *Dos Pintele Yid*, one of his greatest roles, you'll know what I mean. That essential spark of Jewishness that continues to endure in America. That spark is what keeps us alive, no matter how many people want to see us destroyed."

Another couple lived in the back three rooms. They kept to themselves, but there were quarrels over the kitchen. A simple stove that used coal, a small square box with a chunk of ice delivered by an iceman. In winter, they could also use the ledge outside.

Two families crowded together in one place. A tenement filled to overflowing with people on each floor.

*Tenement.*

She'd never heard the word before, in any language. The smells and noise and confusion frightened her at first, the dark hallways, the scratching in the walls at night as though the rats would come out and eat her up alive. One toilet down the hall for all the families on their floor, and privies in the dirty courtyard that were stifling in summer and freezing cold in winter. There was a water pump with a spigot there, too. They could use it for washing, or for bringing water upstairs to heat for bathing or cooking. When it was cold, Rose told them, laundry would have to be hung inside. Otherwise, the lines between the apartments could be used.

When it got too hot, they dragged their mattresses onto the roof, or slept on the fire escapes, the only place where Sonya could see the stars. But instead of dense blackness, there were lights, people all around. Yet a loneliness would creep over her that felt like a stone in the middle of her heart.

Basha was sent to school. She had to go, even though she was a girl. That was the law in this country, Rose said.

Sonya would have to take her. Tirzah was ill and was almost always in her bed. Even the drops of medicine she took failed to help her lungs.

Little Isaac stayed at home, getting into mischief, his mother too sick to take care of him. When she wasn't sick, Tirzah was depressed. It was all of one cloth. One condition led to the other.

Isaac had developed an impish grin, asking everyone for candy, begging for spare change to buy it when Sonya took him to the store. He begged to go outside and sit on the front stoop, to watch the older boys play ball or shoot marbles. He was learning English on the streets. Sonya suspected that some of it wasn't so polite.

Rose, who understood English very well, told him that if he didn't stop they would have to rinse his mouth out with soap.

"He's running wild," she said. "He needs a mother. It's time Tirzah saw a doctor."

When Sonya told Yankel, he shot back, "You only see a doctor when you're dying. A doctor is not for craziness in the head."

Those times when she got out of bed, Tirzah sat all day looking out the tiny window that faced the unkempt courtyard and outhouses, thinking of the place she had left. It was fall. Back home, the snow would have already come in drifts of white clouds and would hang from the boughs like stately crowns.

"Why have we come here?" she asked over and over again, as balky as a child. She was afraid to go outside.

"You have to get out," Sonya said.

She took her mother for walks, but Tirzah was confused by the noise and vehicles, the language, the people rushing by her. The kitchen frightened her, too. She didn't know how to use the stove. Nor did she want to go down the steps to the basement to do the wash or get water from the pump. She was short of breath, afraid that she wouldn't be able to find her way back. She didn't like all of Rose's celebrity customers coming and going all the time. And so she sat like a statue, without talking, repeating the same words.

"I want to go home."

"And what if antisemites come to our door at home?" Sonya asked.

It was not so much a question as a statement. Tirzah had written her aunt to tell her they had arrived. A few months later a reply came saying things had taken another turn for the worse. Money was scarcer than ever. Cossacks were everywhere, terrorizing Jews. Food was scarce. More letters told terrible tales. The family needed their help. The officials were crooked, taking everything. They were waiting for a revolution to right things. Maybe then everything would change for the Jews.

"We are not going back," Sonya said with finality. "There is nothing to go back to."

Her father had finally found a job as a welder, working fifteen hours at a stretch. Sometimes he slept at the factory so that he could be there early in the morning, before the sun rose. Sonya didn't like the way he was drinking.

He had changed his name, too. He was no longer Yankel, he informed her.

"It's an old-country name," he declared.

"What name will you be then?" Sonya asked.

"Abraham," Yankel said. "I'll call myself Abe. A good Jewish name and an American one, too. Have you heard of Abe Lincoln?"

Sonya had begun sewing to help Rose, alongside the other young women who came every day. Working for Rose was better than the big factories, they said, where over a hundred girls just like themselves, fresh off the boat, had died in a fire, trapped by locked doors. Greedy bosses had wanted to make sure they got their money's worth from them. Sonya listened quietly. There was a lot to learn from these women who had been here longer.

She was paid a few cents for each piece she completed, not much, but she decided not to look elsewhere for better pay. She made up her mind not to go to school, either. It wasn't required of someone her age.

The younger women were going to classes to learn English. Maybe she would go, too. The classes were free, and it was not too far away.

Suddenly, the nights turned cold, and it began to rain. Rose gave Sonya scraps to make clothes for her sister and brother. She made a new dress for her mother to cheer her up.

Tirzah tried it on and stood before the mirror. For the first time she smiled. Then she frowned.

"I shouldn't have come. I'm lonely. I don't know anyone. There's too much noise, too many people. I want to go back," she said, and began to cry. "Yankel is never home."

"We can't go back," Sonya told her. "There is no money for tickets. There is nothing left for us there."

"There's more than enough to do here," Sonya went on, and thought about how their positions had been reversed.

Sonya was growing up. She had taken charge of the money, did the cooking every night and the wash on Friday, trying without success to get her mother and Basha to help. It was hard to put a meal together. They scraped by with money from the Jewish Aid society, but they wouldn't be able to get that help forever.

Basha had begun to complain, suddenly asserting herself.

"Everyone makes fun of me. No one wears babushkas on their heads, or old-fashioned shirtwaists. The other girls have ribbons in their hair."

Rose found some ribbons that were used for one of the costumes and fashioned a bow for her.

"How do you like that? Now you look just like an *amerikanka*."

One day Basha came home with a note.

"My teacher wants to see Mama," Basha said.

"Tell her your mother can't come."

That wasn't the end of it. Basha was given another note in the teacher's elegant handwriting. She gave it to Rose, who read it slowly, sounding out each word.

"Someone else will have to come to see me then."

Sonya went herself to find out what was the matter. Miss Novello wore paint on her face and a long dress with stockings and black shoes. Her hands were white and smooth and she wore a gold bracelet on the bony wrist of one hand and a locket at her throat.

She got right to the point. Basha was having a problem adjusting.

"Do you understand what I am saying to you?" she asked Sonya. "Can't your mother come to school?"

"My mother is not well."

"I see."

Miss Novella pressed her lips together, not altogether pleased.

"You mean she hasn't adjusted yet to a new country. Perhaps that's why your sister is having a problem. The shock of a new country, a new language, so far from everything that is familiar."

Sonya nodded.

*Adjusted.*

Judging by the teacher's expression it wasn't a bad word, but it was not a good word either. She didn't understand the meaning, even though she tried to connect one letter to another, until they flew beyond her. It was hard to separate them. Everyone spoke too fast, impatient when she couldn't understand. They were like the automobiles that sped along the street and didn't wait for anyone who was crossing in front of them.

"And your father?"

"My father works all the time. He isn't home."

She had not meant to say this. It had slipped out.

"He comes home to give us money," Sonya corrected.

That was true, but he was gone most of the time. Where did he go? Miss Novello wanted to know. Sonya wasn't sure.

That night, after the children were asleep she closed the door behind her and went out. It was nearly the end of October. A cool edge to the breeze, and if she stood in a certain spot she could see a sliver of moon in the sky. The same moon that she had seen before she came to this country.

What a miracle that it could be in both places, but what a difference here on the Lower East Side of New York, where there was never a need to go to bed. Sonya soaked up the sound of music drifting into the brisk air from the music halls and the voices of the throngs of people rushing along, making their way inside where lamps shone brightly. Newsboys were everywhere, hawking papers, trying to earn a few cents. Boys with small shoeshine kits trolled the streets even after dark, plying their trade anywhere near a light and a bench.

Many people were still sitting on their stoops, despite the chill, to get some air before they had to turn in for the night. But there were also homeless children everywhere, dirty and uncared for, sleeping in doorways or anywhere else they could find a place to lay their head. An epidemic of orphans plagued the city.

Life pulsed among all those buildings, not all of it good, but thank God there was no one beating down their door to mutilate and kill them. She had learned to avoid some of the neighborhoods where occasionally Jews had been taunted or beaten. Yes, they were still Jews, but here they were human, too.

Sonya liked to look into the lit windows as she passed by to watch the people moving about inside. What were their lives like? Surely they were easier than the lives of her own family. She liked to imagine walking up the stairs and being part of the families she saw, who seemed happier than her family. What would happen if she did? Could you walk into another life and trade it for one you liked better?

And if she did, what would God say about that?

She hadn't thought about God for a long time. He must surely be in America, too, still playing his jokes. She thought of him as one of the shadowy forms on the large screen in a movie theater Rose Bender had taken her to one night.

They sat in the dark watching people walking about on the screen as though they were really flesh and blood, but not people you could touch. It was like life itself, Sonya decided. You couldn't touch it. You simply lived it day by day. She had started to feel that she was always on the outside looking in, as though she would never be inside the room that was called America.

A lady in the theater sat at a large keyboard instrument that Rose called an organ. When horses were galloping on the screen she played very fast. The music slowed down when people were crying. It made Sonya cry, too, that melancholy sound that tore at her as though it had come from somewhere deep inside. In the back of her mind, she kept seeing their little village with its forests and streams, the simple life they had lived before they came here.

When the film was over, the figures disappeared and the lights came on.

"Where do they go?" Sonya asked.

'They're in a *reel*," Rose said, emphasizing the word. "When you rewind the reel and play it, they will be there again."

"And how do they do that?"

"It's in the film," Rose explained. "You run it through a *pro-jec-tor*"—a word that Rose said very slowly, drawing it out so that Sonya could learn it. "You can see it over and over again, as many times as you want, and it's always the same."

The past was like that, Sonya thought. She had a pro-jec-tor in her mind. Certain scenes played over and over again. She could take them out any time she wanted to, but they would still be waiting for her. They kept replaying, adding more and more images until her mind was ready to burst with them.

"A miracle," Sonya said.

"There are no miracles," Rose replied matter-of-factly. "There is only what we do ourselves."

"And God?" Sonya asked. "Is he like one of the shadows on the screen?"

Rose thought about it.

"Yes, I suppose that could be true. Sometimes he appears; other times he's absent, and try as we might, there's nowhere we can find him."

Sonya had been thinking about Boris Thomashefsky's offer and kept asking Rose if she was grown up enough now to go see him. Finally Rose gave in.

"Okay, but be careful and don't let him charm you into bed."

Sonya was certain he had forgotten her, but as soon as she walked in the door, he greeted her.

"Aha! My *shayna maidel!*" Boris said. "Somehow I knew you would come. Rose tells me that you are also from a small village near Kiev. I am from Tarasche, not so far away. And so is my wife Bessie, here. So we are all *landsleit!* You and Bessie and myself and half the people in the audience. You don't even need to learn a part for this play. It's a part you've lived in, a play about the ache in the heart for the country where we were born and the difficulty of the new life here that we have all struggled to begin. You are small enough to play one of the young boys."

"She's much too pretty for that, Boris." Bessie said, standing back to appraise Sonya. "Where have you been hiding this beauty, Boris? After she is finished with you, I want her for my own production. I already have something in mind for her."

"You'll have to wait," Boris told her with a firmness that discouraged further discussion.

"Then I'll wait," Bessie replied, just as firmly. "But I won't forget."

Boris was a taskmaster. Everything had to be perfect. They rehearsed, and then they rehearsed some more. He took an interest in every detail—the scenery, the costumes, the music. He coached the actors, listening to their speeches with a careful ear, telling them exactly how he wanted them to sound, directing their posture and gestures.

Sonya felt sheer terror. The one line she had to say seemed to be stuck in her throat. She could feel her heart pounding and prayed that she would die before she had to say it.

One of the boys, Dovid, smiled at her. "It won't be as bad as you think," he said, trying to reassure her.

On opening night, it didn't seem possible that it would all come together. Sonya, disguised as a young boy, played the friend the Russian Jew had left behind in the old country who had waited years to hear from him.

The stage was darkened and a single spotlight shone on her. Stage fright had almost rendered her speechless, but then she saw Boris in the wings motioning for her to breathe. She inhaled deeply and thought of Nadija, whom she had left behind, and her cousin Irina, who had wanted to come with her.

Tears filled her eyes and her voice broke with emotion as she spoke her line: "My friend, I have waited for you all these years, but you have forgotten me as though I was nothing more to you than a stranger." There was a long silence when Sonya was finished. It was so quiet she was certain no one was there but herself until the audience erupted in applause.

"For shame he left you and never even wrote!" someone shouted above the hubbub.

This response, Rose had told her, was the way the audience traditionally showed its appreciation for a performance.

She didn't know what Bessie had in mind for her. But Sonya knew she wanted to do it. She felt heady with the excitement, the thrill of being on the stage and taking bows when the play was over. She had never felt so alive.


Yankel came home less and less.

Little Isaac cried for him. Tirzah continued asking where he had gone. Basha was caught up in the new world that was opening up to her and seldom asked about her father. She spoke English now, and when Sonya asked her a question, she refused to answer.

Sonya was paid very little by Boris Thomashefsky, and the money Yankel had given her was running low. The children were hungry all the time. Rose helped by giving her a few coins to tide them over, and more sewing to do.

Sonya decided to find her father.

"Where does he work?" Rose asked.

"I'm not sure," Sonya answered. She had never really thought about it. He came home late at night and went to work before anyone got up—if he came home at all.

"Find out where he goes when he gets off work."

She asked other men in her neighborhood where her father worked and was told it was at a factory on Water Street.

She found the building, and watched from across the street as the workers came out until at last she saw her father. He had shaved off his beard and was wearing clothes she didn't recognize. He didn't look like someone from the old country anymore. It was hard to believe he was the same person.

She followed him several blocks and waited while he rang a bell at one of the tenements that lined the street.

"Where are you going?" Sonya shouted, heading across the road to confront him.

He spun around to face her.

"What are you doing here?"

"We have nothing to eat! My mother is sick."

"Sick in the head," Yankel said. "Go home where you belong."

"*You* need to come home," Sonya demanded, standing her ground.

"I'll come home when I'm ready," Yankel told her.

"I'll go to the police," Sonya said with a boldness that startled her.

"And what will they do? You're a child."

"What's this, Abe?" a woman asked, opening the door.

"Nothing," he said, "Nothing that concerns you," and disappeared inside.

"Women are abandoned here all the time," Rose reflected that evening. "People change in America. Things change, lives change. We leave the past behind, and sometimes people are left behind, as well." She paused for a moment. "We've gained some things. There are no pogroms here. We don't have to fear the terror when the beast is unleashed and rages against Jews, battering down your doors and killing your children. But other qualities have been lost."

"I am thinking of taking my mother back," Sonya said.

"What will your mother do there? Yankel will never return. And you? You will never come here again. You will be lost forever, Sonya."

The weather grew colder. The months followed each other rapidly as winter settled in. First, the rain and winds came, blowing the leaves down the street until the spindly trees were bare. Overnight it seemed, the snow followed, pristine white at first and then changing to slush and mud as people tramped across the sidewalks and streets.

Sonya thought of the great forests in Ukraine, gowned in fleece, the chalky hills melting into the fresh streams. Where they had once lived now seemed as if it had been a dream that vanished upon waking. Did it still exist?

She watched the world now from her seat before a sewing machine, the rhythm of the click-clack of the needle, her foot on the treadle, turning out clothes for people she didn't know. Some days there was excitement when leading actors came up the stairs, filling the rooms with their presence, nodding to the women, who were afraid to look up, asking that more glitter and flash be added to their costumes, to compete with the other men.

The brooding face of Jacob Ben-Ami, who had arrived from Minsk, captivated her. David Kessler, serious and strong, rarely spoke. The illustrious Sigmund Mogulesko always had a comic quip to share. Rudolph Schildkraut, Rose told her, had been stolen from the German theater by Boris Thomashefsky.

But Sonya loved it best when the women came in their elegant and stylish attire. Rose had taken her to see their performances—the majestic Bertha Kalich in *The Kreutzer Sonata,* which spoke of the need for women to be fulfilled; the temperamental Keni Liptzin in *Mirele Efros*, the story of a powerful matriarch who is estranged from her family. (It was Keni who announced dramatically to Sonya, "I live only for the theater.") And, of course, the vibrant Bessie Thomashefsky, who took Sonya under her wing.

She had never met women like this. They had great talent, but also power and charm. Unlike her mother, they ruled their own lives and promoted their own careers. They were helping to create a new theater that could only flourish in America.

It was all Sonya could do to wait each evening for the performance, to play her small part, standing on the stage and speaking her line, the excitement afterward as the audience leapt from their seats to embrace the entire cast with applause.

"I'm writing a new play," Bessie told her one day. It has a part for you. In fact, it will make you famous."

"What kind of part?"

"It is the story of Abishag," Bessie said, "the beautiful young virgin who was selected to lie with King David when he was very old, to keep him warm. In my play, only Bathsheba of his former wives has survived and is left at the palace, defending her son's right to inherit the throne. But Adonijah, David's fourth son, the child of Haggith, has decided that the throne should be his, instead of Solomon's, after the deaths of his older brothers.

"There were people waiting for David to die. But there was another group that wanted to keep him alive," Bessie explained, "They were determined to find the most beautiful girl in Israel to lie with the king to restore his vitality. Perhaps, who knows, they thought a miracle would happen and she would give birth to a child who would inherit the throne."

Bessie paused, "I will play the part of Bathsheba. You will be Abishag. And the part of David? I haven't decided."

"I'm not sure" Sonya said slowly. "I have only begun. I . . ."

"Nonsense," Bessie replied, taking a script from her purse and motioning for Sonya to join her on the stage. "I was younger than you are now when I ran off with Boris and began acting. You'll speak for young women today in the role of Abishag. She is a pawn in the Bible. She was not allowed to have her own dreams. Her beauty has made her a captive. Wrenched from her family and her home in Shunem she was brought to Jerusalem against her will. But she'll attend to David because she recognizes a kindred spirit, a soul not unlike her own, a man of strength but also great sensitivity. She is a woman with thoughts and feelings, a stranger among these people she doesn't know, no different from the audiences who come to see us, adrift in a new place that she doesn't understand."

Yes, perhaps Bessie was right, Sonya thought. She stood on the stage and looked out at the empty theater. Bessie swept her arm in an arc to indicate the audience.

"Imagine yourself playing the role of a frightened stranger in a strange land who gradually gathers confidence in her own power."

"I'll explain as we go along," Bessie said. "When the physicians are assembled around the ailing king, they decide to order the royal couriers to find the most beautiful young woman in the country. After a great search, Abishag, who lives in the north of the land, is found and brought to the palace amid the fanfare of royal trumpets—a joyous scene with music and dancing in the great tradition of the Yiddish theater. But this is only a prelude to the next scene, when she realizes what the future holds, the bitter knowledge that she will not see her family again. She was never asked, but only told. Her desires no longer matter. She has been informed that her task is to keep the king alive, a man she has never seen and only knows through hearsay.

"This is the darker side of the Yiddish theater," Bessie added unhappily, "the sadness that is always intermingled with joy."

Sonya was silent, thinking of her father. That sadness crept into her reading, no longer a performance, but a sudden melancholy that pervaded her own life. Bessie stood next to her, a noble Bathsheba who bowed and began to speak:

BATHSHEBA

*(Bathsheba bows before David.)*

My Lord, your handmaiden waits.


ABISHAG

*(It is the moment Abishag has been dreading, but as soon as she enters, she falls to the floor and prostrates herself before the king.)*

I pray, My Lord, that I will serve thee well.

*(When she looks up, she sees that the king's eyes are clouded, his skin is the color of thin parchment. All that remains of his famous red hair are tufts of gray circling the crown of his head. Is this the warrior king, the king who vanquished thousands of foes, who ravished Bathsheba? Abishag is so young and he—the king—is so old. The distance between them fills her with grief. It is the distance between her humble country house and David's dazzling palace.)*


KING DAVID

Come closer. I can't see you.

*(He is impatient, too weak to rise from his bed. Abishag hesitates, approaching him timidly. He speaks gently.)*

Do not be afraid. I pray thee, speak.

*(He suddenly spies Bathsheba, who is still standing to one side and dismisses her.)*

Go! Leave us!

*(David reasserts the authority that has deserted him in old age and illness, but the effort causes him to sink back on his bed.)*

BATHSHEBA

Yes, my Lord.

*(Bathsheba reluctantly leaves, looking behind her as Abishag moves closer to the king. David waits until she is gone to speak again. His voice is halting.)*

KING DAVID

From where have you come? A great distance?

*(Abishag reaches out to help him as he struggles to his feet, but then stops. He is still the king.)*

ABISHAG

I am of the tribe of Issachar, from Shunem. Your handmaiden knows only the fields and earth, the plants that grow by the grace of God, the sun and moon, and nothing of palaces.

KING DAVID

A long journey. I remember the way from my youth. I was once a shepherd herding sheep. I, too, knew the sighing of the wind, the light of the stars in the dark of night, the song of the grass beneath my feet.

*(He stops speaking but continues to gaze at her.)*

And will you stay with me?

*(Perhaps it is the yearning of his voice, or the shadow of confidence of a once powerful king that allows her to see the young man in the old and touches her heart. He is only a mortal man, after all. His words pierce the armor that she has built against him.)*

ABISHAG

Yes, my Lord. I am here to be your companion. I pray that I can give you strength and make you well again.

*(David nods and motions for her to approach his bed. She comes closer.)*

KING DAVID

Thou art kind as well as beautiful.

ABISHAG

Thank you, my Lord.

*(Abishag bows again. He reaches for her hand and grasps it, as she lies down on his bed and they embrace.)*

I will not leave you.

The past is only a breath away, Sonya thought, brought back through a power that she did not pretend to understand, but only felt. Yes, on the stage she had become Abishag, who was breathing in her presence as though she was standing with her. The woman's ancient soul had taken over her own, the dead given life.

"I knew the part was made for you," Bessie said, her voice choking with emotion. "I'll finish writing it and you'll become a star, Sonya. Audiences will flock to see you. Your mother and sister will come, too. Think how proud they will be of you." Then she added, "There are people who believe that King David represents the enduring tradition, but Abishag is the youthful infusion of the common touch, Yiddish, that can renew it with vigor."

When opening night arrived, though, her mother and sister were not in the audience. Tirzah disapproved, and Basha, despite her new boldness, was too timid. Instead it was Rose Bender sitting in the first row, beaming at Sonya, and Dovid seated next to Rose, silently reassuring her.

At the sight of them, Sonya's stage fright suddenly disappeared and nothing stood in her way. The stage was hers. Before she began to speak, she slipped on Abishag's skin, gazed through her frightened eyes, and felt the pulse of the other woman's courage, the soft drum of her heart encasing her own soul. So completely had she assumed the spirit of Abishag that she didn't know the play was over until the audience began rising from their seats, cheering and applauding her performance.

Whenever she went out into the streets, the commotion of the city never stopped, the crowds of people, the noise. And beyond her neighborhood and that city, she knew there was a greater, unknown America that lay waiting for her.

She had begun to read, teaching herself English from Basha's books. She would pause at corner newspaper stands, perusing the magazines with their colorful illustrations depicting strange cities far across the continent. New York itself she had barely seen, only the part that was near the East River.

But there was also Chicago, which lay east of another river, a name she couldn't pronounce that reminded her of Po Kip See. And Alabama, another strange name, where black-skinned people lived who had once been slaves, still separated from the people who were white by laws that oppressed them, even in America. And San Francisco, which looked as though it might fall into the sea when the earth trembled, as it had only a few years before.

Then trouble was brewing in the headlines. A war might be imminent. Political parties in Russia were trying to topple Tsar Nicholas II. Letters continued to arrive throughout the winter, another one from her mother's sister begging for their return, one from her father's brother. He had not heard from Yankel.

"You won't hear from him, either," Sonya wrote back. "His name is Abe now, and he has left us. We are alone here, but not without friends who have helped us."

At last the weather grew warmer. The sun shone for most of the day, and sheets drying on lines billowed in the soft breeze. Women began cleaning their front steps of winter grime. The streets became more crowded than ever. People grew livelier, discarding heavy coats and hats. Orange streaks floated on the horizon at dusk, auguring spring.

She had thought about going back to their home for weeks, waiting until Bessie's production was over. What was she to do? Her mother was no better. All winter Tirzah had lain in bed in a cold room like an old woman, refusing to get up even on days when she was well. In the space of a year her hair had turned gray. Her skin looked jaundiced. Little Isaac was always in trouble. Basha declined to help and wouldn't mind her, though she was always asking Sonya to make her new dresses. She had friends now who were real Americans.

A miracle! Sonya thought, looking at these children who came to play. They didn't even look like Jews. They spoke English without an accent. They'd never had to cross an ocean and took their easy lives for granted. Her sister had forgotten her own language, the old traditions, slipping into American ways.

Rose had let them stay in her apartment, but Sonya didn't want to take charity anymore. Despite the applause she earned in the production of Abishag, Bessie couldn't pay her enough to cover all of her expenses.

What a fool she was, Sonya knew, to go back now, just when she had a reason to stay. And yet she decided to go and be done with it. She couldn't take care of her whole family by herself.

"No one goes back," Rose said.

"It's what I have to do," Sonya said. .

Bessie lent her money to help pay for the tickets, even though she didn't want to take it.

"You'll pay me back when you return," she said. "You will return, won't you?"

"I can't promise."

"Don't desert us, Sonya. You have a future here. You were meant for the theater. You have talent. If you continue, you will become the talk of the Lower East Side."

She told Dovid she was leaving. He had offered her friendship and something more that felt like the beginning of love. When he looked at her she could feel his concern. After her performances, he often walked her home and kissed her gently on the lips.

"I will miss you," he said sadly. "I couldn't bear it if you didn't come back. Here is my address. When you return I'll be waiting for you."

They left on a beautiful day in May, almost a year after they had come. Basha was angry and sulked. Little Isaac was not so little anymore. He had stopped asking about his father, but his rage found other outlets. He hit Sonya with his fists and shouted, "Don't tell me what to do!"

"What has happened to Yankel?" Tirzah asked.

"Yankel is not coming back, Mama. He's gone."

That whole terrible trip home was escaping in reverse. They boarded a ship full of what seemed to be undesirables: some clearly insane, others with mysterious ailments. The blind. The sick. The lame. Those who had no means to support themselves. Many were weeping and distraught. They had spent their last money to come to America. Everyone knew the stories of those who stayed and flourished. But these were the failures, those who couldn't make it and had to return.

"Ah," said a man who limped, "So you are returning, too."

"I'm hoping to come back," Sonya said.

"And how will you do that?"

"I don't know yet. Perhaps a miracle."

"I'm hoping for one, too."

The ship was going to Hamburg. From there they would take the train. It was faster; they would arrive sooner. Her cousins would meet her with a wagon. They would stay with her mother's family.

There was only the endless water again, as though it had been waiting for them all along, the food that left them hungry no matter how much they ate, the storms that kept them in bed. Sonya didn't get sick this time either. She walked the deck as they traveled farther and farther away on a journey she didn't want to take. When they finally arrived, it wasn't the same place she remembered. Everything was different. Her native tongue suddenly felt foreign to her ears, even though she continued to speak it, because everyone else spoke it, too.

The people she saw, their clothes, even the foods they ate; the trees that were beginning to blossom, which she had so longed to see again; the snow-cleared streams and grass; the splendid night skies—all seemed strange.

It took her awhile to realize that she was the one who had changed. When she was in America, she'd dreamed of this unspoiled country, but now that she was here, she missed the lights and the noise and activity of New York, the crowded tenements teeming with people and energy, the sense of something coming into being, not only her own rebirth, but the country's, as though everything was being formed before her very eyes: the theater, the people, the sense of excitement, the rapt audience, noisy but awestruck.

She was a divided soul, like the Russian Jew in the play who missed Moscow even as he was becoming an American.

There was ferment here, as well, but it was the wrong kind. Political unrest and hunger, violence against the Jews that had never abated, a tsar instead of a president, a ruler instead of laws decided by the people.

Meanwhile, her mother had begun to come to life again, as though she were awakening from a long sleep.

"I am a chained woman," Tirzah said, "an *agunah*, chained to a marriage that doesn't exist. How will I manage?"

"We will manage," Sonya said.

How could she leave? And how could she have ever thought it would be easy?

"I'll begin sewing to earn money. I can take care of those who need help. I'll see if Nadija's parents want me to come back. I've missed her, one of the few people I have missed."

She passed by the home they had left. Another family was living there. How strange to see other people living in the place where she had been born and grown up. Children were in the front yard playing. They looked at her curiously.

"What are you doing here?" the younger boy asked.

"This was my house," Sonya said. "Yes, the house where my family lived for many years." She stood there for a few moments as though the past would come reeling back like film on the projector. Where had it gone? Had their lives been only shadows, devoid of substance? In her mind she could still see her last image as they pulled away, the house growing smaller in the distance.

"Well, it's our house now," the older brother said. "You don't live here anymore. Why did you leave?"

"My family went to America," Sonya said, "and God willing, I will return."

"Nadija is gone," her mother, Chava, said when Sonya appeared at her door.

"Gone?" Sonya repeated.

"She's dead," Chava said flatly, as though she had repeated it many times before. "She didn't last long after you left. Her heart was not strong. She asked for you all the time. She stood at the window waiting for you, even though I told her you weren't coming back. I told her that you had gone to America. And now you are here and it's too late."

"I wanted to see her," Sonya said. "I have never forgotten Nadija."

"Nor did she forget you. We have grieved for nearly a year. Our lives are hard in many ways. Things continue to get worse. I have no other children. I have no son. He left long ago for America, and I've never heard from him. My letters came back stamped 'address unknown.' And now my daughter is gone as well. We have decided to go, too. There's nothing for my husband and me here except an empty house. Perhaps there's nothing for us there, either, but we will see. And maybe I will find my son."

"It's a large country," Sonya said. "It stretches from one sea to the other, but all I have seen is New York, and of that city, only one small part of it.

It's a big adjustment," she added, thinking of the word that Basha's teacher had used, "It's not for everyone. It wasn't for my mother, Tirzah Danelovich."

"And will you return?"

"Women aren't allowed to come alone. America doesn't want women who might not be able to provide for themselves."

"I can't blame them," Chava said.

"Besides, I can't leave my mother. I thought I could, but how can I? She has no other way to support herself. My father has left us. It happens frequently to families in America and now it has happened to us."

"There are many sad stories. I have mine and you have yours."

"We'll make the best of it," Sonya replied calmly. "There is nothing else we can do now."

"And America?" Chava asked.

"It would be a miracle…" Sonya said, leaving the thought unfinished.

"We are leaving," Chava told her. "My husband and I. It's now or never. We'll set sail at the end of summer, before the cold and snow begin. I'll speak to him. We could take you with us, if you are part of our family." Chava hesitated before she said, "If you are our daughter."

"What do you mean?"

"Your mother will have to give you up so that we can adopt you. We will list you as our own. Others have done it. It's the only way you'll be able to leave. Otherwise you will remain here forever in this forsaken land where Jews are despised."

"Perhaps things will change one day."

"Nothing will ever change," Chava said, "even if there is a revolution."

"And what about my sister, my brother?"

"We can't take all of you. Think about it," Chava said. "We'll leave in a few months, and we're not coming back. We have nothing to come back to. Perhaps it will be your only chance."

"And how will I tell them?"

"You'll have to find a way."

Yes, God plays tricks on us, Sonya said to herself. Things happen to us that we cannot even imagine. She thought about it for months. How could she do it? Just leave and never come back, trading one life for another. Yes, she had considered it now and then, but to actually do it was something else.

She walked about in a daze. She was torn not only between two countries, but between two families. How could she leave her own family? Was such an act permissible? She would never see them again. That much was clear. One day she was certain she would leave. The next, she knew she couldn't do it. It was like choosing who would die between two people you loved.

Basha had settled into the life that they had lived before, seldom speaking of that other country, but Sonya noticed that she clung to her big sister more, as though she suspected that Sonya would abandon them. Little Isaac was growing up by leaps and bounds. And her mother was better now that she was back. The fresh air put a rosy glow in her face. She seldom stayed in bed. She had too much to do, helping her sister with the children.

Sonya was the only one who yearned to return, to take up the unfinished life she had started. When she fell asleep, she imagined that she was walking the streets of New York, dreaming of the life that was waiting for her. Dovid was waiting for her, and Bessie. If she stayed she would surely shrivel up and die.

One morning she woke up and resolved to return.

Her mother wept when Sonya told her, but after thinking about it for a few days, gave her away to Chava, as she had asked.

"You are no longer my daughter," Tirzah said sorrowfully. "Return to America and make a life for yourself."

Sonya embraced her. "I will return and, God willing, I will make a life for myself, but you will always be my mother."

Tirzah was silent for a moment. "And the children?" she asked.

"I'll tell them when the time is right."

The problem was how. Sonya thought about it for a long time. A story. Yes, she would tell them a story. But what kind of story would it be?

She finally decided. One evening as she tucked them in, she told them the tale of a princess who came to a beautiful land where she had never been before. At first it was strange. She knew no one and she didn't know the language, but gradually, she made friends. She found a home and something that she cherished and someone she loved.

"But the princess," Sonya said, "had to leave this place and suddenly return to her former home. She was very sad. All she could think about were the people she had left behind. She knew that she must return to find them. Her prince was waiting in an enchanted forest. She had to release him from the sadness that he felt when she left."

Something else that she had cherished was waiting for her, too. It was the Yiddish theater, where she would act in plays that told stories about the Jewish people.

"Does she return?" Basha asked.

"Yes," Sonya said, "because that princess is myself. The country is America, and I am going back. When you are older, you can come and join me."

"What about me?" Isaac asked.

'Yes," Sonya said. "You can come, too. But Mama must stay here. You will both take care of her until then."

"Will you come and get us?" Basha wanted to know.

"I won't return here again," Sonya told her, "but I will send for you, and we will all be together."

"When?" Basha wanted to know.

"I'll tell you when. I will not leave without saying goodbye. And you will write, and I will write back. We will be together through our letters. We will still love each other just as much as if we were together."

When Sonya was finished speaking, Basha was quiet. Even Isaac didn't know what to say. A vacant space opened up between them as they thought of the future. Sonya refrained from speaking again. They understood. She knew that she did not need to tell them anything else.

Yes, life was full of miracles. Her whole life spread before her as though a path had been laid leading to the future. As soon as she set foot on land, Dovid grabbed her around the waist and kissed her on the lips.

"Don't ever go away again," he said. "I couldn't live with it. I prayed every day that you would return."

"And did it help?" Sonya asked.

"You're here," he said.

He was trembling as he walked next to her, taking possession, when she introduced him to Chava and her husband.

"And the old country?" he asked. "You've left it for good?"

"Yes," she said.

"It was the only way to escape. I did the same thing when I was very young and ran away to join the circus," he said and increased the pressure of his hand on her back so that she felt chills course down her spine. "Thank God you're home."

"My little Sonya," Bessie said, embracing her. "I knew you would come. I was waiting for you. It's your destiny. Once you have tasted the theater, you will never leave. It becomes a part of you."

"I have my own troupe now," she continued. "Boris promised to give me a role in his new production. He gave it to his lover instead. *Regina*." She spat out the name with distaste as her anger exploded. "He broke his promise for the last time, and now I will take over his theater and rename it for myself."

She looked Sonya over.

"A little paint, a new dress and you'll be as good as new. We are Jews. We know how to survive, to take the bad with the good. We have within us the juice of life. It never dies. We pass it on from one generation to the next.

"I have decided to continue playing roles that celebrate and encourage women. Plays that will change them, that mirror their own lives, the lives they are living now and the lives they want to live here, in America. Your strength and youthful enthusiasm will help me."

Bessie reflected on this, as though she could see the future, the passing of the generations in this country.

"I hope that those who come after us will say that we had courage and passion, that no matter what our human failings, we created something new that brought joy and meaning to thousands of our people—that we continued that essential spark of Jewishness. Without it there is no future for us."

"It's one of the reasons I returned," Sonya told her. "It's why I am here."

"There's a role waiting for you in my next production, if you want it. I'm working on it now. But I'm afraid there's also bad news."

"And what is that?" Sonya asked.

"Rose Bender died. She got up one morning and said that she felt sick. She was gone in minutes. I couldn't believe it. She had the energy of two people. How does such a thing happen? There were many mourners. Half the Yiddish theater was there. Yes, they shovel the dirt over you and that's it. But what a void her death leaves in our lives. The good die, too, but when they die they are irreplaceable."

It was not just a hole in the earth, Sonya said to herself, hearing the terrible news. It was a hollow place in the middle of her that would not go away.

One night coming back from the theater she passed Rose Bender's building. She knew every corner of those rooms. A light was on in the flat as though Rose was still sitting there, her foot on the treadle, her hand turning the wheel, bent over her work, sewing another one of her costumes for the theater, or a dress for one of her ladies, pins stuck in her hair and a few between her lips, a pincushion strapped to her wrist.

Who lived there now?

It was too late to tell Rose that she'd come back to repay her for her kindness. A soft rain was falling, stripping the trees of their leaves. Rose had been a light, she had guided her, like that lady with the torch that had welcomed her to this land. She owed her everything, but there was no way to repay it now, not even by telling her.

Can the dead hear? Yes, she thought, perhaps everything is revealed to them, and it's the living left in a fog of mystery that will lift only when they, too, pass into the silence where God reigns and not men.

Dovid came around more frequently each week. He was acting in a play with Jacob Adler, the Jewish *King Lear, Der Yidisher*

*Kenig Lir*, a part that had made him famous, which Jacob Gordin had written, modeled after Shakespeare—a play audiences could relate to: the ingratitude of children, their American children, who were already moving in a different direction from their parents.

Sonya had been cast with Bessie in *Di Shayne Amerikaner*, "The Beautiful American." In spite of their estrangement, Boris had written it for her. She had taken the reins of the People's Theatre, renamed for her. Bessie Thomashefsky's name shone in bright lights. Sonya was the riding instructor who teaches American ways with the comedic touch that the role demanded, while Bessie shocked theatergoers—who were nonetheless intoxicated by her performance—in her role as an emancipated woman wearing riding breeches. She brought to her performance a passion and bravado that captivated the audience.

One night, exhausted, Bessie said she couldn't go on. "Sonya, it is up to you to be Bessie Thomashefsky tonight. Improvise when you can't remember your lines. Fake something! The audience will never know the difference."

"How can I?"

"The baby bird learns to fly by trying it himself," Bessie said. "Tonight you will fly, Sonya."

"And remember, improvise!"

The audience grumbled restlessly before they settled into their seats. She wasn't Bessie—still, she sank into the role and gave it her best, following Bessie's lead but imposing a style that was all her own. And when she came back on stage at the end, she received a standing ovation.

"You see," Bessie said, "I knew you were ready. It is time for you to try out your wings, my little Sonya. I've written a part for you in my new comedy, *The Green Cousin*. Yes, it's what is called slapstick here, but the audience never tires of it. You'll play the role of a hapless immigrant girl, Feigel. I named her for you, the little bird who learns how to fly, with her humorous fumbles as she adjusts to life in America. Everyone laughs at her comic misadventures because they remember their own initial days as greenhorns."

Sonya reflected on her own first weeks just off the boat, only amusing now that they were safely in the past. Finding talent as a comedian that she didn't know she possessed, she performed the role of Feigel brilliantly, and the audience embraced her with adoration, demanding that Bessie bring Sonya back as a star.

Meanwhile, there was a palpable excitement in the air. Stages were alive with Yiddish troupes performing plays written by Yiddish playwrights. Other new leading actors like herself were being groomed. Audiences flocked to the theaters, clamoring for more, creating idols they followed from one production to the next with a passion that moved beyond the final bows, an excitement verging on euphoria. People were ravenous for these plays. They booed and cheered. Sometimes they talked to the actors as though they were sitting in their own living rooms, forgetting that it was theater and not real life.

Weren't they all Jews? What need did they have for formalities?

On the stage life was exaggerated and heightened in intensity, Sonya realized. The actors' speeches were sculpted, as were their costumes and the way they looked. You could see them clearly, the way you couldn't see people in real life. You could discern a deeper truth, the truth that was submerged in the day-to-day chaos of living.

That was what Sonya aimed for, what everyone in the theater wanted, to touch other Jews, to help them to see their own lives clearly so that they would live them more deeply because of what they witnessed. They came out of loneliness and the fear of being in a new country where they had to learn a new language and customs, and to leave behind many traditions of the old world. They wanted to be with other Jews and to see their own lives reflected on the stage.

She moved out of Chava's flat to live with two other friends in the theater.

"I didn't expect you to stay," Chava said, "But we are your family now and you—you are the only family we have here."

One day she went to the building where she last saw her father and stood outside, hoping to catch a glimpse of him.

She continued to stand there as the light changed to dusk, and she summoned courage to go up the steps and ring the bell, practicing what she would say. She would demand that Yankel divorce her mother so that she could be free. But there were still children to take care of and support. She would require that he take responsibility for them. She rang the bell several times, until someone came to the door, a young woman.

"What do you want?"

"I am here to see my father."

"And who is that?"

"Yankel Danelovitch," Sonya said, "He is calling himself Abe."

"Abe is gone," she said. "I haven't seen him for months. And good riddance. If you see him, tell him that he owes me money. He borrowed money from me and the bum never paid me back."

She looked more carefully at Sonya.

"And who are you?"

"His daughter."

"He didn't tell me he had a family. Go away. And don't bother me anymore unless you can pay me the money I lent him."

Then she slammed the door in Sonya's face.

Her father was out there somewhere, but she was beginning to realize that she'd probably never find him, would never know where he was. He might even have taken another wife who knew nothing about the family he already had. She had heard that not a few men had done that.

Sonya didn't believe he was dead. He was too crafty for that. He knew how to take care of himself. And he was still her father. It was not so easy to get rid of the past. He was lost in America, but scraps of memory remained—disjointed images, coming back when she least expected it. She would have to write her mother and tell her.

> Dear Mama,
>
> I feel that you are still my mama. I arrived a few months ago. I am acting in the Yiddish theater with Bessie Thomashefsky. She has her own theater now: The Bessie Thomashefsky People's Theatre. I hope that you are well, also Basha and little Isaac, although I am sure he has grown even more since I last saw him, and I should not call him little anymore. I think of all of you often. I stayed with Chava after I arrived, but now I have taken a flat with two other girls who are also in the theater. I am sending you some money

that I hope will help. I will try to send more soon. I am keeping company with a boy named Dovid. He is also an actor, appearing in another play with the great Jacob Adler.

Sadly, Rose Bender is gone. I felt a great sorrow when I heard the news, remembering her kindness. Also, I have tried to find Papa. I am sorry to say that I have as yet not been able to locate him, but I will keep trying. I have decided to put an ad in the Yiddish newspaper that may yield some success.

Your loving daughter,

Sonya

She sent the ad asking about her father to Abe Cahan at the *Forverts* along with a letter and a description of Yankel. She wrote that Yankel Danelovitch (also known as Abe) had a wife and children who were destitute in Russia, but one daughter had come back to America and was appearing on the Yiddish stage. She waited for information from anyone who had seen him. A few people responded, but by the time the news got to her, it was always too late. Yankel seemed to be everywhere at once and then he was nowhere, like a thief in the night.

One night, playing a scene in *The Golden Bride* as a simple village girl in the old country who sings of a tree that stands deep in the woods, Sonya looked out at the audience and saw her father in the front row.

She stared at him and he stared back. There was insolence in his gaze, as though he was mocking her, and perhaps anger because she had published his name in the newspaper. How could she stop the play to confront him?

When she came out to take her curtain call he had fled and

there was only an empty seat. He had come to see her, Sonya thought. He wanted to see if she was telling the truth about being on the Yiddish stage with Bessie Thomashefsky—and to scold her for what she had done.

She hoped that he had taken a good look. He had come to a new land, putting everyone and everything behind him, even his family.

"But perhaps I have done the same thing," she thought.

Sonya wrote to her family for the first year or two, sending money, telling them that she was making a name for herself in the theater. She took to it naturally, as though she had been born to it. Bessie gave her a start, but she continued on her own. Keni Liptzin's words kept coming back to her: *I live only for the theater.* Sometimes she thought it was no different from the stories she had made up long ago for Basha and Isaac. She could feel the roles she played. She was no longer Sonya Danelovitch, but became the soul of another being so fully that she inhabited their emotions and body, as though she had become a *dybbuk* taking possession.

The theater took over her life. Gradually, the memory of the old country grew dimmer and dimmer—and that of her family who lived there. In her mind they remained unchanged, the way she had last seen them. But they persevered in informing her of births, deaths, and marriages, as though they were reproaching her for her neglect.

Basha married at sixteen. Little Isaac grew up to be a doctor. Her mother, despite her illness, lived to a ripe old age. Sonya put the letters in a box that she kept tied up, unable to sever the last link to them.

They came through the worst of times, the Revolution, the

terrible famine, the wars, Stalin's purges. Somehow they survived. But she never spoke of her family to others. She never even told her children.

Sonya never saw her father after that night. He had disappeared into America as surely as she had. Her life had taken unbelievable turns that she could not have imagined.

Rose had said that there were no miracles, but Sonya was always convinced that her life had indeed been a miracle juggled by a jokester called God.

ACKNOWLEDGMENTS

"VILNA" WAS WRITTEN in memory of my father-in-law, Isaac Berkman, whose recollection of the tragic fate of family members in Eastern Europe made it possible for me to tell their story, and who shared with me his knowledge and love of Yiddish literature. The family photograph featured in the story "In Sudargas" encouraged me to create a narrative that transcended the boundaries of one spring day, and "Miracles: A Novella," a work of the imagination, chronicles the life of a woman, based on a few bare sentences related to me that came alive as I thought of my own father, Lee Schoenfeldt, and his difficult journey to America.

My appreciation to Alan Rinzler, whose editorial artistry was an important part of completing *The Girls of Jerusalem and Other Stories*. I am grateful for his support and friendship. Julie Fry's superb design brought a new dimension to these stories. It was a pleasure to work with her. I would also like to thank Leslie Tilley, Ingeborg Weinmann White, George Rubin, and Marina Brodskaya for their help. My special appreciation to Susan Green for her immense gifts as an editor and her meticulous attention to detail and language that greatly enhanced this book. It was a special joy to learn from her. And to Linda West

Eckhardt, a dear friend and writer, Texas born and bred, from Hereford, Texas, Deaf Smith County, whose background made its way into the story, "How I Found My Life," my appreciation for sharing those memorable years as we learned to make our way as writers.

This book would not have been possible without the help of my husband, Norman M. Berkman, who has given me his unfailing optimism, strength, and love. My son, Stephen Berkman, who has been not only a son but also a colleague in search of the highest standards of artistic integrity, helped to bring this book to publication with his sage advice and assistance; his own book of photographs and text, *Predicting The Past—Zohar Studios: The Lost Years*, was recently published by Hat & Beard Press, Los Angeles. I also want to express my gratitude to my daughter, Cheryl Giddings, who supported me with her artistic skills, thoughtfulness, and enthusiasm for this work. And to Lindsey, Lauren, Tyler, and Paige, who have allowed me to touch the  future, my prayer is that you will not forget the wisdom and experiences of those who have come before you.

Finally, I would like to remember Rabbi H. David Teitelbaum (May 14, 1926–March 8, 2021), a dear friend, whose teaching, guidance, moral courage, vision, and great love for the Jewish people encouraged me to write these stories. His light will continue to shine in the world and illuminate the darkness.

MARSHA LEE BERKMAN has published her prize-winning fiction in literary magazines, journals, and anthologies. Her work has been called "original and powerful," and has appeared in *The Schocken Book of Contemporary Jewish Fiction*, *Writing Our Way Home*, *Shaking Eve's Tree*, *Mothers*, *Lilith*, *Jewish Women's Literary Annual*, *REAL: Regarding Arts & Letters*, *Chicago Quarterly*, and many other publications. She is editor of the acclaimed collection *Here I Am: Contemporary Jewish Stories From Around The World*, published by the Jewish Publication Society and awarded the prestigious PEN Oakland/Josephine Miles Award to "promote works of excellence by writers of all cultural and racial backgrounds and to provide recognition for outstanding literary achievement."

The author graduated from Northwestern University with a Bachelor of Arts in English and holds graduate degrees in English and Creative Writing from Sonoma State University and San Francisco State University. She received a Master of Science and a Doctor of Science degree in Jewish Studies from Spertus Institute in Chicago. Her dissertation examined the historical forces that have shaped Jewish life and the power of memory in the collective consciousness of the Jewish people.

Marsha Lee Berkman grew up in the Midwest and South and has lived in the San Francisco Bay Area for many years, where she teaches workshops in fiction and memoir. She has been honored for her work in the Jewish community with the Eternal Light Award.

www.ingramcontent.com/pod-product-compliance
Lightning Source LLC
Chambersburg PA
CBHW031238310726
48971CB00004B/1073